Includes Bonus Story of
My Beloved Waits
BY PEGGY DARTY

The Prodigal's Welcome

KRISTIN
BILLERBECK

BARBOUR BOOKS
An Imprint of Barbour Publishing, Inc.

The Prodigal's Welcome ©2001 by Kristin Billerbeck
My Beloved Waits ©2002 by Peggy Darty

Print ISBN 978-1-68322-269-9

eBook Editions:
Adobe Digital Edition (.epub) 978-1-68322-271-2
Kindle and MobiPocket Edition (.prc) 978-1-68322-270-5

All scripture quotations are taken from the King James Version of the Bible.

This book is a work of fiction. Names, characters, places, and incidents are either products of the author's imagination or used fictitiously. Any similarity to actual people, organizations, and/or events is purely coincidental.

Published by Barbour Books, an imprint of Barbour Publishing, Inc., P.O. Box 719, Uhrichsville, Ohio 44683, www.barbourbooks.com

Our mission is to publish and distribute inspirational products offering exceptional value and biblical encouragement to the masses.

Member of the
Evangelical Christian
Publishers Association

Printed in the United States of America.

Chapter 1

Natchez, Mississippi, 1866

Y ou've come back." Eleanor blinked back tears but couldn't rein in the emotion that caused her to tremble. The ghost of her past stood before her, as real as any Confederate soldier.

"California was not the land of riches I thought it would be." Nathaniel's sheepish grin confirmed her worst fears. He had squandered everything.

"Things are not as you left them, but I'm sure you've realized that would be the case with the war."

Eleanor hadn't meant to sound cold, but how could Nathaniel expect to pick up where he'd left off? Except for his more manly frame from hard labor, he looked the same. The familiar hazel eyes with flecks of gold stared at her; the warm smile, the knowing look all took her back six years when she had loved this man with her heart and soul.

"My father has welcomed me home, Eleanor. With his blessings."

Eleanor awoke from her memories. Did he expect her to do the same? "I'm sure your brother has other thoughts on the matter. Did you know Andrew became a captain in the war?" She waited for his reaction and watched him flinch. "Did you know he lost an arm?" *Oh Nathaniel, did you know he asked me to marry him?*

Nathaniel's gaze dropped to the rich earth. "I did."

"I hope your dreams were realized in California, Nathaniel." *For ours died a long time ago, when Yankees invaded.* Eleanor picked up her skirt and walked toward Rosamond, her once-stately home. The sight of it forced her to face him again. "Your brother, and men like him, are the reason our homes are standing today." Her firm stance meant nothing against his apologetic gaze.

"Eleanor, please. I was a fool." He touched her shoulder, and she shivered at his touch. Turning to look into his eyes, she felt her heart throbbing under his gaze. Unwittingly, she fell into his open arms, and her body racked with tears at the comfort she found in his embrace. Without thought, she drew closer to his chest.

"I am so glad you've come home, Nathaniel. I'm glad you are safe." His familiar scent filled all of her senses, reminding her of what was, what might have been. No matter what her head told her, her heart still loved this man, still ached to have him near her. But his being home was enough. It would have to be.

"I've come home to stay. I'm done with foolishness."

"Are you, Nathaniel?" She forced herself away, straightening her gown. "But I'll not hold it against you, Nathaniel. Welcome home. I pray you'll make the most of your new life."

Eleanor tilted her chin, summoned her remaining shreds of courage, and turned. If it weren't for the war, she might have stayed in his arms forever—forgiving him and his childish ways—but she was stronger now. She had changed since the war. Everyone had. Everyone except Nathaniel, who remained unscathed by battles and Yankees.

"Eleanor, will you have me?" He opened his hands, willing her to come back to him. "I know I do not deserve you."

Eleanor's breath abandoned her, and she fought the urge to run to him. "You don't know?" she whispered.

"I know you are angry. You have every right, but I've changed, Eleanor. I'm not the boy who left—"

She interrupted him. "I'm engaged to your brother, Nathaniel. I thought your father would have told you." She softened at his wounded expression, and, for once, she felt like the traitor.

"Eleanor." The hollow sound of her name sent a sickening

swirl through her stomach. "My brother? Andrew?"

"Your brother has been here, Nathaniel." She needed to justify herself. How dare he look at her as if she had been to blame? "He fought for me, and my family's home, our heritage. While you ran to seek your fortune in the wilderness, Andrew was steadfast and true. The war has been hard on everyone. I need something to hold firm, to be solid; and that is Andrew." Eleanor stood a little straighter.

"Slaves were not your heritage, Eleanor. You always told me you would fight to see them free. You've been listening to your father for too long."

"Who else was I to listen to, Nathaniel? The idealistic man I thought shared my visions left, without so much as a handshake."

The accusations were flowing freely now. "You were *my* fiancée! You would marry my own brother?" Nathaniel's voice carried so the house servants looked on with interest.

"Keep your voice down. We needn't share our business with everyone." Eleanor waved the attention off and focused on Nathaniel again, clenching her teeth in annoyance. "I assumed our engagement was nullified when you left me a note telling me of your future in California. Why ever would you expect me to be free six years later? Do you find me that unpalatable?"

"Of course not, but I didn't expect you to marry my brother either."

Nathaniel crossed his arms, as though he had a right to be upset. Irritation plunged through Eleanor's veins.

"In case you haven't noticed, there's a shortage of marriageable men since the war, but even if there weren't I would be engaged to your brother. He has proven himself to be a hero, and so much more."

"But do you love him?"

Eleanor gulped noticeably. "Of course I love him."

Nathaniel stepped closer, and she felt his proximity to her feet. She curled her toes in her boots, needing to let off her restless energy. His familiar scent felt too intimate.

"Ellie," he whispered.

"Don't call me that. You have no right to call me that. Think of your brother, Nathaniel," she begged him. "Think of me." She pressed a hand to her chest.

Nathaniel retreated, and she breathed an audible sigh of relief.

"It's not over, Ellie. I came back for you, and I'll make my brother understand. I'll make you understand. God has changed my heart. He has redeemed me from the pit, and I want to share it with you. I want to—"

"It doesn't always matter what one wants, Nathaniel. Think of your brother. Think of all he has been through, all he has endured while you spent your inheritance on what suited your whims and squandered your heritage. The Nathaniel I loved would never have knowingly hurt his family."

The descending sun caught the gold flecks in his eyes, and Eleanor was transported to another time and place. The horses whinnied in the background, while Nathaniel held her hand in the green spring grass. He had looked at her with a man's eyes then, and she remembered how the sun had caught the gold that afternoon as well.

"God has granted me forgiveness, Ellie. Won't you?"

Eleanor was startled from the images of a happier, carefree time. "I forgive you, Nathaniel, but I will still marry your brother in one month. You should wish us every happiness. It is the least you can do."

"Miss Eleanor! Miss Eleanor, your father is asking for you." The shrill voice of Mrs. Patterson, their family housekeeper, called her.

"I must go, Nathaniel. Take care of yourself." Eleanor turned toward her great house, now scorched with remnants of the war and badly in need of whitewash. She willed herself not to turn back and nearly choked on the tears she held at bay. By combining her plantation with Andrew's, she hoped to keep them both alive with the freed slaves who remained. The workers were indeed few. Everything seemed so easy minutes ago, but Nathaniel's return had changed everything.

☙

Nathaniel ambled back toward Woodacre, his family plantation. "I should have known." He shook his head in anger, his teeth still clenched. His brother's triumphant smile at Nathaniel's return suddenly made sense. Andrew's admiration of Ellie had never been a secret. He had always been jealous over the connection Nathaniel and she shared. And now Andrew had managed to end the special bond, once and for all. Nathaniel chastised himself. He had no one to blame but himself.

"Where have you been, big brother?" Andrew's victorious tone caught Nathaniel's attention. "As if I didn't know. You've been to see my fiancée? I could have saved you the trip, dear brother." Andrew smirked.

He still wore his Confederate uniform, his left armhole stitched closed to hide the war wound. Nathaniel felt Andrew's entire appearance was merely a costume meant to taunt him for his past sins, as if he were saying, *Here I am—the righteous brother, the one who did as he was told and earned Father's favor.*

"Why did you keep your engagement a secret?" Nathaniel watched his brother's smile disappear. "I should think you'd announce it to the world. This is quite a victory for you. You'll own Rosamond, too, I suppose."

"I thought it best you hear it from Ellie. I feared you might not believe me. I can see by your face you believe it now. Ellie deserves to be cared for."

The use of her childhood nickname sent chills through Nathaniel's spine. No one but he and her mother had ever called her that until now.

"There are so many women, Andrew. Why Ellie?" Nathaniel couldn't keep the anguish from his voice.

"*Eleanor* has wasted six years of her life, Nathaniel. She's been pining for you, swearing you'd return to her. But I knew differently. I knew you'd come back destitute and probably married with a few children as well. You surprised me there. She finally agreed to marry a man who truly loves her, not just with words, but in action. Something you've failed to do, dear brother." Andrew patted Nathaniel's shoulder.

There was a bit of warmth in the act, and Nathaniel reminded himself it was he who had left. Wouldn't he want Ellie to be happy? Wouldn't he have wanted her to be a mother and share in all that life had to offer her? He was still so selfish. His conversion hadn't changed his desires.

"Will you love her, Andrew? Or just the land she can bring you?"

"I shall not dignify that with an answer."

Nathaniel lowered himself to the rich earth under his feet. Every part of his will had disappeared. Six years in California, and he had come home with nothing. Not the wealth he'd promised himself or the new faith he'd claimed. Or so it seemed. He thought loving this Jesus, this new God, who was more than a weekly visit in the family pew, would change everything, but it hadn't appeared to change anything.

I'll prove my worth, Lord. You did not redeem me for nothing, and I'll show them all out of love for You. I ask for nothing. Nothing, but the chance to be on Woodacre again and see that my brother cares for Ellie. My precious Ellie.

❧

"Eleanor, who was that you were speaking with?" Mrs. Patterson lowered a brow. "It's not proper for young ladies to be conversing with a gentleman alone. Especially an engaged woman."

Eleanor laughed. "Mrs. Patterson, after the war there's hardly anything that isn't proper anymore. Just this afternoon I spent overseeing the tilling of the soil. That's hardly worthy of any belle."

"Well, you shouldn't be out there anyway. You know how your father feels on such matters."

"I also know his overseer wouldn't dare lay a hand on the men when I'm around. So I stay close by. The Bible says we are to submit to those in authority, and President Andrew Johnson is our president. I submit, but that scoundrel taking the overseer's place doesn't seem to."

"Johnson is no president of mine, the traitor."

"The Bible says—"

"Do not try to dissuade my thoughts, Eleanor. You're still your father's daughter, and you're not a married woman yet. Here on Rosamond we still keep up appearances, no matter what the Yankees tried to do to us. If we give up our discretion, why, we're no better than the likes of them."

"Yes ma'am."

"Now who was that man you were speaking with?"

"Nathaniel Pemberton, ma'am. He has returned from California."

Mrs. Patterson mumbled something Ellie was surely better off not hearing, but she spoke the end of her thoughts clearly. "You stay away from that fitful coward, Eleanor. He's not worthy to walk on Rosamond soil."

"His father has forgiven him. He's been welcomed home with open arms."

The older woman pursed her lips. "Well, he's not welcome here. What Mr. Pemberton feels led to do is between him and the Almighty, but as far as I'm concerned, Nathaniel Pemberton isn't worth the rags I saw on his back."

"In case you've forgotten, he's to be my brother in a month's time. I suggest you forgive him for all our sakes. If our plantations are to thrive, we've got to work together in our new situation. The war hasn't helped any of us."

"Nathaniel did his family more harm than the Union gunboats did to our fair city. Your father will not take kindly to Mr. Pemberton's welcoming back such a turncoat. I can tell you he will not be invited to the nuptials."

Eleanor sighed. She knew what her father would have to say

about Nathaniel's return, and it probably wasn't fit for a lady's ears. But she had already forgiven Nathaniel. She couldn't help herself. Nathaniel didn't have a cruel bone in his body. He'd been misguided and wistful about his once-future plans, but who could blame a man for following his dream? It would have been different if he'd come back a wealthy man, successful in his pursuits. All would have been forgiven, but Nathaniel was being punished for his failure. Of that, she had no doubt.

"You needn't worry about him. He'll be Under-the-Hill soon enough." Mrs. Patterson said, referring to the town's seedier part of town. "Coward," she added.

Cowardice had nothing to do with Nathaniel Pemberton. If anything, cowardice had personified the town of Natchez. If it hadn't fallen so early, none of the many buildings would be standing. As it was, Natchez wasn't much worse for the wear, except for the slave situation, a few gunboat marks, and the looting. The money and privilege the town enjoyed were far more important to its inhabitants than fighting a war. They planned to run their town their way regardless of the outcome of any violence.

"Eleanor." Her father's gruff voice halted her thoughts.

"Yes, Father."

"I've had word from Woodacre that Nathaniel has returned." Her father's darkened brow said it all. He was worried she'd run away with the man she once loved.

"Yes sir." Eleanor tried to act unaffected.

"You'll not speak with him. The Lord only knows what terrible ideas he's brought from that forsaken California. Not to mention the diseases known to be out West."

"Father, Nathaniel doesn't mean any harm. He—"He coughed abruptly, and Eleanor corrected herself. "Master Pemberton."

"Eleanor, I know your mother fancied Master Pemberton for you at one time, but that all changed when he showed himself to be a milksop. His brother is far better suited to you, and I'm only sorry we didn't see it earlier."

"Father, Nathaniel—Master Pemberton—couldn't have known there was to be a war. He went before—"

"Everyone knew there was to be a war, Eleanor!" her father bellowed. "When the government tried to exert its will on the states, it was only a matter of time. South Carolina did what we all had to do, and Nathaniel had to see the fire coming. It's probably why he left so quickly."

"Reconstruction has begun, Father. We must move forward." Why was she defending Nathaniel? Hadn't she said the same things to him? But, somehow, hearing someone else speak of her beloved that way was far more difficult than she'd have imagined. She chastised herself for thinking of him as her beloved. Andrew was her beloved. *No, Lord, he is my fiancé, and there is such a chasm between the two. Help me think properly of Andrew, Lord. Please.*

"I don't care what *their* law says—no one's going to tell me how to run my plantation. We'll set up black codes as all our neighbors have."

Eleanor cringed. Black codes were plantation speak for the continuation of slavery. They would make former slaves sign away their rights for the *privilege* of working, with severe punishments for anyone who dared not complete a contract.

"Father, the Negroes just want food and shelter. They're not asking for a lot, but you've got to care for them properly. They're people. The Bible says there was neither slave nor freeman in Christ. The men are not getting enough to eat, Father, and they're having to steal from each other to get enough food for the day's work."

"If they don't like it, they can leave." He looked to the ground. "Until the codes are official of course."

Eleanor thinned her eyes. "It's a new day, Father. You've got to learn to adapt, or the Yankees will be back. We must find a new way of running Rosamond. The way Mother ran it. Lincoln said the Union must reunite for charity's sake."

"And Lincoln is dead for charity's sake."

Eleanor decided it best to drop the subject. Seeing the pain the war had caused, all its death and destruction, it was no wonder her father felt as he did. Although Natchez had been spared the worst kind of ruin, the town had still lost many of its sons. No one could forget that. It was impossible to think of Yankees without thinking of loss.

"Andrew is coming for dinner tonight, Eleanor. You shall not let your beau down. You look as if you've been in the fields all day."

Eleanor smiled nervously. There was a reason she looked that way. "Yes, Father."

She excused herself to go into the house and climbed the familiar stairs, but she stopped on the landing, gazing into an old portrait. Her mother looked back, and Eleanor choked back tears at the sight of her. "You would forgive him, Mother. I know you would." She let her eyes close in reverie. *Oh Lord, give me the strength to marry Andrew.*

Chapter 2

D inner proved to be an odd little affair, and Eleanor tapped her feet incessantly to endure the drawn-out evening. Nathaniel was there in spirit, though unwelcome by all, his invisible presence interrupting Eleanor's every attempt at conversation. She could think of no one else.

"Ellie," Andrew said.

He'd taken to calling her Ellie when Nathaniel returned, and Eleanor didn't like it one bit. It was a childish name, not worthy of a woman who would soon be mistress of Woodacre, and it only called attention to the closeness she and Nathaniel once shared.

"I hear the ladies are organizing a quilting circle again. Will you be a part of it?"

Eleanor pushed the food about on her plate. "I shouldn't think so, Andrew. I'll have much to do preparing the rooms after our wedding."

"It's been a time since Mother was there to add a lady's touch. Father and—" He halted, clearly stumbling over the name of Nathaniel. "Father and his sons are looking forward to having the niceties of life brought back to Woodacre. I daresay the house-keeper has been driven to insanity seeing to us. You may dismiss her if need be."

"That shan't be necessary, I'm sure." Eleanor forced a smile.

An eternity of idle, pointless conversation followed before the men retired to the study. Eleanor promptly excused herself and flew down the back steps, stopping outside the kitchen house. She gasped for breath, grateful for the cold air rather than the stagnant feel of the dining room. She sniffed the crisp air, thankful for the smell of fall leaves in the night breeze.

"Ellie," his voice came to her in a whisper, and for a moment she thought she dreamed it. But Nathaniel stepped from the

13

shadows, and her heart pounded faster. "Do you remember how we'd meet here when we were younger?" His tall frame sent her mind soaring, and she recalled the way his hazel eyes caused flutters in her stomach. Just as it felt now. *Nathaniel has grown into a stunningly handsome man,* she admitted to herself. "Do you remember, Ellie? We'd wait until the men retired, when we were supposed to be tucked away for the night, and we'd come here to the kitchen and play jacks."

She turned away to avoid his warm gaze in the moonlight. "You shouldn't be here. Father would have your head if he knew you were bothering me."

"Am I bothering you?" The self-assuredness in his voice hadn't changed a bit. Nathaniel understood his power over her, and it was all the more reason to squelch it now.

"Of course you're bothering me. If you hadn't noticed, I was having a fine dinner party with my fiancé. A dinner party which you were not invited to, or didn't you notice?"

Nathaniel clicked his tongue. "When has your father ever willingly invited me? I'm going to prove myself, Ellie. I may not be any type of Confederate hero; but I was wrong, and I intend to make up for it."

"I shall be the first to congratulate you when you do. If you'll excuse me."

Eleanor hiked up her skirt and turned to leave, but Nathaniel grasped her shoulders, stopping her.

"Eleanor, I know you believe in me. I know you understand I didn't know a thing about the war."

"You knew *when* it was happening. Don't tell me you didn't know your country was in a war. California is not that far away. Many men returned from the West to fight, and even Europe, but you didn't, Nathaniel."

"I wasn't saved, Ellie. Would you rather I'd died in battle than meet you for all eternity? God had His plan. My selfishness was great, but He has used it to bring me back to Him."

"Nathaniel, do you expect me to believe that God ordained your flight?"

"No, that's not what I meant. I just meant if I had died in the war, I would not meet you in heaven."

"Don't be ridiculous. You've been attending church since you were a boy. What is this talk of not being saved before?"

"I've been fidgeting in the pew since I was a boy. I never knew eternal life rested in Him. Not until a spicy old prospector told me the Gospel, and I grasped it in my heart by confessing my sins."

Eleanor looked into his eyes and knew he spoke the truth. Nathaniel wasn't the dramatic type, especially not about religious conversation. If he said he'd found grace, he had.

All at once a fearful cry stopped their conversation, and her breath caught in her throat. Could it be what it seemed? A tiny baby's wail? Raccoons made similar noises, but something about the insistence of this cry told her it was no animal. Eleanor walked toward the edge of the woods, and the cries became louder and more discernible. It was definitely a baby. She drew closer, but Nathaniel held her back.

"Stop, Ellie. It could be some kind of trick. Let me check first."

Eleanor pulled free. "You'll only scare the baby. Let me go."

She went to the edge of the woods, and Nathaniel held her back again. Wiggling from his grasp, she stepped gingerly into the trees. The light from the kitchen barely lit her path.

On the soft ground, rustling in the leaves, she found a black infant. The baby had been swaddled in a rough blanket. Probably the very blanket given to the child's mother by her master when she was a child.

Eleanor picked up the baby and searched its dark brown eyes in the dim light. "Oh Nathaniel, look." The baby blinked wildly to avoid the light, but upon seeing Eleanor's face, smiled a heart-warming grin, then promptly began crying again. "His mother must be here somewhere. Hello!" she called out. "If the baby's mother is about, please show yourself. I mean you no harm."

"She won't come with me here," Nathaniel informed her.

"Then leave," Eleanor said curtly. Seeing the hurt in Nathaniel's face, she softened her tone. "I'm sorry, Nathaniel, but this baby is so young. I want to help the mother, if possible."

"I'm not leaving you alone in the dark of night without anyone to see to your safety."

His sudden interest in her safety sent her reeling. "I've been fine for six years without you, Nathaniel. Or should I say Master Pemberton? Do you think I cannot do for myself now? Please leave—your presence is only scaring the mother." She cuddled the baby close to her, and the loud wails turned to soft, smacking whimpers. Little sniffles followed, and soon the smile returned—a precious, innocent smile that only a baby could offer.

"I'll be close by," Nathaniel announced before turning away.

Soon after, another rustling in the leaves gave way to a young girl, certainly younger than Eleanor. She had big, round eyes and clearly knew her life was in danger by showing herself at the house. Eleanor approached the girl with the baby. "Is she yours?"

The girl nodded. "He. I got nothin' to eat, ma'am. I can't nurse him with nothin' in my belly. The men, they need food for the work, but my baby, he need it, too. I wasn't going to steal nothin'. I was goin' to see if there was scraps from dinner."

Eleanor cringed at the girl's thin frame. She needed more than scraps. "What's your name?"

"Ceviche," she answered softly.

"I'll get you some food, Ceviche, on the promise that you'll come here every night. I'll leave a basket for you. You eat it here, and don't tell any of the men where you go. Do you understand?"

"Yes ma'am."

"Stay here. I'm going to get you and the baby a warmer blanket."

"No ma'am." Her eyes grew wider. "They'll know where I was

if'n I come back with a blanket. The masser at Woodacre, he'll kill me for certain."

Eleanor looked at the baby and then at her mother. Of course, the girl was right about the blanket, but Eleanor feared for the cold fall nights. Whatever the plantation owners had suffered, it was nothing next to the slaves. Looking into the depths of the mother's eyes, Eleanor could see that now. This girl had no way to protect her baby, and desperation had brought her to the edge of Eleanor's grand home in the dark of night. Could there be a more hopeless feeling? It was the first thing she would change as mistress of Woodacre.

"You're probably right about the blanket. Stay here. I'll get you some food."

Eleanor plundered through the kitchen house, avoiding the strange stares she received from the house servants. She packed the goods in a picnic basket reserved for outings on spring horse days and left without a word of explanation.

"Don't eat it too fast." She warned as she handed the basket to the girl. "And come back tomorrow for more."

The young girl held out a trembling hand but took another look at her baby and grabbed the basket. Curtseying, she ran into the dark night.

"You still feel as I do then." Nathaniel came behind her and touched Eleanor's shoulder. It sent shivers through her spine, and she unconsciously rubbed her arms to stop the feeling.

"I don't know what you mean, Nathaniel. I saw one of God's children hungry, and I fed her. There's nothing more to it than that. She wouldn't be in such a position if it weren't for our fathers and this war."

"What will you say to my father and your future husband Andrew when they employ the black codes, Ellie? Will you sit by and watch them go against the law?"

"I shall help them write the codes if need be. They'll allow for enough food and the ability for a worker to leave should they like." Eleanor squared her shoulders, confident in her words.

But Nathaniel laughed aloud, cutting her off. "And a plot of land to call their own in the corner of the plantation.

"Tell me you aren't still so naive, Ellie. Our fathers blame the Yankees for everything that's befallen them, and punishing the slaves is just what they've done their entire lives. Certainly your father tried to help them when your mother was alive, but what's he done for them since?"

"Freedom is the law, Nathaniel. At some point, our fathers will have to adapt. I have. I've lost everything that meant any-thing to me. All that's left in this house is the walls. We sold all the silver for the war effort. We even sold Mother's jewels that were sewn into my gown for protection."

"Your father let you sell your mother's things?"

"We had no choice, Nathaniel. The South gave up as much as we could to ward off the Yankees. We burned all our cotton and anything that could be considered transport so the Union wouldn't get it. We didn't want to make it any easier for them to kill Confederate soldiers."

"Eleanor, marrying my brother will not help your cause. You will only succumb to their way, their ideas."

"I haven't yet," she answered defiantly. "I've managed to stay quite grounded in my opinions, and I've helped to make the plantation workers' quarters much more livable. Imagine all I could do if mistress of both plantations. Our fathers don't understand that their method won't work anymore. They don't understand that the method to continue their way of life is to treat the men well. They don't want money. They have no use for it. They want land; they want—"

Nathaniel knelt before her, grasping her hand. "Ellie, come away with me. We'll be married in Vicksburg by morning."

Eleanor yanked her hand from his touch, though it took all her strength. "You said you came home to be forgiven. Do you think anyone would offer forgiveness if you stole your brother's betrothed?" She looked deep into the hazel eyes, and she saw remorse there for his words. Eleanor reached out and touched his cheek. "I know you want to please your father, and the way to do that is to let things be. Andrew and I shall be happy, somehow. Since you've squandered your inheritance, I cannot help the slaves as your wife."

Nathaniel flinched, and Eleanor realized he understood the truth in her words. "I need Andrew as much as he needs me. It is the way of life, I suppose. Needs and desires are very different things."

"You don't want to marry my brother, Ellie. You're marrying him because you feel sorry for him. But there's nothing to pity about Andrew, Ellie. He's wanted you from the day you were born on Rosamond. He meant to make the plantations one, and he'll succeed if you give him the honor. If you think your position will help the slaves as your mother's did, you underestimate my brother."

"How dare you, Nathaniel! How dare you accuse your brother of such vile things! He loves me." But deep down she questioned her own words. How could she help but do anything less? Andrew had never whispered words of love to her. He'd never placed gentle touches upon her arm as Nathaniel did so naturally. *But that isn't love*, she told herself. Love was commitment and being there—not a passing emotion. Andrew had been there while Nathaniel flitted about the country.

"He's trained himself to love you, Ellie. Can't you see that?"

"Stop calling me that childish name. I'm not a child, Nathaniel! I'm sorry you feel your brother must be trained to love me, like a circus performer. Is it such a chore? Then why should you want to plow through life with such a dreary task?" Eleanor turned her shoulder to the man she had once loved. Every time he whispered her name she withered a bit. Did Andrew love her? Could anyone after she'd been the object of so much conjecture following Nathaniel's departure?

"I didn't mean—"

"The Nathaniel I knew would never be so cruel. I thought I knew everything about you. I agonized when you left. You showing up before my wedding is hard enough. Don't make me endure more." Eleanor wiped away a tear and tried to still her trembling frame.

Nathaniel reached for her, but she maintained her distance, trying to think of the baby she'd cradled and other more comforting thoughts of the people her marriage would help, but to no avail. She swallowed hard and looked directly into the eyes of the man she had once loved with her whole heart. As much as she feared the answer, she needed to know why Nathaniel had left.

"The town remembers how you departed. They remember me as the jilted bride, and they were right, weren't they?" She waited for the words to sink in, but he didn't answer her. "They said you escaped to avoid marrying me. They said your father had ordered it, and you wouldn't be told how to live your life. I was a laughingstock, Nathaniel, at only seventeen years of age."

Nathaniel's eyes clouded over, and Eleanor felt as though she had been struck. "It's true then? I am why you left."

Nathaniel looked away into the night's sky, and Eleanor had her answer. She marched toward the steps.

"Ellie!" Andrew's voice beckoned her.

"I must go. My fiancé calls." She blinked madly to keep the tears away. *Only a few steps,* she told herself.

As she hiked up the stairs, Nathaniel stood alone at the kitchen house, but it was she who was truly alone. Her heart ached. Nathaniel had never really loved her. He'd never loved anyone more than himself.

Chapter 3

Nathaniel stood on the back stoop of Rosamond until total darkness enveloped him. One by one, the candles and the fire were extinguished in the cookhouse, and the night became blacker. Only the great house remained lit. Eleanor came into sight, and Andrew gathered her close. Pain clenched Nathaniel's heart. *You don't love her, Andrew. Let her go.*

Nathaniel closed his eyes, unable to witness his brother and Ellie together. Andrew deserved her, he supposed, but the thought caused a sour feeling in Nathaniel's stomach. Andrew stayed and fought, Andrew cared for the plantation, and Andrew stood up to be a groom, while fear sent Nathaniel bolting like a frightened catfish.

Where was he when Ellie had grown into a beautiful young woman? Had California offered him anything so special?

"Won't do you no good to stand there feeling sorry for yourself." Eleanor's childhood maid, Hattie, stood at the back step, beating a rug. She focused on her project and spoke of the decorated textile. "Surprised we got anything left after them Yankees stormed through here. A painting here and there, a rug, a few plates. We done hid the silver; they didn't get that." Hattie smiled with what appeared satisfaction.

"You think I feel sorry for myself?" Nathaniel walked toward her.

"Who wouldn't? We done all had a time of it, but thinking about it don't help none." Hattie took a stick to the rug. "Why you men can't wipe your feet outside, I never will understand."

"She's going to marry my brother."

Hattie shrugged. "You're just lucky she didn't do it six years ago. Consider it your penance you should watch the wedding." Hattie placed the beaten rug over the stair rail and came toward him. "Let her be, Master Pemberton. Your brother will make her happy, and the sooner things return to normal, the better. Life's been too hard for too long. A wedding will help things heal."

"Why have you stayed on, Hattie? You don't have to, you know. If things are so hard, why don't you go?"

Hattie laughed. "Where am I going to go? I got nice quarters here, and the missus taught her daughter to treat me right. I got no complaints with Miss Ellie. Mrs. Patterson, she leaves me alone for the most part. Searching for something better is what got you into trouble, Master Pemberton."

Nathaniel wanted to tell her to flee, to run now before Andrew came into possession of Rosamond, but that wasn't fair. His own prejudices probably mingled heavily into his opinions.

"No, and I don't suppose you would ever have complaints with Eleanor. She loves from the depths of her soul."

Hattie searched his eyes. "Where'd you go, Master Pemberton? Do you know how I nursed that broken heart of Miss Ellie's? We all thought she'd get over it, that she'd find someone else to love and cast off her old feelings for you like some worn-out coat. But she didn't. She wore them like a badge of honor, her own Confederate flag, waving torn in the wind. And now that you're back, she's marrying your brother. Life's odd, ain't it?"

Nathaniel thought so. "I went to California, hoping to find gold."

"Did you?"

He laughed. "It was gone a decade before I got there. I sat in grimy mining camps and finally prospected for a mining company. Any measly flake I found belonged to them."

"Did you find what you was looking for?" Hattie asked, with all the wisdom of any educated scholar.

"I beg your pardon?"

"Can't imagine what you was missing here, what with your daddy owning all that land and all. So I figured you went looking for something in particular."

Nathaniel shook his head. "I went looking for a fool's adventure, and that's exactly what I found." What *had* he been hoping to find? Everything that mattered to him was right here in Mississippi all along. Everything, that is, except adventure, and he had found that highly overrated. Wondering whether he'd make it to the next day was no longer a thrill for Nathaniel. Thinking on the American war, he probably could have found adventure in Mississippi as well. Nathaniel sighed audibly. He was no better than a dog chasing its own tail.

"What was you looking for?"

"I guess I had independence in mind, Hattie."

Hattie laughed. "Well, leaving your family high and dry is a way to find that, I suppose. I been here since I was a young girl, and I guess I never did wonder much what was beyond those white fences, so I can't fault you. Miss Ellie taught me to read, to speak properly, and how to pray to God. That's a lot to be thankful for. There ain't much more a woman asks from life but to be forgiven and know there's eternity waiting on her. That makes me happy."

Happiness. Would he ever find such an elusive thing here on earth? The Bible didn't promise it, and Nathaniel highly doubted it. "I'm glad you ask for so little in life, Hattie. I suppose that's a good way to find happiness."

"You want to know what I think?"

"I'm not sure, Hattie," Nathaniel answered with a chuckle.

"I think you're still in love with Miss Ellie, and you're planning to steal her away from your brother."

Nathaniel laughed and shook his head. "No, Hattie. Andrew's won fair and square, and he deserves Ellie. Not that I didn't try, mind you. But Andrew will be good to her." As soon as he said the words, he knew they were untrue. Andrew had never cared for anything unless it served his own purposes. Nathaniel had no doubt that if there were any way to care for Woodacre, other than going to battle, Andrew would have found it.

As if reading his mind, Hattie went on, "You believe that, Master Pemberton?"

"No, Hattie, I really don't."

"I didn't think so. I thought you must have learned something while out in California. I pray you do steal her away, Master Pemberton, even though I could be hanged for saying so. Nothing left for a belle like her any longer. The Yankees, they treated her with the utmost respect. But the Southerners, the gentlemen, they rocked my girl's faith. They spread rumors about her and said she was on Satan's side when she tried to help a Yankee officer in need. But I know she would have helped Satan himself if he lay in a puddle of blood. Miss Ellie's like that. She's got a heart of gold. So see, Master Pemberton—you didn't need to go looking for the precious metal."

"I suppose I didn't, but I disrupted my father's plans once, Hattie. I don't plan to do it again," Nathaniel said by way of excuse, hoping he truly was being a hero letting Ellie marry Andrew. Somehow he doubted it.

"You didn't learn nothing while you was in California. Nothing. Because the Nathaniel I knew was a fighter. He wouldn't just give up the woman he loved because he didn't want to stir up any trouble, but I'm glad you've grown up. It will make things much easier."

Hattie's faith in him bolstered his own. What if God had sent him back in time for the wedding to stop it? What if *this* was God's will?

"Thank you, Hattie. You're a godsend."

Hattie laughed her boisterous, familiar laugh. "I know it. You just keep in mind what I told you."

☙

Eleanor watched Hattie carrying on below with Nathaniel. She had opened her window but could hear only muffled conversation, not the words being said. What were they discussing? No doubt it was she, but in what capacity? Had Hattie told Nathaniel to run again and leave her to be with Andrew? Her maid was far too familiar with her future brother-in-law for Eleanor's liking. And from the looks of it, Nathaniel had easily won Hattie over with his carefree style.

A knock at her door startled her from the window, and she closed it with a *crack*. She swallowed hard and opened the door. Her father stormed into the room with hands clasped behind his back. "I'm sorry to disturb you in your quarters, but Andrew has approached me with an important matter. He is anxious to get on with your lives."

"Of course, Father. That's understandable. We are to be married in a month," Eleanor agreed, hoping the direction of the conversation wasn't headed where she feared it might be.

"He's waited a long time to ensure that you wouldn't be upset by his proposal, and now that you've accepted, he's hoping to begin the marriage as soon as possible." Her staunch father patted his protruding stomach and paced the room. "When I was ready to take a wife, I was anxious to have her under my roof and begin our lives together, but there's the added issue of planting. It won't be long now before it begins. The soil will need a lot of encouragement this season."

Eleanor gulped. "Father, are you suggesting we move up the wedding? We've hardly had a decent engagement period as it is."

"No one's counting the days of an engagement anymore, Eleanor. We've all faced death and survived. Those of us who are left must move on. What with the shelling of the town, the gunboats, no one is worried about a decent interval."

Eleanor's heart beat in her ears, and she had to think fast. The idea of marrying Andrew before she had time to prepare her heart after Nathaniel's arrival suddenly sickened her. It made her feel like the traitor she was.

"Mother would care." The comment stopped her father's pacing, and Eleanor knew she'd hit her target. His brows lowered, and he studied her. "Mother would care, Father. It's odd enough I'm marrying Andrew when everyone thought I'd marry his brother one day, but to do it quickly when Nathaniel's just returned will only intensify the gossip. People will talk, Father. Like they did when Nathaniel left—do you remember?" Eleanor looked out the window again. "I know we've always been called the proud Sentons, but I venture to guess Mother would have wanted me to have a proper engagement." She wished she could see her father's expression but dared not face him.

"I shall ask my sister for her opinion," her father said, then left without another word.

Eleanor fell to her knees as she beseeched the Lord. "I don't even know what to pray for, Lord. But please let Your will be done, and prepare my heart if I'm to marry Andrew sooner than I'd planned."

Her fate rested in her aunt Till, and, for her own sake, Eleanor hoped their opinions agreed. Hattie entered the room with a loud bang. "Are you ready to be undressed, Mistress?"

"Oh Hattie, don't call me that."

"I'm sorry, Miss Ellie. I saw your father leave. I'm thinking about him. Everything all right?" Hattie began her nightly routine of readying Eleanor for the following day. She checked her combs and laid out an appropriate gown for the next morning. Once her ritual was complete, she turned to Eleanor and forced her eyes away.

"Why do you think Nathaniel came back, Hattie?"

Hattie clicked her tongue while motioning for Eleanor to turn around. The older woman began unbuttoning the back of Eleanor's gown and then untying her undergarments. It felt like an eternity before the maid answered. "Can't rightly say, but he means to make a name for himself here in Natchez."

"What do you mean?"

"His father has welcomed him home. That's no small gesture. Master Pemberton's going to prove himself to his father. I have no doubt."

Eleanor turned to face her maid. "Did he say anything about me?"

"Were you eavesdropping, Miss Ellie? During the war, men were shot for less."

"I knew he was out there. He approached me after dinner."

"If your father, or your future family, caught you talking with Master Pemberton, you may as well say good-bye to Woodacre. No war is going to erase that kind of scandal. Natchez hasn't forgiven him, even if his father has."

"Tell me what he said, Hattie," Eleanor begged.

"Just that he's sorry he left without word. He wants to make it up to you, but I think he knows the way to do that is to leave you be." Hattie began to pull at Eleanor's hair, letting it down from the net to fall in red cascades across her back.

Eleanor blinked back tears. "Did he say that? That he was going to leave things be?"

"It's just the way it is, child. Propriety dictates you two stay far away from each other, and he's got a mind to make the most of his second chance at Woodacre. You wouldn't want to get in the way of that now, would you?"

"No, I suppose I wouldn't." Eleanor rubbed her temples. "I have a vicious headache."

"It's too much excitement for the day."

"I'll tell Father tomorrow that it's fine to move up the wedding. I don't suppose there's any reason to keep it a month from now. A fortnight will be plenty. I'm not as young as most to begin having children, you know." Eleanor felt somehow that if she just got her wedding over with, maybe her feelings for Andrew would follow.

Hattie began hanging up Eleanor's gowns. "You'll tell your father no such thing. Just wait, Miss Ellie. Wait and see what happens. God isn't through with you yet."

Eleanor looked into her maid's eyes and saw a certain sparkle. Although she didn't know what the elder woman had in mind, something was circulating in that head. Eleanor drew in a cleansing breath of excitement. Waiting would be the least of her problems. Getting her father and Andrew to agree to terms in hiring the slaves back at an honest day's wage—*that* was her real problem.

Chapter 4

Aunt Till and her daughter, Mary, arrived from Louisiana the following morning. It was a bright and promising day, and Eleanor breathed in the fresh autumn air, glad to think of her future rather than her troubled past.

"Aunt Till!" Eleanor ran to the carriage without a concern for grace or propriety. Her aunt Till was finally there, and Eleanor had great expectations for her aunt's opinions on a hasty wedding. Years had passed since their last visit from her father's beloved sister, but she had little doubt how the woman would view such a societal faux pas.

Aunt Till's home had been shelled and destroyed by Yankees, but she maintained her prestige and respect even without the money usually necessary for such an honor. By all accounts, Aunt Till should have returned to Rosamond, her childhood home, a broken woman, but it hadn't happened. She had remained in Lousiana, hoping Mary would marry a handsome officer returning from the fields. Mary's beau never did return from the battles, and her heart never appeared ready to accept another in his place. Moving became unimportant in the women's shared mourning.

Aunt Till's generous frame exited the conveyance, lifting the strain of the carriage visibly. She lumbered toward her niece with arms outstretched and pulled her into a hug. "Lovely little Eleanor. Look what a beauty you have become. Your cousin Mary has been telling me of your escapades here in Mississippi."

Eleanor looked to her cousin and pen pal. Mary shook her head nominally as if to say that nothing of importance was ever relayed from the letters. Just seeing Mary made Eleanor feel like a carefree child again, wanting to giggle through the fields on her mare and jump fences behind her cousin. Eleanor grabbed Mary's hands and whispered in her ear, "I have the day all planned for us.

We shall have a picnic and ride to our hearts' content."

"I heard Nathaniel's returned. Is it true?" Mary whispered excitedly. "Shall he join us as in the days of our youth?"

"Shh, no. Father has forbidden me to see him."

"So you are set to marry Andrew after all." Mary stamped her foot childishly. "I was hoping the wedding would be called off." Mary smiled sweetly to throw her mother off any trail. "Maybe not called off, but I was quite hoping for some excitement so Nathaniel might carry you off romantically, stealing you from his brother once and for all."

"What are you two conspiring?" Aunt Till asked.

"Nothing, Mother. We are discussing the wedding plans of course."

"Ah, to be a young bride again. Eleanor, where is your father? Is he not here to greet his own sister?"

"He's in the fields, Aunt Till. He shall be back soon. There was some business to attend to, and he could not be relieved of it."

"My! Doesn't he have an overseer?"

"No, Aunt. The overseer has disappeared, but I believe he may have a new one this week." Eleanor hoped that was enough of an answer, for she knew nothing more. She had no more idea of what had happened to Mitchell Rouse than her father, but she feared for the man. He was a vicious overseer, and she couldn't say she missed him; but she also knew the men didn't miss him, and thus her uneasy feeling for him. She hoped he'd left of his own free will and hadn't met with an untimely ending.

"Disappeared, dear?"

"Father shall tell you all about it. May Mary and I ride this afternoon, Aunt? The servants have packed us a fine picnic, and it's such a nice day."

"Mary is probably tired from our journey, Eleanor."

Aunt Till removed her gloves. Gone was the kid leather and in its place a shiny material of lesser consequence. Eleanor winced at the sight of it.

"I'm not tired, Mother. I've never felt finer." Mary's eyes widened in her plea, and her mother relented with a smile.

"Very well, if you two should like to live your last days as girls, who am I to stop such revelry?"

Eleanor and Mary smiled broadly, took each other's hands, and ran to the stables, giggling with glee. They fell in a heap outside the stables, just as they had when they were children. They laid on their backs in the tall grass, gazing dreamily at the clouds above while their gowns stretched out beyond them. "It is such a pleasure to be away from the house and all its chains."

"That one looks like a tulip," Mary commented.

"And that one, a dragon," Eleanor said, pointing to the sky.

Mary lifted herself onto her elbows. "How does Andrew manage without the arm? Is it very strange to watch him? I'm quite nervous I shall stare at him."

"He does fine, I suppose. I pray you won't stare at it. It's nothing really. Just his arm is not there. I guess I don't think of it much."

"Really? I daresay I'd be quite weary of marrying a man with no arm."

"Not if it was Morgan you wouldn't," Eleanor said in reference to Mary's beau who had succumbed to the war.

"Andrew is *not* Morgan, Ellie. That's what I mean." Mary gazed steadily at her cousin.

"Andrew and his father still have enough men at the plantation where he can tell them what work to do. Andrew has harsh words for the Federalists that keep a close eye on his work though. He claims he is barely surviving, and so does my father. That's why we must forge the plantations together. I hate to hear of such matters, but I suppose it's my lot in this life. One can no longer play childish games all day. The war has put an end to that."

Mary sighed. "I don't want to discuss the war. I hate everything it represents. Let's talk of something cheerful. I'm sick of seeing Yankees lurking on every corner. Tell me about Nathaniel being back. Is he quite a criminal?" Mary said dreamily.

"You mean Andrew, my future husband. That is whom you wish to discuss," Eleanor said.

"Of course—Andrew." Mary cleared her throat. "Were you able to get fabric for a gown?"

"I'm wearing my mother's. It's the one she wears in her family portrait."

"It's such a pity she won't be here, Ellie."

It's not a bit fair. "It's probably just as well—this wedding will be small. Appropriate for the circumstances. Besides, I think she'd be disappointed I'm marrying Andrew. She never did care for him much. He was such a serious child, no fun at all. Mother always worried he'd steal the life right out of me if I was allowed to play with him."

"Will he?"

Eleanor drew in a long breath. "Andrew won't, but this plantation might. It's not like it was. There are men out of work, men who want the slaves' jobs, and Father lords that over the slaves. Or freedmen, as the Yankees call them. Things will never be the same, I suppose."

"Maybe we should have married Yankees and said good-bye to the South and all its problems. It might be nice to leave all this behind."

"Perish the thought, Mary. That's high treason." As she said the words, she didn't know if she believed them.

Mary giggled. "Perhaps, but they did look fine in their uniforms." She winked and rose from the ground. "And don't tell me you didn't notice. Come on—let's go to the house and get our riding outfits. The horses are waiting." Mary held out a hand and helped Eleanor to her feet.

In a matter of moments, they were stripped and into their riding clothes. The speed of the horse sent a wave of exhilaration through Eleanor. It had been so long since she'd ridden free, and she pondered why. The wind in her hair wrestled with her net. She wished propriety allowed her to toss the contraption into the air. Eleanor wanted to feel this way again, to feel there was life worth living. She drew in an excited breath.

"Yah!" Mary kicked her horse and went into a full gallop.

"Yah! Yah!" Eleanor stayed with her, following closely behind. "Oh Lord, thank You for sparing Lady!"

Most horses were stolen during the war, but Lady and her partner were kept in the slaves' quarters and spared their natural fate. Eleanor lifted an arm into the sky and wailed her enthusiasm, which brought her cousin to hilarity.

They rode to the edge of the plantation and noticed Andrew bent over the soil at the gate of Woodacre. No doubt he was wondering how the spring planting would be after a disappointing harvest this year. Eleanor wished to veer back home and avoid such painful reminders of life, but it was too late. Andrew heard the hooves, dropped the soil, and waved.

In a flash of energy, Mary jumped the fence like a professional rider and landed laughing. Eleanor couldn't decide whether to follow her cousin or halt before Woodacre's fence. She hesitated a bit too long and pulled on the reins late. Lady veered, attempting the jump, but Eleanor heard her hooves kick the fence and felt the jolt in her back. Everything happened then in slow motion, and she felt herself hurltling through the air, like the firing of a cannon. She braced herself for the upcoming landing and listened in horror as Lady's body hit the ground hard.

Eleanor's twisted frame hit the soft ground with her shoulder first, and she ducked for cover at the lighted silver of Lady's shoe reflecting the sun over her. The horse fell away from her, and she clutched her chest in relief. Then she felt herself jolted by immediate gunfire, and she looked up to see Andrew blocking the sun with a pistol in his hand.

"What are you doing?" Eleanor screamed in terror. "Lady! Lady!" She ran to her horse's side, but it was too late. Andrew's gun had brought the mare to a swift ending. "Are you a lunatic?" she sobbed, grabbing her fiancé by the collar with her arm that didn't throb. "What did you do? What did you do?" She pounded her fist into his chest, and with the gun in his only hand, he was powerless to defend himself against her rage.

She felt her hands pulled behind her and Nathaniel's soothing voice calming her. "It's going to be fine, Ellie. It's going to be fine. Calm down." Nathaniel pulled her away from Andrew, locking her arms together in an embrace. An embrace meant to foil her violent reaction. "Mary, run home to Woodacre and get my father's carriage. Hurry!"

"He shot Lady!" Eleanor wailed, while seeing Andrew with more venom than she knew she possessed. She tried to free her arms, but Nathaniel held steady. "He shot Lady!"

"I'm sorry, Ellie. I'm sorry!" Andrew looked mortified, as if he was scarcely able to believe his actions. "I just reacted. Tell her, Nathaniel. Tell her I didn't mean to hurt her Lady! I'll buy you the finest mare this side of the Mason-Dixon—I promise!"

Nathaniel looked sadly at his brother. "I'll tell her, Andrew," he answered quietly.

She fell into Nathaniel's chest weeping.

"Everything's going to be fine, Ellie. We'll get you home, and things will look different tomorrow. Andrew thought you were in danger. He tried to defend your safety."

She used her good arm to hold onto Nathaniel for comfort. "Lady," was all she could manage for an answer.

"Eleanor, is your arm okay?"

She looked down at her arm, dangling by her side. "It doesn't want to move, Nathaniel." She didn't feel any pain. She was too numb to feel anything other than the emotion of her horse lying dead beside her.

"Andrew, go see what's keeping Mary. Hurry!" Nathaniel called nervously, while smiling calmly at Eleanor. She watched as her fiancé ran toward his house, his long strides belying the weakling she suddenly felt him to be.

"Ellie, let me see your arm." Nathaniel touched her arm, and, as the shock had worn off, she flinched in pain. "It's not broken, but it's pretty badly bruised."

The arm was the least of her worries. Her horse, her one joy left in this life, was gone. Could she ever forgive Andrew? "Oh Nathaniel, has God abandoned us?" Eleanor looked at Lady and began to sob again. Nathaniel turned her face into his chest.

"Never mind, Ellie. Never mind. This, too, shall pass."

"You were right to run away, Nathaniel. I wish for your sake you'd never come back to this forsaken land. There is no reason for us all to be miserable. You should have stayed away. God isn't here in the South anymore. You should have followed Him to the West. I only wish—"

"Shh. Of course He is here, Ellie. You've just lost sight of Him. That's all. He's here, Ellie."

"Where?"

"He did what we couldn't do ourselves. Do you remember how as a child you didn't think it was fair how those children were born into ownership? You said it was just like the Israelites in Egypt—do you remember?"

"Everyone I loved has abandoned me, Nathaniel. Even you." Eleanor didn't want to think of the good the war had done. Right now, everyone was miserable. She was glad for the future generations, of course, but would those better days ever come in her lifetime?

"God has not abandoned you, Ellie." The intensity with which he said this caused her to believe him, but then she remembered her predicament.

"You'll let me marry him, Nathaniel," she said with an accusing tone. "The man who just stole the only joy I had in my life, and you'll stand by and watch me marry him. You're a traitor just like the rest of them." She hoped her vehemence would force Nathaniel into action. She wanted him to steal her away in the night, but she could see by his set jaw he had no such intentions. Eleanor pulled herself up, trying to maintain her last shred of dignity, and began the long walk home.

"Ellie, please wait. The carriage will be here shortly."

Nathaniel tried to stop her, but she'd had enough of the Pemberton clan, and she hoped to rid herself of them forever. If Nathaniel wouldn't help her, she would find a way to help herself.

Chapter 5

Andrew sat in the carriage. His shoulders slumped in defeat. "She'll never forgive me."

"Of course she will," replied Mary. "She's just had a terrible time of it. Give her time to wallow in her melancholy, and our Eleanor shall return to us. Why, I'm sure by tomorrow, she'll be more herself. She is not the sort to stay in a fit."

Andrew shook his head, raking his hands through his hair. "No, no. It's different this time. Did you see her face?" Andrew relived her expression of horror, the hatred he saw in her eyes. "Did you see how she wanted Nathaniel's comfort when she stared at Lady? She never thought of me, her fiancé. I was a fool to think she'd ever love me." Andrew turned his face. "If she knew what a coward I was, she would have never said yes in the first place. I suppose I'm only getting what I deserve." Andrew knew he was being a fool, rambling on so, but he couldn't help himself. It seemed to pour from him without a thought on his part. Perhaps it was all the guilt he'd stored up for misrepresenting himself.

"A coward? Andrew, as you sit beside me with an arm missing from the war, you call yourself a coward? A prestigious medal hangs from your uniform. Your valor could never be questioned. You have just had a miserable day. Tomorrow will be brighter." Mary took his hand and grasped it in her own.

"No." Again, Andrew shook his head. "No, Mary. Things are not as they appear. I'm no soldier."

"You sit beside me wounded from the war," Mary tried to reassure him. Her eyes pitied him, and he hated the thought.

The truth rolled from him like an overfilled cotton car. "I didn't lose my arm in battle, as everyone thinks." He felt a great weight lifted from him.

"Whatever do you mean?" Mary smiled at him, obviously trying to placate his miserable ramblings, but she had no idea. She didn't know what kind of coward stared back at her.

Rumor had it Mary lost her own fiancé, a man who earned the name hero. It wasn't fair that he should be sitting here with her; it wasn't fair that her fiancé had died on a battlefield somewhere, while he was alive, less an arm. Only his fear and cowardice had saved his life. Eleanor had seen the true Andrew when he shot her horse. How would he ever redeem himself now?

"I cannot say what I mean, but I wish I could, Mary. Your beau's efforts should not be in the same breath as my own. I'm not worthy. It isn't fair that I should have another chance at life while he lies in a grave."

"But God has granted you another chance, Andrew. Take it. Take it and hold onto it for all it's worth. I wish Morgan could do the same."

"I never made it to battle." Andrew admitted quietly, unable to hold the guilt at bay any longer.

"Of course you did. You were in Vicksburg. Everyone knows that. Your father is so proud; he boasts of it to everyone from what Eleanor tells me."

"No, I was thrown from my horse, Mary. I fell under the horse. His hoof landed on my arm, gangrene set in, and that's how I stand here today. I never made it to the fight. I am an expert horseman. I fear it was my own panic that threw me from that horse."

Mary's mouth opened, but she snapped it shut quickly. "I don't know what to say. I'm sure you didn't do such a thing purposely."

"There's nothing to be said, I suppose. I don't expect a reply or understanding. But this is the reason I reacted so miserably today. When I saw that horse fly through the air, when I saw Ellie land—it was all I could do not to strangle the horse with my own hands. I suppose I blame the horse for my cowardice. I have never enjoyed riding since."

Mary exhaled deeply, clearly troubled by what she was hearing. "I cannot respond, other than to say I wish Morgan had run, Andrew. I wish he had mounted his horse, galloped the opposite way, and was here with me, known as a coward. As it is, I shall be known as a spinster, but a spinster who once loved with all her heart."

Andrew couldn't look at her, couldn't see the pain she bore. "Morgan was a fine man, Mary. I'm certain of it."

"He was," she agreed.

"Will you tell Eleanor the truth of her betrothed?" Andrew supposed it didn't matter, for Eleanor would never look at him the same way again after Lady's death. Andrew's cowardice scarcely mattered since he had killed her horse, her most prized possession.

"I shall not tell Eleanor anything presently. But you should tell her, Andrew." Mary ceased conversation at Nathaniel's appearance and presented a sweet smile to Andrew's brother.

Nathaniel noticed his brother's blanched expression immediately and felt sick to his stomach for his brother. Andrew's remorse for his actions were painted on his face as clearly as any scar; his usual, angry self-assuredness had vanished.

"We should hurry!" Nathaniel exclaimed. "Ellie has gone on ahead. She's quite shaken." Nathaniel stepped up into the carriage at Andrew's protest. "Move over, Andrew."

"You're not going with us, Nathaniel. She doesn't need you along. She's my fiancée, and I'll take care of matters."

"I'm not the one who shot her horse!" Nathaniel's words pained his brother, just as he'd meant them to, and immediately he felt the guilt. How could any Christian brother watch his brother in so much pain and feel any satisfaction? He hadn't meant to be cruel, but at the same time he wouldn't allow Andrew to focus on anyone other than Ellie. For once in his life, Andrew was going to put someone ahead of himself. "It's not me she doesn't want to see, Andrew. It pains me to remind you of that, but she's the one you need to think of. She will mend if you give her time."

"How dare you waltz back into our lives and—"

"Stop it!" Mary ordered. "Both of you are acting like spoiled children."

Of course she was right, and Nathaniel winced at her words. He was being no better than Andrew. "Mary, you take the carriage and find Ellie. We'll wait here."

Mary stumbled over her words. "I'm afraid I don't remember the path as well as I ought to. I need one of you to come along." Mary faced them both, looking from one to the other. "Nathaniel, I think it should be you. No offense, Andrew, but Ellie would be upset at the sight of you just now. It's better if Nathaniel shows me the way. I shall relay to Ellie your concern for her."

Nathaniel breathed a quiet sigh of relief and climbed aboard the carriage. After a brief hesitation, Andrew jumped from the carriage, his face dark with anger. "Do not take advantage of me, brother. It will be at your expense!" Andrew threatened as the red dust covered his image.

Nathaniel turned his attention to Mary. "You think it was wrong for me to return, too, don't you, Mary?" He didn't want to hear her answer but braced for it.

"I'm inclined to my opinion, Nathaniel."

"What can I do? I can't make it right with Ellie. I thought she'd be here as always when I returned. I was a fool to think of her that way. I realize that now, but I don't want her to hate me for the rest of her life. I couldn't bear it."

Mary's eyes thinned. "To think I practically worshipped you as a child—but you're not the man I thought. Seeing you let Ellie marry Andrew, I've lost any respect I once carried for you."

"I offered myself to her, Mary. She doesn't want me. She said as much; and, besides, I'm doing what's best for everyone by bowing out. My brother will offer her the life she deserves. I can offer her nothing. I've received my inheritance and squandered it."

"Your father said he put you back in the will. At least that's what Ellie was told by her father."

"When my father passes, Andrew will see to it that the lion's share is his. And I don't care for material items, so it is of no consequence to me. I received all that I deserved and more by my father allowing me to return."

"Why did you come back then? Was it only to upset Andrew? Was it to make Ellie feel her life was incomplete somehow with your brother?"

"I came back to share my faith. I'm going to become a preacher. Perhaps it's best for everyone if I become a circuit-riding preacher and leave this place. No one listens to a prophet in their hometown—right?"

"A preacher." Mary placed a hand over her mouth and giggled, then stopped abruptly. "You're not teasing?"

"There's Ellie!"

The carriage rolled to a stop, and Nathaniel jumped out. Her eyes were red, and without a handkerchief she used the back of her hand to wipe her face. Blinking several times, she gazed at him with childlike eyes. Her russet hair was down, surrounding her shoulders and falling in gentle curls down her back. She'd never looked more beautiful to him, and he wondered if he was strong enough to leave Woodacre now. Now that he knew what he was leaving behind. Could he leave Ellie in the arms of another man? His breath left him as he pondered it.

He reached her, and she didn't fight him, as though she were discovering the same feelings. She fell against him and put her ear to his heart.

"I never thought I'd see you again. I'm so glad you came back, Nathaniel. I lied when I said you shouldn't have come. I would have wilted if I never saw you again. I think of Mary and how she felt losing Morgan. I felt nothing less not knowing where you'd gone."

"Ellie, Mary is watching."

"So let her see. Let her know that I love you. Has it ever been a secret? What else do I have to care for now? They'll marry me off as quickly as they're able. I shall be the good little wife everyone wishes. Only I will not pretend I am happy for it."

"How is your arm?" Nathaniel asked, caressing it gently with his hands. His touch caused her to flinch once again.

"Who cares about my arm? My beloved Lady is gone. You shall leave me again. If I should lose an arm like your brother, how fitting. We would be the armless couple that people come from miles around to view. Perhaps we might even join a circus."

"Eleanor!"

She pressed her hands over her face. "I'm sorry. I'm sorry. What a terrible thing to say. Forgive me. I'm not myself. You should leave Woodacre again. It's best."

"I agree," he said, breathing in the familiar scent of her hair.

She pulled away quickly, her deep brown eyes wide and fearful. "When will you leave?"

"Soon. Look at the trouble I've caused being home these few days. You and my brother will live a long life together. It will serve no purpose if I stay. I know you shall be happy without me—that Andrew is best for you." Looking into her eyes, he prayed his brother would whisper sweet words of love to her. He prayed that Andrew was entering into more than a business relationship and that he would cherish Ellie as a beloved wife, not a piece of personal property.

"I'm going to become a preacher. Perhaps a circuit-riding preacher." Nathaniel swallowed hard. He hadn't been called to be a circuit-riding preacher, but it sounded so lofty. Maybe his father would respect him if he succeeded at something other than planting. Whatever he did, he needed to get away from Ellie. Andrew deserved her; he was the one who had stayed and fought for her. And her life would be better with Andrew. He could provide her everything she was accustomed to.

"Please don't leave, Nathaniel. How will I marry him? How will I look him in the eye when I see you, and say 'I do'?" She leaned back into him, and he unconsciously surrounded her with his arms, so obviously pained by her question. It sent a wave of nausea through his stomach.

"Ellie, please don't say such things. It's not proper for you to say such things."

"What do I care of propriety, Nathaniel? My hair is down; my hoop is gone. Do I look as if I care for such manners?" She laughed, an uncomfortable, forlorn laugh. "Perhaps Mother looks down on me from her place in heaven and is encouraging me to run. I'm owned. Worse than any slave, Nathaniel. No one has set me free. I must marry whom my father tells me to marry. I'm chained to that plantation, and no Yankee law is going to help me."

"Eleanor, you are just being spoiled. Andrew will provide a nice life for you. He'll get you a grand mare, and you shall have your happiness once again. The plantations will thrive under the new laws. It will just take effort."

"Do you believe that? That I shall be happy? That a large home shall make me such?" She looked up at him, her pleading eyes begging him for the truth.

But he wouldn't give her what she asked for. It would only make things worse. He knew she wasn't spoiled or self-centered, and with him out of the picture there would be no regrets.

"Mary's going to see you home now."

Nathaniel tried to help Eleanor into the carriage, but she turned and ran. She scurried behind a collection of weeping willows. Nathaniel followed her without thinking. He found her sitting under the big tree with her arms crossed.

"We'll run together, Nathaniel. Who's to stop us? We could get married Under-the-Hill, take a ferry, and be on our way. No one questions such things now that the war has torn everything apart."

It would take one sentence from Nathaniel to silence her. He only had to say he didn't love her in such a way or that he hadn't wanted to settle down, but the words wouldn't come. They stuck in his throat like a great walnut lodged in discomfort.

"Eleanor, come and get in the carriage. A doctor should check your arm."

"Do you think your brother will treat me fairly, Nathaniel? Or do you think he wants the plantation? Tell me—does Andrew want Rosamond, or me?"

"Both, I suppose. There's no one for your father to leave it to. Why shouldn't Andrew run it?"

"There's me, Nathaniel. My father could leave the plantation to me. I would treat the men fairly, and I know just as much about running it as my father. Perhaps more because I listen."

"Ellie, I'm going home. You're talking ridiculously. I shall tell Mary where she can find you."

"Fine, Nathaniel. Leave if you must, but remember this. You do love me. I can see it in your eyes. Only yesterday you were asking for my hand in marriage, and I won't forget that. Not for as long as I live. I'll marry your brother if that's what everyone wishes for me, and I shall be a good wife to him. He is a hero to the South, and that is enough for me. But will it be for you?" Eleanor squared her shoulders. "What shall happen to you, Nathaniel?"

"Eleanor!" Eleanor's eyes opened wide at the sound of her father's bellowing voice.

"Stay here, Nathaniel. Please—my father must not know we were together."

He took her hand and grasped it. "I shall never do anything to hurt you on purpose, Ellie." He watched as her curls bounced away and then closed his eyes in agony. Her father would never accept Nathaniel as a son-in-law. He had to do what he could to make Andrew more desirable to her as a mate. It was the least he could do.

Chapter 6

After two days of bed rest ordered by her father, Ellie yearned for the sunshine and the outdoors. She longed to see the magnolias and smell the Mississippi autumn. Her room felt stuffy and only furthered her feelings of capture. Mrs. Patterson hovered about Eleanor as though she were an invalid. She sighed with relief when the older woman finally disappeared downstairs to eat supper.

"Perhaps we could climb from the windows," Eleanor said with an enthusiastic grin. "Like when we were children!"

Mary answered solemnly, in a tone that reminded Eleanor they were adults now. "Your father is very concerned about you. Why would you give him more to worry over? Your arm could become worse if you don't rest it."

Eleanor exhaled deeply, knowing her cousin was right, but wanting to be childish again, if for no other reason than she would soon be married. Probably children would follow, and her carefree romps through the long grass would cease. "Another day gone. If it weren't for sneaking out in the evenings, I couldn't stand it. To think the men are free all day, and we are locked up here."

"Your father will have a fit if he finds you giving extra portions to that slave girl. You never know what dangerous characters she might bring with her one night."

"They're not slaves anymore, Mary," Eleanor said, springing out of bed and stamping her foot on the floor. No one remembered these were free men and women. "And it's time for me to get down there—the sun is nearly gone."

Eleanor packed up the remainder of her meal. She'd told the cook she was extra hungry with her illness and had a good supply of biscuits and even portions of meat for Ceviche tonight. It would be a treat for the young girl, and Eleanor took pride in saving such a sufficient meal for Ceviche.

"My mother is in the parlor. I don't know how you'll get out tonight." Mary crossed her arms and stretched her legs onto the bed as though taking some pleasure in the thought her cousin might get caught.

"Aunt Till will be talking with her *daughter*." Eleanor smiled and yanked Mary by the hand from her comfortable position.

"Oh no, you've gotten me in enough trouble this week. I've already got the Pemberton boys fretting over you and asking for me to see to your every whim. Now you want me to get in between you and your father? Well, I won't do it. You're on your own if you intend to sneak out of this house. No slave girl is worth all this. My mother is right to worry after you since your father has no idea what you're capable of."

"Mary, where's your sense of adventure? Remember when we borrowed the pony to see the battle at the river? Think of all the excitement we would have missed had we stayed home as Aunt Till and Father ordered."

Eleanor hoped to persuade her cousin in her quest for freedom, which she was usually able to do. She had found her calling seeing to the needs of others, and she hoped Mary would help her do it. Nothing else felt important any longer. Not the color of her dress or the state of Rosamond or even Lady being laid to rest. Eleanor planned to help the former slaves, and she planned to enlist Nathaniel to help her. They still had that in common.

"If you won't help me, at least let me borrow your gown. Perhaps I can slip out that way. Mine are all so brightly colored."

Mary crossed her arms. "I'm not having any part of this, Ellie. You've got no business out in the woods at night. Lord only knows what tragedies might befall you."

"Fine. Stay here, but if you heard that baby wail, you'd help her, too. What right do we have as humans to starve people? I'll tell you—we've got none, Mary!"

Eleanor opened her bedroom door and peeked around the jamb. All was quiet, and she tiptoed down the stairs, leaving her cousin alone. It was the one time she remembered Mary defying what she wanted. She heard her father and aunt arguing in the library but didn't stop to listen. She was just thankful their conversation kept them so busy that they didn't notice her. It was something about the missing overseer.

She passed easily without being seen and climbed down the back steps with her basket packed. Ceviche was waiting for her at the edge of the woods as usual.

"Miss Eleanor, you's so kind." Ceviche held her baby cradled against her breast with one arm and held out the other for the basket.

"May I hold the baby?" Eleanor reached out her arms and took the infant into an embrace. Closing her eyes, she listened to the gentle smacking noises as the baby sucked on his little fingers. "He's getting so big."

"Yes'm. Now that I got me more milk, he's gonna be a big chil." Ceviche rammed the food into her mouth and swallowed huge gulps of milk to chase it down. Her breath was labored from eating so feverishly.

"What's his name? I never asked."

"His name is Frederick. He's named after Frederick Douglass, and he's gonna be just as smart, Miss Eleanor. I'm gonna get him out of here. He's not gonna pick no cotton for his life."

"How do you know about Frederick Douglass, Ceviche?" Eleanor was mystified that anyone so remote might hear of the works of such an outspoken black man. As for Eleanor, she'd heard only derogatory statements about him from her father, but enough to know that he represented everything her father feared.

"It don't matter none. Fact is, I know." Ceviche continued to force food down herself, and Eleanor had to look away. "I also know Masser Pemberton is leaving tomorrow."

"Andrew?" Ellie turned back toward the young girl.

"Not your man, Miss Eleanor—his older brother. He's going to preach about Jesus—at least that's what he says."

"Where did you hear that?" Eleanor's eyes widened in fear that this might be the truth.

"He's packing up his things now. Andrew says it's best he leave before you's over your illness. You ill, miss? Word is, Masser Andrew's happy to see Masser Nathaniel go. Mrs. White is helpin' him pack."

"Are you going back to Woodacre now?" Eleanor bounced the baby nervously. "Can you get a message to Nathaniel for me? A message that no one would see you bring him?"

"I can get one to Jim. Jim, he can go anywhere on Woodacre. He'd see to it that Masser Pemberton got the note."

"Wait here." Eleanor thrust back the baby and climbed the back stairs. She hunted for a piece of paper and found a bit of charcoal to write her note. She scribbled something quickly and took it to Ceviche. "Don't tell anyone you've done this."

"No ma'am."

"I'll see you tomorrow night, Ceviche." Eleanor bent over and kissed Frederick's head. "Get the note to Woodacre as quickly as possible."

She snuck back into the house and walked into the parlor, where her father and aunt were still having words. She acted as though she'd just come from upstairs.

"Eleanor, what are you doing out of bed?" Aunt Till stopped arguing with her father and lowered her brows in a concerned frown.

"I was thirsty. I thought I might help myself to some tea."

"Ring the bell, Eleanor. That's what it's there for." Her father crossed his arms. "Where's Mary?"

"She's in my room," she answered truthfully. "Is there any tea?"

"Eleanor, get back in your room and stay there," her father ordered.

Eleanor could see her father was in no mood for her trifling, and she promptly stood up straight and left. She closed the parlor doors, and the argument started again at once. Despite knowing better, she leaned against the wall and listened.

"Where did they find him?" Aunt Till asked.

"He was in one of the cotton fields. None of the slaves claims to know anything about it, but he didn't get there on his own."

"You've got to get Ellie married as soon as possible. It isn't safe for her to be here. She needs a husband who can keep her safe. No more of this running around on a horse between the plantations. She's had far too much freedom."

"There was a day when chivalry ruled the South. Those days are gone, I suppose."

"I'll take Mary as soon as the wedding is over, and we'll be on our way. It's not safe for her to be running about either, though she's not inclined to adventure like Eleanor. You'll need to have someone with them at all times until the wedding. It's necessary. As soon as Eleanor's arm has recovered, make arrangements with Preacher Cummings to perform the ceremony." Aunt Till clicked her tongue. "I'm so glad Eleanor's mother didn't live to see this. To see what has become of Rosamond."

"You take care of the womanly things surrounding the wedding. I'll handle the slaves, and I'll find out what happened to that overseer." Her father's voice grew louder. "Someone's going to pay with a hanging."

"Shh," Aunt Till reprimanded. "Eleanor and Mary have had a hard enough time of it. They needn't know any of this."

Eleanor clutched her hands to her chest and ran up the stairs, afraid to hear anymore. It served her right for eavesdropping. The overseer wasn't coming back. With fear and trembling she recalled running to the edge of the woods alone each night. Would she be able to go tomorrow? Or ever again? The thought of baby Frederick looking bigger and healthier drove her. She would have to find a way.

❧

Nathaniel closed his traveling pack on the small amount of items he intended to take with him. Mrs. White offered to send a food basket along, and he graciously accepted. He didn't know where he was headed or how long it might take him to find his way. He turned his face to the ornate ceiling and asked for the Lord's guidance.

Andrew stood with his hand in his pocket, studying everything Nathaniel did. "So it looks as though you have everything. You should leave tonight."

"I plan to wait for daylight, Andrew." Nathaniel excused Mrs. White and faced his brother. "You have your whole life with Eleanor. You needn't worry about how soon I go. Your wedding shall be soon enough."

"Eleanor doesn't love you, Nathaniel. You squelched any of those feelings the day you abandoned her and left her to be gossiped about as a terminal spinster. I hope you don't leave thinking you're doing me any kind of favor."

"On the contrary. I'm leaving to do Ellie a favor. You two should have Woodacre to yourselves, instead of extra relatives bumbling about. Father will see to it Ellie is given the proper beginnings of your marriage, and so will I. It's only right that a married couple start out on the right foot."

"Don't ignore my words, brother. Eleanor is not your Ellie any longer, and I'd appreciate it if you spoke of my fiancée in appropriate terms. She shall be your sister-in-law in less than a week. I'll find her a new horse, and all will be right again."

Nathaniel looked at his case before buckling it up. "I meant nothing by it, on my honor. I was only referring to my childhood playmate. I wish that you would get over this anger you have toward me. You are the only brother I have. I'm leaving, so let it be on good terms. You shall have Father and Eleanor all to yourself again. I needed to come back to make amends, but I shall not stay. Isn't that enough for you? What more would you wish?"

Andrew tilted his head to the side, avoiding eye contact with Nathaniel. What had happened to the brother Nathaniel knew? The boy who had spurred him on in races and taught him to ride a horse? Where was that Andrew now? Nathaniel was certain Andrew didn't even love Ellie. He only hated to lose, and in Andrew's mind he had lost. He wouldn't be satisfied until Nathaniel was dead. At least that's what Andrew's scowl said.

"You wish me dead, do you not?" Nathaniel asked.

"I wish you were thought of as dead. Where you go is your affair."

"I'll give you a word of advice, Andrew. Buy Eleanor a special horse, one that tells her how truly sorry you are."

"I have already spoken with a top breeder—"

"Ellie—I mean, Eleanor—doesn't want a top breeder; she wants Lady. I've written down the name of the farm where Lady came from. Perhaps they'll be able to trace the line and find you a horse who's similar."

"Lady was nothing more than a rickety old mare, Nathaniel." Andrew laughed. "She was little more than food for the hounds, and you wish me to replace her?"

"You're thinking like a man and about the value of good horseflesh. Eleanor is thinking of the horse she loved. Buy her a relative of Lady's. Trust me. Just this once. I'll not steer you wrong." Nathaniel shoved the scrap of paper into his brother's pocket. Then he held out his right arm to shake his brother's hand. "I wish you the best, brother. Make Father proud. I know you always have."

To his surprise, Andrew reached out and took his hand. "Good luck, Nathaniel."

Stepping into the hallway, Nathaniel decided to check on his horse and the small conveyance he would take with him. He was probably gathering far too much to make an honest circuit-riding preacher, but he would wait to see where God sent him before he did anything drastic. Perhaps he would find a little church to work out of. He approached the stables and was met by Jim, one of the plantation men.

"I gots a letter for Masser Pemberton." He held out the note, and Nathaniel recognized Ellie's penmanship immediately.

He unfolded the note quickly, thanking Jim for his service. Then he bowed his head in shame at the contents.

Dear Nathaniel,

I've heard rumors that you are departing us again. Tell me it isn't true! Tell me you won't leave me here to suffer alone. My father holds me here because of my arm, but I'm afraid there is something far more sinister at work. Will you leave again without bidding me good-bye? While I am held captive?

Yours affectionately,
Ellie

Chapter 7

Nathaniel!" His father's voice jolted him from his quiet thoughts. "You're needed here. Come back in the house with me."

Nathaniel crumpled the letter into his pocket and followed his father into Woodacre. They climbed the circular staircase into his father's study. The home, while still spacious, stood sparse and empty. All its lavish furnishings had disappeared with the war. If they'd had a mother or a sister, perhaps some of it would have been replaced by now. As it was, it remained a hollow testament to destruction.

He breathed in deeply, surrounded by the smell of his father's cigars. Whatever furniture the Yankees stole, Nathaniel was sure that scent was singed into the wood. How Nathaniel would miss that spicy scent that instantly catapulted him back in years. Back to a time when he hadn't made so many mistakes and people thought of him as a man with promise. A man they'd like to see their daughters married to. Now he was the black sheep, the one who caused whispers as he passed, and certainly no one they'd be proud to call "son". His father entered his library and closed the doors behind them.

"Sit down, son."

Nathaniel obediently sat at the great desk, relishing the opportunity to be called son again. How grateful Nathaniel was he'd been provided such an opportunity. "What is it you need, Father? Is it something Andrew might be able to help you with?"

Nathaniel remembered his promise to the Lord. He would do nothing to undermine Andrew's authority any longer. Nathaniel would humble himself, as the Bible taught. No matter how difficult it might be, it was best for all involved.

"No, it's not something Andrew can do."

"I'm leaving tomorrow, Father." Nathaniel watched his father shift uncomfortably, and he tried to put him at ease. "My things are packed, and I think it's best. I shall be back for visits this time though."

"I'm asking you to stay." He shook his head and slapped his hand on the desk. "No, I'm *telling* you to stay!" It was nearly the same conversation they'd had six years earlier when Nathaniel decided he couldn't be chained any longer and ran. The similarities drove Nathaniel to hear his father out. "We need you here on the plantation."

"I can't stay, Father. Andrew is quite capable, and my staying will only frustrate him." Nathaniel prayed for strength to broach the obvious subject they had never discussed before. "Eleanor cannot rely on me, Father. She has to turn to Andrew, and I fear the only way for her to do that fully is for me to leave."

"Eleanor will do as she's told. That's her father's business, not yours. You're not going to run again because of some woman. I'm asking you for a far more important motive. All our lives could depend upon it. The woman either of my sons marry is not of concern to me, other than the obvious benefit of marrying Woodacre and Rosamond."

"I can't imagine how my staying this time would make anything better." Nathaniel raked a hand through his hair, agitated at the uncomfortable position in which his father was placing him.

"You're soft on the slaves, aren't you? Least that's what they think." His father stood and walked around the desk, sitting on it in front of Nathaniel. "They found Rosamond's overseer, Mitchell Rouse, in a cotton field. They don't know how he got there, but my fear is an uprising. Andrew's been overseeing the workers with a rough hand. I fear it might come back to haunt us."

Nathaniel clicked his tongue. "So treat them right, Father. You don't have to fool anyone if you just treat the men as they should be treated. We're to love our neighbors as ourselves."

"I fear it's too late for that. Look at Mitchell's untimely end. He was a man of thirty perhaps. What if his death was—well, what if he was murdered?" The senior Pemberton could barely utter the words.

Nathaniel knew his father needed comfort, not his anger, over how Andrew had seen to things. Guilt gripped him. How could he leave the plantation in his brother's hands? His father's fears might well become a reality with Andrew at the helm.

"Overseeing is hard work," Nathaniel stated. "I didn't know the man, but perhaps this Rouse fellow filled himself too full with drink before work. It could have been a stray Yankee looking for a meal, Father. Either way—fear is not of the Lord. It won't do us any good to be fearful. All this trouble could be solved by giving the men enough food portions to do their work. Eliminate these black codes you've started. They're nothing short of slavery, Father, and slavery is illegal. Going against the law will only harm Woodacre in the long run."

His father's wrath was stirred. "This plantation has been in Pemberton hands for generations. You think I'll have some Yankee telling me how to run it?"

His face reddened, and he clutched his chest. Nathaniel stood and steadied him.

"Father, you're getting too upset. Sit down."

He choked out the words: "You'll stay."

"I'll pray over it," Nathaniel replied. "I'll have Mrs. White bring you some tea. Have one of your cigars." He went to his father's humidor, a luxury that had obviously been salvaged, and took out a long, brown cylinder, handing it to his father.

"Pray?" His father asked. "Your family home is in jeopardy. Our very lives may depend on your being here, and you tell me you'll pray? What kind of preaching got into you in that forsaken land? Religion is for weaklings, Nathaniel."

"I've been weak, Father. The Lord is for those who need strength."

His father grunted, and Nathaniel knew it was best to abandon this line of conversation.

"What makes you suspect Mr. Rouse met with an untimely death?" Nathaniel asked calmly, unwilling to discuss his prayer life when his father was so angry.

"He was found in the field with a bottle of drink beside him. He'd been missing for over a week." The senior Pemberton ran the cigar under his nostrils, breathing in deeply. He didn't light the cigar, only savored the smell. "Rouse wasn't a popular man."

"Name me an overseer Master Senton has hired who was popular. Eleanor's father has always ruled with an iron fist, Father. No one's disappeared yet."

"Now that the Yankees got it in their heads that these men are free—well, there's no telling what will happen."

"They are free, Father."

"Your brother keeps close tabs on what the men eat. It will be no secret to the slaves who it was who ordered the portions." His father's voice was weak. "If you leave, I fear your brother may be next."

Nathaniel closed his eyes and dropped his head into his hands. *Lord, what are You telling me? If I don't go, Andrew and Ellie may never have the marriage they need. But if I go, Andrew's and Ellie's lives may be in peril.*

Nathaniel excused himself and made no commitments. He would talk to Jim and find out if the slaves knew anything before he reacted rashly.

"Wait on Him. Wait on Him," he repeated aloud to himself as he entered the hallway.

"They teach you to talk to yourself in the West?" Mrs. White held a silver tea tray and smiled at him. "Your father's expecting tea. Will you join him?"

"I'm leaving, Mrs. White, but thank you. I need to go into the fields for a bit."

"Is it safe?" she asked fearfully.

"I don't know what superstitions you've been filling your head with, Mrs. White, but it's perfectly safe to be in the fields."

Nathaniel nodded his good-bye and closed the door behind him. Outside, he mounted a horse and rode to Rosamond as if chased by a great fire. He needed to be close to Eleanor if only to ensure her safety; even if he never spoke to her again, he would see she was taken care of properly. Her nightly escapades to bring food to Ceviche weren't safe, though Ellie wouldn't care if it meant helping a wounded soul.

Riding to the edge of the wooded area, he saw her illumined by the light streaming out of the kitchen window. She was huddled next to a wrought-iron bench in the garden.

"Ellie!" He ran to her side, putting his arms about her. She shivered at his touch. "You're frozen to the core." He removed his coat and wrapped it around her shoulders. "What are you doing out here?"

"Ceviche told me you were leaving. It's true, isn't it?" Ellie's red-rimmed eyes looked at him.

He felt like the ultimate betrayer at the sight, and his natural instinct was to comfort her.

"My father is asking that I stay. I'm praying over the matter."

"Your brother was here earlier. He's asked that we move the wedding up. Was that your idea?"

"Andrew was here?"

Eleanor nodded. Again her hair was down in luxurious curls, and Nathaniel thought he would languish over the intimate sight. It took all of his willpower to keep his hands from caressing the locks and feeling the silky strands between his fingers.

"He kissed me," she said shamefully. "Not the kind of kiss you and I ever shared, Nathaniel. It hurt."

Nathaniel clenched his fists tightly, and his jaw tightened in anger. "What do you mean he kissed you, Ellie?"

She shook her head. "I don't want to talk about it. It was awful, Nathaniel. Is that what marriage is like? I always thought it would be like that idyllic way I felt when I saw you run across the field. You know, that sweet, butterfly feeling in my stomach. But it is not going to be like that, is it, Nathaniel?" Her wide coffee-colored eyes blinked at him, looking for hope in his answer. "I thought a woman could make herself love any man she chose as her husband, but that heavenly swirl in my stomach won't ever come with Andrew, will it, Nathaniel?"

"Ellie, I don't want you coming out here alone anymore."

"I don't want to be married to a man who kisses me like that," Eleanor whispered, almost to herself.

Nathaniel's gut turned at the innocence in her voice. He would see his brother dead before he would let him touch Ellie harshly again. He closed his eyes, remembering his vow before God. He was supposed to help Andrew be a proper husband to her. Was that possible?

"Did you hear me, Ellie? It's not safe for you to be here alone anymore. You stay in your room. Tell your father you still don't feel well, but stay there until you hear from me. I'll send a pebble to your window when I return."

"Where are you going?" she asked, her voice shaking.

"I'm going Under-the-Hill to ask a few questions." Nathaniel couldn't be more specific than that. It was bad enough he admitted to going where the bars and brothels thrived.

"Why must you go there?"

"It's something I must do."

"You are coming back, aren't you, Nathaniel? You won't leave me again? I won't hear from Ceviche that you've abandoned us?"

"Ellie, don't look at me as if I was born to deceive you. It's not like that. You know I have to do what I must. You know that Rosamond and Woodacre need each other to survive."

Nathaniel couldn't look at her when he said the words. How could he tell her it was all right to marry a man who made her feel ill? That she wasn't entitled to a man who made her stomach swirl sweetly? How could he tell her the very sight of her sent his own heart racing and made him want to forget any vow he'd ever made?

"Nathaniel, will you kiss me?" Eleanor's face was mere inches from his own, and he felt her warmth to his inner soul. But sin felt good before one committed it. "My stomach is swimming now. I need to know if it only feels that way for you."

Nathaniel stood abruptly. "No, Ellie, I won't. You're my brother's intended bride. This is wrong."

She stood beside him, leaving her hair to whip around in a way that reminded him of all he might lose. "You're going to change that, aren't you, Nathaniel? You're not going to let me marry him." Eleanor pressed her cheek against his chest, and he knew his pounding heart betrayed his calm front.

"Stay in your room, Ellie. I'm promising you nothing." Nathaniel turned on his heel and didn't look back for fear she would know what he really felt.

Chapter 8

Eleanor forgot to breathe as Nathaniel's horse drove into the dark night. It seemed she had spent a lifetime watching Nathaniel leave. Always wondering if this was the time he would never return to her. It never got any easier to watch him go, but she was resigned to it now. One day it would be forever, and it was time she got used to the idea. She stood and walked to the back porch.

"Ellie?" Mary's hand touched her back gently. "Hattie is up in your room. She's been putting off Aunt Till. But I fear your days are numbered if you don't come in now. You don't want them to know about you feeding the slave girl, do you?"

"I'm coming."

"What's happened?" Mary's tender voice caused a flurry of emotion. The tears began again for Eleanor, and she embraced her cousin.

"I'm not going to marry Nathaniel," she said, by way of recognizing the fact.

"No, Ellie, you are not," Mary answered gently. "It is for the best."

"You seem to like my fiancé. Tell me why." Eleanor hoped that hearing something positive about Andrew would help her focus on him and not on the slim chance of Nathaniel's returning to her. Woodacre's and Rosamond's future depended upon this marriage. Nathaniel's reputation was scurrilous. She was engaged to marry his brother, and her father would never put their beloved plantation in the hands of a Yankee.

Her father, Master Senton, called anyone who didn't help with the war effort a Yankee, because if you did not help, you hindered. Nathaniel was the coward who had left his family, and nothing would change that in her father's eyes. As the wedding loomed, Eleanor's hopes diminished. Seeing Nathaniel again was only torture to her wounded heart.

"Andrew is not Nathaniel, Ellie. He will not run at the first sign of trouble. He'll save your land," Mary said brightly, and Eleanor realized she'd been speaking. "He's serious and thinks more of the future than Nathaniel does. He will provide a good life for you. You cannot compare the two brothers. It's like comparing cotton with tobacco." Mary squeezed Eleanor's hand for reassurance.

Eleanor wished she had her cousin's sense, but she wore her heart out in the open. Hiding her feelings would come soon enough. "How can I help but compare them?"

Mary seemed to search her mental libraries for something good to say about Andrew. She did not take nearly as long as Eleanor might have. "Andrew is handsome and dashing if you'd only see him that way, Ellie. He is a proud Confederate warrior, with medals to prove it. I'll admit Andrew has lived in Nathaniel's shadow, but he's a fine man. I know any number of women who should be happy to call him their husband."

Eleanor recalled the harsh kiss he had planted upon her and couldn't imagine ever being happy for the opportunity. "Do you know such women?" she asked sincerely.

"I do," Mary answered. Her words were slow and deliberate. "Andrew loves you, Eleanor. He'll be a good husband. I know I've always been partial to Nathaniel, but who hasn't? And this trip I'm wondering if I hadn't made a mistake in that. Nathaniel is easy to love, I'll grant you that, but Andrew is steady and true."

"Steady? It sounds as though you're describing a field horse, Mary." Eleanor couldn't help herself; she giggled like a schoolgirl. It felt like the finest luxury to laugh through her tears. "Surely you can think of something better to say of my fiancé than he is steady."

"I can say he is alive, Ellie. Which is more than I can say for my dear Morgan. You are blessed to have a decision of any kind.

I had none. Death took my love from me, and I shall have to wait to hold his hand in heaven."

"You think I have a decision?" Eleanor stifled a shudder. She wondered if Mary might see things differently had she been the recipient of Andrew's harsh kiss. "I'm so sorry about Morgan, Mary. It's not right that you should have lost him, but so far you've told me my fiancé is steady and alive. It's not exactly the feelings that inspire passion in a woman."

"Passion is exaggerated in importance, Ellie. It shall cease. That's what my mother says."

"I should hope it doesn't. Maybe I am a fool, Mary, but I would rather have a fleeting year of passion than a lifetime of *steady*. What is there to a dull, fixed life? Especially after the excitement of the war, I fear I will not be content as a wife. I have watched shells fly by my family home. How can I live with dull? I wish my mother were here to question on the matter. She would tell me if I was doing the proper thing."

Mary sighed. "I long for a steadfast life. How sick I am of the ups and downs, the riches and poverty, the starvation and plenty. I should love to live a simple life with a steady husband, but I fear Mother would be lonely without me at her side."

"You do not think you'll ever marry then?" Eleanor wrinkled her face, confused at the notion. It seemed she had no other options besides marriage, and here Mary sat free from the prospect because her fiancé had been lost to the war. Eleanor's true love had disappeared to the West. Why was she expected to marry?

"Now that the prospects for marriage have dwindled so, I must say I doubt it. I never was as popular as you are with the opposite sex, and since there are so many women fairer than I, my chances are slim. I fear I don't have the lush curls and batting eyelashes men seem to favor. Morgan was different. He was attracted to my intellect. He thrived in it, but I'm afraid most men find a bookworm useless in this time of our history."

"You survived, Mary. And don't forget it. God has put us here for a reason, and we have to believe He has a plan. I'm only lamenting that His plan may not match mine. It's selfish of me, I admit." Eleanor hoped to encourage her cousin. "But how like God that is, and He always seems to wrap His gifts so much prettier than I ever could. His hands stretched over darkness and created the world. I suppose I cannot question what He has for me now." She knew her words were never truer, although she had been selfish in her pursuits.

"I suppose I cannot question God in this."

"I wish I wasn't at the mercy of my father. He thinks only of the plantation since Mother died. He'll not care if Andrew is a suitable match for me."

"I don't think that's true, Ellie. Your father loves you. He wants to see you well taken care of after his death. That's a noble trait, and remember *who* put him in charge of your life."

"Let's not talk of sad things any longer. I'm to have a new gown for after the wedding. Would you like to see the pattern I've cut?"

"I'd love to! I'm so glad we shall be able to create gowns and have fabrics of luxury once more. What a mean spirit those Yankees must have had to come in and destroy our gowns for sport and our china for target practice. Have they no shame to go into a woman's bedroom and tear through her things?"

"Let God be their judge. I'm just glad they're gone. Once we combine the plantations, things will be normal again. We'll have cotton and fabrics and food and servants. We shall even replace things that have been lost."

Eleanor forced a note of cheer to her voice. Maybe things would be better as she said. She looked at her cousin and saw the melancholy there. Immediately, she chastised herself for her careless talk.

"I'm sorry, Mary. I know things will never be the same for you. Not with Morgan gone. How thoughtless of me to say such a thing."

Eleanor thought she heard a horse's hooves and looked into the dark night, but only blackness stared back at her.

"Never mind, Ellie. Never mind," Mary said, and Eleanor was left to wonder if she referred to the night sounds or the loss of Morgan.

⟂

Long before Nathaniel reached the infamous Under-the-Hill port, he could hear the raucous noise from Silver Street. Its brick buildings teemed with sailors, drunkards, and bandits. Nearly every night someone was murdered, and Nathaniel prayed tonight wasn't his night as the boisterous sounds came closer. It was a dark night with no moon in sight, and the Mississippi appeared as only deep blackness. But Nathaniel knew it was there. He could hear the echo of drunken men's voices bouncing off the calm waters.

The vile scent of the town, something like coal, molasses, and foul liquor, mingled under his nose. Slowing his horse to a trot, he prepared to step into Mississippi's underworld. He hoped his intuition was wrong, that Andrew had no business here.

As he came onto Silver Street, the noisy tin pianos and fiddles belted his senses. Women offered themselves to him from the boardwalk with a coquettish nod of the head. Nathaniel turned his eyes away, disgusted by the overt display. Rabble-rousers lined the streets, yelling obscenities as he passed. He ignored everything until he reached his destination.

He climbed from his horse and paid a man, who looked as respectable as any he'd seen on Silver Street, to watch his horse, offering more if it was there when he returned. Luckily, horse thievery was still punishable by death, and even drunk men weren't likely to play with such a heavy sentence. Nathaniel entered the Rumbel and Wensel store, which was just another bar. But this place had nothing on the dirty mining camps of California, and Nathaniel took comfort in the fact that God was beside him.

Approaching the grocery clerk, who was a bartender at night,

Nathaniel was careful not to give himself away. One sure way was to order something other than liquor, but Nathaniel had played this game before. "I'm starving. You got any grub back there?"

"I can have the missus cook you up something. You just get off a flatboat?"

"Nah. But I'm hungry just the same." Nathaniel took out some cash and flashed it. Answers were much easier to get when the prospect of making an easy dollar was obvious. "Been up to Natchez. I'm looking for a man named Mitchell Rouse. You know him?"

The man's eyes thinned, and he motioned for his wife to cook something. She hurried back to the kitchen. "What do you want to know?"

"His boss is looking for him. Ran off the job, and they want their pay back. You heard anything?"

The bartender bent toward Nathaniel, grabbing a bill for himself. "I might."

Nathaniel pulled the remainder of the cash toward him. "Word on the plantation is the slaves might have pulled a Nat Turner," Nathaniel said, referring to the slave who pulled a revolt killing several owners and their families. The story was infamous, and many owners ruled with an iron fist out of fear that such a thing could happen to them. Nathaniel wanted to offer something to the bartender to throw the man off any trail of his identity.

"Slaves most likely got nothing to do with it." The bartender looked around him before resuming his wiping of the counter. "Rouse was here about a week ago. He was fighting with a man over a shipping tax."

"What would an overseer have to do with a tariff?" Nathaniel froze at the slipup. No street dweller would use such a term, but the bartender didn't seem to notice. The man was still salivating over the dollar bills in Nathaniel's possession.

"He wasn't just an overseer, from what I hear. He ran a business here at night. A certain business dealing in trade, if you know what I mean." The man motioned with his brows and looked to a nearby woman drinking with a patron.

Nathaniel's stomach turned at the thought of dealing in human flesh, and it took all his willpower to keep his disgust from showing in his expression. "Ah," Nathaniel said casually.

"When a man don't pay the tax, his haul gets confiscated. No goods, no cash. No cash, your credit catches up with you, if you know what I mean. Rouse probably threatened the wrong man."

"You think Rouse is dead?" Nathaniel feigned ignorance, knowing the man had been lying in his cotton field the day before.

"That's what the man said. You're the second guy who's been here looking for him today. Some one-armed guy was here this afternoon saying Rouse was dead. Was there any kin?"

"One-armed?" Nathaniel was stunned at the description of his brother.

"He acted like he didn't know what Rouse was up to, but I seen him in here before. He knew why Rouse was dead; he just wanted to know who did it." The bartender dried a glass, and his wife appeared with a plate full of potatoes under a slop of gravy.

Nathaniel smiled at the woman. "Do you know who did it?" he asked the bartender.

"I got my ideas. But you ask that one-armed guy. He knows more than he's saying. I can taste it."

Nathaniel handed the man three dollars and started in on the feast before him.

Chapter 9

Doctor Hayes glanced over his spectacles. "Your arm looks fine, Miss Senton. I'll tell your father you are cured." He stood up, placing his instruments back in his bag. "Anxious to be married, I suppose?" He smiled at her as though she were a lovesick girl waiting for a happy diagnosis.

"What about the color of my arm? Will it go away?" Eleanor asked, hoping to remind the doctor and those concerned that her arm still looked like a ripe blueberry. Surely, no doctor would approve such a vicious bruise on a bride.

"Give it a few weeks," he answered. "A long-sleeved gown will take care of it presently."

Eleanor faltered at the advice. A long-sleeved gown wouldn't hide her heart, which seemed to beat only at the sight of Nathaniel. At least that was the only time she noticed she had a heart, when it thundered as he approached. Her quiet night jolted her back to the present. No pebbles were thrown at the window, although she couldn't sleep for thinking she might miss Nathaniel. Perhaps this was the time he had gone for good.

"I'll see myself out, Hattie. She may get into her hoop contraption and rejoin the land of the living," Doctor Hayes advised.

Eleanor blushed red at the thought of this man discussing her hoop, but she dismissed it. Chivalry hadn't been the same since the war. It probably never would be. Suddenly, the thought struck her as funny, and she giggled out loud.

Mary came to her side. "Whatever is so funny, Ellie?"

"The war has certainly changed things. Doc Hayes has commented on my hoops. I daresay he wouldn't mention such things before. I guess we have all seen too much."

"Andrew is downstairs. He wishes to speak with you."

Eleanor swallowed hard, and the folly immediately left her voice. "Andrew?"

"Yes, Andrew, your *fiancé*. I think he may have discussed the wedding date with your father. They seem to be in quite good spirits."

Now Eleanor's heart beat rapidly, but it wasn't the pleasant feeling she anticipated. It was fear. Chances were, she would be married before she ever saw Nathaniel again, and the answers he went searching for would serve them no purpose. After tightening her corset and fastening her hoop, Eleanor checked her reflection in the mirror and practiced a smile. She clenched and grimaced until she saw teeth. When she was satisfied with her playacting, she started down the circular staircase. Her father and Andrew waited in the foyer, and the closer she got, the farther away they both felt. When she stood beside them, it was as though another body had taken her place.

Andrew smiled pleasantly enough, and Eleanor again forced her lips in an upward fashion. "Hello, Andrew."

"I have a surprise for you, Miss Eleanor." Andrew clicked his heels together and motioned toward the door.

He followed Eleanor out, and her eyes opened wide, hoping it was not a mere figment of her imagination. Her jaw dropped at the sight of a horse that appeared identical to Lady. She was a chestnut beauty with a black mane, and Eleanor instinctively went toward her.

"She's beautiful!" Eleanor exclaimed, patting the dark mane. "Whose is she?"

"She's yours. A cousin of Lady's. I purchased her from the same horse breeder."

"You did?" Eleanor was taken aback.

This was something she could appreciate about Andrew. He had figured out where Lady came from and purchased a family member. She looked to the horse's deep brown eyes and felt a bond. Lady lived on in this mare. She ran to her fiancé and threw her arms about him.

"I'm speechless, Andrew. I don't know how to show my gratitude. No one's ever given me a more thoughtful gift."

She smiled and noticed Andrew's shy, sheepish grin. This was the kind of gift Nathaniel would have given her. She shook the thought from her head. Perhaps she'd been too harsh on Andrew. This proved he was more than steady, and it was time she started focusing on the future, not her past. Nathaniel was her past.

"Thank you," she managed. "I'm sorry I was so emotional and uncivil the day of my accident."

"Never mind, Eleanor. You deserve this horse. I wish you understood how sorry, how truly sorry, I am about Lady." Andrew bowed. "This mare has been broken. Are you ready to ride her?"

Eleanor brightened. "I can hardly wait." She dashed up the stairs, with Mary at her heels. "Oh Mary, can you believe she's such a fine mare? I wish it were Lady of course. But I shan't act spoiled anymore when Andrew has done me such a service. I should be truly grateful for such a beautiful horse, and I shall be."

Eleanor ran to her room where Hattie was spreading out her dinner gown. "Hattie, forget about that gown. I need my riding clothes. I have a new horse!"

"A new horse?" Hattie questioned. Eleanor knew her father didn't have the money for such luxuries right now, and probably Hattie did as well. "You haven't got time to gallivant before dinner."

"It's a wedding gift—from Andrew," Eleanor explained.

"A gift? Is that what they call it when a man replaces what he shot?" Hattie mumbled.

Eleanor's gaze fell, her spirits sinking like a spent gunboat to the bottom of the mighty Mississippi.

"He *had* to shoot Lady, Hattie. Her leg was broken most likely, wasn't it, Mary?" She looked to her cousin—to someone who could make her believe things weren't that bad. Mary's eyes flickered and strayed about the room. Her eyes focused everywhere but on Eleanor. "Right, Mary? He *had* to shoot Lady. He's a hero. Tell Hattie, Mary."

But Mary didn't answer, and Eleanor looked at Hattie's disapproving scowl.

"Rosamond is going to go to the codes, Miss Ellie. Make no mistake about it," Hattie stated, as though it were a known fact.

"What does my new horse have to do with that?"

"If a horse can make you forget what you've been fighting for—"

"No, Hattie. There will be no codes here. Father will see to it that the men are given their freedom. Mississippi may not see them as people, but Father does. I know he does, Hattie. Rosamond would never turn to the black codes. It's simply another form of slavery, and Father never treated his men like that."

"That may well be true, Miss Ellie, but when Master Pemberton owns things, things are going to change."

Mary interrupted. "I think you've stated your opinions quite plainly, Hattie. That's enough."

"It won't. You have my word on it," Eleanor protested.

"Your word. Has your word stopped you from feeding that poor starving girl from Woodacre? I know what you are doing, Missy. I didn't raise you from an infant to be fooled by your nightly exits from this house. Why do you think she's coming here if things are so good at the Pemberton house?"

Eleanor felt the blood drain from her face. She had meant for her marriage to solve problems, not create different, worse problems. Looking at Mary and Hattie, she suddenly felt as if she were a traitor, and that her new horse had chains draping from its hindquarters.

⁂

Nathaniel sat on the docks watching as the flatboats and paddle wheelers maneuvered around the Port of Natchez. It had been a long night, and Nathaniel wasn't any closer to learning the truth about Mitchell Rouse than he'd been the night before. Nathaniel rubbed the back of his kinked neck and tried to stretch out his tired shoulders. On the trail for Rouse, Nathaniel had discovered something unsavory about Andrew's dealings. Woodacre wasn't nearly as bad off as Rosamond, and Nathaniel had thought it was Andrew's tight ledgers. But now he wondered. While most Southerners had burned their cotton rather than let the Yankees get it, Andrew had sold theirs at a healthy profit, not caring who purchased it. Had he done worse?

If the town knew of these scalawag dealings, Woodacre's reputation would be dashed. It was one thing that Nathaniel had tarnished the family name by "running" rather than fighting in the War between the States, but to know Andrew may have profited from the South's misfortune would seal their fate forever. In the future no one would do business with Woodacre knowing they were scalawags. It was worse than the carpetbaggers of the North.

"Who you lookin' fer?" A gruff voice met him, and Nathaniel looked up, thinking Goliath lived again. A huge beast of a man blocked the sun completely, and Nathaniel stood up for fear of getting trounced upon.

"I'm waiting for Jeremiah Coleman. You know him?" Nathaniel stammered.

"What d'ya want with him?"

"I want to know what business he's had with Mitchell Rouse." There was no sense playing cat and mouse with this man. Nathaniel knew decidedly who would lose.

The man laughed and spit tobacco into the water. "There's a name I haven't heard for a while. I'm a seaman, mister. Don't do nothing but haul cotton and molasses upstream." The man walked toward his flatboat, which had just docked, and heaved a box onto the dock.

"Did you haul cotton for Rouse?"

"Maybe some. Who wants to know?" The man turned and

held a meaty palm upward, and Nathaniel obliged with a five-dollar bill.

"Nathaniel Pemberton."

The man looked him up and down and crossed his arms. Then he laughed. "You're most likely related to the one-armed Pemberton? Why don't you ask him?" Jeremiah dropped his box, and the dock shook with the action.

"I'd rather hear it from you, if you got a notion to talk." Nathaniel took out a wad of bills and fanned through them. He watched the man lick his chops and wipe away the remaining saliva.

Jeremiah nodded. "What's the one-armed scalawag to you?"

"He's my brother," Nathaniel admitted.

"Ah," Jeremiah noted. "You're the deserter."

"I left before the war."

Jeremiah's eyes widened in disbelief. "I ain't your judge, boy. Tell it to God."

"God's forgiven me," Nathaniel said, thankful for the chance to be bold in his faith.

"Yeah, but your brother ain't." Jeremiah laughed. "I can't say I care much for that brother of yours. He'd just as soon cheat you as look at you. Losing his arm didn't do anything for his soul."

Nathaniel swallowed uncomfortably at the thought. His brother lived for himself. Would he ever humble himself to God? "So does that mean you're willing to talk?"

Jeremiah handed back the five-dollar bill. "I'll tell you what you want to know, Pemberton. You're a fellow brother in the Lord, and I got allegiance to Him." Jeremiah looked up to the blue sky, and Nathaniel nearly fell backward at his luck. "What do you want to know?"

Chapter 10

Mary, please tell me. I know you." Eleanor pleaded with her cousin, her palms sticky from her desperation. "You know something you're not divulging. If I should marry Andrew and some dark secret should come about, some dark secret that you have knowledge of, what then? Will your guilt haunt you like a field ghost for the rest of your days? This is for you, as well as for me." If there was a way out of this predicament, Eleanor wanted to know it. How dare her cousin stand in her way!

Mary pursed her lips and gnawed on them a bit before speaking. "I gave my word, Eleanor. Someone not holding his word is what killed my Morgan. If the Yankees hadn't known his men were advancing, he might be alive today." Mary shook her head rapidly. "I won't do it."

"So you are willing for me to embark on a marriage such as this one, while you hold this secret to your breast." Eleanor used every tactic she knew to try to break Mary, but nothing worked. At this moment, she hated the fact that her cousin had such character and devotion to the South. Where was Mary's devotion to her? Where was their sisterhood?

"If I thought you were in any kind of danger, I would divulge my secret without a care, but you are not in any danger, Ellie. My secret is of the past, not your future."

"But the Negroes might be in danger, Mary. Will your conscience allow them to suffer? I have worked hard to see that Father complied with the new laws without harming the plantation."

"What I know has nothing to do with Andrew's running of the plantation. I know nothing of such things. You can rest easy, my dear cousin." Mary bent over her knitting, her sterling silver needles clanking wildly as she worked.

"But I cannot rest easy, Mary. Downstairs beckons a beautiful horse, and she is calling my name and my future. Do you know of a reason I shouldn't accept such a present?"

"Hattie's just talking, Ellie. She is just trying to make trouble, and she is overstepping her boundaries."

Mary looked at Hattie, and the older woman nodded her head slowly.

"You all keep me out of it," Hattie said, "if you know so much."

"Hattie!" Eleanor exclaimed. "Do you know what Mary knows?"

"I don't know anything but my feelings, and my own feelings say that horse is poison. Anything that man touches is poison. Rosamond will be next. That's all I'm saying."

"Hattie," Mary chastised, "Eleanor is going to marry this man. You need to mind your place."

Hattie went about the room, straightening up. She closed her lips firmly over her teeth and said nothing more, but Eleanor understood her silence. Her silence meant Eleanor was a traitor to Nathaniel. A betrayer to Rosamond, the Negroes, and her, and it was how Eleanor felt. The beautiful mare was only a bandage to the pain. It would do nothing to heal her hurts or mistrust of the man she was soon to call her husband.

Mary dropped her needles to her lap. "Very well. I will not tell you the exact knowledge I carry, but I will tell you Andrew is not what he seems. That is not to say I think he is of poor character however. I believe he would make a fine husband for you, Eleanor." Mary looked at Hattie with a scowl. "Would you like it if she should be a spinster like me, Hattie? Nathaniel certainly isn't fit to marry. He hasn't two pennies to his name and no more right to Woodacre than you or I. Would you rather she marry him?"

"Yes." Hattie had clearly had enough and bolted from the room, slamming the door behind her.

Eleanor had never silenced Hattie in the past, and Mary's

insolence because of Hattie's color obviously perturbed the elder woman to no end. And with good cause. Eleanor had always been taught to respect Hattie and that, no matter what happened, Hattie would always tell her the truth.

"That woman has more nerve." Mary sighed and looked at her cousin. "I think you should marry Andrew without reservation. I must admit, when I first stepped out of our carriage and saw Rosamond's grounds again, I thought only of you and Nathaniel together. I was so charmed by the memories of Nathaniel. But I know he can't be the same man any longer. California would have changed him. Poverty has changed him."

"Who is to say I want Nathaniel?" Eleanor crossed her arms defiantly, hoping to keep her heart to herself, but her cousin continued.

"Eleanor, haven't you lived a poor life long enough? The Yankees have done their damage, but Andrew has triumphed. Don't you want to share in that? To see Rosamond transformed into its former glory with its fine furnishings and lavish luxuries? Andrew has the means to do all of that. Nathaniel doesn't."

Did her cousin know her so little to think she thought of such trifles? Surely Mary knew honor and love were far more important than material goods. "I should think I have more character than to worry only about pretty gowns and fine furniture."

"Of course you do. You also care about the former slaves. You don't want to see them abandoned, do you? Combining Rosamond and Woodacre—"

"Is exactly what the Federals are trying to halt. President Johnson wants to limit the size of farms so that slavery is abolished completely, including the black codes. Combining the plantations will put us under a Yankee microscope."

"It will also make you rich enough not to care, and you know it."

Eleanor did know it. Marrying Andrew was by far the easiest way to help the Negroes, but Hattie's words haunted her. What would God have her do? He would want her to help the slaves, wouldn't He? As much as she desired Nathaniel, that didn't make it God's will.

"I'm going to accept the horse, Mary. I want to ride today without a care in the world. I want to see the countryside and forget all these problems today."

Eleanor started down the stairs and met her fiancé's gaze with a happy grin. His mount stood beside hers, and she suddenly felt trapped.

"I was hoping to get to know my horse today," she said by way of excuse.

"Well Eleanor," Andrew stammered, "it has only been a week since you fell. I'd like to be certain you are up to the ride. Besides, it isn't safe for you to be alone. A chaperone is quite necessary."

"I shan't go far. I will return before lunch—I promise."

She stepped on the foot ladder to her new mare and proudly trotted away against Andrew's protests. As soon as the shade trees covered her, she clicked the horse into a full gallop and streamed like the Mississippi. She pulled her hair from its net and shook it out so it fell down her back. The wind on her face, the scent of the magnolia, the bright green of new grass—all caused a stirring sensation within her. Every part of her felt alive and refreshed. As long as she had these moments of freedom, she could endure anything.

The sound of hooves met her ears, and Eleanor's heart sank. Andrew had followed her, taking her dreamy state far away. She pulled her horse under a magnolia and stayed there, hoping Andrew would pass her by and leave her to relish her solitary ride. Her breath was labored from her run, but she patted her new friend and spoke softly to her. They were going to get along well.

The hooves sounded closer, and Eleanor tried to act as though she were only taking a rest for a moment should Andrew happen upon her. She looked up at the grand magnolia and remembered as a child her days running under these trees. She and Mary and

Nathaniel would have a rousing game of hide-and-seek while Andrew looked for snails and other such discoveries. The oncoming horse slowed its pace, and Eleanor's stomach lurched joyfully at the sight of Nathaniel.

She dismounted from her horse, as did he, and she ran toward him, clutching him for what would probably be the last time. Without thinking, she kissed his rough face, running her hands over his jaw. "Nathaniel. Take me away from here." Where such bold words had come from, she did not know, but she meant them, every one.

Her words shot through him like a bullet, for he pulled back quickly. "Eleanor, don't say such scandalous things."

"We shall be married," she said, breaking every law of womanhood her mother had so laboriously taught her. "I shall become the perfect preacher's wife, Nathaniel. I will learn to cook and clean and keep a proper house. We shall find a nice little parish somewhere and settle."

"Ellie," he whispered her name. By his eyes she knew he wanted to kiss her, and she made the most of his moment of weakness. She placed her lips on his and felt the firm line of his lips return her kiss with vigor.

Again he pulled away. "Ellie, stop it! You were born to live this way on a great estate. Even the Yankees can see that. They've allowed your home to stand. They've moved upriver because they know you belong here. The *Essex* dared not interfere with you—how shall I?" Nathaniel said, referring to the gunboat that had attacked their fair city long ago. "I only ask that you stay here on Rosamond, but do not marry my brother."

"Tell me what you've learned, Nathaniel. Tell me why you've come back to me. Why you would wish for me to be alone forever."

"I don't wish for you to be alone. I just ask that you not marry my brother. I'd rather see you marry a Northerner."

"Tell me why."

"I cannot."

"Then I shall marry Andrew." Eleanor crossed her arms, but she broke under Nathaniel's gaze and fell into his broad chest. He smelled of the river, but she didn't care. She knew this might be the last time she ever held him again. "Take me with you, Nathaniel. Please."

She looked up into his hazel eyes, which were filled with tears. He tried to blink them away but could not, and she triumphed in thinking that she was breaking him. More tears appeared on the horizon of his gold-flecked eyes with each closure. "I cannot take you," he said again.

"My father will make me marry him, Nathaniel. If you leave, you leave me with Andrew. I'll have no other options to me. The black codes will be employed on Rosamond as well as Woodacre, and you will run from it. For once, Nathaniel, I ask you to be the man I know you to be."

He clutched her arms tightly. "Do you think I'm weak, Ellie? Do you think it's easy for me to leave knowing whom I leave you to? I leave because I'm strong, Ellie. And it's not my strength that propels me; it's His."

"But you'll still leave." Eleanor couldn't mask her scowl. This wasn't about getting her way. This was about their future. The legacy of their family estates. "You think Andrew is a better choice for running Woodacre than you."

"It doesn't matter what I think. My father has chosen."

"Your father didn't choose. Your father was never given the chance, Nathaniel. You left him no choice when you packed up for California. Give him a choice now. For all our sakes. Mary knows something of Andrew; you know something of him. All of you keep your secrets while you leave me as the sacrifice."

"Better I leave you than stay. That you resent me now rather than later when we must raise our children in the washhouse, with only a spinning wheel and loom as our furnishings. When you have a baby on your hip and an iron in your hand, would you still find me so wonderful? I have nothing to offer you, Ellie."

"You have yourself, Nathaniel. Why does everyone think I care for things? I watched the Yankees take most of them, and I survived. I did not wilt at the first sign of poverty."

"You know nothing of poverty, Ellie. Poverty is not eating corn bread rather than biscuits because there is no flour to be had. Poverty is not having the corn bread at all."

"You think I'm a spoiled child."

"I think you are wonderful," he said, grazing her cheek with his hand. "But I also believe you offer more to Rosamond without me. The Negroes will come under the black codes, and things will be as they were. Not enough food in the cookhouse, no hoecakes for the workers, nothing. Is that what you would have?"

"That has nothing to do with my marrying you, Nathaniel!"

"It has everything to do with it. Do you think your father will be happy with such a marriage? When you might be mistress of a great house like Woodacre?"

"I do not think my father would make me choose."

"Then you are naive. I'm not willing to take the chance with your future. Your father has made his opinions of my character well known. I'll not gamble with your life as well as my own."

"I'll marry a Yankee if need be, but I will not stay without you. The Negroes have been fending for themselves for a long time, and they can continue to do so. Once I'm married, there's nothing you or anyone else can do to undo it. Let it be on your conscience, Nathaniel! I won't do what's best for me. Nor will I live by your will or my father's. For once I'll do as I please."

Eleanor mounted her horse like a man, not caring for propriety's sake any longer. She kicked the horse and was off, blinded by her tears.

Chapter 11

Eleanor bent low on her horse, racing alongside the Mississippi against its fierce current. The thunderous shelling began in her head again. Her mind brought back the fearful attack by the Yankee gunboat *Essex*. All that the Yankees succeeded in doing that day was killing a young girl, Rosalie. How the town mourned her loss. Northerners invaded that day, and Natchez allowed it without protest.

Eleanor didn't plan to surrender so easily to her own battle. She would disappear from sight before she went back willingly. Something about Andrew was dark, yet no one would tell her what. Marrying him to find out his secret frightened her to no end. How could Nathaniel tell her not to marry his brother but not tell her why? It felt cruel.

The bustling port of Natchez came into view as she pushed her way through Water Street. The river was to her right; the great bluff to her left. She was officially Under-the-Hill without a chaperone. A rush of excitement pulsed through her. She slowed her horse and tried to appear nonchalant. But as she approached the wharves and warehouses, it was readily apparent a woman in riding clothes was not a typical sight along the rough-hewn streets.

Men shouted obscenities, showing their terribly boorish manners, but Eleanor held her chin high, ignoring them all. The sound of horses' hooves closed around her, and feeling surrounded, her confidence waned. She casually picked up her pace, heading toward the piers where countless ships were docking. Being without a chaperone suddenly didn't feel so freeing. She hoped to meet someone who might recognize her. Surely there would be people of society there traveling—someone who might help her find her way on the pier.

The wooden structure jutted out from the banks of the river, hanging ominously over the water. Eleanor knew of the countless deaths associated with life on the river, but she took faith in the fact that she had survived the war.

In her blue merino gown with the white bodice, she suddenly felt improper with no hoop as she jumped from her horse. She held tightly to the reins, trying to ignore the eyes staring at her. A huge man, wearing an open cotton shirt that showed more than it hid, started toward her; and Eleanor straightened herself to appear taller than she was. Her effort was to no avail since the man still stood more than a full foot above her. His arms were so enormous that they looked like the flanks of a horse, and Eleanor gulped, preparing for his approach.

"Horses ain't allowed on the pier, miss. They scare the live-stock, not to mention the travelers. What's your business here?" He took her horse and tied it to a nearby pole.

"I'm looking for passage up the river." She unconsciously smoothed her skirt. "Are you in possession of a boat?"

The big man laughed but stopped when he realized she was serious. "Where's your lady's maid? You don't look like the type to be traveling alone. You running from home, little girl?"

"I am not a little girl. I'm looking for passage up the river. If you cannot help me, would you kindly point me in the right direction where I might purchase a ticket?"

"Missy, there ain't a flatboat or ship out there that will take you out of Natchez. Somebody's going to be looking for you, and we don't like questions down here at the docks. You just run back home before you cause any trouble."

Eleanor's heart pounded in protest. She had not come this far to be turned away. She didn't care how big this man was.

"I can pay you." She fingered the gold bracelet on her arm and let the sun catch its sparkle. "This bracelet was my mother's, one of the only possessions left after the war. It's very expensive. I'm sure it would bring in a tidy sum."

The giant man came toward her. "Missy, this is a dangerous

place for a woman alone. You just take your pretty mare and find your way back home."

She shook her head. "It's more dangerous for me there. I'm engaged to a man I fear is dangerous," she blurted out, pressing her fingers to her mouth. "Will you help me? I'll find a way to pay you if you're not interested in the bracelet, though I don't see why you wouldn't be."

The burly sailor laughed again, not mean-spirited, but jovial. "I think that fiancé of yours has reason to fear for himself. Looks like he found himself quite a keg of gun powder."

Eleanor crossed her arms. "I'm quite capable, sir, much more so than I look. The home guard ran screaming before the Yankees pulled me from my home."

"I don't doubt it, miss."

The big man tipped his hat, focusing behind her. "Nathaniel."

Eleanor turned to see Nathaniel waiting beside her.

"This a friend of yours?" the man asked, nodding toward her.

"You two know each other?" Eleanor asked, feeling as if she had been betrayed yet again. Just her luck on an entire dock to find a friend of Nathaniel's.

The two men smiled at each other.

"Jeremiah and I met yesterday," Nathaniel said.

"Well, run along now." Eleanor shooed him away with her hand.

"Ellie, I am not leaving you here alone. Jeremiah has work to do. Let's go."

"Why are you following me?" she demanded, grasping his shirt in her frustration. "You've made your intentions known, so leave me be! If you won't help me, I'm determined to help myself!" Her father would simply see her flight to freedom as an immediate need for her marriage, so there was no going back now.

"Did you think I'd just let you run to Natchez Under-the-Hill alone?" Nathaniel laughed. "Really, you must think better of me than that."

He grasped her waist and turned toward her negotiating partner. "This is my brother Andrew's fiancée. Jeremiah Coleman, may I present Miss Eleanor Senton."

"Nice to know you, miss." The brawny gentleman tipped his hat again.

"A pleasure," Eleanor said flatly.

"She's quite pleasant when she gets her way," Nathaniel said.

Just then Eleanor had an idea that bubbled to her mouth without her giving it thought. "Mr. Coleman, could you take Nathaniel and me upriver? I'm sure my bracelet would allow for both of us, would it not?"

Jeremiah shook his head. "Miss Senton, as I told you before, I'm not taking anyone's fiancée away from town. Not to mention some high-falutin' daughter of a wealthy plantation owner. What Nathaniel does is his business, but I'm havin' no part in this scheme of yours."

She turned in desperation to Nathaniel. "Please, Nathaniel. This is our chance. Run with me and don't look back." She clutched his hands. "You'll have your dream of being a preacher, and I'll find some way to help the Negroes up North. Come with me."

Eleanor tugged on Nathaniel's hands, but the firmness in his stance dictated he was not moving.

Jeremiah did her a service by looking away and pretending not to overhear her pathetic attempts to woo a man into marriage. She peered into Nathaniel's eyes with tears streaming down her cheeks. "Please, Nathaniel," she murmured. "I'll be a good wife."

He pulled her closer by her waist, whispering in her ear. "I love you, Ellie. With all my heart I love you. That's why I need to take you back."

Eleanor felt as if her bones were crushed within her, but Nathaniel held her steady. She had allowed herself to believe freedom was within her reach. If only she'd found a sailor willing to take her bracelet, perhaps then Nathaniel might have asked the right questions and followed her. If only she had stolen away, maybe he would have come after her, and they would have been married quietly. Nathaniel's upright character was her stockade. No garrison or militia could save her now.

Ear-piercing screams broke her from her mission. It was a high-pitched squeal from a voice Eleanor knew. "That's Ceviche, Nathaniel! I know it. I'd recognize her voice anywhere. It came from that boat."

Nathaniel ran with her up the dock to a steamer ship that was forced low to the water with extra cargo. The screams were silenced as they approached.

A man stepped across the boat's entry with huge fists to his hips. "You want something?"

"I believe that's my Negro calling, and I want to see her," Nathaniel said.

Eleanor uttered a prayer that her instincts were correct, and they wouldn't both end up at the bottom of the Mississippi.

"That ain't your Negro. Negroes is free, or hasn't anybody told you?" the man said flatly. "You git on out of here before—"

"Before what?" Jeremiah appeared behind them, his huge stance as fearsome as the river itself.

"Now, Jeremiah, you got no business here. This is between me and the gentleman here."

"Let him see who's screaming. You didn't take her? You got nothing to worry about. It won't hold you up none, and you could be turned in if you don't let him on. You want the Federals searching your boat?"

The man's face turned ashen, and he stepped aside. Jeremiah entered the plank only to be knocked on the head by the end of a rifle. He swayed but never lost his footing. He rubbed the back of his head, clearly steaming over the violence. He picked up the man as though he were just another bale of cotton and threw the flailing limbs into the river below.

Eleanor looked over the pier to see the man clinging tightly to the posts. "I can't swim," he called out.

Good, she thought.

But Jeremiah dove in and retrieved the man. The two of them came up on shore with Jeremiah holding the man by his collar. He met a Federal officer and handed the man over, wiping his hands of him before returning to the boat. Nathaniel had long since disappeared into the bowels of the steamer and come back up with Ceviche. Eleanor ran to her and comforted her sobs.

"They's got my babe."

"We'll find him, Ceviche. I promise," Eleanor said.

Looking into Ceviche's dark tear-filled eyes, Eleanor knew she couldn't just leave Rosamond. Without her, who would care for the former slaves? Her father would simply give in to Andrew's wishes, and the black codes would become a certainty. She looked to Nathaniel's knowing eyes. He had more wisdom than she possessed in her little finger.

A tiny wail was heard, and Eleanor saw Jeremiah running up the pier. It was baby Frederick wrapped in his worn blanket. Jeremiah held the infant away from his wet clothes and out toward his mother. Ceviche ran sobbing toward Jeremiah and cradled the baby to her cheek, thanking God aloud for taking care of her son. Eleanor could barely look at the young mother for the emotions it stirred within her.

Nathaniel towered over her, his muscular frame breathing hard from his rescue, which obviously involved some violence. Eleanor stood and rubbed his rough cheek.

"You were right about going back," she admitted. "But then you knew that all along, didn't you?"

"I don't want to be right, Ellie." Nathaniel looked at her with the eyes of a man who by sheer will held her at arm's length. "You know that, don't you? I want to be your husband."

Eleanor nodded. "I know, Nathaniel."

"Will you trust me and not marry my brother?"

"How can I escape it?"

"I don't know, Ellie. But I know the Mississippi wouldn't have stopped you if I hadn't, so I just pray you're as resourceful with my brother."

Eleanor laughed, then gasped. "I forgot. I promised I'd be back for lunch."

Nathaniel took out a pocket watch. It was two o'clock. Nearly teatime. "They'll have a search party out for you."

"Yes," she agreed. "Whatever will I say?"

"Say you went after Ceviche. That ought to send a scare through somebody. Watch their eyes, Ellie."

"Will you come home with me?"

Nathaniel shook his head. "I don't want your reputation in question. Go home. I'll find out who took Ceviche."

"Will you see to it she gets home? And that she gets food?"

"Of course." Nathaniel set his jaw, forcing his gaze from her.

But she wouldn't leave him without saying her piece.

"No matter what happens, I love you, Nathaniel."

"Don't—"

"I should have followed you to California years ago. You would have had no choice but to marry me then."

He let out a short laugh. "You deserve so much better. I'm going to do what I can to ensure you have a husband worthy of your love, Ellie."

"So am I, Nathaniel. So am I," she announced before turning away with a single, coquettish look back.

Chapter 12

"Eleanor!" Andrew rushed toward her, helping her from the saddle. Her fiancé didn't look the least bit winded, and the ice in his tea was still fresh. Yet his words were frantic. "Where have you been? We've got a rescue party out looking for you. When you didn't come back at lunch, we organized one right away!"

Eleanor searched Andrew's eyes and wondered if his fear stemmed from legitimate concern for her person or fear that she might be lost without their marriage to seal his future. Noticing his tea cakes on the veranda, his comfortable position didn't speak well of his true devotion.

"I'm fine," Eleanor answered, unable to remove her gaze from his picnic. "I just had a long day getting to know my horse. I shall name her Tiche. It's a nickname. Do you like it?"

She was certain Andrew would know Tiche was a shortened version of Ceviche. His eyes flickered in acknowledgement, but she couldn't read if there was guilt in them or not.

"Eleanor, it's a slave name," Andrew said quietly.

"There aren't any more slaves, Andrew. Remember?" She smiled and moved toward her cousin, who wore a concerned frown. "If you'll excuse me, Andrew, I haven't seen my cousin all day, and I must dress for dinner."

She hurried toward the house, its great columns beckoning to her. Looking back over her shoulder, she called out, "Thank you for the horse. She really is a beauty."

Eleanor raced up the grand staircase until her father's angry voice halted her last step to the landing. "Eleanor Sarah Senton. Stop right there!"

She turned, revealing her mud-stained gown. Its fine wool would never be the same. Shame washed over her at her father's rebuke.

"Is it your intention to ruin the reputation of this family?"

"No sir." She rubbed the cashmerelike fabric, certain its original softness would never come back.

"Is it your intention that our family name should be associated with Natchez Under-the-Hill?"

"No sir."

"Eleanor, you were seen Under-the-Hill today. Would you care to tell me why?"

She swallowed hard. If she had been seen in Nathaniel's arms, he might be sent away once and for all, and she would have little to say for her reputation.

"Yes, Father. I rode my new horse along the riverbank, and I ended up at the port."

"Eleanor, you are to be married in two days' time. I've given my consent for a quick marriage, which I think is best under the circumstances. I have let you run wild for far too long. It's time you began acting as mistress of a great home, the life you were meant to lead. The war has put things off long enough. Your mother would be disappointed if she knew you were still unmarried and running about like a schoolgirl. I pray she doesn't know of your escapades."

"Yes, Father." Eleanor curtsied, turning toward the top of the stairs.

"And Eleanor—"

"Yes sir?" she asked over her shoulder.

"I'm glad you've returned."

Her heart raced as she fell onto the bed. If she had been spotted with Nathaniel, he would be sent away. At least until she was safely married. She eyed her maid suspiciously.

"Hattie, who saw me today Under-the-Hill?"

Although Hattie never left the house, she possessed a wealth of knowledge. Somehow anything that happened within twenty-five miles of Rosamond was transferred to her head without any sensible way of its getting there. Eleanor had never known Hattie to leave their property.

Hattie looked at Eleanor's cousin, Mary, before resting her eyes on her mistress. "I don't know, miss."

Eleanor caught the stressed use of *miss* and looked for some way to dismiss her cousin, to be alone with Hattie's secrets. "Mary, would you mind leaving me to dress? I'm a dreadful mess, and I am quite humbled by my appearance."

Mary sighed. "Very well; I'll go entertain Master Pemberton. I fear you were dreadfully rude to him after his generous gift, Ellie."

"I'd be most grateful if you would, Mary. Tell him I'm sorry, won't you?" Eleanor waited until the door was safely closed and glanced at Hattie. "What do you know? Who saw me Under-the-Hill?"

Hattie rearranged Eleanor's toilet on the vanity as though she had nothing of importance to say. It was just as she acted when a grand tidbit of information would escape her. "The new overseer went to meet with some shippers for the cotton. Word is you were on the docks with Master Pemberton."

"Did he tell my father that Nathaniel was with me?"

Hattie shook her head. "I don't think so. You have to understand Rosamond's people don't want you marrying that Andrew, Miss Ellie. I think they're secretly hoping that prodigal of yours might eventually win your father over. That new overseer will probably be looking for a job if you up and add Rosamond to Woodacre. Work isn't as easy to come by as it once was."

"Why did this new overseer tell my father anything then?"

"He doesn't want you dead either, Miss Ellie. Under-the-Hill is no place for a lady. I'm sure you'll hear all about it from Mrs. Patterson later, so I'll save me some breaths. Why were you there with Master Pemberton? He proposing marriage again?"

"Hattie, how on earth do you know all this? That I was Under-the-Hill, I mean? Who told *you*?"

"Hattie has her ways," she answered mysteriously. "You

weren't thinking of running off now, were you?"

Eleanor clutched her stomach, sickened by the knowledge that she was so transparent. "I love my father. I love Rosamond, but I also love Nathaniel. Every time I look into his eyes, I wonder how I will live without him. And I don't love Andrew."

"Don't go practicing for the theater on me. You got along fine for six years without that man; you'll be fine this time. Women have married for a lot less than love. At least Andrew has the means to keep you happy."

Eleanor stamped her foot childishly. "No, I won't be fine, Hattie, because now I'll be forced to look into Andrew's dull eyes. Eyes that lack Nathaniel's sparkle and a speech that's meant for me alone. His unspoken manner that tells me everything I must know without uttering a word. Would God give us such a gift and not allow us to open it?"

"I don't rightly know where God is in this mess, but I do know that your mama would not have liked to see you a spinster, and that's exactly what you'll be if you keep disappearing alone. A spinster or dead in the ground."

"My mother wanted me to marry Nathaniel, Hattie."

Hattie nodded. "Oh, your mother did love that boy. Every day he was allowed to break from his studies to play, she'd make sure there was sugarcane for him to eat. His father was so stern that he was never allowed to have sugar or popped corn. Your mother loved that boy as if he were hers. She always hoped. . . well, that's neither here nor there now. God doesn't want you to sin, Miss Ellie. I know that much. If you are engaged to Andrew Pemberton, the Bible says you are betrothed." Hattie stripped Eleanor of her gown and threw it into a heap on the floor. "Much as I hate to confess it."

Eleanor sank to the floor. "I cannot marry Andrew."

"You very well can, and you will. Your father says in two days' time—"

"Is that what you want for me, Hattie?" She crossed to the

bed in her petticoat, throwing herself on the great mattress.

"Of course not, Miss Ellie. But what we want isn't always what's best for us."

A loud sound halted their conversation. "What was that?"

"It sounded like a shelling," Hattie said.

"But the war is over—what on earth?"

"You stay here. I'll check the balcony." Hattie opened the French doors and stepped boldly onto the portico. "It's Ceviche's man! He's gotten himself a rifle."

Eleanor stood, gripping the post on her bed. "What does he mean to do with it?"

Her pulse raced. Although it had been over thirty years ago, and before her time, the Confederacy had not forgotten the killing rampage of 1831.

"What does he mean to do?"

"He's pointing the gun at Andrew!" Hattie said. "He's speaking to him, but I cannot hear what he says."

Eleanor could not help herself. She made her way to the French doors, forgetting her half-dressed state. "Is anyone else with him?" she asked, worried for her family. "Where's Mary?"

"Miss Ellie, get back. You've got nothing but a petticoat on. Andrew's alone. Mary must not have left the home yet."

"Did Andrew take Ceviche? What is he saying to Andrew?"

"Shh!" Hattie warned. "Let me hear."

Eleanor whisked on her afternoon gown without care as to its appearance. The pagoda sleeves hung carelessly since she couldn't reach the buttons herself. "I must see if Father is all right."

"Miss Eleanor! You'll do no such thing."

"Button me up, Hattie. Now!"

Eleanor's tone left no room for argument, and her maid fastened her up. Without a hoop, the skirt sank dangerously low on the floor, but there was no time for formality. She rushed down the stairs, careful not to trip over the extensive fabric. Her father, Aunt Till, Mary, and the household staff crouched warily in the foyer.

"Get upstairs, Ellie!" Her father's voice boomed.

"I think I might be able to reason with Ceviche's man, Father."

"You've done enough."

"But Father—"

"I lost your mother to the slaves. She gave her life for the ungrateful lot of them. Do you think I'd let you do the same? Get back upstairs now! Or you'll end up dead as your mother."

The angry scowl of hatred changed her father's entire face. He looked monstrous and bent on revenge. He held up a revolver, filling its last chamber.

"I said, get upstairs!"

Her father opened the double doors of cut glass and stepped outside.

Eleanor backed up, unable to believe the sights before her eyes were really happening. All she could do was pray. Pray that her father would return and this beast who dwelled within him would leave as suddenly as he came. She fell to her knees on the stair landing, lacking the strength to make it to her bedroom.

"Lord in heaven, bring peace upon this household. Please. I don't know what I'm doing wrong, Lord, but I shall humble myself to You now. I shall marry whomever You please. Only spare my father from this wrath—and Ceviche's husband, Lord. Help him run like the wind, and don't let him hurt anyone. He only wants to protect his family, Lord. Please help him. Help us all."

Another single shot peeled through the air, and silence followed. An eerie, beckoning silence. Eleanor ran to her balcony where Hattie crumpled to the floor, crying out. Stepping past her maid, Eleanor gasped at the sight. Lying limp on the ground was Ceviche's man. Behind him was Nathaniel on his horse with a smoking revolver in his hand.

"No!"

Eleanor's scream was heard, and Nathaniel peered up at her. He avoided her gaze and went to the dead man. Eleanor's heart broke for Ceviche, who had lost her baby's father.

"How could you, Nathaniel?" she muttered. "How could you kill a man who fought for his family?" The room went dark, and she remembered no more.

Chapter 13

The sun had set by the time Eleanor blinked back to life. In the darkness, she had forgotten why she had slept in the afternoon, but recognition came with a thunderous bolt. She sat upright, but her throbbing head willed her back onto her bed, and she groaned.

"Hattie?"

"Hattie's not here, Ellie." Mary came out of the shadows and pressed a cold towel to Eleanor's forehead. "She's seeing to your father. How are you?"

"My father—is he alive?"

"Of course he's alive. He's out at the slaves' quarters flushing out anyone he thinks may cause us further trouble. He hopes to instill the black codes immediately to gain control over the men. Heaven forbid this type of thing should ever happen again."

"What do you mean?"

"Nathaniel having to shoot that lunatic. Right on your front lawn. Why, it's just wicked that such a thing could happen in the broad daylight of such a beautiful afternoon." Mary dropped her nursing duties and took up her knitting needles again. "I'm telling you, Ellie—you are fortunate to marry a man such as Andrew. He tried to reason with the man, but he went on and on about his wife and baby. As though there's any legitimacy to that at all."

"Mary, what are you saying? I thought you were against the codes as I am."

"Only because I was ignorant—well, I shall not be fooled again. Andrew has your best interest at stake when he employs the codes. That should be obvious from today's treachery."

"What about Nathaniel? What did he do with Ceviche's husband?"

"I assume he threw the man in the river where the criminal

belongs once and for all. Imagine threatening the owners of Woodacre and Rosamond and assuming he'd live through the siege."

"Maybe he didn't hope to live," Eleanor said defiantly. "Maybe he hoped to prove his wife and baby are not refuse to be carted off at Andrew's will."

"Andrew? Andrew hardly has anything to do with her disappearing. She was probably anxious for the chance to get away from here and thought she'd plan her escape. She might have stolen away were it not for Nathaniel who caught her red-handed on a cargo boat Under-the-Hill."

Eleanor rubbed her throbbing temples, hoping to will her nightmare away. But each time she opened her eyes, Mary sat calmly with her clanking needles, rattling on and on about Andrew's heroism.

"Where is Nathaniel?"

"I'm not certain, but his father was quite proud of his rescue today of Andrew. I daresay Nathaniel might get a bigger part of Woodacre after today. Should he want it of course. Perhaps after his kill today he's thinking twice of becoming a preacher."

Eleanor could listen to the chatter no longer. "I must find Hattie."

"I told you, she's at the slaves' quarters, and, with your escapades of late, your father had best not find you out of the house. He's trying to prevent an uprising as we speak. Should a slave find you now, your life might be worth more to them if it was extinguished."

Mrs. Patterson entered Eleanor's room with a tray of tea. "Get back in bed, Eleanor. You need to be resting so you're not peaked for your wedding. Andrew told your father today's adventures only prove your immediate need of marriage. It's for your very protection now."

"Where is Hattie?" Eleanor asked again, hoping for a different answer from Mrs. Patterson.

"They're at the cookhouse now. Your father wants to see to it that the workers don't get ideas in their heads. Today was a very dangerous sign. It is a good thing Master Nathaniel happened upon the scene, or your fiancé might very well be dead."

"Instead, Ceviche's husband lies at the river. It is all my fault, Mrs. Patterson. All my fault. If I hadn't been so concerned about myself, so selfish in my thinking, Ceviche and her family might be together tonight."

"You're rambling on about nothing, Eleanor. Don't let your father hear such strange utterings. He already blames the slaves for your mother's death. It won't do you any good to take responsibility for something that is just a way of life."

"Is it a way of life, Mrs. Patterson? To be so uncaring and immoral toward human beings? Jesus said to love even the least of these. My mother did that, and I'm proud to be like her."

"And look where your mother is today."

"She's with Jesus," Eleanor said confidently. "I must speak with Nathaniel."

"Nathaniel is being honored at a family dinner tonight, Eleanor. He's a hero."

Eleanor couldn't imagine Nathaniel shooting a man in the back. It was so unlike him, so out of character; and it certainly didn't make him heroic. Had she brought such confusion by begging him to find a way for them to marry? Had this been his way to prove his loyalty to his father and hers? She prayed it wasn't so—that Nathaniel had his own reasons for shooting Ceviche's husband. Her stomach lurched vigorously each time she pictured young Ceviche with no father for her baby son. She relived the infant's desperate cries of the night she met him, his precious dark-as-coal eyes gazing wondrously at her and his calming sucking sounds as he nibbled at his fingers.

She had to find a way to help, but first she needed to escape her stifling room. Her cousin's interminable clicking needles and Mrs. Patterson's overbearing ways threatened to send her to the asylum if she didn't flee.

"Eleanor, where are you going?" Mrs. Patterson questioned as Mary's needles ceased.

"I'm going out for air. It's stifling in here." Eleanor opened her French doors and sucked in the chilled evening air. When the clicking resumed and Mrs. Patterson busied herself, Eleanor shut the doors quietly behind her.

Leaping over the veranda, she caught her boot in the trellis and worked her way to the lawn. Once on the expansive stretch of grass, she stole away into the heritage oaks and countless magnolias under the starry canopy.

A guard dog barked at her, but Eleanor calmed the beast with her soft voice and soon resumed her run. She ran past the cookhouse and into the stables. Peeking over the stalls, she spoke softly to Tiche. "Are you up for a ride, girl? A pleasant ramble under the evening sky. We shall have a grand time." She spoke to calm herself as well as her new mare.

Only once had she been out this late into the night. It was the evening following the battle of the *Essex* against her city. She and the neighbors had promenaded to the levees to watch the great battle, never understanding that her beloved Confederate forces might fall victim to the Yankees. Numb, she and her compatriots returned home at a slow pace, no one speaking a word.

"Miss Ellie!" Hattie's firm voice jolted Eleanor from her solitude. She placed a palm over her heart.

"Oh Hattie, you gave me such a scare. What are you doing out here?"

"The question is, missy, what are you doing out of your room?"

"I wanted to see if Tiche was all right after the gunfire this afternoon. You never know how a horse will react to such circumstances."

She focused on patting the horse, afraid to look up for fear of getting caught in her lie. Hattie needed no such assistance however. Eleanor's lies were few and far between, and without practice one did not become very accomplished.

"You need a saddle for that now, do you?" Hattie held a candle to her face.

"Are you going to bring me back to the house, Hattie? If you are, just say so."

"That all depends. Where do you think you are heading on this dangerous night?"

"I have to find Nathaniel, Hattie. I have to know why he shot that man. He knew what Ceviche meant to me. How could he do what he did for Andrew's life? Ceviche cradled her baby before Nathaniel. I need to know how he could take that infant's father so readily."

"I'll admit it's not the Master Nathaniel we've known. But one never knows what a prodigal might do to prove his worth."

"I just can't believe he'd kill for it. He would leave before he'd do that. So why didn't he, Hattie?"

"I don't know, but I expect you'd better find out." Hattie grabbed Eleanor's saddle and threw it over Tiche. "You stay off the path and listen for the sounds of anyone following you. And if your father or your aunt or Mrs. Patterson asks, I never saw you, you understand?"

"Oh Hattie!" Eleanor raced into Hattie's wide-open arms and grasped her with all the strength she possessed. "Thank you."

"You come back into the cookhouse in the morning, and I'll have a story concocted by then. You let me handle the fibs to your aunt and father. Your lying will only get us all into trouble. You are a terrible liar, missy." Hattie laughed.

Eleanor smiled. "I'll see you in the morning." With a click of her tongue, she was off into the starry night. Her horse's *clip-clop* was softened as she trod through a soft, grassy field. She eased her mare away from the house before picking up her speed and pushing the horse to a full gallop.

Woodacre came into view. Candles lit the interior of the great brick house brightly. Eleanor dismounted, tying Tiche to a nearby magnolia, and hesitated a moment to formulate a plan. Where might Nathaniel be?

A hand suddenly gripped her mouth, and Eleanor tried to scream before hearing Nathaniel's gentle voice in her ear. "Ellie, it's Nathaniel. Shh! Shh!" He said, bringing her into his arms. She turned into him, allowing his warmth to calm her pounding heart.

"Nathaniel." She held her ear against his steady heartbeat, which inexplicably quickened. Neither of them uttered another word for a long stretch of the night. Together they held each other under the bright, full moon against a heritage magnolia, relishing their stolen time as if each star were placed for their view.

When Eleanor's eyes became heavy, she realized she must accomplish her task and finally found her voice. "Nathaniel, I need to know how you could have killed Ceviche's husband."

"I didn't kill him, Ellie. It wounds me that you would think so little of me."

Eleanor sat up. "I saw you, Nathaniel. I saw you with the smoking revolver."

"Faith is being sure of what you cannot see, Ellie. Do you think I mortally wounded that man? After I saw his baby crying out for its mother that very morning? Do you think I could be so callous as to rid that baby's father from our earth?"

"No, no, I do not. That's why I don't understand what I saw. I had to know what happened. Tell me and put my mind at ease."

Nathaniel unleashed her comb and ran his fingers gently through her hair. "Ceviche and her husband and little Frederick are on Jeremiah's boat to the North. Jeremiah has friends there who will find the family work."

"No, I saw his limp body."

"It's amazing how one can act when one's life depends upon it," Nathaniel explained.

"But I heard the shot!"

"A blank."

"They are alive?"

"More than alive, Ellie. They are truly free."

Eleanor sank into his chest. "Something I will never be."

"There's only one way I can protect you." Nathaniel continued to brush his fingers through her hair, and she delighted in his every touch.

"Not by going away."

"No, Ellie. By marrying you before it is too late. I cannot let your wedding to my brother take place. Perhaps I'm selfish or simply unwilling to sacrifice all of myself to the Lord, but I cannot let my brother have you as his wife. I cannot let another man touch you. I have no peace or rest thinking of such things. The Lord says it is better to marry than to burn with passion. I cannot burn this way while you marry another. It is not too late, Ellie, but by Saturday it might be."

Eleanor closed her eyes and played the song again and again in her head. Nathaniel had finally consented to marry her, and her giddiness knew no bounds. "We shall be poor?" she giggled.

"Most likely destitute."

"I shall wear muslin year round?"

"There will not be a silk in sight."

"I shall say good night lying beside you each night?"

"That one thing is certain, my love." Nathaniel reached for her chin and pulled her into a kiss. Eleanor had never known such bliss.

Chapter 14

After a long night, sitting under the heritage magnolia, Eleanor forced herself away from Nathaniel's soothing voice and their lively conversation. She galloped toward home, where smoke billowed up from the cookhouse chimney. She smelled the delicious scent of bacon lingering in the moist, morning air. Her stomach's growl was hardly noticed, as her heart pounded for fear of what awaited her had she been discovered missing.

Samson, Hattie's nephew, waited outside the stables and took Tiche. He motioned for Eleanor to run, and run she did toward the delicious scent and her lady's maid. Hattie anxiously awaited her outside the cookhouse, her nervous foot tapping wildly. Dawn hadn't yet broken, and the cover of darkness shielded Eleanor from a deeper fear.

"Get upstairs," Hattie ordered. "Everyone's still asleep, and I made your excuses last night. You were under far too much trauma for an appearance at dinner," Hattie informed her.

It was not an untruth, and she would have little trouble corroborating Hattie's story. She had been too affected by yesterday's events to attend supper. Why, she was so affected that she wouldn't be able to appear at her own wedding on Saturday. The thought brought a smile to her lips.

Entering her room, Eleanor quickly inspected her gowns and climbed into one that Hattie had set out. She must decide which ones she could take with her to elope. The word sounded so sinful. She hated to think of starting her marriage with such a devious plan, but what hope did she have? If she didn't elope, she would marry Andrew. A man she didn't love, who felt it his perfect right to sell human beings. Even when the law disallowed it, he had created his own laws under the black codes. The war and all its death taught Andrew nothing. Not even the loss of his arm had broken through his hardened pride.

Eleanor swept her arm across her vanity, pulling her silver comb set into the fabric folds of her skirt. She would have to sew her valuables under her hoop secretly after everyone was asleep. The idea soon struck her as ridiculous, and she poured her valuables back onto the walnut table with a clang. There would be no need for silver comb sets on the preaching circuit.

Hattie appeared momentarily after the noise. "Are you trying to wake the entire state of Mississippi?" She quickly shut the door behind her. "What are you up to?"

"I was just straightening my vanity." She reached out and placed her toilet in proper order.

"What did Nathaniel tell you? You did see him, I take it."

Eleanor nodded. "He didn't kill Ceviche's husband. They performed a play for Andrew and his father. Ceviche and her family are on a barge up North. A friend has found work for them."

"Oh praise Jesus!" Hattie exclaimed.

"I'd appreciate it if you let the workers know he's not dead."

"I wouldn't dream of keeping such news from them."

"Hattie, I'm leaving." Eleanor looked into Hattie's intense brown eyes. "I'm running away and eloping with Nathaniel, and I can't leave without telling you how much I love you."

Hattie shook her head firmly. "You can't leave. Think what it will do to your father. He's already lost his wife. What will he think when you leave him, too?"

"I hope he'll think he was wrong to force me into marrying Andrew," she answered, crossing her arms. "I have done everything my father has ever asked of me. Only now have I asked something of him, and he denies me. He will force me into a life of unhappiness if I stay."

"Have you asked him, Miss Ellie? Does your father know you wish to marry Nathaniel? Now that the man has returned, have you told your father you feel differently?"

"My father is not exactly one to discuss my feelings. I scarcely think he cares what the depths of my emotions are."

"If you haven't asked your father, you cannot be sure of his answer. Running off with a man who's not your husband is sinful, and it will bring dishonor to this home. Is that what you want?"

"I cannot ask him. If I ask him, I risk Father finding out what Nathaniel and I are planning."

"He cannot force you to say 'I do' the day of your wedding, Miss Ellie. You forget you have more to say in this situation than you think. I'll not have you playing the victim. Your mother did not raise such a woman."

"Father will not leave Rosamond to Nathaniel. Without a marriage to Andrew, this plantation has a chance of treating its workers right. You have more to lose than anyone, Hattie. Do you want to see your nephew owned again? Your sisters?"

"Your mother saw to it that we were never treated as property," Hattie explained.

"And who will see to it when Father is frail? It certainly won't be Andrew."

"Ask your father, Miss Ellie. I'll not have you sin to make things right. God will not honor such a decision. Your mother taught me to read my Bible, Miss Ellie, and I do read it religiously."

Eleanor looked at the cashmere carpet that had escaped Yankee confiscation. Its design was intricately woven, and small replicas of the cross danced before her eyes. "I'll pray about it, but I'm confident in my decision. I love Nathaniel."

"It may take more than love if you defy your father. Don't forget that. I cannot support this, Miss Ellie. It's dishonest."

Anger raged within Eleanor's small frame. She wanted to please everyone, to continue working for the weakest as her mother had, but God seemed to be providing a choice. And it was a choice Eleanor didn't want to make. Her beloved, or her life's ambition. One or the other would perish in her decision.

Hattie quietly removed herself from the room, opening a Bible on Eleanor's dressing table. Eleanor approached it but feared what it might tell her, and she closed it without scanning a word. Voices mingled in the hallway, and it wasn't long before her door opened.

"Ellie? It's Mary. May I come in?"

Opening the door, she saw her cousin's tearstained face. "Mary, what is it?"

"I've been up all night sobbing." Mary still wore her night-dress, and her hands trembled. "What if something had happened to Andrew? I might have seen him die, shot before my very eyes. I cannot get the Negro's face out of my mind. There was so much hatred there. He would have killed Andrew. I know it by the sheer repulsion in his eyes."

Eleanor took her cousin's hands and spoke gently. "Mary, the man's wife and child were taken from him. Whether or not he had the right man, I do not know, but he thought Andrew sold her, and his anger was justified."

"How can you defend such a beast?" Mary shook her head rapidly. "When your fiancé might have been dead two days before your wedding. How could you be so unfeeling? Are there any womanly emotions inside you?"

Not for Andrew there weren't, that she would admit, but Eleanor didn't elaborate on her emotions. Mary thought poorly enough of her presently. "I am only trying to let you see *why* someone might have so much anger. If you could find who took Morgan from you, would you be content to go about your day the same way?"

"We are not discussing the civilized. We are talking about slaves."

Mary's expression held a frightening righteousness, and Eleanor realized her cousin had long been tainted by Confederate rhetoric. She had not the wiles to read both sides. Mary hated the Yankees for what they had done to Morgan, and slowly it had withered away her heart toward anything the Federals stood for.

"Family is family regardless of skin color." Eleanor spoke her view quietly and looked away so as not to punish Mary further. She fussed with her toilet and then bent over to splash her face with water and pat a towel on her face.

"You are not worthy of Andrew's love," Mary spat out the words, "if you can find any sympathy for that man—that man who might have killed Andrew. He's dead as he deserves to be."

"Thanks to Nathaniel." Eleanor couldn't help herself. She needed to point out to Andrew's greatest admirer that he was a coward, and nothing more. Nathaniel had followed Eleanor Under-the-Hill, ensuring no danger would come to her, while Andrew, her supposed betrothed, luxuriated over a tall iced tea.

Mary's eyes thinned. "Did *your* precious Nathaniel fight in the war? Did your Nathaniel ever do anything but rely on his daddy's reputation in Mississippi? How dare you marry a man on Saturday when your mouth betrays him this day! I repeat, dear cousin, you are not worthy of Andrew Pemberton."

Mary reached for the doorknob, but Eleanor stopped her with words that tumbled out angrily.

"And you are worthy, Mary? That's what you are hoping for, isn't it? That I shall give Andrew up for you? And you shall be mistress of Woodacre. You'd like that, wouldn't you? To fawn over my fiancé and remark endlessly on his medals and washed-up uniform that he wears ridiculously about town. How well suited you would be, spending a lifetime trying to make the South rise again."

"You traitor! You may have been born in Mississippi, but you are a Yankee through and through. I shall tell Andrew everything. You may pretend to be an insipid, sweet belle, but you harbor a heart that beats at zero. I pray no man finds himself wed to you, least of all Andrew!"

Mary slammed the door in such a violent manner that the entire house most likely awakened. Eleanor's feelings would be secret no longer.

Her breathing was rapid and strained. She fell against the back of the door and covered her face, sinking to the floor in a trembling, fearful cry. Mary and she were like sisters, but life had torn them apart just as the war of America had divided the states. Why had God made her so different? Most women would happily marry a plantation owner of any acreage in their post-war desperation. What was it about her that made her think she deserved anything more? She cried out to the Lord in her pain.

"Heavenly Father, do I sin to ask for love? The Bible says to flee from temptation, but where would I go, Father? If I stay here, my father will marry me off; but if I go, I will never be able to return. But how can I marry a man I do not love? One I do not even respect? Do You ask that I humble myself and deny everything I know to be true? Or will You honor my love and be with Nathaniel and me in our deception? Tell me, Lord. Please tell me."

Hattie pushed against the door and knocked Eleanor from the kneeling position. Looking at the closed Bible, Hattie shook her head. "You won't get any answers from God if you don't listen."

"Is Mary okay?" she asked timidly.

"She's locked herself in her room. I don't know what went on between you, but I can tell you she sounds as if she's packing to leave."

"She loves Andrew." Eleanor picked herself off the floor and sat down hard on her desk chair. "If she marries him, she'll punish every Negro in sight for Morgan's death and Andrew's near death."

"You cannot leave, Miss Ellie."

"I know, Hattie." Eleanor covered her face again. "I know."

Chapter 15

Nathaniel slammed his Bible shut. He had tried everything he could think of to deny that the seventh commandment applied to him, but coveting his neighbor's wife, his brother's wife, was exactly what he was guilty of. Engagements in the South were not mere formalities. They were a bond as serious as marriage. Yet he had given his word to Ellie, and since the Bible also cautioned to let your yea be yea, Nathaniel would run away with her and not look back. He would pay for it later, when he tried to find work or when he preached. Of that he had little doubt, but he would not let his reputation be ruined with her again.

He took out the latest map of the Mississippi and began to trace a possible route for them. Jeremiah would return the following day, and Nathaniel would discuss arrangements with him. Jeremiah wouldn't like taking Ellie out of Mississippi, but if she were Nathaniel's wife, he would have little choice.

The library door opened, and Nathaniel's father, looking haggard and blanched, leaned against the doorjamb. Nathaniel pondered how aged his father now appeared. Master Pemberton no longer stood an astounding six feet. His body had bent in the years Nathaniel roamed California, and the son couldn't help but pray his absence hadn't caused the hollow look that swept his father's expression.

"I was right about Andrew," his father said solemnly. "The slaves do want to kill him. If it weren't for you, he'd be dead by now."

A wave of guilt lapped Nathaniel, recalling how his one-act play struck fear in the heart of his father. "Andrew is not giving the men enough to eat. We have so few workers left. Andrew shall be picking cotton himself before the year is out."

"That's why the codes are necessary, son."

"The codes fix things now, but they won't fix things forever. You've got to think of Woodacre for longer than this generation, Father. Would you want Andrew's children to be destitute when the Federals seize our plantation for lack of complying with the law? Because that is what will eventually happen. The United States government will own this land if we don't submit to the authorities."

"You're talking nonsense now. Woodacre survived the war. How many plantations were cut into tiny farms, but we have prospered, and we will continue to do so." Master Pemberton stood tall, as proud as any peacock. "Yankees will never touch Woodacre. I'll die before I see that happen."

Nathaniel shook his head. "Father, I'm not trying to upset you. I'm only trying to give you another viewpoint. As someone who didn't witness the ugliness of war, I can testify to the Yankee stronghold Under-the-Hill."

"The Yankees have been here since 1862, Nathaniel. They haven't gotten us yet. Listen—enough of this nonsense. I came to speak with you about your future on this plantation."

Nathaniel shook his head. "Before you go on, you must know I've decided to leave. Andrew will be safe now that the attempt on his life was tried and failed. I'm glad I came home for a time, but I don't belong here."

His father hadn't heard a word he'd said. "I've decided to rewrite my last will and testament, Nathaniel. You are entitled to half of Woodacre again. Saving your brother's life yesterday proved to me that you are a changed man, and you are once again my true son. Of course, it is only right that when Andrew brings Eleanor home, she will be mistress of our plantation, but there shall be room for a wife of yours."

Nathaniel nearly laughed aloud. His father could give him all the riches in the state of Mississippi, but the only treasure he wanted was Ellie. The one jewel his father saw as worthless was the single solitary desire of Nathaniel. Andrew could never appreciate her rare beauty or her marked intelligence. Andrew only desired her for Rosamond, and in his greed he had missed what was truly of value.

"I'm not staying, Father." Nathaniel neglected to add that he was taking the supposed mistress of Woodacre with him.

"I'll not give you another penny if you leave, son."

"I know."

"I cannot give your rights back as first son. It is only fair that you should be under your brother's authority. Andrew deserves that much after losing his arm to fight for the South. Surely you wouldn't deny him that."

"I don't deny him anything." *Anything except a wife in Ellie, a woman Andrew could never appreciate anyway.* "I'm going to preach, Father. I want to tell the country how I've been forgiven and comfort those who have seen the wages of war."

Andrew appeared behind their father. "Please, dear brother, by all means go and spread the Word, and spare us your hypocrisy."

A chill spread down Nathaniel's spine. *Lord, help me to love my brother.* "I have changed, Andrew. I'm sorry you cannot see it."

"You have lost, Nathaniel. That's why you leave—because you know Eleanor would never marry a downtrodden, disinherited scalawag like you. Or should I say Ellie." Andrew smiled wickedly. "But don't worry, brother. I shall take good care of her."

It took every ounce of self-control not to grab Andrew's neck and squeeze. Nathaniel closed his eyes in prayer, asking the Lord to fill him with the Spirit. When he opened his eyes, his brother looked like nothing more than a taunting weasel to Nathaniel. His lack of appreciation for Ellie's discerning nature was exactly what would allow them to escape together.

"I am glad you took my advice and bought a cousin of Lady's for her." Nathaniel focused on the positive aspect of his brother. The only one he could conjure up.

Andrew laughed. "I found a horse that looked like Lady. I didn't go through much trouble. Matching up that old guard dog meal wasn't too difficult. Eleanor is not exactly a horse scholar, dear brother."

"I'm sad for you, Andrew. Ellie is a fine woman, and you are quite fortunate she consented to marry you. I had hoped you would treat her as such. Lady was with her for a long time. Poor Ellie."

Andrew licked his lips lecherously. "Now that cousin of hers, on the other hand—"

"Andrew!" Their father's horror at such words was readily apparent. "You shall not discuss your future wife in such a manner nor compare her to another woman. It's sinful, and you'll bring ruin upon this house with your lustful, coarse talk."

"I only meant—" Andrew was silenced by his father's remonstrance.

Nathaniel had had enough. "What happened to Ceviche?"

Andrew winced at the name. "Who?"

"The slave girl with the infant—Ceviche? Sammy's wife. Sammy, the one who tried to kill you yesterday."

"How on earth would I know what happened to a useless slave girl?"

"Because word Under-the-Hill is, you received payment to sell her. Is that true?"

Andrew looked to his father, then back to Nathaniel. "I'm not in the business of contraband. Is that why her lunatic man came after me yesterday? And died for his trouble?"

Nathaniel gritted his teeth, wanting to shout with all his breath that Sammy wasn't dead. He was aboard a freighter to freedom on the Mississippi. "I'm just repeating what's being said Under-the-Hill."

"If you weren't hanging about in such a vile area, you'd know nothing of such lies."

"Both of you, stop it!" Their father reprimanded, clutching his chest. "Nathaniel, I am giving you half of Woodacre," he said through strained breaths. "You two must learn how to coexist peacefully on this land."

Andrew's face twisted at the pronouncement. "What do you mean?"

"Nathaniel is my son, Andrew. And as much as I'd like to reward you solely for your bravery for the Confederates, I cannot deny my first son his rightful inheritance. You shall receive the lion's share and final say, but Nathaniel and his wife will receive half of the plantation and live here as well."

"You must be toying with me, Father. Nathaniel and I could never share Woodacre. Why, he'll give the slaves beefsteak and potatoes for dinner each night. We'll be run into the ground before the first year is up. Is that what you would have happen? That this would become a freedman's camp? Because your soft son will turn it into an afternoon club for slaves."

"He proved his loyalty to me and this land yesterday when he shot that man. When he saved your life, Andrew."

Nathaniel swallowed the walnut-sized lump in his throat, knowing his father did not know the real story. He started to correct his father and tell Andrew that he didn't want the land when he realized Andrew did want it, that he desired it more than anything on earth. Including Ellie.

"I had a pistol on me. He just saw the villain before I did," Andrew said. "I am a Confederate captain. Clearly, I have far more experience than my cowardly brother."

Nathaniel started at a thought, before scrambling back to the map stretched across his father's desk. Scratched into the bottom of the map were the words *"Corporal Andrew Pemberton"* and the date *"April 1865."* Knowing the uprising had ended by then, Nathaniel mentally calculated that Andrew could not have become a captain as he had been portraying.

"Who was it that made you a captain?"

It was all Nathaniel would ask him for now. He had more important things to think of, like how he would get Ellie tomorrow night and steal her away up the mighty Mississippi River. He would let Andrew explain things to his father.

"Excuse me," Nathaniel said, bashing shoulders with his brother as he exited the room.

Yet Andrew followed closely, pointing a pistol in Nathaniel's back as they made their way down the hallway. "Keep walking."

"Would you shoot me, brother? Here in the hall of your father's home? When I saved your life yesterday?" Nathaniel smiled. "Don't worry, Andrew. I have no intention of staying and working Woodacre. You can put your pistol and your threats away."

The stabbing pain in his back dissipated as Andrew put away his gun. "I don't just want Woodacre—I want Rosamond. And by Saturday I'll have it."

Nathaniel tried to reason with his brother. "What will such greed accomplish, Andrew? What more could you want?"

"To prove to Father he has only one son who will bring glory to this household. And to rise up against the North once again with financial ways the Yankees will respect."

"You've done business with the Yankees through the whole war. Do you think I'm blind, Andrew?"

Pulling out his pistol again, Andrew traced his thumb along the intricate design of the firearm while twisting it playfully in his single hand.

"I have nothing against you, Nathaniel." Andrew looked straight into Nathaniel's eyes. "Go out into the four corners of the earth and spread your religious babble—I send you out with my blessings—but relinquish your rights to Woodacre before you go."

Nathaniel stepped back and crossed his arms. "Very well, Andrew. I'll grant you that request, in writing. On one condition. Let Ellie go, and marry her cousin. Mary is the one you want anyway."

Leaving with Ellie would solve the immediate issue, but stealing her from her father and inheritance was not how Nathaniel preferred life to be.

"Mary," Andrew laughed. "Mary hasn't two coins to rub together. Why should I be saddled with a wife who has nothing to offer me when I can have Eleanor's fortune?"

"Andrew, I pray your heart isn't that dark. I pray you would see the need for love in your life. You were always Mother's favorite. How she cradled you until you were far too old for such snuggling."

The recollection brought tears to Nathaniel's eyes when he gazed into his brother's blank eyes. There seemed to be no emotion, no depth of life left. The war had left its mark on Andrew. No matter what lies Andrew told or what illegal dealings he was involved with, the fact was, he was not a child of God. And that broke Nathaniel's heart.

"Pray to your invisible God all you want, Nathaniel. In the meantime, I shall be rich and embracing the woman you love."

Chapter 16

Father, I do not wish to marry Andrew," Eleanor said in her most solemn voice, careful not to show any depth of happiness. "I do not love him, nor do I think he will do what's best for Rosamond. I am asking that you support me in my sundering of the engagement." She lifted her chin, practicing a stern expression. She only hoped her father was as easily convinced as her mirror.

"Are you quite through talking to yourself?"

Hattie waited with her arms stretched out, holding a morning gown for Eleanor. It was a crimson merino and just the color to inspire all the strength she would need. Everything depended upon her ability to reach her father.

"I'm not talking to myself. I'm rehearsing. Aren't you the least bit anxious for me, Hattie?" She shook her hands to release the excess energy she possessed.

"I'm content in all circumstances. Your mother taught me that. She says I'll have a mansion built for me in heaven and walk on streets of gold, so I'm content with what He has for me here."

"Hattie, I don't know how you do that. I wish I had the presence of mind to be happy wherever God placed me." Eleanor smoothed on her white, kid leather gloves. "But I fear I shall not be content without Nathaniel, without something to call my own."

"You act as though contentment is a magic pill, but there's nothing to it, Miss Ellie. Sometimes having nothing is a blessing. I wait with wonder each day for the Lord and what He has. When I learned to read, I could be anyone on a moment's notice. I remember a quote I once read: 'The wealthy try to control their destinies only to be disappointed when they're rendered utterly useless against the wave of fate.'"

"You think my marrying Andrew is fate?" Eleanor removed

her gloves again, wringing her hands.

"Now I didn't say that. I said it's in your best interest to be content if that's God's plan. I was born a slave, Miss Ellie. I've never been off this plantation except through the books your mama gave me. I saw your daddy grow up, and now I've seen you grow up." Hattie nodded her head with her eyes closed. "I'm content."

"Well, I'm not a victim, Hattie, and I'm not going to marry a man I don't love without a fight. And a harrowing one it shall be."

"Just a few short weeks ago, you were happy to marry Andrew. Nathaniel's appearance changed all that in a matter of two short weeks?"

Eleanor sighed. "It changed everything. It's one thing to marry when your future is without hope. It's quite another when the man you love stands in the witness box."

Three loud knocks rapped on the door.

"Here's your chance. I'm praying." Hattie fastened a lace collar in Eleanor's décolletage and stood beside her charge with hands at her side.

"Good morning, Father."

Master Senton walked toward the French doors with purpose, hands clasped tightly behind his back. "My sister and my niece tell me they are leaving before the wedding. When I ask them what such nonsense is about, they tell me I must speak to you. Do you have something you wish to speak to me about, Eleanor? Why are our relations leaving?"

Eleanor looked to Hattie and sucked in a deep breath. "Father, I don't wish to be married to Andrew, and Mary knows it."

Her father rubbed his gray beard and pursed his lips. "Is there a reason for such a decision the day before the wedding?"

"I didn't know you were going to move the wedding date up, and when you did, I realized how much I do not want to spend the rest of my days married to Master Andrew." Eleanor breathed deeply, trying to keep the emotion at bay. One crack in her consternation and her father would turn away from her hysterics.

"What would you wish to do with your days? Would you like to begin college? Or maybe you'd like to take over as the new overseer on Rosamond? Tell me, Eleanor—what is it you wish for?"

Eleanor cringed at her father's sarcasm. She did wish for an education and also the chance to see to the workers' needs to ensure a future under the Federal, republican government. But she was a woman, and, as such, she would ask for what was possible.

"I wish to marry Nathaniel." Eleanor tilted her chin high toward the delicately inlaid ceiling. "I wish to marry him and see him run Rosamond."

Her father burst into laughter. "Would you like to sleep on a star, my dear Ellie? Perhaps I can arrange for your mattress to be taken by sky train." But his laughter ceased upon her tears.

"I love Nathaniel, Father." Eleanor wiped her eyes with a handkerchief, angry with herself for her tears. The monogrammed letter "P" on the cloth sent a flurry of courage to her sickened heart. "Nothing will ever change that. Do you wish for me to marry the brother of the man I truly love? I tell you I cannot do it. I won't do it."

"I wish to do what's best for you, my dear. Young women are put under their father's care for a reason. Men are much more logical and more scholarly on such matters, while women tend to be of a softer nature, as God intended. Your mother's father ensured that I was a proper selection many years ago, and I shall do the same for you." Her father came close to her and patted her cheek. "I know it feels bleak, but you have had all the finest possessions in life. You have lived on Rosamond your entire life. Nathaniel became a different person when he lived as a nomad. Your troubles together would be endless. With Andrew, your life will change very little."

"Is that how one decides upon a spouse? By who will effect

the least change in one's life? Hasn't the war changed me as well, Father?"

"I want you to apologize to your aunt and cousin. Mary is very distraught, and you shall never forgive yourself if she is not there to stand by you at your wedding."

"Mary will not come to my wedding, Father. Of that I am certain, and there will not be a wedding. You cannot force me to accept my vows. The words will not come, Father. I know they won't."

"You will do what you must to make sure Mary is there, standing beside the bride. A wedding on Rosamond without my sister and her daughter, our only living relations, would cause scandal and ruin. Now run along and apologize."

Eleanor took one final stand. "I love Nathaniel, Father. Andrew does not want me. He wants Rosamond."

"And who better to have it than a man who succeeded in the midst of a battle? While gunboats and cannons raged, Woodacre stood and prospered. The same shall be said for Rosamond. Together they shall be invincible."

Eleanor opened her mouth to speak but snapped it shut at her father's silent reprimand. Her arguments would only trouble her escape. Turning toward the door, she left her father with one last memory. "I love you, Father."

Eleanor prayed for the words to speak to her cousin. Making her way down the hallway, she stopped at a miniature of the grand portrait on the landing of her mother. There was a light in her mother's eyes that seemed to shine even in death. A knowledge and well of strength that went beyond the physical. It was as though her mother's image calmed, humbled, and prepared her to meet Mary again.

Mary loved Andrew. How was her cousin any different from Eleanor? It wasn't wise to love Nathaniel, and yet every bone in Eleanor's body yearned to go to him and leave her comforts behind. Did Mary feel the same for Andrew?

Eleanor tapped gently on her cousin's door and listened to the excited chatter that followed. The door crept open, and Mary stood in the tiny crevice between the doorjamb and the door. "I have nothing to say to you."

Eleanor stopped the door with her hand. "Mary, wait! I'm sorry. Please hear me out."

"What is it?"

"I apologize for my harsh words and bitter accusations against Andrew. I had no right."

"He loves you, Ellie. How can you be so cruel to a man who gave up everything to fight for you?"

"I am a selfish creature, Mary. It is not right that I marry Andrew, not when I don't love him as you do."

"You think I love him?" Mary tried to laugh.

"Don't you?"

Mary's cheeks blushed, and she paused before answering, "Yes, I believe I do. As sinful as I know it to be when he is betrothed to my very own cousin. And it is not the way I loved Morgan," she added quickly. "It is different somehow. I feel a kinship with Andrew because of all we've lost. You and Nathaniel have prospered over your misery, but Andrew and I have suffered greatly. It is not merely his arm that's wounded, but his heart most of all. Can't you appreciate that, Ellie?"

"I do appreciate Andrew, as I appreciate all Confederates, who so gallantly fought for the South and our way of life. I am not a Yankee, as you suppose—only a woman who sees both sides. I suppose that is strange for a woman of my little education."

"It is not strange—only proof that you did not suffer during the war. Your great love has come back to you because he fled. How I wish Morgan had done the same. But since he did not, I cannot help but feel Andrew's pain."

"You know I cannot marry him, Mary. It will be a life of misery for both of us."

"I do not see as you have any choice, and I do hope you'll

learn to appreciate his sadness and take pity on him."

Eleanor pushed her way into Mary's room and motioned for the servants to leave. "Do you really hate the slaves, Mary? Do you blame them for Morgan's death?"

"Why shouldn't I?"

"Because they were pawns in the Federals' game, and we cannot spend our remaining days punishing them for it. It is not Christian."

"Why do you care what I think about the slaves?"

"Because when you marry Andrew, I want your promise you will not support him in the codes."

"Marry Andrew? Ellie, I think your fall from that horse did far more damage than we first suspected."

A pounding on the door interrupted them. "Miss Eleanor, Miss Mary, come here at once."

The two women looked at one another and hurried to the door. Mrs. Patterson's red cheeks popped in and out in the old woman's fatigue.

"What is it?" Eleanor asked.

"There's been an accident on the road. A young woman was thrown from her open carriage. She is not complaining, they say, but she is in and out of consciousness. Miss Mary, I'm going to move your things to Miss Ellie's rooms, and you girls shall share while this poor miss recovers. Your father has sent for the doctor."

Mary looked at Ellie, then at Mrs. Patterson. "Is there a reason she cannot stay downstairs for her infirmary? Why must she be brought up to the family quarters on the eve of a family wedding?"

"They say she is quite the beauty, Miss Mary. We are trying to protect her from male callers. She has an audience around her now, and I'm quite sure she will appreciate the privacy while she recovers. She appears quite distraught over the attentions."

"Well, how long will it be?" Mary asked.

"I cannot say, Miss Mary. They are being very careful in

moving her. She may have broken her back."

"What about the wedding?"

"Why, it will go on as planned, Miss Mary. We shall just have to rearrange plans for our guests. Miss Ellie, I'd appreciate it if you'd help Miss Mary with her things. Hattie and I are preparing bedding for our patient."

"Of course, Mrs. Patterson." Eleanor bit her lip. *How on earth will I escape my quarters with Mary sleeping beside me? Only one day remains until my fate is sealed. Will a wounded stranger stand in the way of my future?*

Chapter 17

Sarah Jenkins grimaced in pain as her strong cousin lifted her up the stairs. She said nothing, but her expression said it all for her. Her blond hair, which extended to her ankles, fell loose and hit each stair as the two young people climbed up. Silence draped the foyer with shared melancholy.

"Doctor Hayes is coming up the drive now!" Mrs. Patterson exclaimed. "Miss Eleanor, you go meet him, and I'll see to the young lady's needs."

Eleanor ran across the summer porch, taking the steps two at a time, and met Doctor Hayes, taking his horse's reins. "She's upstairs. Mrs. Patterson will help you."

Doctor Hayes only nodded, then sprinted toward the house while Eleanor tied his horse to a low-hanging magnolia branch. She watched as the inhabitants of the entryway huddled around the doctor. Innocently, she took one step backward and then another, until she turned and broke into a hastened run. A run that led her to the stables and the freedom Tiche could provide her while everyone was busy. Eleanor's crimson merino hardly warranted riding clothes, but she placed a sidesaddle on her mare, coughing at the dust from the huge animal, and shimmied out of her hoop. She left it lying scandalously on the basin of Tiche's stall.

She mounted her horse and stole away quietly from the house for one last, leisurely ride along the magnolias before her possible elopement. Workers stared at her, but she avoided eye contact, not wanting to give herself away. A pleasant morning ride, her smile told them, while her deep red gown belied another occasion: one more in tune with a morning breakfast on the veranda as a bride-to-be. The invalid had served a special purpose for Eleanor. It allowed her to avoid living the lie of preparing for a wedding, which she had no intention of seeing through to its conclusion.

Galloping to the end of Rosamond's long drive, Eleanor saw the crowd still lingering about the overturned black carriage. Its wheels spun in the air, and the sight reminded her how badly hurt the young woman must be. She involuntarily shivered thinking about the poor woman. Not far from the sight, a pink silk ribbon fluttered in the wind. Its length could only mean it must have been used as a garter. Eleanor jumped from her horse, placing the ribbon in the small pocket within the folds of her dress. She would return it to the young woman quietly.

Eleanor's movement caused the mingling men to turn around and stare at her. She nodded in acknowledgement, stepped on a tree stump, and mounted her horse once again. Making her way toward the path along the river, her arm began to ache, and she stopped to rest under a large oak tree at the top of the levee.

She rubbed the still-purple limb until the gallop of a single horse disturbed her quiet. Eleanor turned to see Andrew riding his buckskin mare, and her heart beat rapidly. She hoped he wouldn't question her. Hadn't Hattie said she was the worst liar in Mississippi? He wore his uniform as usual and a slight, cockeyed smile. Mary's recriminations haunted Eleanor, and she forced herself to take pity on Andrew.

"Good morning, Andrew."

"Good morning, Eleanor. Out for a morning jaunt?"

"Yes. And you?"

"I came to inspect the overturned carriage and what might be done to right it. Why aren't you at the house with the invalid as everyone else is?"

"There was so much confusion, and I feared I wouldn't get another chance to ride Tiche—before my wedding of course."

"Of course. How sad you will be to leave your childhood home, but how remarkable that you should live but a stone's throw from the great house."

Eleanor picked at the grass, looking wistfully at her childhood home. "Do you really think the plantations should be combined, Andrew?"

"They shall be after tomorrow, regardless of my thoughts." His crooked smile broadened.

"I don't think they should be. Paperwork could be drawn up to prevent it. I think the Federals may seize the properties and break them apart, leaving them smaller than they are now."

"You've been listening to too much gossip if you think that could happen."

"The taxes will go up, possibly to the point we cannot pay them. That's what happened to the Landers place. I read—"

"Eleanor, why would you worry your head over such things? Those are a man's worries."

"I am just the supplier of the inheritance, is that it?" Eleanor shielded her eyes from the sun.

Andrew raised his arm, and Eleanor flinched as though he might strike her. Upon sensing her fear, he grazed her cheek roughly with his hand. "Of course not, my darling."

Feeling as though he might press one of those painful kisses to her lips, she backed away.

She put her hands on her hips. "The black codes will ruin Rosamond. Our people will flee. They have been treated far too well to go to such inhumanity now."

"Was it humane for that slave to try to murder me in broad daylight? They are savages, Eleanor. They don't duel or fight as a proper man. They attack in the night like stray soldiers without enough to eat. The codes will ensure our safety."

"I won't let Rosamond go to the black codes, Andrew." Eleanor steeled herself against the tree. "I'd die before I let that happen. My mother fought her entire life to ensure our plantation treated its slaves with dignity."

"Your mother was a fool, and she died for her ignorance." Andrew's eyes widened. "Eleanor, I'm sorry. I was repeating Nathaniel's words. I should have known better."

Eleanor looked directly at Andrew. It was the first time she'd really looked into his coal black eyes and tried to find what Mary pitied about him. She couldn't see it. His eyes were dark, not just in color, but in emotion. They were as lifeless as the men in make-shift graves along the roadway.

"Nathaniel loved my mother, Andrew. He would never speak ill of her. Your own mother—well, never mind. It is wicked to say anything against the dead."

Mrs. Pemberton, their mother, was a callous woman who crouched over Andrew at every sniffle but denied Nathaniel's basic needs. Had it not been for favoritism by his father, Nathaniel might not have grown to a man at all. To hear her own mother spoken of as insane was blasphemy in light of his own mother's sins.

"Perhaps it's best we not discuss this now. On the eve of our wedding, we should be speaking of much happier things, such as the wedding trip I've planned. Would you like to hear of it?"

"No. Surprise me." Eleanor turned away from his empty eyes, torn between saving the slaves of Rosamond and saving herself from a life of misery. She hated that she was such a selfish creature and wouldn't give a moment's hesitation to the choice.

"Eleanor, I know we've had our differences, but it's time they came to an end. I shall run the plantations as I see fit. As for you, you may buy your furniture and turn Woodacre back into the showplace it once was. You may hire as many servants as you like and throw as many balls as our fair house can stand, but you really must leave the business to me."

"Andrew, I am asking you one final time to reconsider our marriage. What if you were to marry another and continue to build up Woodacre as you hope to? Two plantations will only be a headache to you."

"Your father will have no part in such a plan. Eleanor, you are just nervous. I know it has been difficult for you having my brother return before our wedding. I know that you fancy you once loved him, but I can assure you his appearance means nothing. I am offering you the future that any Southern woman would cherish. Do not miss the opportunity over a foolish dream."

"I only meant—"

"Enough. Eleanor, you will be at the wedding tomorrow as scheduled, or my brother will pay with his life."

He looked directly at her with his cold, empty eyes, and she had no doubt he would follow through on such threats if they gave him the opportunity. But they wouldn't. She and Nathaniel would run into the dark night before Andrew ever got the chance.

Eleanor shook her head. "Is that a threat, Andrew? Do you threaten me?"

"Do not misunderstand me. I mean you no harm. But I have worked long and hard to make a success of Woodacre, and I shall do the same for your family plantation. But I will not stand for this infatuation with my brother. It must come to an end. And it shall, one way or another."

"Andrew, you don't mean such vicious words. Take them back."

"Neither my father nor you has ever understood Nathaniel for who he really is. Now he comes back six years later, a walking ghost spouting his preacher babble so my father will forgive him. It's really inconceivable how he's found a way to break through my father's shell and be written into the will again. I do pray you're not falling for his excuses, Ellie. He wants Woodacre, and if he had his way, he'd have you, too, so that he might combine them as I plan to. Thank heavens, your father sees though him. Everything Nathaniel touches turns to poison. The ground will wither and die under his care."

"No, he doesn't want the plantations. He's leaving it all behind, Andrew. He told me so. He will preach." *With me at his side,* she added silently.

"He will not leave Woodacre, Eleanor. He will play on my father's sympathies and remain with us forever. He will live in our house and eat of our table until we put an end to it. But, as I said, it's not your worry. You'd best get back to the house and see to your invalid." He mounted his golden mare and clicked his tongue.

"Andrew, wait."

But his horse was galloping down the magnolia-lined drive. Eleanor dropped her face in her hands. After a few moments had passed, she took Tiche's reins and walked slowly back to the house. Mary stood on the porch, waving with a friendly smile, as though all were forgotten between them.

"Ellie, why, you're as cold as ice. Where have you been?" Mary took her hands. "Miss Jenkins is truly in pain, Ellie. She must lie on her stomach, propped up on her elbows. I'm afraid there's not much Doc Hayes can do for her."

"How is her cousin? The one who was traveling with her? Has he suffered much?"

Mary shook her head. "It doesn't appear so. He received a welt on his forehead, a great strawberry-colored thing, but he seems more concerned about Miss Jenkins than anything else."

"I shall visit her and welcome her. I have something of hers left at the accident site."

"She's been asking for you. It seems she feels terrible about troubling a young bride on the eve of her wedding. I'm sure you can set her mind at rest."

"The wedding should be postponed. How callous of us to celebrate while she lies in agony. She'll need her rest, and the music and merriment will only disturb her. I shall talk with Father presently."

"He has no intention of canceling the wedding, Ellie." Mary's green eyes darkened in a challenge. "He has already spoken of it to my mother. He is worried for your reputation."

"Why is it *you* wish for me to be married, Mary?"

"Because I wish for Andrew to be happy. That shall make him so."

"Only God can truly make him peaceful and happy, Mary."

Mary rolled her eyes. "You've been listening to Nathaniel and Hattie far too long. Save the sermons for Sundays, my dear cousin. You have hospitality to see to." Mary stepped away, allowing Eleanor to enter the great home.

Eleanor's father spoke in the study with Aunt Till. Their conversation seemed of the utmost importance, and Eleanor nodded in recognition while heading up the stairs, but her father called out to her. She entered the once-lavish sitting room and sat on an opulent, red velvet chair that now wore the knife wounds of a Yankee bayonet.

"Mary has updated me on Miss Jenkins's convalescence. I shall see if the young woman has further needs that only an equal might understand." Eleanor referred to the garter, knowing that if she had lost such a personal item, it would alarm her more than any pain until it was returned safely to her care.

Aunt Till cleared her throat. "The wedding shall be a quiet affair out of respect for Miss Jenkins. We shall hold the events outside on the front lawn so as not to disturb her any more than possible."

The wedding would be quieter than they imagined. For the bride would turn up missing as dawn broke.

Chapter 18

The sunny yellow curtains were drawn, and a somber ambiance filled the usually cheerful guest room. Miss Sarah Jenkins moaned in agony, and Eleanor nearly turned back for fear of upsetting the young invalid. A creaky floorboard gave the visitor away, and slowly Sarah turned around. The rumors were true, for she emanated beauty, even in ill health. Her cheeks were a fresh petal pink, and her luxurious blond hair fell about the floor, surrounding her like a halo.

"Good morning, Miss Jenkins. I am Eleanor Senton."

The young woman stretched out a hand. "Miss Senton. I am so dreadfully sorry to have interrupted your wedding festivities. Forgive me, please."

"Think nothing of such nonsense, Miss Jenkins. Your health is far more important. Is there anything I can get for you? Would you like tea?"

"No, thank you. My mother is being sent for, and they shall decide if I may be taken by ambulance to our home in Vicksburg."

"You mustn't trouble yourself. You shall stay as long as necessary to recuperate." Eleanor found herself staring, for she had never seen such loveliness. "Where were you heading, Miss Jenkins?"

"My cousin was seeing me to Baton Rouge. My sister has settled there with her husband."

Eleanor reached into her pocket and brought out the pink silk ribbon she had found at the scene. She tucked it under the woman's hands without a word.

"Thank you," she said, letting out a deep sigh.

"If it is of any consequence, I heard the men speaking, and they said your fall was quite graceful. You did not show so much as a foot."

Miss Jenkins smiled, while closing her eyes in obvious relief.

"It is of enormous consequence. Thank you, Miss Senton. Please do not waste more of your day here with me. You have a wedding to prepare for. But before you go, would you tell me about your fiancé? Is he handsome? What do you love most about him?"

Eleanor thought only of Nathaniel. "He is strikingly handsome. He is tall with dark, wavy hair and green-gold eyes. They are the warmest of eyes and seem to dance with amusement without his uttering a word. He is impossible not to love."

"Did he fight in the War between the States? Was he a hero?"

Eleanor's countenance fell. "No. No, he didn't."

"I'm sorry. My mind must be swimming. I thought I was told he was a captain."

"Yes, yes, of course he is. Forgive me—my head is not clear from the preparations."

"I should love to meet him when I'm feeling better."

"What about you, Miss Jenkins? Are you engaged, or do you have a beau?" Eleanor could simply imagine the throng of men who followed at the young woman's heels. Eleanor was thought quite attractive, but she felt like a toad beside this woman even in such a fragile state.

"I was engaged to be married before the war, but my fiancé died at Paducah in Forest's Calvary Department. He died a hero. It was a Confederate victory. It was a small battle, but it will have enormous consequences for me throughout my lifetime."

"You will marry another though. Someday—"

"As far as the government is concerned, I was already married, and I am a widow. It seems Franklin took out a marriage license, and although we never had any type of ceremony, I shall be known as a widow."

Eleanor blinked. "What? What did you say about the marriage license?"

"It is a man's business. I am sure your fiancé has taken care of it, but it legally binds you before the wedding. The records clearly state you are married whether or not an actual ceremony took place. So I am a widow."

Eleanor searched the floor, breathing with difficulty.

"I'm sure your captain has acquired one, Miss Senton. Is that what rattles you so?"

"What would happen if your fiancé was found alive, Miss Jenkins? And you had married another after the license was drawn?"

Miss Jenkins twisted her face at the absurd question. "Why, I'd be guilty of bigamy, I would guess. Either that or I would not be considered married at all and living in—well, I shan't discuss such scandal, as we are ladies."

Eleanor clutched her chest, trying to gain control of her breathing. "Excuse me, Miss Jenkins. I shall return to check on you later."

Flying down the steps, Eleanor ran past her father's and aunt's concerned calls and out to the lawn. She had to find Nathaniel. Surely he would straighten this out. To her unparalleled relief, Nathaniel waited for her on the lawn, dressed for dinner. She struggled toward him with dread, as though her legs were caught in a quagmire. They buckled underneath her, and she battled to stay upright before she reached her destination.

"Nathaniel," she said breathlessly. "The marriage license. Has Andrew obtained a license?"

"That is what I came to tell you." Nathaniel's brow lowered. "I did not think my brother would obtain it before tomorrow, but it seems he has. He has shown it to me and threatened that if you were to leave now, you would be his wife forever."

"No," Eleanor shook her head. "No, Nathaniel. Tell me this is a nightmare, that we shall still run this very evening."

"I cannot take another man's wife, Ellie."

"You would take his fiancée! I fail to see the difference."

Nathaniel flinched. "The difference is our ability to be married legally. I'll have to find another way, Ellie. We cannot start our life in sin. I would rather see you married honorably to my brother than living with a scandalous title attached to your name. I love you far too much to let such a thing happen."

"But you will let him win, Nathaniel! How can you give me up so easily? He will ruin Rosamond, and me. Will you go on and preach without thinking of me again? You may escape a life of ruin, but I shall live it either way. I would rather live it with you."

"All is not lost, Ellie. I will find a way for us. If there is such a path, I will take it by the reins and steal you away as my bride. But I must do it honorably. I have brought far too much shame on my father to do this to him, or you."

"All is lost, Nathaniel. He shall have me tomorrow, just as he always planned. Why, oh, why did you stay gone so long?" Eleanor heard her father call from the veranda and lowered her voice. "Please do not forget me." Despair clutched at her breast. To be so close to her heart's desire only to have it ripped away was worse than cruel. The thought of Andrew's harsh kisses made her shudder.

"I'll do whatever I can."

Nathaniel's brown eyes spoke to her. His deep, jutted jaw left her breathless. She could not imagine life without him, and she wouldn't. Hattie said her father couldn't force her to say "I do," and suddenly she knew she would cut out her own tongue rather than mouth the words to a man who had threatened her beloved. Andrew possessed not an ounce of love or chivalry in his wretched heart, and Eleanor would not believe God willed her to be married to such a man.

"Eleanor!" Her father's terse use of her name broke Nathaniel's warm look.

"Do not give up hope, Ellie. Pray without ceasing." He threw a leg over his horse. "Yah!"

Eleanor turned and made her way toward where her father stood on the veranda. "You cannot make me accept Andrew! You cannot!" She sprinted up the stairs and retreated to her bedroom.

Hattie waited for her with freshly baked cake and a warm pot of tea. "Eat something, dear. You've lost all your coloring."

"I'm not hungry, Hattie. I shall starve myself."

"I've left your Bible open again, Miss Ellie. You call Hattie if you need anything."

"How do you stand it, Hattie? The feeling of being owned?"

Hattie laughed. "I guess I just think about my future. If we wallow in the pain, that's all there is."

After the older woman had left the room, Eleanor pushed away the tea cart and once again closed her Bible.

✍

Nathaniel rode to Natchez Under-the-Hill with a pounding urgency. Riding up to the county clerk's office, he pulled his horse to a rough stop. "Whoa! Whoa!" Haphazardly, he tied up the horse, uttering a prayer Ellie would be there when he returned. In the cramped office a single clerk huddled over paperwork at a desk.

He stood immediately. "May I help you, good sir?"

"I need to see your records on Captain Andrew Pemberton. Apparently he's taken out a marriage license."

The clerk nodded. "I remember him. Missing an arm, right?"

"That's him. Do you have a copy of the record?"

"Who wants to know?"

"I am his brother and will be standing beside him for his wedding. He stands to inherit a great deal of money upon this marriage."

The little man squeezed his eyes shut and then studied Nathaniel for a sense of honesty. "It's been filed already. I'm sorry."

"So it is legal." Nathaniel felt the life drain from him.

"As legal as it can be. I do my job with honor, dear sir."

"Of course you do." Nathaniel slammed his hand on the counter. "Thank you for your time."

"Enjoy the wedding," the man called after Nathaniel.

Oh Lord, how will Ellie and I be together now? What is it You wish for me to learn? You tore apart a sea to save Your people from slavery, and I cannot believe You want Rosamond to hold Your people in bondage. And I hope You don't mean it for Ellie. Speak to me, Lord.

Nathaniel snaked his way down to the riverfront and noticed Jeremiah's boat docked at the central pier. He paid a stable master to take his horse and jogged down the craggy bluff toward the water's edge.

The air over the Mississippi was breezy and filled with the stench of steamers and their cargo. Nathaniel could see Jeremiah heaving great bales of hay onto his boat, and his stomach lurched at his predicament. He had planned to hide on that boat this very evening, sheltering Ellie, who would have been his bride, from her captors. They would sail away at the first sign of light. He had imagined it many times. Now nothing in his life was certain.

As he drew nearer, Jeremiah threw one last bundle onto his boat and stood up straight. His lumbering form was drenched from the physical labor, causing him to lift his shirttail to wipe away the beads of sweat. "Nathaniel. What brings you here, brother?"

"Can we talk on the boat?" Nathaniel looked about him, and although he recognized no one, he trusted no one either. Information at the docks paid good money.

"Come aboard." Stepping back, Jeremiah moved toward the bow and entered a small, private room used for steering the boat. Shutting the door behind them, he grabbed a tin pot from the stove. "You want some coffee?"

Nathaniel shook his head. "I came here because I need your help, Jeremiah. Again."

"Are ya still plannin' on bein' here tonight? I can marry legally. You assure the future Mrs. Pemberton of that. I don't want her frettin' about that."

"There's going to be no wedding, Jeremiah. At least not my own. Andrew has already secured a marriage license."

Jeremiah slammed the coffeepot down. "I knew your brother was no good."

"He's only doing what I should have done. He's thinking ahead, ensuring Ellie will belong to him. If I had been more forthright and forceful with her father, I would have thought to do the same thing. As it is, I'm paying for my lack of action. I moved slower than the sludge in a Mississippi puddle."

"So you just goin' to give up? Let 'im marry her?" Jeremiah scratched his head. "She seemed pretty desperate to avoid such a weddin', offerin' me her bracelet and all."

"I know, Jeremiah. She is desperate, and I need to take care of her before she does something rash."

"What's more rash than running off with her groom's brother?"

"I'm not sure, but I know Ellie, and she'll do what feels right if she's trapped."

Jeremiah laughed. "You sure God ain't doing you a favor by takin' that little spitfire off your hands?"

Thinking of her fiery spirit only brought joy to his heart and a smile to his face. "I'm quite sure."

"All right then. I'll help you. What is it you have in mind?"

Chapter 19

Hattie had come into the room and opened Eleanor's Bible again. Hebrews. Eleanor scanned it before closing it again. She didn't need a sermon. She needed God to act—and quickly. She still held hope that her hero would return for her and that he would overlook the troublesome marriage license. After all, Andrew would be as stuck as she was if he didn't cancel the license. Did Andrew hate Nathaniel enough to spend his life alone? To make them pay for her sins of leaving him at the altar? Eleanor couldn't answer such questions, and she supposed Nathaniel couldn't either.

Through her walls, she could hear the gentle moans of pain from Miss Jenkins, and Eleanor quickly entered the shared door to see if she could be of any assistance.

"Miss Jenkins?"

Quiet sobs emanated from the stricken woman, and when she peered at her visitor, her eyes were round and full from crying. "Did I disturb you, Miss Senton? I'm so very sorry."

"Hush, I'm just concerned about you. Is there anything I can do to ease your pain?" Eleanor took a cloth and dipped it in the washbasin, wringing it and placing it on the woman's blistering hot forehead. "You are so warm. You must have a fever."

"Call me Sarah, Miss Senton. I do feel dreadfully hot. I do hope I cool down so they don't cup and bleed me again with that butchering apparatus."

Eleanor winced at the notion. "You've had such a trying day. I wish I could give you something for the pain. I understand that tomorrow they will have an expert and a homeopathic physician visit. Is that right?"

"You shouldn't even be thinking of me. You will marry your prince tomorrow. I hope the ambulance will come and take me away before the nuptials, and I shall not further trouble you."

"No, I won't marry my prince." Eleanor wanted to add that she would marry the toad, but she kept her animosity to herself. Her attitude was less than Christian. She chastised herself but still allowed the truth to come rolling out. "I shall marry the brother of my prince."

Sarah perched herself higher on her elbows and smiled, showing the first sign of light Eleanor had seen from her. "This is just the type of story to take my mind off the pain. Will you share with me? It sounds terribly exciting. Your words shall not leave my lips, if I should live to tell anyone."

Eleanor willingly told her long and detailed story, and Sarah listened with vigor. How nice it was to share the story with someone who wasn't tainted by the past. Sarah finally lowered herself back to bed. "I am exhausted by your life, Ellie, but Nathaniel sounds romantic beyond measure. I should be surprised if he does not rescue you. He does not sound like the type of man to leave you with your troubles, not anymore anyway."

"If he does not rescue me, I shall introduce you, Sarah. There is no sense for both of us to be unhappy, and I think Nathaniel would make the finest husband this side of the Mason-Dixon line."

Sarah laughed. "Ellie, he shall come for you, and I daresay any man would not be thrilled with the prospect of an injured wife. I shall perhaps remain a spinster forever." Sarah's eyelids appeared heavy, and it was obvious sleep was overcoming her. "Will you read to me from the Bible? I should like to listen to scriptures as I fall asleep. My Bible is there on the nightstand."

Eleanor picked up the great, black book and opened to where Sarah had marked with a scarlet silk ribbon. Hebrews. If she didn't know better, she would think Hattie had planned this. She read a few chapters before Sarah fell off to a peaceful sleep. Once in the chapter, however, she stopped at the words before her, and her heart pounded at the message.

"Marriage is honourable in all. . .but. . .adulterers God will judge. Let your conversation be without covetousness; and be content with such things as ye have: for he hath said, I will never leave thee, nor forsake thee."

Eleanor's breath left her at the searing admonition. She had complained without ceasing. She believed Nathaniel would save her, but he couldn't. Only God could save her from her lack of contentment; and until she made things right with Him, they could never be right within her heart. That is what Hattie had tried to tell her. She hurried to her own bedroom and found Hattie packing her trunk for the wedding trip.

"How is Miss Jenkins?"

"She is sleeping peacefully. Hattie, I believe I read what you wished me to. The scripture, I mean, in Hebrews—was it about contentment?"

Hattie smiled. "I believe you read what God wished you to as I see your Bible is sitting there untouched."

Eleanor looked at the Bible and walked toward it. Her hand flew to her mouth with a gasp. "It is the same page."

"Don't act so surprised. God is mighty and willing if we draw near to Him."

"Everything points to the fact that I should marry Andrew. I can protect Rosamond, I can protect the slaves, and I can protect Nathaniel's life. But if I don't marry him all of those things will fall into his hands. Especially the black codes. Mother's wishes will be long forgotten."

"They already are being forgotten, Ellie. But you must allow God to work. He doesn't ask that you do everything by yourself— only that you rely on Him."

"There's only one reason to marry Nathaniel—for my own selfish desires. I must fight that, Hattie. Perhaps God's will is different for my life than what I had hoped. I must accept His will for my life."

"I knew God was working on you, dear."

"I'll be at the heritage magnolia." It was her favorite place to pray. "Please tell anyone who's looking for me where I'll be. I won't leave shouting distance of the house."

"Very well, but you must be back to dress for dinner. We're expecting all of the Pembertons and a few neighbors as well."

"Is Nathaniel invited?"

"Yes, Ellie. He shall be here, according to his father and your aunt. God will give you the strength, Ellie, whatever you decide. I know He will."

✍

Eleanor dressed in her finest bare-shouldered silk for the preparation dinner. The soft pink color induced a rosy glow to her cheeks, and her fear slowly dissipated as she gazed at her reflection. She drew in a great breath. "If this is God's will, let it be."

Descending the staircase, she fingered the banister, taking in the details of the ornately carved balusters. Had she ever noticed there were pineapples carved into each base? As she reached the entryway, candlelight danced on the Italian marble, and she was mesmerized by the fiery reflective dance.

"Ellie?" Nathaniel's deep voice met her.

Looking up, she willed herself not to fall straight into his arms. Nathaniel never appeared finer. Clean-shaven for the occasion and looking dashing in his black suit of clothes, she marveled at what a handsome groom he would be. With his dark, wavy hair combed neatly, he smiled, showing elegant white teeth and an aristocratic carriage. The light of the candles shone a brilliant bronze into his hazel eyes, and Eleanor squeezed her eyes shut, willing herself to remember every detail of him this night.

I can't do this, Lord. I am not strong enough.

"Eleanor," Andrew stood before her, finally in something other than his Confederate uniform. He also wore a black suit.

"Good evening, Andrew."

"May I say you are a perfect vision this evening. Why, you shall have the entire town of Natchez hoping to marry you."

At this comment, Andrew looked callously toward Nathaniel, who hadn't taken his eyes from Ellie.

"Thank you, Andrew. You are most kind."

"I have taken the liberty of selecting a wedding gift for you." Andrew produced a long, velvet box. He opened it and inside lay an emerald necklace with dropped stones and gold encasing. Eleanor gasped at its beauty, but she instantly regretted her reaction when she saw Nathaniel turn from her. "It was my mother's. We buried it during the war so that my bride might have it."

Eleanor turned away from Andrew, and he placed the necklace around her neck. It suddenly felt like a shackle to her, and it took every ounce of strength not to rip it from her neck.

"It's beautiful, Andrew. Thank you."

He placed a harsh kiss on her cheek and whispered in her ear. "See, I can be quite agreeable." His breath upon her sent a shiver down her back.

A seven-course dinner and dull conversation dragged on until Eleanor could barely hide her impatience. She listened as Andrew told guests exploits of the war. Some new, some he had repeated endlessly. When the last guest left, Eleanor bid good night to her father and aunt and snuck quietly down the back stairs for some air. The cookhouse was alive and vigorously churning out smoke for tomorrow's festivities, and Eleanor used its light to find her way to an iron bench which decorated the garden. It wasn't long before Nathaniel joined her.

"I knew you would come."

"You look beautiful, Ellie. You shall make the most extraordinary bride. I wish I might be here to see it."

Any emotion ceased. Eleanor felt only numbness as she faced Nathaniel. "You are going then." She lifted her chin and played with the folds in her gown.

"Yes."

"I shall miss you, Nathaniel."

"And I, you. I've threatened my brother's life if he mistreats you, Ellie. He's given me his word he shall treat you as a queen."

"As he treated Ceviche."

"We don't know he had anything to do with that."

"No, that's right. We won't take the word of a slave girl over your upstanding brother."

"You're only making this more difficult."

Eleanor faced him for the last time. Powerless against his brother, she currently despised him for his weakness. No matter how strong he pretended to be by leaving her a reputable woman, she would remember him for his lack of courage. "I shall be fine, Nathaniel. I have reconciled myself to such a marriage. I was once very used to the idea until you came back and teased me. Do not worry. I shall make the most of my match and do what I can to help the people of Rosamond and Woodacre."

"One day you shall thank me for my sacrifice."

"I doubt that very much, Master Pemberton, but as I said, I shall be a good wife to your brother. It appears God is teaching me a lesson in contentment, and I shall learn it well. I am thankful we had this romantic tryst, that I might be the heroine in a Charlotte Brontë novel for a time and remember the days of my youth with folly. For two short weeks I was the belle of the ball."

"You will always be the belle, Ellie. Always." He bent down and brushed a kiss to her cheek.

Chapter 20

Eleanor's ivory satin wedding gown with its wide skirt, worn over layers of petticoats and a full crinoline hoop glistened with elegance in the morning light. She fingered the handmade lace neckline, thinking such extravagance was wasted. Dressing had been a chore, beginning with the embroidered chemise, topped with a restricting corset, and finally the laced closing on the back of the bodice. She could barely breathe from all the layers, but she was thankful her wedding was in early November, rather than the stifling heat of summer.

She placed the floral motif Limerick veil atop her crown of auburn hair and sighed. "I shall forget Nathaniel was ever here. That is the Christian thing to do."

"Yes," Hattie agreed, though her mood had been less than Christian today. With every step she forced her foot to the ground, and when lacing up the wedding gown Eleanor thought she might die from the elder woman's aggressions. Although Hattie had preached to her endlessly on contentment, watching Ellie marry Andrew was like giving her own daughter up to a sworn enemy. Its toll upon Hattie grew obvious.

"Hattie, do not look at me in such a way. I am no traitor. If I don't marry him, we shall all suffer. I must marry someone, and it may as well be Andrew. I thought you told me you could be content in all circumstances."

"I can be, but I hoped for better for you, Ellie. I hoped you might find true love rather than settle for a life with Andrew Pemberton."

"I shall persuade him in regards to the workers. Give me time."

"You are far too generous with his nature. Your mother despised him as a child, and I think it was with good reason."

"My mother never despised anyone."

"True," Hattie said. "But if she was close to despising anyone it would be that strange boy who always had a snail in his pocket." They laughed together.

"All little boys like snails and frogs. It's quite a normal experience for boys."

"It was not normal to talk to them. And he talked to that snail just as I am talking to you this morning. Called it Rudolpho."

"Hattie, are you quite finished?"

"I am finished."

"Nathaniel is gone. There are no options left to me, and we shall soon depart for Woodacre to live, so I suggest you get used to respecting Andrew as master of our home and not bring up Rudolpho again."

Eleanor knew her tone was cool, that Hattie only had her best interest at heart. But the day was hard enough to endure. She needed Hattie on her side. A strange sense of calm had enveloped Eleanor. With Nathaniel gone, and no escape possible, she was determined to see God's will through to its rightful end.

Hattie's booming voice interjected, "As I said before, I'm content, and when I enter his home as a servant, I shall forever be silent."

A muffled cry emanated from the next room. "Excuse me, Hattie. That's Miss Jenkins. I need to check on her this morning."

"In your wedding finery?" Hattie asked.

"Unless you care to unlace me and start again." Eleanor laughed at Hattie's grimace. "I didn't think so. I shall return shortly for my bouquet, and we shall get on with this wedding."

Eleanor knocked quietly on the guest room door. "Sarah? Sarah, it's me, Ellie; may I come in?"

"Please, Ellie. Come in!" Sarah turned toward the door, still in her stomach-down position with her blond hair cascading about her elegantly. "Oh Ellie! I have never seen a more beautiful bride. What a sight you make this morning. I was feeling so depressed until I got a glimpse of such beauty. My spirits are lifted now."

Eleanor twisted and turned to model her exquisite gown. "It is lovely, isn't it?"

"Not the gown, Ellie—you. Smile, Ellie—it is the only thing that's missing."

"I'm not sad, Sarah, really. I'm resigned. I'm resigned to getting married today, and I shall make the best of it because that's what the Lord would have me do."

"You are a better woman than I."

"How can you say such rubbish as you lie in agony and make nary a sound, Sarah? This gown would be twice as beautiful on you. Your golden hair is being talked of throughout the town. I've been asked if you might part with a few strands for a souvenir."

Sarah laughed. "Such folly. Men are naive creatures, more vain than you or I."

"This gown would be beautiful on you," Eleanor repeated.

"Perhaps I shall get the chance to wear it someday if I'm not a certified cripple for my entire life. I fear no one would marry an invalid."

"You will recover, Sarah. I'm certain of it. Doc Hayes has called in the best specialists, and when you do you shall wear my gown and do it proper justice. I should like to see this gown worn by a bride who glows with happiness, as you certainly shall."

"Prince Charming did not come last night?"

"No, and he won't be at the wedding. He has left Mississippi and my life forever."

"Such a pity. It was so romantic to think he might sweep you away in the night and make you his bride, leaving his brother terrorized from the deception."

"It did make a romantic tale, didn't it?" Eleanor took a cloth and wrung it out in the basin.

"No! You shall ruin your satin. Your groom would not appreciate droplets of water on your gown."

"I can see you perspiring from here, Sarah. I cannot leave you like this."

"Call for my cousin. You are a bride today, not a nursemaid!"

"Pshaw! I cannot have a man standing over you. Your position is perilous enough as it is, and I know that would be my undoing to have a man see me in such form."

"We are too alike, dear Ellie. Vanity first!" Sarah giggled.

Eleanor's heart ached as she watched Sarah struggle with each movement, yet laugh through the pain. "I have nothing to complain about. I know that now. Nathaniel is a far-off dream. Andrew shall be my reality."

"Sometimes our second choices are truly better for us. God knows, Ellie, and He will care for you."

Eleanor nodded. "Doc Hayes has sent for a chair with wheels. Do you think you might be able to attend the wedding? I should feel so much better if you were there."

"Such a kind invitation, but I wouldn't dream of intruding on your day. You shall be the belle of the ball today, Ellie, not a foreign invalid who is more fit for a circus act than a witness to a wedding."

"Pray for me. It shall be a harrowing day. My cousin Mary shall watch every move I make all the while she cries at Andrew's vows."

"Mary has lost so much, and now this. Sometimes, life simply isn't fair."

"I know one thing. God provided your friendship for me, and I needed it to get through this day. To be able to tell someone, in all this finery, that I feel more like I'm attending a funeral than a wedding is such a great weight off my heart."

"If I am not here when you get back from your wedding trip, I shall write, Ellie."

Squeezing the cloth for one final sweep of perspiration, Eleanor kissed her new friend's forehead. "Wish me luck."

"All you'll need rests in Him."

Eleanor left and shut the door quietly. Mary met her in the hallway.

"Your dress is divine, just as we imagined. Won't Andrew be happy?"

"Won't he," Eleanor said flatly.

"I'm sorry for our misunderstanding, dear cousin. I should have never expressed my emotions for your future husband. Forgive me for such impropriety."

"You are forgiven, Mary. You were only doing what you thought was best. Trying to make me realize what a fine husband Andrew would make."

"I'm glad you've come to the realization. He is far too valuable to mishandle. Mitchell Rouse made that mistake."

"Mitchell? What did you say about Mitchell, my father's overseer? Or should I say former overseer?"

Mary's eyes grew wide. "Nothing. I said nothing about him. Only that he misunderstood Andrew's strength and saw his loss of an arm as a sign of weakness."

"How would you know, Mary? Mr. Rouse was dead before you and Aunt Till arrived."

"I've only heard things."

"What kind of things, Mary? Does this have anything to do with Ceviche or Sammy?"

"Oh my, no. What would it have to do with a slave girl or her—" she stopped to clear her throat, "her husband."

"How did you know Sammy was her husband?"

"I—I just assumed."

"Mary Louisa Bastion, you tell me what you know. Or I shall announce to the wedding party that I cannot marry such a black heart and tell the congregation of your love for my groom."

"Don't be ridiculous, Eleanor. You would do no such thing."

"Why wouldn't I? I have nothing to lose, or did you fail to notice that Nathaniel left for good last night? Don't pretend with me, dear cousin. I saw you on the veranda last night." Eleanor grabbed at her cousin's wrist when she tried to escape. "I know you know everything that took place between Nathaniel and me.

145

You hoped for the opportunity to sweep in on Andrew, but he will not marry you, Mary. You are penniless, and Andrew's heart is as black as the bottom of an overloaded flatboat."

Mary looked straight into her eyes, testing her to see if she would follow through on her threats, and Eleanor held firm, never relinquishing the gaze. Mary soon backed down. "Very well. I shall tell you what I know, but only because it will have little bearing on your future now. Andrew has collected the marriage license. The only way you would be free from this marriage now is to ruin your good name, so I am confident my words will not harm Andrew in the least."

"Tell me what Andrew had to do with Ceviche."

Mary held her chin high. "He traded her for taxes on Woodacre. While your neighbors scrambled to stay as one plantation and not be divided, Andrew made a deal. He gave free cotton to the Yankees during the war. But only because he is a true Confederate and knew he would see the day when their money might enable him to spit in their faces. Ceviche had caught the eye of a young Yankee, and Andrew traded her for the right to be left alone by the Federal administration in Natchez."

"You seem to take an ill pleasure in that, Mary. Can you imagine being sold to a bidder who thought you beautiful?" Eleanor looked into her cousin's darkened eyes. What had happened to her childhood playmate? "Does that give the man a right to own you?"

"Ceviche is a slave girl, Ellie. She's quite used to being sold."

"She grew up at Woodacre. She's no more used to it than you or I."

"It was shameful how you risked yourself to feed her. Andrew was right to be rid of her and now, thanks to Nathaniel, rid of her man, too. We lost everything because of the slaves. When will your stupidity allow you to grasp that? That the South is no more because of slaves."

"The South is no more because we had more pride than gunpowder, Mary."

"Traitor!"

"And just for your information, Mary, Ceviche was not sold. Nathaniel rescued her and her husband who was supposedly shot before your very eyes. The family, including their precious son, moved North to freedom this week." Eleanor squared her shoulders. "If I cannot be free, I shall do all I can to ensure others can."

Mary's eyes thinned in rage. "I shall tell Andrew everything."

"Go ahead, Mary. You shall be gone when we return from our wedding trip, and it would be quite inappropriate for you to have an audience with a married man."

"You will stand before him and God, vowing to love him?"

"Have you left me any choice in the matter? When you think back on this day and how Andrew has been saddled with a great beast of a wife, I ask you to remember who put me there." Eleanor lifted her skirt defiantly, grabbing her bouquet from Hattie. "If you'll excuse me, I have a wedding to attend."

Chapter 21

Eleanor had no intention of being a "great beast of a wife," but she could not resist the temptation to show Mary how meddling in another person's affairs would lead only to trouble. The guests milled about the lawns, and music filled the air. Eleanor's heartbeat intensified as the reality of her wedding finally took hold.

Looking out the second-story window, she saw Andrew shaking hands and meeting with guests. She had never seen him appear more social, and he had a smile for everyone. "Is that smile for me, Andrew? For capturing me, or because you have finally captured Rosamond?"

"It won't do you any good to be talking to yourself now, Miss Ellie." Hattie closed the shutters and whirled Eleanor around to check final appearances.

"I prayed diligently this morning, Hattie. God's will be done." Squaring her shoulders, she willed herself to believe the words.

"Everyone is getting into their places. Are you ready?" Hattie had tears in her eyes, but Eleanor forced herself not to fret.

She felt her thundering heart and drew in a thorough, cleansing breath. "I am as ready as I'll ever be."

The wedding march began, and Eleanor met her father at the stair landing. "You look lovely, Eleanor. So much like your mother on her wedding day. She was queen of the court. I have never seen another bride that held a candle to her. Until today."

Eleanor smiled and squeezed her father's hand. "I am sorry I've been so defiant, Father. About Nathaniel and the rest."

"Never mind. It is all finished now. A woman's heart gives itself so rarely. I just have to remember how young you were when he charmed you. But Andrew shall make a good husband, Ellie, and a good owner for Rosamond."

Eleanor nodded, unable to speak, for she still thought Andrew would make a terrible overseer of Rosamond. Perhaps her father was right though. What did a woman know of such matters? Eleanor's heart was always swayed by the plight of the slaves, just as her mother's heart had been. Yet her mother still loved and respected her father, and she would learn to do the same for Andrew.

The wedding march began again, and Eleanor descended the final stair, turning toward her father. "I wish Mother were here."

"If she hadn't nursed those slaves with the fever, she would be." Her father must have realized his harshness, for he squeezed her hand and looked into her eyes. "Your mother's soft nature got the best of her, Ellie. That is why I wish for you to marry Andrew. I know he will not let your kindly nature kill you. If only I'd put my foot down," Master Senton said, lowering his head, "she would be here with us now, watching her daughter get married. My weakness killed your mother."

Eleanor shook her head. "Oh no, Father. Mother died the way she lived, loving others. Andrew," she couldn't help herself; she spat his name, "Andrew, may well remember her as a fool for her kindness, but I shall always know her as one who gave herself up for others. There is no higher calling than that, Father. Mother would not wish it any other way." Finally, Eleanor understood why her father was so adamant about Andrew as a husband.

As the wedding march trickled into their conversation, Eleanor wrapped her arms around her father, and his tight, answering hug gave her the strength she would need to follow through with this wedding mockery.

Starting down the makeshift aisle between garden seats, she saw Andrew standing at the end of the altar beside Preacher Cummings, dressed in black. Eleanor wished her own dress might match her mood. Andrew smiled his crooked smile, as if to tell her he had won. She needed no reminder. Reaching her place before the preacher, she could not look at her groom. His gloating was too much for her wearied heart.

The roar of horses overpowered the preacher's introductions, and Eleanor looked up to see several Federal officers in full dress. A colonel jumped from his horse, and the others followed. They approached the young couple with resolute steps.

"Master Andrew Pemberton?"

Stepping back in fear, Eleanor answered for him. "This is Master Pemberton."

"You are under arrest for impersonating an officer."

Eleanor's knees were suddenly weak, and she giggled nervously, catching her inappropriate action and covering her mouth. "Under arrest?" She bit her lip to force back the relief that bubbled within her. "Is there some mistake?" How she hoped there was not. Her heart beat faster with hope, and she turned to see Andrew's face blanched with his shock.

"No mistake, miss. We are sorry to have selected such an inopportune time, but it has come to our attention that your groom has been impersonating a Confederate captain. He has signed federal documents regarding your marriage with a false title. He is under arrest for impersonating a captain and submitting false documents to the federal government."

Mary shrieked and nearly swooned but was caught by her mother who fanned her daughter, pulling her back to a standing position. As Andrew was being escorted away, Mary grasped at his arm, and he returned her look.

"Nathaniel is behind this!" Andrew exclaimed, before turning on his heel and running from his captors.

"Andrew, no!" Mary screamed.

"Halt!" The Union officer readied his gun while a collective gasp went up in the gathering. But Andrew was far too much of a coward to be shot, and he stopped immediately, holding up his head proudly as the Federals reached him.

Andrew looked at his jilted bride. "I shall return when this is sorted out, and I shall have you as my wife. You, and Rosamond."

"I shall wait for you, Andrew!" Mary called, waving her lace handkerchief.

Eleanor stepped to Andrew's side and whispered in his ear: "I shan't wait for you. A criminal and a coward will never own Rosamond!" A wash of betrayal came over her, as she recalled how Andrew had accused Nathaniel of such evil, while portraying the perfect brother and son. The sense of release nearly made her giddy. Free. She was free of his suffocating determination.

Andrew's eyes thinned in his loathing of her, challenging her that all was not lost, that he would be back. She turned away, certain her father would never trust him again. Eleanor's heart warmed to memories of Nathaniel. While he may have left, his legacy lingered. He had saved her from a perilous life. For that and so much more, she would always love him. No other man would ever have her, save the man who had turned his own brother over to the law, rather than risk her married to a man who despised her.

She threw off her veil and faced her friends, trying to feign disappointment and humiliation. "There shall be no wedding today. I'm dreadfully sorry you have witnessed my fiancé on his way to jail."

"May you rot for this, Eleanor!" Mary nearly jumped on her but was held back by her mother's lumbering frame.

"Mary! Control yourself this instant!"

Eleanor stepped to her father's side. "I'm sorry I have let you down, Father."

He stared at the rich earth. "You have not let me down, Eleanor. I cannot believe Andrew did not earn the rank of captain."

"He is unscrupulous, Father. He fooled us all."

The sound of hooves alerted them to another rider's arrival, and Eleanor saw at once that it was Nathaniel. She felt her breathing stop. She closed her eyes and pinched herself. Opening them several times, she finally convinced herself he was no apparition. She ran toward him without thought to propriety or her bouncing hoop, only her trail of satin and lace. His full smile reached her, and she called out his name as she drew near. Jumping from his horse, he took her into his arms and embraced her with such strength she thought he might never let her go. His heart pounded against her ear, and she returned his embrace with all her might.

"What is the meaning of this?" Her father came beside them, looking back to the awestruck audience. "I demand you remove your hands from my daughter this instant! She shall have nothing to do with a Pemberton from here on out."

"I'm afraid she has little choice." Nathaniel took out a piece of paper from his pocket and shook it out, handing it to her father. "I have obtained a marriage license in our names, and I am sorry, sir, but I shall not release her. She shall be my bride or nobody's."

"This is blackmail." Master Senton's eyes narrowed. "Didn't your father raise a proper Southern gentleman? You shall not own Rosamond, if that's what you are thinking."

"I shan't care. It is not Rosamond I want."

Nathaniel looked down upon her, his gold-flecked eyes sparkling above his smile. Although her father was standing beside them, they were never more alone, for his intimate gaze spoke only to her.

"I should never have doubted you, Nathaniel."

"I lost you once, Ellie. I am not shallow enough to do it twice."

"They'll not hang him, will they?"

"No. If he had impersonated a Federal officer, they would have. But as it is, they are more concerned about his taking out a government marriage license, which would have caused them to falsify documents. He made them out to be fools, and the Union is far too concerned about reconstruction to let that happen."

"That was quite clever," her father interjected, his eyes still narrowed. "But tell me why you would go through such trouble if it is not Rosamond you want?"

Nathaniel gazed upon Ellie before turning to Master Senton.

"How can you possibly question me, sir? Which is more valuable to you, Rosamond or Ellie? To what lengths would you go?"

Her father dropped his head into his hands. "The ends of the earth, Nathaniel. The ends of the earth."

"As will I, sir. I love your daughter. I know I am not what you would dream of for a son, but is my brother? His true image was cast behind smoke, and he never truly valued your family or Ellie. I shall value her with my whole being with the Lord's help."

Her father still did not appear convinced. "Andrew valued the South and tradition. He would not allow Ellie's emotions to get the better of her."

"She would have no emotions if she married him. They would all fail her to avoid the misery he would have placed her in. Is that what you wish for her?"

Her father looked at her with a tear glistening in his eye. "I thought that's what I wished for her, but she is so like her mother. I should say that asking Ellie to stop feeling for others is asking her to die."

"Precisely."

"Her life is what I tried to protect."

"I shall protect it. With all that is in me. Leave Rosamond to whomever you deem fit—it makes no difference to me, so long as I spend my days with Eleanor. We shall live on the North Sixty my father has willed to me, in a tiny cabin. We shall not be there for long. Ellie deserves to live as a queen, and I will make it so, but it may not be the way you seek. I have spent far too long searching for riches, only to discover the Lord's grace is worth more than any earthly fortune. I am home now. Home to stay, and I have never been wealthier." His arm came around Ellie, and he squeezed her tight.

"Do you mean to state you will not release my daughter from this marriage certificate you have unlawfully acquired?" Master Senton frowned, but Eleanor saw the light in his eye.

"I do," Nathaniel said.

"Then we may as well take advantage of the preacher's presence," Master Senton said.

"Daddy, really?" Eleanor looked at her father, who hid his smile. She embraced him, releasing tender kisses all over his face. "You are a romantic, Father. Just as Mother always claimed you to be!"

"You are all I have left of her, Ellie. To think I almost killed my own little girl trying to protect her from her true fate. To see your light extinguished would most certainly mean the death of the true Ellie. Go and marry your prince, but remember me as wanting only the best for you."

"Another opinion never crossed my mind," Eleanor said.

He cleared his throat and turned to her groom. "You shall have Rosamond, Nathaniel. You are a true prodigal, worthy of the inheritance."

Master Senton shook hands with Nathaniel, and Eleanor grasped their handshake, smiling for the world to see.

"We must tell our friends before they all leave, Father."

"Let them go. They will only talk."

"Let them talk, but they shall never witness another wedding where the groom loves his bride more," Nathaniel said.

"It is bad luck to see the bride before the wedding!" Eleanor suddenly exclaimed.

"No, Ellie. I have brought the bad luck upon you, and I shall be certain it ends." Master Senton kissed the top of her head.

"I must grab my veil. Father, meet me in the foyer, and we shall start this day again!" She sprinted toward the house, picking up her veil on the way. "There *is* to be a wedding today!"

Her unabashed smile caused a rush of nervous laughter through the small crowd. All except her aunt and Mary, who stood with crossed arms waiting for her father, ready to offer him a piece of their minds. *Well, let them complain,* she thought. *Father shall not listen today.*

Joyfully, she skipped to the house.

Chapter 22

Sarah! Sarah!" Eleanor burst through the guest room door to find her friend biting her lip in pain. "Oh dear Sarah, you are miserable today. Aren't you?"

Sarah shook her head and smiled. "Tell me your happy news. Has he come for you?"

"He has. Andrew has been sent to jail. He was never a Confederate captain."

"I do not wish to hear of him," Sarah answered. "Tell me about Nathaniel. Will you marry him?"

"He has obtained a marriage license. According to the government, I belong officially to Nathaniel. The marriage ceremony is a mere formality, but one I shall readily welcome. Will you come down, Sarah? It is to be in a few moments. As soon as they pull the preacher off the floor from his shock," she said, giggling.

"Ellie, how I would love to, but I fear I cannot sit up in my chair. Doctor Hayes thinks I may have broken my spine. My cousin tried to move me today, and it was not successful. But I shall have him move my bed to the window and watch from here. Would that be all right?"

Eleanor's shoulders slumped. "I wish you could be there, Sarah. It shall not be the same without you and with my cousin Mary looking over my shoulder."

"Ellie, don't say such things. Mary cannot help herself. She has seen so much grief in her short lifetime. Something about Andrew touches her. Who are we to judge?"

"Of course, you are right. As much as I resent it. Nothing shall steal my joy today. Shame on me for allowing it to."

"The next time I see you it shall be as a married woman. Oh, I do hope you won't find me here upon your return."

"I do as well, Sarah—only because I want you to run down

our staircase in victory." Eleanor bent and kissed her beloved new friend. "I shall wave from below."

"Good-bye, dear Ellie."

Eleanor bounded down the stairs and greeted her waiting father.

"Are we ready?"

"I can hardly wait!"

Looking outdoors, Eleanor spotted Nathaniel. His dark, wavy locks blew in the slight breeze of the unseasonably warm day. He smiled to all around him, shaking hands and nodding his head. The joy in his eyes could not be denied, and Eleanor wondered what she had done to deserve a life with this man.

He had left a mere boy with unrealistic dreams and lofty goals but come back a welcomed prodigal. A spiritually mature man, who finally loved the Lord more than himself. Eleanor watched him with awe. How his leaving had changed him, and how she had prayed he wouldn't run to California. But if he hadn't, her handsome prodigal wouldn't be standing here this moment. Ready to marry her and cherish her always. How unlike the spoiled child who left.

She drew in a deep breath and looked at her father. "This day is better than I possibly imagined it. God takes our dreams and multiplies them."

Her father kissed her cheek. "I was thinking exactly the same thing. I know if your mother could be here, she would have tears in her eyes watching you walk this aisle. Only a few short moments ago, I was ready to give you away to a man I knew didn't love you properly but who I felt would take care of you. Now I give you with my blessings, with no reservations, Ellie."

"I am so glad, Father. Aunt Till still thinks Andrew is the better Pemberton, doesn't she?" Eleanor wished her aunt and cousin saw Andrew for who he truly was, but she couldn't let their lack of support steal her joy.

"He will probably still inherit the lion's share of Woodacre.

To your aunt, who lost everything in the war, that means stability." He squeezed her hand. "Wouldn't we all wish to stand on solid rock if given a choice?"

"There is only one though."

"How true, Ellie. I think I forgot that for a while. You have grown to be such a fine young woman." He brushed her cheek. "Your mother's efforts, though short, have paid off. You have her beauty and her heart. But it is time I must part with you, for Nathaniel seems to be pacing nervously like a wild cat."

Eleanor giggled. "I cannot believe I am ready to marry him."

"Here we go."

The wedding march began for a third time, and Eleanor's stomach fluttered with excitement. Her gown trailed magnificently behind her, and she felt Hattie tug at it, so it would lie just right. Straightening her veil, she moved toward Nathaniel as though pulled by an unseen force. She was certain an ample audience still remained to witness the strange proceedings, but she couldn't name a single person. For her eyes never left him. His squared jaw and regal facial structure remained solemn until she reached him. Then he looked upon her with a smile colored by heaven above.

He held her hands and repeated the preacher's words.

"I take thee, Eleanor, to be my lawfully wedded wife. To have and to hold."

His whispered words seemed only for her and the Lord. She blissfully wrapped her memory around each syllable, storing it for future use. She would remember always the warm expression on his face, the sparkle in his eyes, the warmth from his hands.

"I take thee, Nathaniel, to be my lawfully wedded husband."

The ring ceremony was next, and Eleanor's eyes widened. Do you have a ring? her expression asked. But without hesitation Jeremiah, Nathaniel's best man, pulled a gem from his pocket.

Rather than the simple gold band Eleanor expected from her pauper groom, Nathaniel held out a gold filigree crown-shaped ring, which held an elegant emerald, but in a brilliant green circle.

She couldn't help her thoughts from tumbling out. "Where did you get this?"

"It was the one thing I brought back with me from California." He slipped the gorgeous ring onto her finger. "You are the only reason I returned."

Eleanor wiped away a tear and sniffed as the preacher glared at her until she echoed his words: "With this ring I thee wed."

Finally, they were pronounced man and wife. Together they turned and faced their friends and smiled at one another.

"We are married, Ellie. I thought this day would never come."

She peered up at him, his startlingly handsome face sending a fresh wave of exhilaration through her stomach. "But it has come, and I shall cherish this day, and you, for always." That feeling. No longer did she fear harsh kisses and coarse talk. Nathaniel's very presence set her heart at rest.

"We shall start our lives together as we should have done years ago." Nathaniel kicked the ground. "I'm sorry my folly stalled us for so long, dear Ellie."

Ellie's lips trembled. "I should have waited forever once I saw you return from California, even if it meant I might be a spinster. I knew then my heart could never truly belong to another."

"How could we have known what God would use for good? My father has restored me to half of the inheritance as before I left. With Andrew in jail, I daresay we'll have to live at Woodacre for a time. And we shall have Rosamond as well, thanks to your father's change of heart." Nathaniel shook his head. "I am truly a prodigal son, and I have our Lord to thank for it. I shall spend my days preaching on His infinite grace."

Eleanor smiled. "And I shall be at your side, Nathaniel. Whatever life brings us, wherever we might dwell."

"Do you trust me, Ellie? Do you trust God to lead us?"

She felt her head nod up and down. "I do."

Nathaniel drove Eleanor to Woodacre in an elegant, open

black carriage strewn with yellow roses and white silk ribbons. As the carriage turned up the drive, she caught her first glimpse of the mighty house where she would be mistress.

"Oh Nathaniel, I don't know if I'm ready for this." She drew in a deep breath. "Woodacre is so massive, and it's been such a long time since a woman saw to it properly. I don't know if I'm the one—"

He silenced her with a kiss. "You are the only one, my sweet. God ordained you personally. He's returned us to one another for life. I love you, Ellie Pemberton." He caressed her face in his strong hands. "Welcome home, my love."

Kristin Billerbeck is a bestselling, Christy-nominated author of over forty-five novels. Her work has been featured in *The New York Times* and on "The Today Show." Kristin is a fourth-generation Californian and a proud mother of four. She lives in the Silicon Valley and enjoys good handbags, hiking, and reading.

My Beloved Waits

by Peggy Darty

Enjoy Your
Bonus Story

Chapter 1

Grace Cunningham shoved the hoe deeper into the potato patch and yanked off her threadbare gloves. "I hate this broken-down hoe!"

"Thou shalt not hate," Elizabeth Cunningham called from the porch.

"And thou shalt not hoe with a splintered handle!" Grace rallied, picking at the splinter in her thumb.

"Thou shalt not hoe isn't any kind of command," Elizabeth called, smiling at her daughter.

Grace pushed the wide-brimmed straw hat back on her blond hair and looked at her mother, who was, as always, reading her Bible.

"Neither is thou shalt not hate," Grace muttered, "but I do."

She couldn't resist getting in the last word, and she felt a whiplash of guilt in her conscience. After losing her father and brother to a senseless war that had destroyed their lives and devastated Riverwood, their little farm, Grace just couldn't have the kind of faith her mother had.

She leaned against the hoe and studied her frail mother.

Mama's pride is damaged, too, she thought. The brown hair that had turned gray the past year looked only half-brushed and now slipped carelessly from the chignon, dangling about her face. Grace's father, Fred Cunningham, had promised her that they would always be taken care of, but in spite of his promise, they had ended up broke and alone, struggling to survive.

Her father, always conscious of his duties, had worked hard to provide for his family. That sense of duty had compelled him to join Commander Braxton's army in the fall of 1863 when the

Union troops were moving deeper into southern territory.

Grace took a deep breath and glanced up at the sky. The noon sun was moving westward, and a gray cloud thickened overhead. The kind of dense heat that usually preceded a thunderstorm was enveloping her like a steam tub. Her scalp itched, and wisps of damp hair bobbed around her cheeks. She yanked off her straw hat and tossed it toward the grass; then she wound the ends of her thick hair around her fingers, skewered it back in a chignon, and adjusted the hairpins.

As she did, her eyes scanned the land bordering the backyard. A dusty, whitewashed cabin had been converted to a storage shed, and the barn, her father's pride, was sadly in need of paint and repair, with buckled boards along the side. Knee-high weeds filled the pasture where a lone mare tossed her head to chase away a horsefly. Mr. Douglas, their neighbor at Oak Grove, had loaned Molly to Grace after the Yanks took their last horse. Molly had a slight limp and could no longer pull a wagon, but Molly and Grace got along just fine. The faithful old mare carried Grace into Whites Creek to trade unused farm tools for garden seeds and food supplies.

Beyond the pasture, paint-chipped fences outlined barren cotton fields stretching to the Tombigbee River. Those fields were the reason her father had brought them from Sand Mountain to Pickens County five years before the war. His dream of growing cotton had come true on the five hundred acres of rich, river-bottom land. In the old days, farmers could get their cotton loaded on boats going downriver to Mobile. But cotton no longer grew along the river's edge.

Grace turned and surveyed her garden. Okra, beans, onions, corn, and potatoes grew in the rich soil, holding for her and her mother the promise of better days to come.

"Mother, we're going to have fine Sunday dinners, just like before," she called. "We'll spread the dining table with one of the nice lace tablecloths you treasure, and we'll eat to our heart's content. I can see it now." She swept a hand through the air. "Ripe tomatoes sliced thin on a platter with green onions and sweet pickles. We'll have fried okra, fresh snap beans, creamed corn, and boiled potatoes. Lots of sweet iced tea."

"And fried chicken," her mother offered, her head tilted slightly, her eyes staring dreamily into space.

Grace glanced back at her mother and sighed. She hadn't the heart to remind her there were no chickens to fry and no way to raise their own. Their last six chickens had been taken by Union soldiers. Grace had watched in horror as the soldiers strapped the chickens onto their saddles and rode off with them squawking and flapping. She later learned it was a common practice for soldiers, particularly those in a hurry. At the time, however, she could not believe her eyes as their prize chickens were swept away.

She heaved another sigh, squared her shoulders, and reached for the hoe with new determination. She was finished with the potatoes; time now to thin the corn. Despite the cloud of gloom that hung over the farm she loved so dearly, Grace began to feel a sense of comfort as she thought about the seeds she had planted just a month earlier.

She looked over the neatly weeded rows and remembered how she had waited with anticipation and pride as the seeds began to sprout. Other women could rave about their beautiful flower gardens, but to Grace, true beauty came in vegetables, all colors, sizes, and shapes. She and her mother couldn't eat flowers, but vegetables had half a dozen monetary rewards. She could sell them, cook them, preserve them, swap with her neighbors, or barter with Mr. Primrose at the market in Whites Creek. She could even dry some of her vegetables on cheesecloth over the root cellar and string them on a rope to decorate the kitchen. But that had become a luxury she rarely enjoyed. Nope, these vegetables were for gracing their table and their stomachs, and she smiled at the thought. She picked up the hoe and went back to work.

A few minutes later, Grace heard the whinny of a horse out on the front drive. She glanced at her mother, who was so deep in her reading that she didn't look up as the horse whinnied again. Grace wouldn't bother to tell her they had company until she went around front to see who was riding the horse. Rarely did anyone come up the drive to their house these days, and that was just fine with Grace.

While she was only nineteen, she had earned the right to be recognized as the boss of Riverwood, and she quickly prepared herself to act in that capacity now. She brushed her hands against the side of her father's overalls to freshen up a handshake, then she hurried around the two-story frame house to the front lane.

Accustomed to the sight of neighbors, or even the occasional beggar, she came up short as she met the eyes of a stranger riding tall in the saddle on a fine black stallion. For a split second, she was more interested in the horse than its rider, for it was exactly the kind of proud, muscled horse she had always longed to own. The horse had a white blaze on his forehead and three white-stockinged feet.

Her eyes moved from the horse to the man. From the looks of both, it had been a long journey. While the man's dark frock coat and pinstriped trousers were of quality broadcloth, wrinkles in the cloth suggested time in the saddle. He tipped his top hat, revealing dark brown hair that tucked under just above his collar.

She studied his face—long with broad cheekbones and eyes the blue of an October sky. Then he smiled at her, a smile that lit his eyes and showed off a row of even, white teeth. Grace wondered who he was and what he wanted from them.

"Good morning," he said. "My name is Jonathan Parker."

At the sound of his greeting, all admiration of horse and rider fled. Immediately, her spine stiffened. A Yankee!

"What do you want?" she asked bluntly.

He did not flinch at her rude words. Instead, his blue eyes, fringed with thick black lashes, looked toward the front porch.

"I'd like to speak to Mrs. Cunningham." His tone was polite yet formal.

"She does not receive visitors. My name is Grace Cunningham, and I'm her daughter. What do you want?" she repeated, her gaze slicing up and down his fancy suit and coming again to rest upon his face.

Not a muscle moved in his face in spite of her blunt talk, and she gave him credit for that. Either he was not easily shocked, or he had the ability to conceal his emotions.

She watched him take a long deep breath. She decided he must be reconciling himself to the fact that he would have to deal with her, however unpleasant the task might be.

"I'm on a mission from your father," he said, looking her straight in the eye. "I left him in the military hospital just outside of Chattanooga about three weeks ago. He asked me to return something to his wife."

Grace gasped. "You left Father? In Chattanooga? I thought he was. . .is he. . . ?"

She choked on the words, unable to say more. Two years had passed since his last letter; then this February she had seen his name on the list of wounded soldiers in Tennessee. There had been no further word about Fred Cunningham, and he had not returned from the war that had ended just last month. While her mother had never lost faith that he would return, Grace had given up hope.

She blinked, staring into the stranger's face, unable to ask, afraid to hope. Her heart pounded so hard that she pressed her hand to the base of her throat. She could feel the drum of her pulse against her fingertips.

"I'm sorry, but he was dying when I left the hospital, Miss Cunningham."

She swallowed hard, felt her world dip and sway for a moment before she could speak. Then she remembered her manners. "Won't you. . .come up and sit down?" she asked, turning to climb the porch steps and feeling the weakness that had suddenly taken over her legs.

"I'm sorry to be so blunt," he was saying from behind her.

"I left you no choice," she answered, sinking into the cushions on the cane-back rocker. So her father was not coming back home after all.

She sat there, staring at this stranger, Jonathan Parker, as he swung his long frame down from the saddle and tethered his horse to the rail at the corner of the porch. Then he walked back to his saddlebag and lifted the flap.

She watched his every movement. She had not asked for proof that he had been with her father. His level gaze and sincere manner left no room for doubt. She believed him.

Her eyes widened as he withdrew the black leather Bible she had seen in her father's hands on so many occasions. Then he turned and walked slowly up to the porch. Grace could see the broad muscles of his shoulders straining against his dark frock coat as his climbed the steps and took the chair she had indicated, opposite her.

He was close enough now that she could look him straight in the eye. She realized with a sudden flutter of her heart that he was even more handsome than she had first realized. Her nose twitched at the new scent he trailed over the porch as he passed her. He smelled of fresh pine, as though he had just come from the woods. She liked the smell, and she watched him carefully, taking in everything about him.

"It's been so long since we've had any word from Father. It's just so. . .amazing to think you left him less than a month ago. I have dozens of questions to ask you—"

"Who is it?" Her mother's voice floated from the hallway.

Again, Grace's heartbeat quickened. She looked from the door to Jonathan Parker. "My mother is very fragile now," Grace said under her breath, her eyes imploring this man to understand her meaning. "My only brother was killed at Vicksburg.

Then, when it seemed that things could not possibly get worse, our neighbor, Mr. Douglas, saw Father's name on the casualty list at the town hall in Tuscaloosa."

She glanced over her shoulder to the front door to be sure her mother was not on the porch to hear what she was saying. "She. . .has never been the same since we got the heartbreaking news about Father. In some ways, she has lost touch with reality," she finished quickly just as the creak of the door signaled Elizabeth's presence.

Jonathan nodded, turning in his chair to look toward the door where the little woman stood, hesitating to come out.

"Mother, we have a visitor," Grace said. "You will want to hear what he has to say." She looked back at Jonathan. "I think it's time she faced the truth, and I won't shield her from it any longer."

Elizabeth stepped out onto the porch, her head lowered slightly. She glanced quickly at Jonathan Parker.

He stood up, removing his hat. "Hello, Mrs. Cunningham."

Like Grace, the sound of a voice that was not southern startled Elizabeth. She took a step back from him, her hand clutching the door.

"Mother, he brings news about Father."

Elizabeth's eyes widened in shock. It seemed to take a moment for the words to register with her. Then a sob broke from her throat, and she rushed toward Jonathan, reaching for his hand.

"You've seen Fred?" she asked eagerly. Her entire countenance had been transformed by the news. An expression of hope lit her eyes, tilted her mouth upward, and colored her cheeks.

Watching her mother come back to life with false hope, Grace was astonished, and for a moment she felt her heart would break in pieces. Pain racked her emotions, and Grace wanted to scream in agony and rage at the injustice that the war had hurled upon their loving family.

"I left your husband in the military hospital up in Chatta-nooga," Jonathan Parker said to Elizabeth, speaking in a kind, gentle voice.

Grace went over to stand beside her mother. "Mother, before you get your hopes up," she felt compelled to say, "Mr. Parker has already assured me that Father. . .did not survive."

Her mother shook her head, as though warding off the verbal blow. "No, I won't accept that. Will you please tell me about my Fred?" she asked, still clutching Jonathan Parker's hand as her eyes searched his face.

For a moment, he said nothing. He seemed to be choosing his words as he studied the little woman who clung to him, then he gestured toward the other vacant chair. "Why don't you sit down, Mrs. Cunningham?"

As Jonathan spoke to her mother, Grace smiled sadly. She was touched by his sensitive nature. She wanted to tell him how grateful she was for the way he so tactfully delivered the heart-breaking news.

"Allow me to explain, Mrs. Cunningham," he said, as they took their seats. "Your husband saved my life. I was a soldier in the Union army. I had been captured in north Georgia by a Confederate officer. We were on our way back to his camp on the Tennessee line. Late that evening, while he was asleep, I man-aged to break free of the ropes. I took his uniform." He paused, glancing at Grace. "But I did not harm him. He had fed me and treated me decently. I tied him up and took his horse, but I knew his men would find him the next morning."

He paused, turning his eyes toward the overgrown front lawn. "That night I had to work my way through a dense briar thicket, and I ended up with scratches on my hands and face." A grim little smile touched his lips as he glanced back at Grace. "I looked as though I'd been in battle. My right hand was bleeding, so I cleaned my hand with a handkerchief, then tied the hand-kerchief about my throat. The blood-stained handkerchief appeared to serve as a bandage, supporting my hand gestures to indicate a throat injury. I knew if I were to escape enemy territory. . ." He broke off, glancing from Grace to her mother, as though regretting his choice of words.

"Go on," Grace prompted, scooting to the edge of the seat as she waited to hear the rest of the story.

"It was convenient for me to point to my throat and pretend to be unable to speak. Under this guise, I rode into a Confederate camp on the outskirts of Chattanooga. Your father was the first person who befriended me. That night we were attacked by another battalion of Union soldiers, and before I could explain who I was, I was beaten senseless." He paused and dropped his head, silent for a moment. Then he looked back at Grace. "When I regained consciousness I realized I was imprisoned with the Confederates in a Federal camp in Chattanooga. I was in the cell with your father, and he was very kind to me. In fact, he was willing to share his last piece of bread with me. I'll never forget that," he said quietly.

"That's the way Fred is," Elizabeth said, smiling through her tears. "He always considers the needs of others."

Jonathan hesitated and glanced across at Grace. She knew he had caught the use of the present tense when her mother spoke of the man she loved with all of her heart.

"I had identification papers in my boot," Jonathan continued. "When finally I convinced the guards who I was, they provided me with a horse and allowed me to take your father to a military hospital. By this time, of course, he knew the truth about me, but it no longer mattered."

"I'm sure he was just so grateful that you saved him," Grace said, fighting to hold back her tears.

Beneath her tomboy-tough exterior, she was almost as sensitive as her mother. But she was younger and hardier, and she knew she had to be strong for both of them. Yet as she sat listening to the story, the image Jonathan portrayed to them of her dear father, starving in a prison camp, had almost broken her heart.

"We had no idea what he had been through," Grace said, feeling the quiver of her lower lip. She caught her lip between her teeth and looked quickly at her mother. She had tried for the past two years to shield her mother from more heartache. Yet this man seemed to understand exactly how much he could say and the manner in which to say it. For her mother had not dissolved in tears or cried out at the cruel fate of her husband.

Grace looked from her mother's sweet face to the tall, dark-haired man who sat beside her, turning the rim of his hat around and around in his hands as he told the story. In the last hour, he had ridden up their drive and turned their entire world upside down. She had lost all sense of time and place; she was vaguely aware of the mourning dove in the oak overhead. Its plaintiff little cry seemed a fitting accompaniment to the words Jonathan Parker spoke.

"I appreciate your coming here, Mr. Parker." Elizabeth's voice filled the momentary silence. "I have prayed so many times for my husband's safety," she said, turning in her seat, casting her gaze toward the front drive that wound beneath the canopy of oaks and disappeared around the curve.

"I count it a privilege to be able to visit you, Mrs. Cunningham. I promised your husband that I would return and tell you what had happened to him. Oh, and I have something to give you." He reached for the worn Bible that had been placed on the low wooden table beside his chair.

As her eyes followed his gesture, Grace realized that she had been so caught up in the story that she had completely forgotten he was returning her father's Bible. Now all eyes were on the book that Jonathan held carefully in his hand.

Elizabeth gave a small cry. "It is my Fred's Bible," she said, staring at the chipped leather.

"Yes, it is," Jonathan said, extending it to her. "Your husband gave it to me and asked that I bring it to you, that I put it in your hands. I believe those were the words he used."

Elizabeth stood up and walked over to accept the Bible.

"I tried to be very careful with it," Jonathan said, and as he spoke his brows drew together in a frown, as though he might have accidentally damaged the precious Bible on the long trip to Riverwood.

Elizabeth examined the Bible from front to back, then briefly flipped through the pages.

"Oh yes, it's in good condition. Thank you so very much," she said, hugging the Bible to her breast as one would welcome a lost child.

"I'm sure this Bible was a great comfort to my husband," Elizabeth said, looking back at Jonathan.

"Yes, it seemed to be. Many men kept Bibles with them during the war. In fact, I heard of one incident where a soldier was carrying a Bible under his shirt, and it stopped a bullet." He looked down, as though he had said too much.

"Thank you for bringing this to me," Elizabeth said softly, then she turned and opened the front door and went back inside the house. Her steps echoed down the hallway, and Grace could hear her climbing the stairs to her bedroom.

Grace took a deep breath and looked at Jonathan. "It's been very difficult for her to accept the truth that Father isn't coming home. She still sits out here every afternoon, watching the lane, expecting him to return. I've tried to convince her otherwise."

"I'm so sorry," he said. The blue eyes seemed to deepen as he spoke to her. He tilted his head to the side and looked at her.

She shook her head and blinked, trying again to absorb everything he had told them. As the silence stretched, she felt such gratitude to him for being so kind to her father that she knew what her father would expect in return.

"Please, come inside and allow me to prepare a meal for you." She glanced at the black stallion, nipping at the thick grass on the neglected lawn. She was glad that it was benefitting this man's horse. "What about water for your horse? And feed?" she asked.

"Both would be welcome. Please don't go to any trouble. I don't want to impose on you."

"You're not. This is the least we can do for you. We owe you a debt of gratitude," she said, looking at his handsome face and trying not to feel overwhelmed by a man so kind and caring, yet so handsome and appealing.

As though he felt he needed to break the spell, he stood and looked around. "Shall I take General—er, my horse—around back?"

She remembered the watering trough and the feed bucket. "Yes, the barn is in poor condition, but you are welcome to it. We lost all of our cattle and horses, although we never had a lot. Father was a small landowner compared to the others in the area. He came to this area from North Alabama with his parents, who were migrant workers. He worked hard and saved his money; eventually he was able to buy land here. With each successful cotton harvest, he bought a few more acres, or he and Mother did some work on the house."

Grace thought back over the years. Her father had always wanted the best for his family and had done everything he could to be sure that she and Freddy went to church, attended school, and grew into responsible people.

"As you know, my father was a very good man," she said, remembering the long hard hours her father had toiled. She stood up, thinking of her promise. "Make yourself at home while I prepare lunch."

As she opened the front door and stepped inside the hall, she could see Jonathan speaking affectionately to his horse. He seemed to be a kind man, and she liked him very much. She was so grateful that her father had miraculously met a man like Jonathan Parker to take care of him and fulfill his deathbed wish. She swallowed hard and hurried on down the hall.

When she entered the kitchen, she was suddenly aware of how empty and lonely the large room seemed to her. This room had for many years been filled with people, and it was a joyous place. The echo of laughter from this room had seemed to flow through the entire house. Her mother loved entertaining neighbors and friends, and she had done it often and with exceeding grace and kindness.

Grace's gaze wandered to the trestle table, pushed into the far corner. If a large group of children were not invited as well, she and Freddy often dined in the kitchen while their parents entertained guests. Most of the time, however, entire families came and stayed for several days. Those had been wonderful days and months and years, and all of it seemed to Grace like a wonderful and special dream to cherish for the rest of her life.

She took a deep breath and closed her eyes. All of that was gone now, and even though she was happy to have met Jonathan Parker, he had just confirmed one more sad and devastating truth: Her father was never coming back to Riverwood.

"I just can't think about it," she said. And she couldn't. For a moment she wondered if at times she was running from reality as much as her mother was. She shook her head and forced her thoughts to the business of preparing a meal. Turning, she headed toward the pantry.

The pantry was a small room that reeked of green onions and pepper and spices from the floor to the ceiling. The long side walls held deep sturdy shelves which in years past had held an entire winter's supply of preserved vegetables and fruits. The end wall had hooks and nails from top to bottom for hanging baskets and buckets of kitchen items.

But these days, the room that had held such an abundance of food looked empty and forlorn. At least they still had jars of dried beans and preserved apples and a basket with new potatoes and some green onions from the garden. Grace cheered herself with the vision of all the vegetables in her garden lining the shelves after the harvest. This winter she and her mother would have better food. She would see to that. There would be snap beans to string, potatoes to peel, and tender young corn that could be prepared half a dozen ways.

For now she would make do with what she had. And she would grease a skillet and bake up a batch of her crusty corn bread. She smiled to herself. Mr. Jonathan Parker would not leave Riverwood with an empty stomach.

Chapter 2

When Grace, her mother, and Jonathan were seated at the dining table, Grace watched with satisfaction as Jonathan ate heartily and exercised the table manners she had been taught to appreciate.

"This is a wonderful meal," he said, looking across the table at her.

"Thank you." Grace shifted in her chair, suddenly aware of how stiff the overalls felt against her skin. She imagined she must look quite unladylike to this man, who had obviously been well reared and was probably accustomed to dining with ladies in fine gowns.

"I enjoy cooking," she said, trying to forget her silly idea of ladies in gowns. "I'm just grateful Ardella left behind her recipes. She was the best cook in all of the world," she added, her eyes clouding over as she spoke of Ardella. "Ardella and William lived here with us all of their lives, but they were never slaves," she added quickly. "Father paid them well and told them they were free to go whenever they wanted." She shook her head. "Fortunately for us, they never wanted to leave."

"I can hear the affection in your voice when you mention their names," Jonathan said.

Elizabeth pressed her lace handkerchief to her eyes and dropped her head. Jonathan was quick to notice, and he quickly lifted his cup and began to inspect it. "This is a beautiful cup," he said. "It looks as though it may have been handcrafted in England."

"Fred ordered the set for my fortieth birthday," Elizabeth announced, looking up with shining eyes.

"He was a very thoughtful man," Jonathan acknowledged.

Grace cleared her throat. "Where is your home, Mr. Parker?"

"Please call me Jonathan," he said and smiled at her. Then

he looked back at her mother, as though reminding himself to include her in the conversation as well. "I was born and raised in Kentucky. Our farm was 480 acres on the edge of Louisville. We used three small fields to grow all the vegetables to eat; one large field was for growing corn for our feed for hogs, chickens, cattle, and of course for corn meal. The farm was primarily used for raising cattle. My father furnished beef for the riverboats up and down the Ohio and for passenger trains traveling through Louisville."

"That sounds like a good life," Elizabeth said thoughtfully.

Jonathan nodded. "It was until '60 when my father came down with a lung disease and required a lot of medical care. To pay medical expenses, I sold most of the cattle we owned. He died a month before the war broke out. . . ." His voice trailed for a moment, and Grace watched him closely as she listened. She wanted to know everything about him, and she was very curious about the family he had mentioned.

"Do you have brothers and sisters?" she asked.

"I have two sisters. An older sister, Louise, is married to a furniture merchant in Louisville. They have five children. Katherine, my younger sister, was only twelve when I left for war. In my last letter from Mother, she wrote that she and Katherine had moved to Louisville to live with Louise and her husband."

As always, Grace was thinking of the land. "Who's taking care of your farm for you?"

He frowned. "I don't know, and I must admit I'm quite concerned about it. I wrote my brother-in-law, asking him to hire someone to go out and take care of things, but I haven't heard back from him in months."

Grace watched his frown deepen, and she could imagine he must be very worried about his home. "I expect you need to get back to Kentucky," she said.

"Thank you so much for making this long trip to bring us news," Elizabeth added, looking at him with sincere appreciation.

"Yes, we appreciate you keeping your promise to Father."

He smiled at her, that sad, gentle smile that was beginning to tear at Grace's heart. "As I told you, your father saved my life. Making this trip was not much to do in return. I'm only sorry I couldn't bring you good news."

Grace glanced at her mother and saw her drop her gaze. Hoping to change the subject, Grace asked, "So what plans do you have for your farm when you return?"

"I'm hoping to restock the cattle," he said. "And in time I'd like to raise horses. Kentucky is thoroughbred country, and its always been my dream to have fine horses."

Grace stared at him. *It's been my dream, too,* she thought. But of course she would never admit that to him. Still, it was nice to think that someone might be able to make such a dream come true.

Jonathan looked from Grace to her mother. "Everyone must put the past behind them and go on, although I'm certain that is a very difficult thing for you to do."

"Yes, but you're right," Grace joined in. "We can't go on living in the past." She glanced at her mother, hoping she would take those words to heart.

Elizabeth smiled as she reached for the small jar of pear preserves they had put up last fall.

"Every woman in the South is taught to preserve the fruit on our many trees, Jonathan. Grace, how many fruit trees are left?"

"We had a bad storm last fall that damaged some of our trees," Grace explained. "Two of our apple trees still bear fruit, and of course the pear tree down in the corner of the yard."

"And you were able to preserve the fruit?" Jonathan inquired.

Grace smiled easily at that. "Oh yes. Apple butter, applesauce, dried apples for pies, and pear preserves. Lots of pear preserves."

"Every southern girl carries the special family recipes in her hope chest," her mother said, looking at Grace with obvious affection.

"And do you have a hope chest?"

No, because I have no hope, she thought, giving their guest a penetrating stare.

Jonathan had laid down the linen napkin and was looking at Grace with those blue, blue eyes that had begun to make her a little bit nervous, particularly when they seemed to take in every feature on her face. She wondered what he thought about her sunburned nose and her plain face, void of pressed powder or rouge or any of the items fancy ladies wore. Then she remembered his question and delighted in her independence. It was her one claim to being her own person.

"No, I don't. I'm afraid I defied tradition when it comes to keeping a hope chest," she said, aware of the edge to her tone. She gave a light shrug, and the pale blue work shirt beneath her overalls scratched at her right shoulder blade. "It always seemed a bit silly to me. No offense, Mother," she added quickly.

"You never wanted a hope chest," Elizabeth said, looking rather sad.

"Miss Grace," Jonathan said, startling her with the formality of his address, "do you have friends living nearby?"

Grace hesitated. She had preferred the company of Freddy's friends, even though they were five years older, to the giddy-headed girls in the community who were closer to her own age.

"We were quite young when the war broke out," she answered, looking him squarely in the eye. "Some of the girls accepted proposals from neighborhood boys heading off to war. It was their way of aiding the cause."

She watched Jonathan's head tilt slightly, and she knew he was following her line of sarcasm, while her mother merely smiled, looking pleased at the idea of aiding the cause.

"Sue Ann, my closest friend, moved to Mobile to live with her grandmother, and Rose Marie, our closest neighbor, married Charles Raymond Anderson, whose farm adjoined theirs near Whites Creek. It was a nice way to unite families and land, particularly the land," she added, smiling sweetly as her gaze traveled from Jonathan to her mother, who smiled back.

When she met Jonathan's eyes, however, she saw the slight quirk of his lips, and she sensed that she hadn't fooled him for one minute. This man was smart, very smart, Grace told herself. Her veiled sarcasm would not be lost on him. She even suspected that he was very good at reading minds, and at that, she began to fiddle with her silverware.

Distant thunder rumbled over the roof of the house. Elizabeth began fidgeting in the mahogany chair. "I think it's going to rain," she said, looking disturbed. "And now we can't sit out on the front porch this evening." She turned back to Jonathan. "Every day I sit there, watching and waiting for Fred. He promised me he would return from the war."

Grace stared at her mother. Was she going to pretend that Jonathan had not told them her father was dying when he last saw him? She glanced across at Jonathan and saw that he was looking toward the window. She guessed he was trying to avoid the subject.

Grace opened her mouth, then closed it again. This was no time to remind her mother of the cruel truth, she decided. Instead, she followed Jonathan's gaze to the window where the mimosa bush had begun to tremble as the breeze picked up into a steady wind.

"Mother is right," Grace said. "You shouldn't be out on a stormy night. It will get dark early, and there are deep ruts in the road when it rains. Sometimes thieves lurk in the woods along the roads."

"And you two ladies live here alone?" he asked, looking from one to the other with a deep frown rumpling his smooth brow.

"The neighbors are very kind to look in on us," Grace explained, "although we manage just fine."

He studied her face for a moment, as though weighing her words. "I imagine that you do," he said with a smile.

Grace was grateful that he didn't respond to the sharp tone

in her voice; when her independence was questioned, she had learned to rally back.

"I will accept your kind offer on the condition that you allow me to do something for you in the morning before I leave."

"Like what?" Grace inquired.

"Forgive me for saying so, but I noticed as I turned up the lane this afternoon that the gate is broken. Your reference to thieves in the woods concerns me. I'll stay if you allow me to repair the gate. It shouldn't take long, and I promise not to overstay my welcome."

"It's settled then," Elizabeth said, looking extremely pleased— a look Grace rarely saw on her mother's face.

Another explosion of thunder shook the teacups in their saucers. Grace glanced through the lace curtains to the side lawn, where an eerie yellow light tinged the afternoon. Pale white light flickered and zigzagged past the window.

The mimosa bushes quivered, and overhead the thick branches of trees heaved as debris flew about.

"It's getting worse," Grace said, glancing at Jonathan, who had walked over to stand beside her. She was surprised to see that his face had turned pale, and his eyes had widened as he stared out the window. He looked as though he were becoming ill.

"What is it?" she asked.

He turned to face her. The muscles in his face clenched, and his blue eyes held a terrible kind of fear.

"What's wrong?" she touched his sleeve.

He shook his head and passed a hand over his eyes. "Just a bad memory. Forgive me."

"Of course," she said, wondering why the storm affected him so.

Then the very foundation of the house seemed to quiver as thunder blasted again and again. Something crashed in the front of the house, and Grace rushed out of the dining room and down the hall to see what was happening.

In the parlor, she felt the rush of the wind. A corner of the drape flew about the east window, and as she hurried in that direction, she saw shards of glass strewn about the floor. The empty tea pitcher she had left out on the window ledge had been blown back against the window, shattering a small corner of it. Now remnants of the glass pitcher and the window were being tossed about like dust bunnies.

Seizing a small pillow from the sofa, she stepped around the edge of the glass and quickly stuffed the thick pillow into the gaping hole. Immediately, the wind softened.

"What is it? What's happened?" Jonathan asked from the doorway.

She turned to see that he looked more pale than before, and she began to feel alarmed for him. He was obviously fighting some illness.

"I'm afraid I carelessly left a tea pitcher out on the window ledge when I was pruning the shrubs yesterday," she explained. "The wind blew it against the window and broke a pane of glass. It's okay," she said, trying to keep her voice calm and soothing. "Why don't you sit down? You don't look well at all."

He sank into the chair and again passed his hand over his forehead. Grace noticed the frayed threads along the sides of the chair and the chip in the mahogany arm. The furnishings were in sad condition, but there was nothing she could do about it, and Jonathan seemed not to notice.

"I must apologize," he began.

"Perhaps I am the one who should apologize. I fear my food has poisoned you."

"No, it's not the food."

"I'll get you some water."

She hurried back to the dining room, where her mother was getting up from the chair. "Is everything all right?" she asked calmly. Despite the fierce storm taking place outside, her mother did not look troubled.

"Yes. Mother, why don't you go up and lie down? You always

say you sleep best when it is raining."

"Oh, I do. Will Mr. Parker be staying overnight?"

She nodded. "Yes, I think so. The storm is too bad to allow him to leave now."

Grace hurried into the kitchen to pour a tumbler of water from a pitcher. What was wrong with him? she wondered. Had he been injured in the war?

As she passed through the hall, she saw her mother climbing the stairs. At least her mother was not aware of the man's sudden illness. It would be like her mother to try and put him to bed and insist he stay on for a week.

When Grace returned to the parlor, Jonathan was standing before the broken window, surveying the damage.

"Here's some water for you," she said, as he turned and crossed the room to her side.

"You seem to have temporarily repaired the damage," he said, indicating the pillow. He accepted the glass of water, drank it, and handed the glass back to her. "I'm afraid the war is still with me," he said, glancing back at the gray day beyond the window. "Whenever I hear heavy thunder, for a moment I'm back in battle."

She sat down on the settee and looked at him. "Would it help to talk about it?"

He sat down in the chair again, cradling his head in his hands. "It's the same memory every time. We're camped for the night after a thirty-six hour ride. Men were falling asleep in the saddle, and we had to stop and bed down for the night in a wooded area. We were awakened from a dead sleep by the sound of cannon fire at daybreak. When I looked around, we were surrounded by Confederate infantry; it didn't seem we had a chance. We tried to move deeper into the woods while soldiers were coming at us with clubbed carbines and sabers. We had masked our guns in pine thickets the night before, and we opened fire. The wounded began to fall. . .gray coats, blue coats, soldiers piling up together. . ." His voice was softly muffled by his fingers covering his face.

The keening wind and biting rain hit the window as he spoke, but he didn't seem to notice. Even Grace scarcely heard it as she stared at the man relating a memory that was obviously horrible to recall. He had stopped talking, and she took a deep breath.

"How did you manage to escape?" she asked gently.

"I'm not sure. I just remember firing and backing up, further and further into the woods. Then I heard a bugle, and I barely made out a column of our cavalry riding into the battle. Somehow they turned the Rebs back just in time. I stumbled down a bank to a creek and fell in. Then. . .when I looked around, I saw the water was red. . .and I saw some of my men lying there. . .their heads in the water. . . ."

He stopped talking, and Grace said nothing. He had painted the scene quite vividly for her, and she felt sick just thinking about it. When he spoke of Federal and Confederate soldiers dying together, it was almost too appalling to imagine; yet in her mind's eye she had seen it all. She wondered how he could possibly have survived.

"I am so sorry," he said, removing his hands from his face and looking at her with sad, bleak eyes. "I have no right to tell you such a horrible story. I have forgotten my place," he said, coming to his feet. "I will leave now."

"No, that isn't necessary," she said. "It is late, and Mother wants you to stay."

Grace realized as she spoke the words that she was using her mother's wish to justify her decision, but it didn't matter. He had told her something quite personal—she knew that—and in doing so, had somehow bridged the awkward gap between them.

She looked across at the broken window and saw that the pillow had worked wonders in keeping out the wind and rain. The rain had stopped, but the storm laid a bleak gray light over the land. Grace got up and lit the lamps. She smiled as she realized that for once, she would not awake in the night, jumping at a strange sound, worrying that a thief might be breaking in. She would feel protected with Jonathan Parker staying in the guest room.

She was borrowing misery if she took comfort from the thought of having a man under their roof. He would be leaving tomorrow, and she would never see him again. That realization felt as heavy in her mind as the thick humidity settling over the room after the rain.

"Will your mother be joining us?" he asked.

"No, probably not for a while. She tires easily and usually goes to bed rather early. But then, she is so glad to have you visiting that she may surprise me and come downstairs for more conversation."

"I hope she does."

He cleared his throat, and his voice was stronger when he spoke. "I know the news I have brought about your father is painful."

"Yes. But it feels good to be able to talk with someone who was with Father at. . .at the end." She leaned forward. "Tell me more about him."

Jonathan was quiet for a moment as his eyes lifted over her head to something outside the window. "He spoke of you and your mother constantly. I soon came to realize that he was an amazing man."

She swallowed hard. "What was wrong with him? Other than starvation, I mean."

"He had dysentery. It was rampant among the soldiers, and conditions in the hospital left something to be desired. But it was the fever that had begun to take his life. I would not have left him alone at the end, but the nurse convinced me that the outbreak of fever was contagious. I had to think about returning to Kentucky."

"Of course," Grace said, wondering if her father had suffered very much. But she couldn't bring herself to ask anything more. The pain was too great. Then she thought of one more thing, still holding onto one last hope. "Was he. . .conscious when you left?"

Jonathan looked at her with compassion. "No, he was not."

Silence filled the room until he sighed. "After he gave me the Bible, he seemed to fade away. I'm. . .so sorry."

The bitterness that had festered in her heart like an ugly sore suddenly burst open. Grace jumped up from the love seat, hugging her arms around herself.

"It's all so unfair!" she cried, pacing around the room. "I don't know how Mother keeps her faith or why she bothers. Good people die; horrible people kill and go free. Nothing makes sense to me."

"I know. I was always amazed at your father's faith. My parents were not as devout, and I learned quite a bit from him in the short time we were together."

The words he spoke fell into the tense silence, and for the first time all evening, Grace was conscious again of the difference in his voice and her own. She thought about the difference between his background and hers and the fact that he had fought opposite her father and brother. Yet, she had sat and listened to his horrid account of fighting between her side and his, and for a moment, both sides had seemed to blend into one terrible tragedy. But they were separate tragedies, and the South had suffered defeat.

"You look troubled," he said, watching her closely.

She blinked and looked away. "Tired," she replied. "I'm tired. If you'll excuse me, I think I'll go on up to my room. It's been a long day."

"Yes, of course."

"Mother has prepared the guest room for you. The third door on the right upstairs." She glanced toward the darkness beyond the window, then back at him. "Well, good night."

Turning, she hurried down the hall and up the stairs to her room, desperately needing her privacy. She was grateful her mother had faithfully lit the upstairs candelabra, for its soft glow offset the gloom. Yet it did not reach the shadowed corners of the long upper hall, which greeted her every evening.

With each step, Grace's feet felt heavier. Her heart seemed to be dropping to her feet as she lit the lamp on the table beside the door in her bedroom. Then slowly she turned and closed the door.

Exhaustion crept over her as she walked to the armoire and pulled out her nightclothes. She was tired of dealing with the conflicting emotions that were a part of her every waking moment. War, death, poverty, loneliness. And now she had spent several hours with an interesting man, a *Northerner*, who was sure to set the tongues wagging throughout the county.

That didn't bother her. What bothered her was the fact that she had been cheated once again. Fate had dangled an enticing dream before her, then just as quickly, and as cruelly, yanked it away. She had no hope of having a husband and a family. The future that stretched before her was bleak and unexciting.

As she tied the strings on the bodice of her nightgown, she began to wish she hadn't asked Jonathan Parker to stay overnight. It would have been so much easier to thank him for his trouble, then send him on his way.

She walked to her bedroom window and stared out at the dark night. The wind sighed through the branches, a low moan that seemed to echo the mood in her heart. Despite the humidity of the May evening, a chill crept over her skin as she turned from the window and walked across the room to extinguish the light.

She would be relieved when Jonathan Parker climbed on his black stallion and rode out of their lives, she thought as she crawled into her feather bed and settled into the softness. She closed her eyes, but in the next second, deep blue eyes looked into her own, and the handsome face of the stranger under their roof lingered in her memory.

She rolled over and flopped against the pillow, angry again. She didn't need to be reminded of what she was missing for the rest of her life.

Chapter 3

When Grace stirred against her pillow the next morning, she knew before she opened her eyes that something had changed in her life. Something was different about today. What was it? She stretched her slim body against the linen sheet as her memory settled in place. Suddenly, she bolted upright. *Jonathan Parker!*

Tossing back the covers, she hurried to the washstand, lifted the china pitcher, and poured water into the bowl. The morning ritual of splashing water on her face to wake up was unnecessary today. She was wide awake as she began to bathe, using the special lilac soap she hoarded.

Her eyes fell on the sweat-stained overalls, crumpled in a heap in the corner of the bedroom. Sniffing, she tweaked her nose in disgust. Mr. Jonathan Parker wouldn't be seeing her in overalls today. No sir! Her mind moved on to the possibilities of her wardrobe, though they were slim.

When she finished her bath, she stepped over the overalls and hurried to the armoire, determined to feel the softness of a dress against her skin. She had not worn crinolines in a very long time, one of the advantages of their distressed situation, but today she intended to enjoy every minute she had with their charming Kentucky guest. Today she would enjoy being a woman. She felt surprisingly good about their northern house visitor in the bright sunlight of a new spring day. The morbid thoughts of the night before had been washed away by a deep sleep, just as the hard rain had polished the leaves of the magnolia tree to a waxy green and scrubbed up the sky to a fresh clean blue. She was ready to be up and about her business, to face life again.

Reaching inside the armoire, she withdrew a pair of lacy pantaloons. Turning to the wardrobe, she chose the dress with tiny pink rosebuds that always made her think of flower gardens in the spring. While she dressed, she studied her reflection in the mirror.

She had been blessed with clear skin. While her nose always managed to hang onto the first sunburn, the rest of her skin turned a light golden tan once she adjusted to the sun. Wide-set hazel eyes beneath sharply arched brows stared back at her as she lifted a work-roughened hand to the deep hollow in her cheek. She had lost more weight, and dark circles showed beneath her lashes. Another year of drudgery and she would be skin and bones, she thought, frowning suddenly. She reached up and smoothed the little wrinkle from her brow. There was no point in thinking about life's unpleasantness now; she wanted this to be a good day.

She reached for the silver-handled hairbrush and worked it through her tangled blond hair as she thought about the day ahead. Why not relish gazing at the handsome man, talking to him, maybe even flirting a little bit? After all, he would soon be only a memory, so she should make it a good one.

She whisked her hair back from her face and secured it with a black grosgrain ribbon at the nape of her neck. Then her fingers darted up to fan the wavy ends out across her shoulders. The vinegar rinses she put on her hair kept the shine in it, which always surprised her, considering how little time she had to take care of herself.

Placing her hands on each side of her narrow waist, she whirled before the mirror, satisfied that she achieved her goal: She looked and felt like a woman.

She hurried out of the room and down the steps, led by the sound of voices from somewhere below. At the bottom step, she turned her head toward the open front door. Following the voices, she sauntered up the hall to peer out onto the front porch. Beyond the round white columns that rose to the roof, Grace could see raindrops, like crystal beads, glimmering on the thick grass in the yard. While the yard was pitifully overgrown, like all of the land, a timeless beauty lingered in the massive oaks with their brawny arms and in the creamy blossoms on the magnolia tree.

"*Weeping may endure for a night, but joy cometh in the morning. . . .*"

Grace winced. Her mother was quoting scripture again, probably boring their guest to death.

"You are a very inspiring lady," Jonathan was saying.

Grace quirked an eyebrow. He didn't sound bored; there was even a pleasant note in his voice.

Curiosity tingled through her, as titillating as the fresh breeze from a light east wind. She opened the door and stepped out onto the porch.

"Hello, dear."

Grace turned to study her mother. Her hazel eyes were glowing, and a smile slipped easily over her lips. The look of happiness on her mother's face warmed Grace's heart.

"Good morning," she said, glancing at her father's Bible, which lay open in her mother's lap. She imagined her mother probably sat up half the night, reading the Bible her father had sent back with Jonathan.

"Good morning." Jonathan rose to his feet as she approached.

"Good morning," she said, meeting Jonathan's friendly smile.

He had changed into a fresh white shirt, and his hair was neatly combed. He seemed taller, even more masculine, she thought, as she passed by him on her way to the rocker.

"Jonathan is a Christian, Grace. He was telling me how, as a boy, he sat at his mother's feet while she read scripture."

Grace looked from her delighted mother to Jonathan. A nagging suspicion rose in Grace's mind as her eyes lingered on Jonathan. He was not at all embarrassed by her mother's reference to him being a Christian. Grace knew that Freddy would never want anyone going on about that, even though he had been baptized in Caney Creek years ago at the age of eleven.

She tilted her head and looked at Jonathan more closely, trying to figure him out. He merely smiled and turned back to her mother, who was absolutely doting on him.

Elizabeth was as excited as a little girl at a tea party. "I favor the Psalms," she was saying. "Grace, do you remember how your father and I loved to read those passages?" She glanced at Grace.

"Oh yes," Grace replied, still watching Jonathan, although she had not managed to make him uncomfortable. Since he didn't seem perturbed by her staring, she decided to take a good long look in the bright sunlight of morning.

He had broad cheeks with prominent cheekbones and a smooth straight nose. She had a fleeting desire, a rather crazy one, to show him off to Rose Marie, who had spent most of her teenage years doting on the male population. Then as Jonathan made a comment to her mother, she heard his voice and realized that Rose Marie would have something ugly to say about his being a Yankee. She sighed and turned her attention back to her mother.

Elizabeth was looking out across the lawn, and for a moment it seemed that she was watching something that no one else could see.

"Grace, do you recall how you and Freddy would play on that swing for hours at a time?"

Grace followed her mother's eyes to the huge oak in the corner of the yard. From the lowest branch, the rope swing hung, lonely and unused through the years. She blinked, as the vision of a little girl giggling while her older brother pushed the swing filled her mind.

"Yes, I do," she answered, feeling the first threat of sadness. The day had started so perfectly. Why did her mother have to go and ruin it? But then she was merely recalling a fond memory, and that should not ruin a day. But a happy memory merely emphasized how unhappy so much of her life had become.

Jonathan cleared his throat. "How old was Freddy when he joined the army?"

Grace dragged her memory back through the years. She

looked at Jonathan, and a sad little smile touched her lips as she recalled her headstrong brother. "Freddy had just turned seventeen when he and the neighbor boys got all worked up about being soldiers. Father pleaded with him to wait another year. There were crops in the field and dozens of chores left undone. But Freddy was strong willed."

"Our little boy turned into a soldier overnight," Elizabeth mused, still staring at the swing.

Grace nodded. "He couldn't wait to tell us good-bye and meet up with the Walkers and the three Estes brothers. They were all so eager to gallop off to war." Her voice was mocking as she spoke. She felt the bitterness welling up inside her.

She looked back at Jonathan. "Like Freddy, the Estes brothers never returned."

"Are you going to make coffee?" Elizabeth asked suddenly.

When Grace looked at her, it seemed her mother had not heard the sad words she had just spoken. Sometimes she longed to be like her mother for a short while, to blot out all the bad memories and cling to the good. She supposed it made it easier to hang on to her faith.

It was not until he stood that she realized she had made Jonathan feel uncomfortable. "I'll get busy on the gate."

"And I'll make coffee," she said, thinking that they would all go on about their business now. Yet it was a relief to have something simple to do, anything to occupy her mind and her hands. She headed toward the door, glancing again at her mother, who was staring out across the lawn, deep in thought. She did not appear troubled or even unhappy. She was simply lost in her own world.

Grace hurried toward the kitchen. Strong coffee was exactly what she needed to jolt some sense back into her befuddled brain. Maybe Jonathan Parker was the most handsome man she had ever seen and maybe even the nicest, if she didn't count her father. But he was a Yankee, she reminded herself as she poured water from the teakettle into the iron pot and placed it over the low fire in the hearth. Despite her silly notion about flirting with him and having something to remember later, she realized that she had to be practical. She couldn't lounge about the porch daydreaming like her mother. Someone here had better face reality.

From the pantry, she removed the small tin canister of coffee, so precious during the war that she and her mother rationed themselves miserably. She had derived great satisfaction from bartering an old saddle from the stable in exchange for some much-needed staples. When she'd accompanied her closest neighbors, the Douglas family, to Tuscaloosa, she had enjoyed herself tremendously. Like her father, she loved to trade, and now she made a mental note to gather up anything she could find in the barn and outbuildings. She would plan another day of trading, and that thought helped to lift her spirits.

She walked back to the pot and poured out a small portion of the freshly ground coffee. Maybe she'd check with Eva Nell Douglas to see when they would be returning to town. It would be something to look forward to after Jonathan left.

The heavy tread of boots in the hall reminded her that the man in question had not left and was, in fact, headed toward the kitchen.

"Where might I find some tools?" he asked politely.

She walked to the kitchen window and pointed out the small building huddled near the barn. "The few tools we have left will be there. To be honest, I haven't even been in to look around lately. For a while, I checked every day to be sure no one was hiding there."

He stared at her in dismay. "Do you have a gun, Grace?"

She smiled, pleased that he had called her by her first name. "I have my father's rifle, and I'm a very good shot, if I say so myself."

He shook his head. "I still can't believe that you and your mother live here all alone, with no help and no men to protect you."

She shrugged. "Our men were sacrificed for the war," she replied, then hated herself for the remark when she saw his eyes darken. "I'm sorry," she said.

Her words hung heavily in the air. Grace knew she was behaving badly, but she couldn't seem to help herself.

"I'll go out and have a look."

"I hope you can find what you need," she called pleasantly, hoping to offset her bitter words.

He turned, and their gazes locked for a moment before he nodded and walked out.

Grace stared after him, touched again by his kindness. Something mean in her spirit prompted her to keep making snide little remarks. At first she had even tried to dislike him, but he made that difficult by not taking offense to the bitter words that kept popping out of her mouth. He was a true gentleman who seemed intent on helping them any way he could.

She moved about the kitchen, automatically assembling what she needed to make biscuits. All the while, she stared into space, seeing nothing but Jonathan Parker in her mind's eye. She had never met anyone like him. The local boys had never appealed to her. They had always seemed to be badly in need of learning the basics of etiquette. This was the South, where everyone cut their teeth on being a lady or a gentleman. Before the war, the young men thought of nothing but racing horses, playing pranks, and trying to hold their liquor, and not doing a very good job at any of it, in her opinion.

She rolled out the dough and turned a cup over to cut out biscuits.

A movement beyond the kitchen window caught her eye. Jonathan Parker was carrying a few tools that looked as rusty as she had feared. Yet there was a lilt to his step and a pleasant expression on his face.

Grace stared at him, unable to resist watching his every move when he was unaware of her. He walked with a long purposeful stride, as though he always knew exactly where he was going and what he was doing.

As he disappeared around the side of the house, Grace thought about how eagerly he had spoken of his farm in Kentucky and his desire to restock cattle and horses.

She swallowed hard, not wanting to hope or dream, but she couldn't help herself. She was only nineteen years old, yet she felt at least the age of Agnes, the spinster neighbor, who was thirty-one and had had no offers of marriage.

Grace bit her lip as the frustration of her endless conflict gripped her again. No matter how many times she reminded herself that it did no good to wail about life not being fair, at times like this she wanted to scream at the top of her lungs about how cheated and disheartened she felt.

Why did she have to live out her life at Riverwood with a mother whom she loved dearly but who seemed determined to live in the past?

She grabbed up the bread pan, dipped into her lard bowl, and swabbed the pan generously. Then she began to place each biscuit onto the greased pan.

A fierce ache squeezed her throat, and she swallowed hard against it. She would not cry over something as silly as a lost dream. A dream was an elusive thing. People were flesh and blood and a part of her soul. She had lost a father and a brother, and now her mother just sat on the front porch and waited for "her Fred" to come home. Grace was left to worry about the neglected farmland that needed to produce crops to pay their taxes and put food on their table. It had taken the kindness of a total stranger to make even the most basic repair: the front gate. Yet that same kindness had strangely twisted her heart, flirting with her, reminding her of how lonely she had been throughout the past years.

She'd be better off not to know that there were men like Jonathan Parker walking the face of the earth, returning to a wonderful life he would share with. . .well, she was sure he had his pick of lovely Kentucky women.

"But I'm not going to think about that," she said aloud. She no longer worried about talking to herself. She had grown to like her own company.

Chapter 4

"How far is the nearest hardware store?" Jonathan asked as they sat at the table, eating breakfast.

"About three miles down the road at Whites Creek."

He looked from Grace to Elizabeth, who was seated at the head of the table, sipping her coffee, watching Jonathan appreciatively.

"Then I'd like to ride into Whites Creek and pick up a new hammer and some nails. I want you to have a sturdy gate. And you do need some new tools," he added gently.

"How nice of you," Elizabeth smiled.

Grace stared at him. "You don't have to go to that much trouble."

"I insist. If you don't mind, that is."

She shook her head. "No, I don't mind. In fact, I need to make a trip in to pick up some more seeds for my garden. I'll saddle up Molly and tag along."

"Is Molly up to the trip? I noticed she has a limp."

"Oh yes. She's had a limp ever since I've known her. Mr. Douglas loaned her to us because she could no longer pull a wagon or work in the field. But Molly is just fine to ride. As a matter of fact, we get along very well. Next to Mother, Molly is about my best friend," she said with a grin.

He chuckled softly, and Grace's grin deepened into a smile. She liked the sound of his laughter. It was full and deep and exactly the way a person should sound when amused. She had never liked the shallow little laughs of Farrel Watson, down in Whites Creek, who was always trying to flirt with her but never quite figured out how.

"Well, I'm glad you and Molly understand one another. I was a little concerned when I fed her this morning."

"Thanks for feeding her." Grace spoke quickly, pleased to have someone to help her. "Then we'll go into Whites Creek. Mother, you need to make a list for me."

Grace watched her mother carefully, wondering if she would object to Grace riding into town with this man whom they scarcely knew.

"All right." Her mother smiled. Grace realized everything had changed. The old rules no longer applied, or at least Grace didn't think so.

Later, dressed in the wrinkled riding habit she had retrieved from the trunk, she met Jonathan in the drive. He had found her old harness and saddle and thoughtfully saddled Molly up, and now they were ready to ride. She watched as he swung onto the big stallion with ease.

"Are you okay?" he asked, looking back over his shoulder as they started off down the drive.

"I'm fine," she called back, silently admiring General, the big stallion, as he pranced down the drive. Feeling disloyal to Molly, she leaned over and stroked her mane.

It was a beautiful spring day. After the storm, the air was lighter and sweeter. The honeysuckle blossoms were in bloom, flavoring the air with their special fragrance.

As they reached the end of the drive, Grace took another look at the pitiful old gate and felt embarrassed. It half hung from the hinges, but there was nothing she could do about it. She would be grateful to Jonathan Parker for repairing it. She looked across at him, ready to express her appreciation, but he was already speaking.

"You're very kind to your mother," he said. "I'm sure these have been difficult years for her. And for you."

"The years have been difficult, not just for us, but for everyone. All anyone thinks about anymore is trying to survive. It's the way of war, I suppose." She glanced at Jonathan. "You must be anxious to see your family."

"Yes, I am. And yet—"

"What is it?"

He was silent for a few moments. Then he looked at her and shrugged. "I guess I'm dreading to see the condition of the farm. I know its been badly neglected, and with everyone gone, I'm not sure it will feel like home anymore."

Grace frowned. This idea was something new to her. She had never left Riverwood except for visits to relatives in other parts of the state when she was small. She cast her gaze out across the oak woods, watching a red-winged blackbird sail to a lower branch. The sound of birdsong filled the air, along with the scent of wild-flowers. This was home to her. She tried to imagine how it would be for Jonathan, having been away for so long, then returning to an abandoned home. She lifted her eyes toward the blue skies, admiring the soft puffy clouds skimming about.

She made a promise to herself that she was going to quit complaining so much. In fact, she had begun to feel so good that she now regretted wishing that Jonathan had never come to their door. She was so happy to have a friend and to actually be going someplace, if only to Whites Creek.

She looked up at the man whose horse was a few paces ahead of her. He was a good rider, swaying easily with the horse's gait.

"You ride as though you've spent lots of time in the saddle," she called to him.

"I was in the cavalry. And before the war, we rode horses on the farm."

Her eyes swept up his back, clad in a dark coat, then lingered on the wave of dark hair that brushed his collar.

"I can see this is the heart of cotton country," he said, turning his head to look out across the fields.

"Yes." She followed his gaze to the land bordering the road, land as level as a table, stretching as far as the eye could see.

"This was the Abernathy place," she said.

Just ahead, only a blackened chimney remained of the grand

home, a sordid reminder of the war and what it had done to families. There was no point in saying more; it was obvious the big house had been burned to the ground. She noticed that Jonathan was looking at the ugly pile of rubbish that marred the tranquil landscape.

"How did you manage to save your place?" he asked.

She took a deep breath, feeling a deep relief when she thought about what had happened. "We were fortunate. Only a few soldiers came to search our place. Of course, the soldiers had already taken our horses and cattle and the wagon. On their last foray, they realized there was little of value for them, and our farm is smaller than those around us. The officer in charge was a kind, older gentleman who took mercy on Mother and me. They left us alone."

"Thank God," Jonathan said, breathing a deep sigh.

"Yes, Mother thanked God every night after that. And for a while, I did, too. I guess I forget to be grateful."

Beyond the next field, tumbled shanties that had been slave quarters were now rotting wood with birds nesting in the rafters.

"I'm glad the slaves were freed," she said, staring at the dismal reminder of their lives before the war. "I always got into arguments about people owning slaves. Father always hired Irishmen to do our work, once he managed to buy enough land to raise cotton. And Ardella and William were like family. They stayed with us until they both died."

His interest in their home led her thoughts toward his farm in Kentucky. "I do hope you find your farm in good shape when you return to Kentucky," she said. "Perhaps your brother-in-law has seen to it that the farm has been kept up."

He turned his face sideways to answer her. She saw his profile from a different angle and noticed that his nose was perfectly straight. The jaw was broad with prominent bones capping his cheeks.

"I have my doubts about my brother-in-law. James has no

interest in the farm. I suspect Mother may have trouble dragging Katherine back to the farm if she's become spoiled to city life. Katie is spoiled anyway, being the baby," he said, chuckling softly.

He hesitated as they rode on. "It's hard to believe that the redheaded pixie I left is now a lady of sixteen. She may even have a beau."

"What does she look like?" Grace asked, curious about his family.

"She's a fiery little redhead given to temper tantrums. I doubt if Mother has managed to curtail that temper through the years. But the war may have changed Katie, too." He sighed. "It would really make me sad to return to find my spunky little sister is now a very serious woman."

"She probably has a beau; she may even be married," Grace said. "And I imagine she's very pretty. Are her eyes like yours?" she asked, then wished she hadn't when she heard the admiration in her tone.

Jonathan didn't seem to think anything of the question, however. "As a matter of fact, they're exactly the same color of blue. That's the only resemblance. She has small features and pretty hair, very thick. . .like yours," he added softly.

Grace perked up. Automatically, she lifted a hand to touch a strand of hair curling over the shoulder of her dress. So he had noticed her thick hair, which she always thought was one of her best features. That pleased her.

"What plans do you have for Riverwood?" he asked in a sudden change of subject.

Her thoughts moved back to the home she loved. She couldn't imagine being separated from it, as Jonathan had been. "Well," she began, then paused to ponder her future. "The main thing is to keep the taxes paid so that carpetbaggers don't buy our land for next to nothing." She shook her head, recalling the horrible stories she had heard. "With Confederate money worthless, and no way to make money on the land, it's very difficult to pay the taxes; but if they're not paid, the land can be sold off for as little as a dollar an acre. My father and Mr. Britton, the banker, were best friends, and because of that, Mr. Britton has been generous and patient."

Grace pressed her lips together to keep from saying more. The truth was Mr. Britton was having financial problems himself. He couldn't afford to keep holding her note. She would have to figure out a way to pay him back by the end of the year.

"You mentioned that a neighbor married for the sake of the family, to extend the land lines—I believe that's the way you put it. I imagine you have been presented with offers."

Grace shrugged. "I would never marry for that reason."

"May I ask why not?"

"Because I will never marry unless I truly love the man."

"You seem quite certain of that," he said, tilting his head sideways again, as though trying to read her expression.

"I am. And furthermore, it won't be easy for a man to live with me."

He chuckled at that remark. "And may I ask why you would say something like that?"

She smiled to herself, remembering an old argument. "Father used to say, 'Grace, with that strong personality, you'll never find a man who can live with you.'" She gave a short laugh and looked out across the barren fields. "It was my thirteenth birthday, and I had thrown a temper tantrum because Mother insisted on a tea party to celebrate my birthday. What I really wanted to do was go with Father to Tuscaloosa to a horse and cattle auction."

"At thirteen you wanted to do that?" he asked, laughing.

She thought he seemed overly amused at her honest statements, but she took it good-naturedly. "I hoped to talk Father into buying me a fine horse," she explained. "I had already chosen a name. Darkfire."

"So what happened?"

"Father agreed with Mother, and I had to endure a silly tea

party. I never got the kind of horse I wanted."

"Well, I'll bet your father was secretly proud of your spirit. I think it's admirable for a woman to be a bit independent."

She was pleased by that remark, one so different than she would have heard from most of the boys she had known. They would expect her to be meek and mealy-mouthed like—

She broke off her train of thought, reminding herself not to be unkind about Agnes.

"I was independent for sure," she said, laughing with him. It occurred to her that it was good to hear the sound of her own laughter ringing in her ears.

They rode on in silence, and Grace relished the smell of wildflowers and the feel of a horse moving beneath her. Having Jonathan Parker riding in front of her was no hardship. She sighed to herself. This was turning into a perfect day.

All too soon they were approaching Whites Creek, so she sat up straight and thought about what she had to do.

The main street was flanked by twin rows of small wooden shops with oak trees behind them for shade. Long wooden hitching rails paralleled the front of each shop, and Grace counted three sorrels and two bays tied out front. A fancy buggy was parked in front of the general store, and further down the street near the livery, she saw a team of mules and an old wagon.

Along the uneven boards that served as walkways, a few women, in dark calico and frayed sunbonnets, sauntered along, their market baskets swinging from their arms.

"The general store is the second building there," she pointed.

As they turned toward the hitching rail in front of the store, Grace was suddenly aware of bold stares sweeping over her. Across the street at the livery, a stranger had appeared beside the wagon. He stood with his hands on his hips, his eyes narrowed on Jonathan.

Grace glanced away, scanning the boardwalk again. She recognized the faces of some of the merchants, peering from doorways, but they were not smiling at her.

Mrs. Primrose, who helped her husband at the store, was crossing the street from the bank. A look of curiosity worked over her face as she stepped into the street and struck a path toward Grace.

Jonathan had dismounted and had extended his hand to help Grace down. She had a sudden urge to refuse his help, knowing that Mrs. Primrose was trained on her like a hawk swooping down on its prey. Looking into Jonathan's nice eyes, however, Grace took his hand and dismounted.

"Grace?" Mrs. Primrose yelled, trying to catch up. "How is your mother?"

Grace took a deep breath and forced a smile as she turned to face the older woman, who wasn't even looking at her. The beady eyes studied Jonathan, taking in every detail.

"She's all right, Mrs. Primrose."

Grace was about to turn in spite of the fact that the woman stood directly in their path, still staring at Jonathan.

Grace averted her eyes to her riding skirt, brushing it carefully as though too preoccupied to introduce her traveling companion.

Jonathan merely tipped his hat, saying nothing, for which Grace was thankful. She dared not introduce him, for if he opened his mouth and Mrs. Primrose caught one Yankee syllable, she might flog both of them.

Jonathan seemed to understand as he fell in step beside her, and they stepped up onto the boards leading into the general store. Glancing over her shoulder, Grace saw Mrs. Primrose turn to speak to a couple passing by in a wagon.

"I'll do the talking," she said, under her breath.

She had hoped the beautiful day would send everyone to their fields and gardens, but many had chosen to make the trip to town to restock supplies.

The smell of leather and plug tobacco was strong as the door of the general store swung back at Jonathan's touch. In the rear, seated on upturned nail kegs, Grace spotted several men she recognized. They were huddled up around the hearth. In winter, the hearth at the general store was the meeting place for drinking coffee and swapping tales. There was no fire in the hearth today; still they sat and talked. One of the men, wearing the gray trousers of his uniform, was heatedly relating a story to the others.

"The Yanks took all our horses, our mules, the brass-trimmed carriage, and ever' last wagon we had. They raided the smokehouse and pantry and left us nothing. Had three bales of cotton down in the shed—"

He stopped in midsentence as all the men noticed Grace and Jonathan. From the corner of her eye, she could see all heads swivel toward her, then Jonathan. She lifted her chin and headed toward the counter. "I need a hammer and some nails," she said as Mr. Primrose walked up to the counter. "And do you have any tomato plants?"

"None today," he said, looking from Grace to Jonathan, taking him in from hat to boots. "Could I help you, sir?"

"He's with me," Grace answered quickly.

Everyone in the store was looking and listening now. She stole a glance at Jonathan and saw that his expression was solemn. He pursed his lips and looked around, meeting each stare directly. Nodding briefly at those who were gawking, he turned to Grace.

She breathed a sigh of relief until her supplies were spread over the counter. Grace froze. There was no point in reaching into her handbag; she hadn't enough money to cover the purchase. She could feel the blood rise to her cheeks as she stared at the sturdy new hammer, unsure what to do next.

Jonathan had wandered over to a shelf where jars of homemade pickles and relishes had been placed with a sign that read PLEASE HELP THE WIDOWS OF THE CONFEDERACY. Jonathan removed a jar of each and returned to the counter.

Mr. Primrose totaled the bill and announced the amount.

Saying nothing, Jonathan placed some money on the counter. Mr. Primrose examined the newly minted bills, looking pleased.

"Thank you, sir," he said, looking at Jonathan.

Jonathan nodded as he picked up the package, and they headed for the door. Grace felt the boards vibrate beneath her feet as Sonny Jackson lumbered up to her. He must have been hunkered down somewhere in the back of the store, for she hadn't seen him before. If she had known the town bully was lurking about, she would never have entered the store. Sonny spent his time looking for someone to pester, hoping to stir up a fight.

His pale, watery blue eyes were set between straggly brown brows and thick cheeks. Thin brown hair straggled down from his soiled derby hat, and as usual, his clothes were wrinkled and soiled, though he no longer worked in the fields.

"Hello, Miss Grace. You and yore ma doin' all right?" He stood beside the door, his fat thumbs hooked into the loops of his belt.

"We're fine," she said curtly, sidestepping him as Jonathan reached out to open the door.

"As a friend of Freddy's, I hafta look out for his little sis. Who's your fancy friend here?" He had followed them out onto the sidewalk and was standing directly in front of Jonathan, making a show of looking over Jonathan's frock coat and pinstriped trousers.

"Sonny, I think you need to mind your own business," Grace said. "You and Freddy were never friends; in fact, he hated your guts."

She could have bitten her tongue once the words were out, for this was all Sonny needed to urge him on.

"Yeah, well I still say Freddy would want me lookin' after his kin. Don't believe I ever seen you around these parts, mister."

"You wouldn't have seen me unless you were a soldier in the army," Jonathan said coldly, glaring into Sonny's eyes. "And I doubt that you were." He was taller than Sonny by three or four inches, and the fact that he could look down on Sonny seemed to gall the bully even more.

Sonny sputtered for a moment before muttering a curse and diving into Jonathan's chest. He caught Jonathan off guard. Jonathan's hat toppled, and the package in his arms spurted from his grip as he was knocked back against the door.

Grace dived for the package, then reached for his hat. Like bees to a hive, a crowd was gathering, whispering among themselves. "A Yankee," someone muttered.

Grace took a firmer grip on Jonathan's hat and their package and yelled at Sonny. "Stop it," she cried, just before Jonathan ducked beneath Sonny's swinging fist.

Moving with the grace of a cat, Jonathan sidestepped him, then slammed a fist in the center of Sonny's sagging belly. Sonny groaned and bent double, his arms swinging wildly.

In the next instant, Jonathan's arm shot out again. His fist caught Sonny on the chin, and the bully reeled back. He landed in the street, doubled over, an expression of disbelief on his face.

The men raised their voices, urging Sonny to get up. Grace hurried to Jonathan's side, handing him his hat. "Please, let's get out of here."

Then Ned Whitworth stepped around the corner, and Grace had never in her life been so glad to see the stern sheriff. He stepped in front of Jonathan, whose eyes were narrowed on Sonny. Grace could see that Jonathan was ready to finish the fight. She turned to the sheriff, tugging his sleeve.

"Sheriff, this man is a family friend and—"

"A Yank," someone snorted.

"A no-good, slimy Union soldier," another joined in.

"Stop it!" Sheriff Whitworth snapped at the crowd. "If Miss Grace says he's a friend of hers, then you people better mind your manners."

Sonny was stumbling up, swiping a fat lip with the back of his hand.

"Ned, he started it."

"That's a lie." Jonathan glared at him, doubling his fist again. Then he took a deep breath, as though trying to calm himself as he dropped his hand to his side. "Sheriff, I didn't start this fight, but I won't run from it either."

The sheriff looked into Jonathan's eyes, glanced at Grace, then regarded Jonathan again, nodding his head. "I believe you. But the fight's over." He glanced over his shoulder as Sonny moved behind him. "Don't take another step," he warned. "Or you'll be charged and taken to jail."

Sonny was sputtering with rage, but the sheriff ignored him.

Grace looked from Sonny to the sheriff, then the crowd. She was furious that Jonathan had been treated so rudely, and she was determined to get a word in.

"This man saved my father's life," she said. "He took him to a hospital and befriended him before he died. You should be ashamed of yourselves, all of you!"

Jonathan had taken his hat and the package from her. Placing a hand on her elbow, he walked her back to her horse.

Sheriff Whitworth followed and stood beside them as they mounted their horses.

"Thank you, sir," Jonathan said, turning to the sheriff.

"Don't judge everyone here by Sonny," Sheriff Whitworth said to Jonathan. "Fred Cunningham was a fine man and respected by everyone who knew him. I'm glad to know that someone repaid his kindness."

Grace smiled at the sheriff, appreciating his words more than he could possibly know. "Thank you."

Then they turned their horses around and rode out of Whites Creek without a backward glance.

Chapter 5

Jonathan had said nothing in the hour since they had left Whites Creek. When Grace could stand the silence no longer, she spoke up.

"Let's rest a minute."

He nodded and pointed to a grove of oaks near the road. When they had reached the trees, Jonathan swung down from the saddle. Grace let him help her down, although she could have managed on her own. But she was beginning to enjoy the feel of his arms about her, and she liked the consideration he showed her.

He took off his hat and hooked it onto the saddle horn as he picked up the horses' reins and led them toward a hickory sapling. Grace removed her hat and adjusted the hairpins in her chignon. Then she walked over and sank onto the grass, enjoying the cool shade. She felt hot and parched and thoroughly out of sorts.

"I forgot to offer you water," Jonathan said. "I drew fresh water from your well before I left," he explained, removing the lid from a canteen. He handed her the canteen and sat down beside her.

Grace drank greedily of the cool water. When she had finished she handed the canteen back to him. He reached out, and for a moment, his hand lingered on hers.

"Thank you," she said softly.

"You're welcome."

His gaze trailed down her nose and rested for a moment on her lips. The pine scent that seemed so much a part of him touched her, and it was hard to determine if it were the man or the deep woods nearby that captured her senses. Her glance swept the smooth curve of his chin, then moved up his slim nose to the eyes, which he closed as he drank the water. She could see that he was as thirsty as she.

Aware that she was staring, she turned and looked out across the landscape. A doe stood at the edge of the woods, its ears perked. Something moved behind the doe, something small and light brown. The doe had a little one.

"I'm sorry," Jonathan said, breaking into her thoughts.

She leaned back on her arms and looked across at him. A worried frown creased his brow, and his eyes were troubled.

"For what?" she asked.

"For brawling with that idiot when I knew better."

"You put him in his place," she countered, thinking how she had respected his actions, once she had had time to think about them.

"It was a mistake. It will give some of them a reason to hate me more. And I don't want anyone bothering you after I'm gone."

"After you're gone," she echoed, then caught herself. She looked back toward the woods, hoping to see the doe again. She didn't want to think about Jonathan leaving. Not now.

"I'll be leaving soon," he said, as though to emphasize his point.

"Why?" She looked into his eyes and felt her heart quicken. She didn't know if it was his kindness to her dying father or his gentleness with her mother, but something about Jonathan made it easy to love him. Despite the fact that he was a Yankee. She swallowed and began again. "There's no hurry. You don't have to leave after you repair the gate. And you don't have to fix the gate, you know."

"I want to. But. . ."

"But what?" She searched his face, longing to read his mind, to know exactly what he was thinking.

Without looking at her, he stood up and gazed at something in the distance. "It wouldn't be a good idea for me to stay any longer. You see the hostility people feel toward me."

She thought about that. "But it would probably be the same if I were visiting in your area."

He reached out a hand to help her up. A wry grin touched the corners of his mouth. "You're too pretty to pick on."

"You know what I mean." She grinned, still holding his hand.

"I'm not sure of anything anymore," he said, squeezing her hand. "I do know that you and I live in different worlds. Still. . ." He turned, leading the way back to her horse as they held hands. "Still, I'm glad we met," he said as she leaned against him to place her foot in the stirrup.

Because she was a bundle of nerves, her boot slipped out of the stirrup, and she lunged even closer to him. The arms that had steadied her pulled her closer. She tilted her head back to look into his face. His blue eyes captured her, and she felt her senses whirling. She moved closer to him, wanting him to kiss her, hoping he would.

He hesitated for a moment, as though reluctant, but then he lowered his head, and his lips brushed hers, gently, sweetly. The kiss lasted only a moment, yet time seemed to stand still for Grace. She had never before felt such sweet longing. But Jonathan's blue eyes deepened, and he turned toward the stirrup, holding it firmly.

Taking the hint, she placed her boot firmly in the stirrup and swung herself into the saddle. He gathered up the reins, stroked his horse's neck for a second, then mounted.

Nothing was said as they rode back to Riverwood. Grace stared at the barren fields bordering the road, but she was no longer thinking of the doe and the little one, or the landscape, or the war, or anything else. Something was happening between Jonathan and her, and she was afraid to think about it. She told herself not to get serious about him, but her heart refused to listen. She was falling in love with him, and she knew it; worse, she couldn't seem to help herself.

"Your mother is sitting out on the porch," Jonathan said as they rode up the lane.

"Yes, I suppose she'll go on sitting out there every afternoon, reading the Bible and hoping Father will magically appear."

She studied her mother, sitting very still in the cane-backed rocker, her little face tilted toward them. Grace was amazed at how peaceful her mother looked. Grace rarely felt at peace, and she certainly could not sit still long enough to loiter on the porch.

"Maybe she's only waiting for us," she said, hoping that at last her mother had decided to accept the sad truth.

Jonathan pulled the reins back on his horse and alighted from the saddle, and again she let him help her down. *Might as well enjoy it while I can,* she thought, stealing a look at him. Their eyes met and held, and she remembered the kiss and looked nervously at her mother.

Once Jonathan had helped her down and she'd brushed off her skirt, she stole another glance at her mother, whose smile was still in place.

"Mother, we got what we needed," Grace called, walking up the steps to the porch. She glanced over her shoulder, watching Jonathan remove their package from his saddlebag. "And Jonathan bought some jars of pickles and relish that the Confederate widows are selling."

He approached the steps, looking a bit embarrassed by her compliments.

"That was a very nice thing to do, by the way," Grace added.

"Would you two like to sit on the porch for a while? Grace, you could make some lemonade." The older woman looked from Grace back to Jonathan. "I sit here every day, waiting—"

"Mother. . .you know what Jonathan came to tell us," Grace said, beginning to feel exasperated by her mother's behavior. "You have to accept the truth. Father is not coming home."

Elizabeth shook her head, her eyes still focused on the lane. "God has assured me Fred will come home."

"Mother, stop it!" Grace cried out. "Please don't do this. You're only hurting yourself. And you're hurting me."

Her mother acted as though she had not heard her daughter's anguished words. She said nothing, yet she never stopped scanning the lane.

Grace fought back tears of frustration. She whirled to Jonathan, who had climbed the porch steps and stood at a distance, looking slightly embarrassed.

"Jonathan, tell her Father is dead, that he isn't coming home."

His blue eyes darkened as he looked from Grace to her mother. For a moment, he seemed to be locked in an inner conflict over what to say. Then he looked back at Grace. "I can't say for sure that he is never coming back, Grace."

Grace glared at him. "What do you mean? You came all this way to bring the Bible, to tell us he was dying."

"Yes, he was dying. But he was alive when I left, and even though I doubt he could have lasted long, I can't say for sure that your father is dead."

"Don't do this!" she lashed out at him. "Of course he is dead. If not, we would have heard from him. Father had an iron will; I know that. If he had any hope of living, he would not have sent you here." Tears were streaming down her cheeks, tears of anger and hopelessness borne from having to endure so much heartache.

"Fred will come back to me," her mother said softly from behind them. "In the meantime, I will cling to my faith, and I will wait for him."

"Oh Mother," Grace sobbed, turning back to her. "I guess you can believe whatever you want. But I'm sick and tired of hoping and trusting and praying and trying to do the right thing and still ending up miserable and unhappy. I keep thinking every day will get better, but it doesn't."

"Grace, the war is over," Jonathan said. "Don't you consider that an answer to prayer?"

She lowered her head, ashamed that she was whimpering like a child. Dashing her hand across her cheek, she sniffed and shrugged. "Other folks' prayers have been answered, I guess." She blinked back the tears and looked into his face, feeling a rush of anger when she thought about how he would go back to

Kentucky to a family. "Your family's prayers."

"Yes, He has answered our prayers. And I pray that in time God can heal your anger. I think you are a very brave young woman."

She blinked. This was not the response she had expected, but before she could frame a reply, he had turned back to her mother.

"Mrs. Cunningham, I don't think I have ever known anyone as strong in their faith as you. I see why your husband spoke so fondly of you. And his last words reflected his faith and yours. He spoke of the church."

"Oh yes," Elizabeth sighed. "We loved our little church. When he returns we will start services there again."

"Mother—" Grace bit her lip. How could she keep on living in the past, hoping and believing and never once considering how they were going to eat, how they were going to pay taxes. And Jonathan Parker was making her worse.

A cardinal had sailed down from the live oak to perch on the porch rail. It chirped peacefully, which seemed an odd background for the conflict raging on the porch.

"Come inside, please," Grace said through gritted teeth, glaring up at Jonathan.

Leading the way into the house, she charged down the hall to the dim kitchen. Once she had stepped inside, she whirled, waiting until he crossed the threshold.

"How dare you encourage her in this. Mother is losing her mind, can't you tell? I had hoped you could convince her to accept the truth so that she would stop escaping reality. But now you've made things worse. You've given her encouragement to keep on playing this silly game. You have no right to come here and do this to us."

He leaned against the doorway, narrowing his eyes at her. "Come here and do what? Return your father's Bible? Say a few kind words? Whether you like it or not, you aren't going to change your mother's feelings. Nor will I. I'm not going to be cruel to that dear woman, and you're being cruel to take all hope from her."

While he had not raised his voice, his blue eyes were cold, slashing her up and down.

Grace took a deep breath and met Jonathan Parker's gaze. She was in the throes of a good fight, and she was not about to back down.

"Then if you don't approve of my manner of handling things, I suggest you be on your way. You've done your good deed—you've fulfilled your obligation. Don't let us detain you." She practically spat the words at him as she rushed past him, brushing against his shoulder on her way to the stairs.

"Grace," her mother's voice caught her on the second stair. "I'm ashamed of you."

She whirled, seeing her mother standing in the hall, her hands clasped before her. Her hazel eyes were sad, yet no anger showed in her face or voice. She had merely stated a fact. Elizabeth turned to Jonathan, who was trying to pass her in the hall without being obtrusive.

"Jonathan." She laid a hand on his arm, "I want you to come back and have a bite to eat before you leave. Fred would not want you to leave our home without a gracious good-bye. I'll expect to see you back." Her voice was firm, and Grace could only stare at her. It was as though her mother had suddenly emerged as the woman she had once been. For a moment Grace believed that she was as sane as ever, that she only escaped to her world of fantasy to hide from her heartbreak.

"Thank you, Mrs. Cunningham. I'll do that."

Without a glance toward the stairs, Jonathan hurried up the hall.

Grace turned and flew up the stairs. She had to get to her room fast. Her mother's words had drained the anger from Grace's soul, and she was stung by the reprimand. In the depths of her conscience, she regretted the words she had spoken to

Jonathan. Even more, she was sorry her mother had heard what she had said about her. Her mother was like a fragile little bird with a broken wing; Grace had no right to be cruel to her. For all of Mother's talk about faith, God hadn't changed things after all. He had merely shown her someone she could never have for her own.

Grace trudged into her room to change clothes. She still had time to work in the garden, and it always calmed her down to put her hands in the soil. She would stay busy out back, avoiding Jonathan Parker. After he repaired the gate and came back for his horse, she wouldn't have to speak to him again. And she would be glad when he was gone.

She grabbed up some clean work clothes and changed out of her riding habit. As she dressed, her mother's words continued to haunt her.

"Just forget it," Grace snapped to herself. She took a deep breath and made her way outside to the row of beans. At least there was plenty to keep her busy.

An hour later, she heard a familiar voice. "Miss Grace?"

She turned to see Reams standing at the corner of the house, holding a small brown sack. He wore faded overalls and a clean gray shirt, and below his felt hat, silver hair framed his dark face and highlighted large dark eyes. He grinned, warming Grace's heart.

"Hi, Reams." She dusted her hands on her overalls and walked up to the backyard. "How's Chloe?"

"She's her usual cantankerous self," he said chuckling. He and his wife adored one another even though they constantly teased. "Sent you some fresh eggs. You know, Mr. Douglas bought more hens."

"How thoughtful of you. Come on inside. It's time for me to take a break."

"Yes'm. I was just talking with that fella down there fixing your fence. He seems mighty nice."

Grace lowered her eyes as her conscience indicted her once again. "He saved Father's life," she said, leading the way to the house.

"Yes'm. I spoke to Miss 'Lizbeth on the front porch. She told me about it. Said she was about to make him some lunch."

Grace could hear the clatter of dishes from the kitchen and guessed her mother was already preparing the food. "Why don't you stay and eat with us?"

"I reckon Mr. Douglas won't mind."

"Of course not," she called over her shoulder. Reams and Chloe had been at Oak Grove for over twenty years. They were treated like family and had no desire to leave.

As she scraped her boots on the back doorstep, she heard her mother talking, then she heard Jonathan's deep voice. She hesitated. Reams was coming up the steps behind her, and she remembered she had invited him to lunch. She wasn't going to hide down in the garden as though she were afraid to face him, so squaring her shoulders she led the way into the kitchen.

Her mother was pouring coffee for Jonathan. He sat at the trestle table with a plate of biscuits and preserves.

"Reams is going to join us." Grace spoke quickly, trying to cover her embarrassment about her treatment of Jonathan.

"Good. Have a seat, Reams." Jonathan said, avoiding Grace's eyes as well.

Reams settled down on the bench beside Jonathan.

"I was just relating a story that Mr. Cunningham told me about crossing the Warrior River back during flood days. He was a very brave man," Jonathan said, looking at Reams.

"Yes sir, he was," Reams said. "And Mr. Fred was a good man. I feel sorry for you, Miss Elizabeth. And for you, Miss Grace."

Grace turned and smiled at Reams. "We're managing." Then she turned to finish washing her hands, wishing she hadn't sounded so defensive.

"We are grateful to Jonathan for traveling a long way on a mission from Fred," Elizabeth said. She had not poured coffee for herself, nor was she eating anything.

"Yes'm," Reams said quietly.

A moment of silence hung over them as everyone suddenly seemed at a loss for words. Then Reams cleared his throat and nodded. "Sir, could I ask you something?"

"Sure."

Grace poured herself half a cup of coffee. After rationing themselves on coffee for so long, it still seemed wasteful to have more than one cup a day. But this was a special occasion, she told herself, sneaking a glance toward the table where the men sat.

"Well," Reams continued slowly, "we being admirers of President Lincoln, we been grieving about the assassination. What do you know of the man who shot him?"

"Oh, you mean John Wilkes Booth." For the second time since she had known him, Grace watched Jonathan's jaw clench in anger. "Booth was a madman who professed loyalty to the South, although he was never loyal enough to join the Confederate Army. He had a burning hatred of slavery and of Abraham Lincoln. I've heard that he had concocted some wild scheme to kidnap President Lincoln and take him to Richmond with the intention of exchanging him for prisoners. But then he decided to kill the president instead."

Silence settled over the kitchen as everyone listened to Jonathan. Grace found herself admiring his intelligence and his strong, yet gentle spirit. She had never met anyone like this man, and she was feeling terrible about what she'd said to him. She didn't want him to leave. Not yet. But how could she keep him here? What could she possibly say or do to change his mind when he was determined to go?

"Reams, Mr. Cunningham told me he had never owned slaves, that he never would. He said he employed Irishmen to work the fields. Where did these men go?"

Reams sat back and shook his head. "I don't rightly know."

Grace spoke up. "Once Father left, they scattered. I think

some joined the army; others went to seek relatives. None are in the county. I wish they were," she said, taking her seat on the bench opposite the men.

No one spoke for a few minutes, as they drank their coffee and pondered the nation's plight. Then Jonathan spoke up again. "I know there are men who need work. If we could get a few good men to clear some of your fields and plant cotton—"

"But we have no money to pay them," Grace said.

Reams sighed and looked from Grace to Elizabeth. "I'd better be going." He stood up slowly and Jonathan extended his hand.

"It was nice meeting you," he said to Reams.

"Will you be staying a few days?" Reams asked.

"I've asked him to please stay another day," Elizabeth spoke up, her voice soft and gentle.

Grace stole a glance at Jonathan and saw that he was watching her reaction to the news. She realized that her mother and even Reams were looking at her as well. She fiddled with a strand of hair brushing her cheek. She didn't know how to backtrack on her order for him to leave. Then Reams spoke up, saving her from an awkward situation.

"You were asking about help here. I'd been thinking of riding over to see two of my cousins at Jina. Mr. Douglas could use two more hands, and maybe they could kind of help out."

"Good idea," Jonathan said. "Reams, what do you think could be grown here on a small scale?"

Reams hesitated, looking from Jonathan to Grace and back again. "Lots of folks is planting corn. It don't bring what cotton did, but it's cheap enough to plant and tend. And I could help out. Mr. Douglas would let me do that, I reckon."

"How kind of both of you." Elizabeth turned to them, a new light shining in the hazel eyes that had so often looked weary and distracted.

"Corn," Jonathan said, grinning as though he remembered something.

"What are you thinking?" Grace asked.

"I was just thinking of all the times as a soldier I would go into a cornfield and get half-ripened corn and eat it to keep going."

"Half-ripened corn?" Grace stared at him.

He nodded. "Believe me, if you're hungry enough, it isn't bad. In fact, I preferred it over flour and water fried in lard. That was our meal many nights. I watched one soldier eat a bullfrog," he said, making a face.

"Ain't bad," Reams said, chuckling. "I've eaten a few frog legs in my day. Quite tasty."

Suddenly they were all smiling and laughing with Reams. Grace felt the tension from their argument slipping away as she met Jonathan's gaze, and he smiled at her.

Then Jonathan turned and looked at Reams. "You have a good idea about growing corn. Let's see what we can do about that." He looked back at Grace and smiled.

As Grace returned his smile, she considered his offer of helping to get some corn planted. If he wanted to do them a favor, why not let him?

"Since I haven't finished with the gate, I'd better get back to work," Jonathan said, standing up.

"And I'd better get back to the garden," Grace said.

"And this evening I'll prepare the meal," Elizabeth announced, smiling at Grace.

Grace smiled back, pleased to see her mother being active again. Jonathan whistled as he went out the back door. And as Grace returned to the garden, she felt a sense of relief that she had not experienced in a very long time.

Chapter 6

After supper, Elizabeth suggested they sit out on the porch. It seemed to be the place where she was happiest, and Grace and Jonathan thought it a good idea.

They sat on the front porch for an hour, talking in generalities. Elizabeth asked Jonathan about Kentucky, and he spoke fondly of his home, giving them an interesting look at another part of the country. No reference was made to the war.

When Elizabeth decided to go in, Jonathan looked at Grace. It was obvious he was unsure if he should stay with Grace or go inside.

"We can sit out for a while longer, if you want," Grace said.

He smiled and leaned back in his chair. Neither spoke. Grace suspected he was still feeling awkward about their argument, and she decided it was time to make her peace.

"I'm sorry about today. I. . .regret what I said to you."

He was thoughtful for a moment. "It's okay."

Silence stretched between them again, and Grace felt compelled to explain her position a bit more. "I just get tired of wishing that Mother could accept reality. Father isn't coming home, and we have to accept that and go on with our lives."

"I can understand how you feel about that. Yet I'm fascinated by your mother's strength. I believe she's in full command of her senses, Grace. I've had the opportunity to spend some time with her, and I sincerely believe that she needs to think about your father returning in order to cope with the. . .loss. She believes there is still some hope, and who's to say she isn't right?"

Grace felt a tug of war starting in her heart. "But I can't feel that way, don't you see? It's as though we never get out of the past, but we have to move on, even though we hate what has happened."

"I understand, and I think you are very brave."

She sighed. "Oh Jonathan, I'm not that brave. I'm just like thousands of women who are trying to survive. We go on because we have no choice. As for Mother and her faith. . ." She paused, thinking.

"Mother clings to her faith, spending hours with the Bible and trying to get me to do the same. But God and I have had a falling out. He doesn't seem to be listening to our prayers. I can understand Him not paying attention to mine, for I've been rebellious and sassy. But my folks have always been very religious, attending church. They even helped build a church up on Sand Mountain before we moved here. Why has God let all these terrible things happen to our family?"

"Grace, as you said a few minutes ago, thousands of women have endured the kind of tragedy you and your mother are facing. Some women have lost their husbands and their sons. It's happened in the North as well as here. Who can explain it? As human beings, we have no answers. To me, it seems useless to try and figure it out."

She looked across at him, studying his chiseled features in the moonlight. She knew what he was saying made sense, that he was probably right, but it didn't make her feel better. Yet in another way, she did feel better.

"Thanks for listening to me," she said. "It helps to talk. I know that. There just hasn't been anyone to say these things to because I sound so bitter. And you're right; everyone has suffered from the war."

He turned and smiled at her. Though nothing was said, it seemed they had made their peace and learned more about each other in the process.

This silence between them was peaceful. A light breeze stirred through the trees, and a full moon poured silver light across the landscape.

"It's beautiful here," Jonathan said, staring out at the trees.

"I do love it," Grace replied. "Even though I do a lot of fussing, it doesn't really mean I don't love Riverwood. I'm as tied to the land as Father and Freddy were."

"When you speak of them, I can see that you remember happy times."

She nodded. "Good family times. I'm grateful we had that." She looked across at him, thinking again how nice it was to have someone to talk to, someone like Jonathan, who was kind and sympathetic.

"And you should be grateful," he said. "During the war, I met all kinds of men. Sadly, some seemed to have no attachment to home and family; others were planning to go out West rather than return to the homes they had left before the war."

Grace was curious about his part in the war. She hadn't wanted to ask earlier, for she didn't want to think about him fighting on the opposite side. But he had shown only kindness to her family, and she was grateful he had survived.

"When did you join the army? And where did you fight?"

Even in the shadows, she could see her questions had startled him, but he did not hesitate in answering.

"I joined the Union Army after the Battle of Bull Run."

There was no need to ask why. Grace knew the Confederates had won the Battle of Bull Run, or Manassas as Southerners called it.

"I think the North was shocked by that victory," he continued. "People realized this was going to be a difficult war. At first, I didn't want to be a soldier." He spoke slowly, looking out into the darkness. "I hated the idea of fighting in a war where family members actually fought each other. We had heard of this with our neighbors who had just settled in Kentucky from Georgia. They knew they would be fighting their cousins." He leaned his head back against the chair and closed his eyes. "But I had no choice. I had to defend my beliefs."

As she listened to him, she began to see the war through the eyes of someone on the other side. He had not wanted to go to war, nor had he rushed in at the very beginning, as Freddy had. She shook her head and closed her eyes. "What a long, pitiful battle it was—for everyone."

They sat in silence. Only the distant call of a whippoorwill filled the moonlit night. Grace opened her eyes and saw that Jonathan had stood up and was reaching for her hand. "You are an amazing woman. You've been so strong for your mother. I know it's been difficult."

"Yes," she whispered, stepping closer to him. She was hoping he would kiss her again and they could stop talking about sad things. There had been enough sadness in their lives. She tilted her head back and looked up into his face, wondering why he didn't kiss her.

"Grace," he said gently, "I like you very much, more than I want to think about. But we can't feel this way. There is no future."

She caught her breath. Her mind rushed for words, but she could find none. She wished he wouldn't try to be so sensible. Maybe there was no future, but they still had the present. And she so wanted to be happy for a change.

"You're much too serious," she whispered, searching his eyes for hope. She found none.

"I have to be serious when I know the facts. There is so much bitterness, so much hatred. We both saw it today."

"I don't care," she cried. "I just want to be happy."

"So do I," he said, dropping her hand. "But we each have to find happiness in a different way. I have to return to Kentucky."

"Why do you keep reminding me?" she lashed out. "You seem to want to be miserable and to keep me that way. Can't you forget for a moment all the sad terrible things out there? Can't you look at me and pretend to care about me?"

"I don't have to pretend," he said huskily, staring down into her face.

It was all the encouragement she needed. She stood on tiptoe and kissed his lips, and in a moment he was responding. His arms circled her waist and pulled her closer as the kiss deepened. He pulled away, shaking his head.

"I can't do this. I'm older than you, and after all I've witnessed the past four years, I should know better than to hope for anything between a Northern man and a Southern woman."

But Grace smiled. In her heart she knew she was going to change his mind about everything. She loved him, and it was only a matter of time until he admitted that he loved her, too.

Chapter 7

When Grace awoke the next morning, the sunlight streamed over her bed, and a bird sang sweetly outside her window. Her first thought as her eyes opened to a new day was Jonathan Parker.

He was a wonderful man, she decided. Then she remembered the way he had kissed her. A lazy grin crossed her face, and she shivered with delight. She doubted that she would ever forget that kiss. And she would probably never enjoy another kiss as much. She nestled into the pillow, relishing the memory of standing with him in the moonlight, feeling the tingle of first love from her head to her toes.

"So that's what love is all about," she said to herself, and a feeling of joy flowed through her. She had heard girls talk about being in love, but she had given up all hope of it ever happening to her. Now it had.

She sat up in bed and peered into the mirror. Her thick blond hair was tousled about her face, but her eyes were wide open and glowing like the full moon last night. That silly little smile kept tugging her lips up. She was pleased with her reflection as she turned and tossed the covers back and padded barefoot to the washstand.

Later, when she sauntered down the stairs to investigate the whereabouts of Jonathan Parker, she found her mother in the kitchen, puttering around the pantry.

"Good morning, Mother."

Her mother peered around the pantry door. "Hello, dear," she smiled. "He's down there fixing the gate."

"Already?" she frowned, wondering if he had slept at all.

"Dear, it's nine o'clock. You really slept late." Her mother smiled at her. "Are you hungry?"

Grace spotted some leftover biscuits on the cabinet, along with the pot of coffee. "I'm so grateful for coffee," she said, remembering how it had been rationed during the war. They still were unable to buy sugar.

"I could smell the coffee when I came downstairs. Jonathan was sitting out on the porch, drinking coffee and eating a biscuit." She paused, looking at Grace and smiling. "I guess he likes your biscuits."

Grace merely grinned as she reached down to pluck a fat brown biscuit from the plate. "I like them, too," she said. Then she reached for a mug and poured herself a cup of coffee.

Elizabeth had emerged from the pantry with a pan of potatoes and a paring knife. "I'm going to start lunch."

"Thanks," Grace said, biting into her biscuit. She was relieved to see her mother busy. Some days all she did was read her Bible and stare out the window.

Finishing her biscuit, Grace sipped her coffee and wandered toward the front door. Pushing it open, she stepped out onto the porch and sat down in the chair. As she did, her eyes lingered on the spot where Jonathan had kissed her. She felt as though she had swallowed all the silver light of the moon from the night before.

She sat back in the chair and looked down the lane. She could hear the sound of the hammer pelting wood as Jonathan worked on the gate. Then Grace frowned. What would happen when the gate was fixed?

Grace's thoughts hung in suspension for a moment. Then his words from the evening before filled her mind. *We have to find happiness in a different way. . . . I have to return to Kentucky.*

Her eyes closed with pain. She would think of something to detain him. She needed him here. His family was managing their lives without him; his father had died before the war began. And he had said his mother and his sister would want to stay in Louisville.

She opened her eyes, feeling better. Suddenly she remembered what he had said to Reams. He had asked about finding someone to help Grace and her mother. A pleased little smile tilted her lips. Mr. Jonathan Parker might find out that obtaining farm help would not be so easy after all. She had heard Mr. Douglas complaining about how difficult it was for him to find field hands.

She frowned. If they did find someone to work, how was she supposed to pay them?

She stood up and began to pace the porch. For a minute she almost wished they could stay in the stalemate they were in, just to keep Jonathan with them. Yet she knew they had to get on with their lives. That meant she needed help in getting the land cleared and replanted. After all, there was a limit to how long Mr. Britton would wait on his loan, and she and her mother couldn't depend on their little garden to feed them forever.

Grace paced back and forth, seriously concerned. She hated having to be the head of the house, worrying about all the decisions that a man should rightfully make. She wanted to be a woman in love with a man; she wanted to think about marriage and a family. Her pacing stopped as she reached the end of the porch. Leaning against the rail, she stared out at the overgrown cotton fields. She took a long deep breath and felt herself age another year or two. She knew she would have to deal with reality, not lounge around in her daydreams, as her mother so often did. Bitterness welled up again, putting a bad taste in her mouth.

She turned and walked inside the house. In the hall, she spotted her father's Bible on the mahogany table. Something prompted her to reach for it and hug it gently against herself.

She had not read her Bible in a very long time, not since she had been carrying on this personal war with God. Now, she traced her fingers on the leather cover, seeing the chipped places and wishing the Bible could talk back to her. How she longed to know what Father had experienced, where he had been, what had finally happened to him.

Holding the Bible, she walked back outside and sat down in the chair once again. She opened the Bible to the center and began to read Psalms, always her favorite book. She had learned Psalm 23 by heart as a little girl, and she had made her parents proud by reciting it to them. As she read the chapter again, each word seemed to speak to her personally.

She looked up from the Bible and stared blankly across the yard, thinking. If the Lord was her shepherd, truly *her* shepherd, then He was supposed to guide her through the valleys, beside still water, and He was to restore her soul.

Restoring her soul would be a major task, she thought, yet the verses brought pleasant memories of childhood with her family seated together around the hearth. Her parents were deeply religious, and she had always marveled that they could be so trusting of God.

For years, she herself had thought God had forsaken them, yet. . . She felt a wave of tenderness sweep through her. Yet Jonathan had come to them; her earthly father had sent him, or perhaps the heavenly Father had a hand in it as well.

For the first time, a small glimmer of hope began to flicker within her, like a tiny delicate flame sputtering to life. If she nurtured that hope, believed in it, trusted God as her parents always had, maybe He would prepare that table of plenty before them, maybe their cup would run over again. Maybe He would somehow restore their souls.

She turned the page and saw that her father had marked verse five; she looked at it, wondering why. Frowning, she read on.

"Thou preparest a. . ." He had marked through *"table"* and written *"treasure."* Then the text continued *"before me in the. . ."* Here he had marked through *"presence"* and written *"New Bethany Church."*

"You anoint my. . ." He had marked through *"head with oil"* and written *"field with apple trees."*

As Grace read on, she saw that none of the other verses were marked. At the end of the psalm, he had written the words: *"October 3, 1863."*

Staring at the date, an odd chill began at the base of her spine and slowly worked its way up her spinal cord and settled in the nerve center at her neck. She reread the passage again. And again.

The door opened behind her, and her mother stepped outside.

"I've peeled the potatoes and covered them with water. They're on the hearth now," she said with a smile.

Grace hadn't heard a word. "Mother, did you see what Father wrote in the Bible he sent to you? Here in Psalm 23? Does this mean anything to you?" She fired the questions at her mother so fast that at first her mother seemed confused.

Looking from Grace to the Bible in her lap, then back at Grace, her mother sat down in the nearest chair.

"Here, Mother. Look at this again."

Grace watched the tiny frown of concentration slip over her mother's forehead as her eyes moved over each verse and then lingered on the inscriptions. She looked up at Grace. "When Jonathan gave me your father's Bible, I read Psalm 23 right away because this psalm was our favorite."

She looked back at the verse. "I didn't understand why Fred had written those words in; then I finally decided he was making a reference to the apple trees we helped plant in the churchyard. You remember how he loved apples?"

Grace reached over and gripped her mother's hand. "Mother, I believe this is a code. Look at the date at the end of the chapter."

"Yes, I saw that, too. I assumed that was the last time he read it."

Grace jumped out of the chair and began to pace the porch, her mind jumping from one word to another, and ending up again on the date he had written at the end of the psalm.

"Mother, why would Father be so insistent on Jonathan bringing that Bible all the way back down here to us? He told him to put the Bible in your hands, remember? Why would he ask a stranger, for he was a stranger in some ways, to personally deliver the Bible to us? That doesn't make sense unless he had a very strong motive for. . .as he said, putting the Bible in your hands. He knew you would read that psalm, which had been a favorite of yours and his; and he took a chance that you would understand."

Elizabeth gasped. "Oh Grace. If you're right, it would have been a terrible thing for me not to interpret his message. But remember the other thing. Fred wanted Jonathan to let us know. . .what had happened to him."

"Yes, but Jonathan also said he kept mentioning the church. Don't you remember? We thought he meant go to any church, or perhaps to the church down the road. But he meant for us to go back to New Bethany Church to look for the treasure under the apple tree. Oh Mother, it all makes sense now."

Elizabeth nodded and looked at the inscriptions again. "Freddy used to dress up and pretend he was an explorer when he was a little boy. He always had your father send him notes about buried treasure—"

"You see, that's it! I believe with all of my heart Father was sending a message to us. And I intend to go to New Bethany Church and find that treasure, just as he intended us to."

"But a treasure?" her mother asked, reading the verse again.

"I don't know what's buried there, Mother, but if it was important enough for Father to get the message to us, I owe it to him—and to us—to see what he left there."

She looked down the lane and saw Jonathan walking back toward the house.

"What are you going to do, Grace?" Her mother stood up, looking anxious for the first time.

Grace laced her fingers together, pressing against her palms, and considered the choices she had, which were indeed limited. Her eyes followed the slow easy gait of the man who had come on a mission from her father, a mission that could change their lives.

"If Father trusted Jonathan Parker, then I think we have every right to believe he thought we could trust him as well." As Jonathan grew closer, she whispered her decision to her mother. "I'm going to ask Jonathan to go with me to Sand Mountain. If I'm right and Father hid any kind of treasure there, then I'll offer to share it with Jonathan in return for his help."

A frown worked its way over her mother's forehead. "Grace, we can't be sure about this. And I don't want to risk losing you." She reached out, gripping her hand and looking at her with pleading eyes.

"You aren't going to lose me, Mother," Grace said, hugging her mother and feeling her ribs beneath her fingertips. Her mother had lost more weight. In her father's absence, Grace knew she had to be strong for both of them.

She placed her hands on her mother's shoulders and leaned back to look into her kind hazel eyes. "Your faith has kept you strong and courageous; this morning, I decided that it's time for me to start acting more like you. Please forgive me for doubting your faith," she said, watching the sheen of tears appear in her mother's eyes.

"I love you, Grace," her mother said, looking frail and vulnerable again.

"And I love you. And we're going to be all right, Mother. We will get through these hard times, and we'll be strong again."

"Grace, you've always been strong. Just like Fred."

They were smiling through their tears as Jonathan reached the porch. Looking from one to the other, his face registered surprise.

"Is everything okay?" he asked.

"Everything is just fine," Grace said, smiling at him.

"That's good. Well, I have the gate repaired," he said, looking very pleased about it.

"Thank you so much," Grace said. Her heart was beating faster as she watched him climb the steps and settle into the chair beside her. He had changed into work clothes, and in the faded blue shirt, he was just as handsome as he had been in his nice suit.

"Reams is going to ride over to visit his cousins this afternoon. You remember he mentioned they need work. Maybe he can talk them into coming here and between you and Mr. Douglas, you can come to some kind of agreement with them."

"Thank you." Grace looked at him, wondering for one last time if it were safe to trust him. She was certain that God had sent him to them; after all, he had been the one to bring the Bible with the important message. In her heart, she knew that it was safe to trust this man.

"Come inside," she said to Jonathan, glancing at her mother. "We need to discuss something with you."

Jonathan took a look at her and hesitated. "You sound very serious."

"Yes, please come in so we can talk," she said, automatically glancing around her. She was constantly looking over her shoulder, even though with Jonathan at their side, she felt more safe than she had since the war began.

Once they were in the dining room, seated at the table drinking coffee, Grace opened her father's Bible to Psalm 23. She handed the Bible to Jonathan.

"Read these verses, and notice what my father has marked. Then tell me what you think."

Elizabeth had entered the dining room and sat at the end of the table, watching Jonathan as he read the verses.

Grace watched his eyebrows lift. He stopped reading for a moment and looked at her but said nothing. Then he began reading again. When he had finished, he shook his head.

"In a way, this is pretty confusing to me. It does strike me as odd that he has marked through these verses and made some notations. What seems strangest of all is the date here. October 3, 1863."

"That's exactly what I think."

Jonathan looked over Grace's head to the window, as though

pondering something. Then he looked back at Grace. "Your father told me he joined up with General Braxton Bragg when he came through northern Alabama after leaving Shiloh. Your father would have been in the Battle of Chattanooga and Chickamauga in the fall. That's when he wrote this date in the Bible."

"Then he wasn't too far from Sand Mountain at that time," Elizabeth interjected. "Jonathan, we moved down here to Pickens County from Sand Mountain, where we had lived for eleven years. While we lived there, we helped to build New Bethany Church at Pine Grove. Fred and I planted an apple tree in front of the church."

"You see," Grace turned back to Jonathan. "I'm absolutely certain this is a code from my father. I don't understand its full meaning, but I believe with all of my heart that my father left something at New Bethany Church for us. And Jonathan. . ." She paused and took a deep breath, gathering her courage to ask. "I know you need to get back to Kentucky, but I want to make a deal with you."

"A deal?" he asked, looking from Grace to her mother.

She hesitated, wondering for a moment what kind of deal he thought she was going to propose to him. "Yes, a deal." She plunged on. "Obviously I cannot go that distance by myself." She hesitated, glancing at her mother. "Well, if I had no choice, I would probably strike out on my own, in spite of Mother's protests."

"You know I wouldn't allow you to do that," Elizabeth spoke up nervously, her gaze darting from Grace to Jonathan.

"You want me to go with you," Jonathan said, sparing her the discomfort of having to ask.

"Yes, and if Father has hidden a treasure there, I will share it with you for helping me. Whatever it is."

He shook his head. "I wouldn't feel right doing that. Your father saved my life and—"

"And you saved his life before that. Please, Jonathan, tell me you'll go with me. Then after I satisfy myself as to whether or not there is something there, I promise not to ask anything more of you. In fact, we can part company at Sand Mountain, and you can go on to Kentucky."

He shook his head. "I can't allow you to make the trip back alone. But Grace, before you get your hopes up, I have to tell you something. It's quite likely that your father buried money, not knowing for sure that Confederate money would lose its value."

"That's true," Grace sighed. "But even if that's what is buried there, I still will be glad to go and find out for myself."

Jonathan nodded. "I wish we could find someone else to go with you, Grace. Or go for you. I've been out of service for a month now. I really need to go on to Kentucky."

Elizabeth spoke up. "Jonathan, I wonder if you could send a wire to your family, letting them know that you are safe but that you've been detained."

Grace brightened. "Yes! That's a good idea, Mother." She looked at Jonathan. "The telegraph is back in operation in some areas. Surely along the way. . ."

He raked his fingers through his dark hair as though wrestling with his decision. For a moment, Grace had a terrible feeling that he was going to say no, but then as he looked back at her mother, he slowly began to smile.

"All right. I'll wire my brother-in-law at the first place we come to." He heaved a deep sigh. "Grace, we'll go to this New Bethany Church and see if you're right about this. If your father buried something there, we'll do our best to find it."

"Maybe he buried gold," Elizabeth said quietly.

"But where would he get gold? That's the only part that bothers me," Grace said, trying to figure it all out. "I believe he did send us this message, and I think it all makes sense. But where would he get gold, or even enough money to consider a treasure, for that matter? He was fighting in a war."

"An officer gave me a horse," Jonathan countered, looking

from Grace to her mother. "Maybe someone paid your father for saving a life or just for helping. Or did he have something he could have sold?"

Again, Grace looked to her mother for answers.

"He had his gold watch, which wouldn't be that valuable," she said. "I honestly don't know. But I believe this is a message from God." Grace's mother folded her hands together and smiled. "God began to answer our prayers when you came to us with news from Fred, Jonathan. And I believe those answers are just beginning."

She took a deep breath. "Grace, after thinking about it, I would like to ask Jonathan to go without you. That's a long trip, and it would be too hard on you."

"No, Mother." Grace frowned. "I want to go; I have to go."

"But Grace. . ." Elizabeth looked from Grace to Jonathan. "I hesitate to mention this, but we must consider how it will look to other people, the two of you traveling alone."

Jonathan looked at her mother, understanding her meaning, then back at Grace. "She's right. I can make the trip alone."

"No." Grace stood up. "Mother, this is no time to be worrying about what other people think. I'm going, and there's no talking me out of it."

Jonathan grinned at her. "I can see there's no point in trying. Mrs. Cunningham, I think I need to assure you that I will take very good care of Grace. I will not say or do anything to reflect badly on her. Or upon me," he added.

Grace felt her cheeks flush as she darted a glance at her mother. They were all talking about the same thing: if Jonathan could be trusted not to take advantage of her on this long trip.

"I believe you," Elizabeth said, "and I don't want to offend you."

He smiled and touched her hand. "You are just being a good mother, and I certainly respect that. I promise you," he said, looking into her eyes, "that I will behave as a gentleman at all times."

"That settles it then," Grace said, wanting to get on with

planning the trip. "Jonathan, while we're making deals here, you must agree to accept half of whatever we find."

"Grace is right," Elizabeth said. "You must accept half of whatever you two find there. We have always dealt fairly with people, and to ask anything more of you would be completely unfair."

Grace looked at Jonathan. She could see the inner battle he was waging. But then he began to shake his head slowly, and he put his hands out, palms up.

"How can I refuse two charming, persuasive ladies? Grace, can you be ready to travel at daylight?"

"I'm ready now," she answered eagerly.

He chuckled. "I'm sure you are, but we need to make some plans. I have some maps in my saddlebag, and I want to study the terrain. Also, we need to get the horses ready and. . ." His voice trailed. "I forgot you only have the gray horse."

"Molly will take me wherever I need to go," Grace said, feeling totally confident in Molly's ability.

"Are you sure?" He was obviously not as confident.

"Yes, I am. But if Molly quits on me, I can always ride behind you, can't I?"

"Well, yes. But—"

"Or if we do find gold, I can buy another horse. You see, I have it all figured out."

"I believe you do. It's settled then. We'll go. Mrs. Cunningham, how long will it take us to reach the area where you lived?"

Elizabeth pursed her lips. "We came in a wagon with extra horses, and it took us four days."

"So you camped three nights on the road," Jonathan said, glancing worriedly at Grace.

"Yes, but one night we stayed with some friends along the way who had been neighbors at Sand Mountain. And that reminds me, Grace, you know the Copeland family up around Jasper. You could stay one night at Ethel Copeland's house. Ethel would be pleased to have you. She's a very nice person."

Grace nodded. Ethel Copeland was a sister to Mrs. Douglas, and she and her husband had visited at Oak Grove during the summer and again at Christmas every year before the war began.

"Yes, I think we would be welcome at Mrs. Copeland's house. But I don't know if I can find her place."

"Just stop somewhere in Jasper and ask. Everyone knows Ethel Copeland. Her husband worked at the bank until he died."

Jonathan was deep in thought as they discussed the Copelands, but at the first opportunity he spoke up again. "We need to think about the route we'll take to get to Sand Mountain, Grace. I came down from Chattanooga through Huntsville, but it took three days of hard riding."

His blue eyes were filled with concern as he faced Grace. "Are you sure you're up to that kind of travel?" He began to smile for she had already begun to roll her eyes. "On second thought, I guess you can do about anything you put your mind to, am I right?"

"You are exactly right." She grinned at him.

"You'll need to take food," Elizabeth said, getting out of her chair to go into the kitchen to check the shelves in the pantry.

Jonathan and Grace got up to follow.

"I traveled with dried beans and salt pork in my saddlebag," Jonathan said. "There's still a small ration there. I keep a couple of cooking pans with me as well. Of course, we can stop at a store along the way and pick up rations as we need them."

"We have plenty of biscuits in the kitchen," Grace said, recalling how much he had enjoyed her biscuits.

"And I'll make up some corn dodgers," her mother called from inside the pantry.

Jonathan was puzzled. "Corn dodgers?"

"They're fried cornmeal but very tasty," Grace explained. "Not like that mixture you ate with the army."

"I used to prepare them for Fred when he was going to be

out for a while." Elizabeth's head popped around the door of the pantry. "You remember how he loved my corn dodgers, Grace?"

"Yes." Grace was thinking about clothes. "What else do we need, Jonathan?"

"I'll make a list," he said. "And I'll check your saddle and harness to see if they need any patching. I'll refill the canteen." He paused, then looked toward the pantry where they could hear Elizabeth rummaging around. "What about your mother?" he asked, shaping the question with his lips so that Elizabeth wouldn't hear.

Grace turned and looked toward the pantry. Why hadn't she thought of this sooner? She couldn't go off and leave her mother by herself. Then she thought of the usual answer: their neighbors, the Douglases.

"Jonathan, could you ride over to Mr. Douglas's place and see if Reams and his wife could come stay with Mother? I'll send a note saying. . .I'm not sure what I'll say."

"Why don't you let me think of something?" her mother suggested as she stepped out of the pantry. "In fact, don't worry about it now. I'm sure Reams will be over sometime today, and I'll ask him."

Grace nodded in agreement to the plan. "A note from you will be much more convincing, Mother. Mr. Douglas isn't about to say no to you."

They laughed together, and Grace breathed a sigh of relief. It seemed that finally God was beginning to answer their prayers.

Chapter 8

They left at first light the next morning. True to his word, Jonathan had both horses ready for travel, and he had stocked saddlebags with rations and drawn out a map for them to follow.

Grace was thankful they were traveling north and would not have to return to Whites Creek. For now, she wanted to put as much distance as possible between them and Sonny.

They set off at a brisk pace and had ridden for over an hour in silence. Grace had promised herself not to be a chatterbox or worry Jonathan unnecessarily. They had agreed to ride faster the first few hours while the horses were fresh, so conversation was scarce as they cantered their horses up the main road.

Only once did Grace worry about their safety. They had rounded a curve and come face-to-face with a man riding toward them on a sway-backed mule. He was the worst looking man Grace had ever seen. Beneath a cap of animal fur, his skin was blackened from smoke; the smell of fire was strong upon him. His clothes were filthy and ragged, and there was a strange glint in his hard eyes. Once they were close to him, he looked away as though avoiding their open stares.

After he was well behind them, Jonathan turned to Grace. "I've seen several men like that along the way. Bummers, they're called. They're thieves who roam the country, stealing, killing. You see now why I'm concerned for you and your mother."

Grace glanced back over her shoulder as the old mule and the strange man disappeared around the curve. "I think I'm better off not knowing about people like that," she said, wishing that she had never seen the man whose image was sure to haunt her memory, particularly in the middle of the night when she jumped at the slightest sound. "I hope Mother is all right," she said. She had hated to leave her mother for whom she felt so responsible.

"With Reams and his wife there, she'll be safe while we're gone."

Grace nodded. "Yes, thank God for Reams and Chloe."

Every bone in Grace's body ached by the time they reached Jasper, but she would have bitten her tongue off before she complained. They stopped to ask directions to Mrs. Copeland's house once they reached the outskirts of Jasper. As it turned out, they were only a short distance from their destination, and it was a relief to Grace to turn Molly up the circular drive to the brick house.

Grace studied the house, sitting at the top of the hill, recalling the fun she and Freddy had enjoyed when her parents had visited the Copelands. For a moment, her throat felt tight when she recalled those days, but she forced her mind to the task at hand: reminding Mrs. Copeland who she was so they could stay overnight.

Darkness was settling over the front porch as she wearily climbed the steps and knocked on the front door. She could hear footsteps moving quickly, approaching the entrance. Then the door opened, and Mrs. Copeland stood before her, looking as though she knew Grace but couldn't quite place her.

In the two years since Grace had seen the woman, Mrs. Copeland's hair had turned gray. Also, she was much thinner, which was not a surprise to Grace. Almost every woman she saw was thin because of the hardships they had faced during the war.

"Mrs. Copeland, I'm Grace Cunningham. My family lives on the farm adjoining the Douglases in Pickens County. Do you remember me?"

"Of course I do!" Mrs. Copeland responded. "Land's sake, what a beauty you've become. Do come in," she called, looking over Grace's head to Jonathan.

"Mrs. Copeland, this is Jonathan Parker," Grace made the introduction as he removed his hat and bowed. "Before he opens his mouth, I must tell you that he's from Kentucky, but he befriended my father during the war. And now he's doing a great favor for my mother and me, seeing me back to Sand Mountain."

"Hello, Mr. Parker. Come inside, both of you."

After a day spent looking at rough terrain for miles on end, Grace welcomed the feel of the cozy little house, where crocheted doilies, comfortable sofas, and chairs gave a sense of home.

Just then another woman came to the doorway of the kitchen, surveying them curiously.

"This is my older sister, Edith," Mrs. Copeland said. "Edith, come say hello to Grace Cunningham and her friend, Jonathan Parker."

"Cunningham?" Edith repeated, staring at first Grace, then Jonathan.

"Yes, you remember Elizabeth and Fred Cunningham. How are they, Grace?" Mrs. Copeland asked, smiling.

Grace took a deep breath. "Father died last month in Chattanooga," she replied. "And Freddy was killed in battle in '62."

Mrs. Copeland shook her head sadly. "I am so sorry, my dear. My Robert died before the war. And you know we never had any children, so I don't know the agony of losing a son in the war. Your poor mother." She sighed and began to lead them into the kitchen. "Come in."

"Now which Cunningham is this, Ethel?" Edith inquired, looking blank.

Grace glanced at her and decided the woman was well into her sixties and obviously a bit forgetful.

Ethel went into more detail about how she and her husband had been neighbors. Meanwhile Grace looked around the kitchen. A teapot and cups sat on a small table covered with a white cloth.

"We don't want to impose," Jonathan spoke up, when at last he had an opportunity.

"Not at all. We have plenty of room here, with only Edith and me to rattle around in this big house."

They laughed together, then sat down at the table for a meal of meatloaf and potatoes. Grace tried not to eat too much food, but she gave up when Mrs. Copeland brought out an apple pie. After stuffing themselves and chatting for another hour, Jonathan stood.

"If you ladies will excuse me, I'll say goodnight."

"Your room is at the far end of the hall upstairs. Last door on the left."

Jonathan thanked her again and left the women alone to talk about happy times during the summers they had visited. Within the hour, Grace began to nod. Mrs. Copeland showed her to her room, and Grace only had time to admire it briefly before collapsing into bed and sleeping like a baby.

They saddled up and rode out of Jasper early the next morning after saying good-bye to Ethel and Edith. Both knew it would be a long, hard day, so they decided not to waste time and energy with conversation. They rode hard, stopping only for a quick lunch by a stream where they could water their horses and rest the animals for an hour. Then they were on the road again.

By midafternoon, Grace was wondering how much longer she could stay in the saddle. She was not accustomed to such long rides, but she didn't remind Jonathan of that. If he were willing to go to the time and trouble to take her to Sand Mountain, the least she could do was be a good sport and not complain. She had known the trip would be difficult before she'd left home, and she had been determined to go. Yet a deep ache was settling into her bones when she spotted a small community at the next bend in the road.

"Let's stop here and check supplies," Jonathan suggested. "I'll ask someone about the road ahead. I thought we'd camp tonight, if you feel you're up to it."

"Sure." Grace forced a smile, but all she could think about was how comfortable Mrs. Copeland's bed had felt the previous night and that she was already twice as tired as she had been then.

The community turned out to hold no more than basic shops, but they picked up some dried apples, and Jonathan spoke with the man at the livery about the road north where they were traveling.

As they rode out of town, Jonathan promised only another hour of riding before they would stop. This time Grace agreed. "I'll be ready; I don't think I can go much farther."

When Jonathan led the way off the road and through a grassy meadow toward a small stream, Grace heaved a deep sigh of relief and began to feel better. She was pleased to see that Jonathan knew what he was doing when it came to finding a good camping spot for the night. He had chosen a level spot near the small creek. They were about three hundred yards upstream from where the wagon road crossed the creek.

"We'll be safer if we don't camp too near the road," he explained to her as they picketed their horses. "Do you mind dipping a can of water from the stream over there?" he added as he gathered up leaves and pine straw.

"What are you doing?" she asked, looking at the pine straw.

"This will keep the ground from being too hard beneath your quilt," he answered and kept working.

She smiled to herself. He was such a considerate man. The longer she was with him and the better she got to know him, the more she liked Jonathan Parker.

Later, settled down before the fire, they sipped their coffee and enjoyed the feeling of a full stomach for the first time all day. After a meal of dried apples, beans, and salt pork, Grace began to relax. Just sitting beside Jonathan and staring at the low campfire was comforting to her. She was no longer nervous around him or even shy. She felt like she had known him all of her life. It was strange for her to think about him that way, when they had come from such different parts of the country and had been on opposite sides of the war. But none of that really mattered to her now.

Jonathan Parker was the kind of man she had always dreamed of meeting, but she had begun to believe that she never would. She stared at the flickering flames of the campfire, still amazed by all that had happened.

"Are you okay?" Jonathan asked.

"Fine." She looked at him, admiring the way the firelight danced over his handsome face and lit his deep blue eyes. "I'm sorry I was so rude to you when you came to our house," she said, suddenly thinking about the first time she ever saw him.

"I didn't expect you to greet me with open arms, certainly not when you heard me speak and realized I was a Yankee."

She reached over to touch his hand. "You are such a kind and tolerant person. You are slow to anger, slow to take offense, and always willing to give people the benefit of the doubt. I really admire you for that, Jonathan."

"And you are quite a woman," he said, squeezing her hand. "You have a beauty that shines from your heart, and I admire you very much. I think you're probably the most courageous woman I've ever met."

She laughed. "Courageous? You mean the way I struck out on this crazy mission to the north of Alabama?"

"Let's hope it isn't crazy. Yes, I admire you for that, but I also respect the way you've taken charge of your situation at home, trying to make the most of a terrible ordeal. And I admire the way you have taken care of yourself and your mother."

"Thank you. Oh Jonathan," she said, staring into the fire, "I hope Father has something important waiting for us. If so, maybe there's hope of saving the farm and starting over again."

She leaned back and hugged her knees. Her riding habit was wrinkled and soiled at the knee, but she didn't care. She felt so happy sitting beside Jonathan, daring to hope and dream once again. Tilting her head back, she looked up at the stars. It was a black velvet night with a thousand tiny lights twinkling across the heavens.

Jonathan reached over to press a kiss to her cheek. She leaned closer, but he pulled back from her, chuckling softly. She turned and looked at him. "And just why are you laughing, Mr. Parker?"

"I was just reminding myself of my promise to your mother to behave like a gentleman. And that means its time to pitch my bedroll on the opposite side of the campfire."

"Don't get too far from me," she said, glancing at the spot where he had laid his bedroll. She would feel safe with him there.

He stood up, still holding her hand. "Sweet dreams, Grace. I hope they're of me."

She smiled up at him.

Later, as she snuggled down into her quilts and drifted off to sleep, she thought how good it felt to sleep out under the stars. As she listened to Jonathan's steady breathing from the opposite side of the campfire, she hugged her pillow and slept even better than the night before.

✑

The next morning, they left at daybreak with a fierce determination to make it as far as they could. At noon, with the sun high in the sky, they stopped beside a stream to water and graze their horses and to rest and snack on a light lunch.

"You've been a good companion on this trip," Jonathan said, as they dropped down on a grassy spot under the wide branches of a leafy oak. "You haven't complained about sleeping on the hard ground or riding for miles on end without stopping. I feel certain if I were with my sisters, I would have heard a lot of complaints long before now. But then, neither of my sisters would have the backbone to make this kind of trip. On second thought, Katherine might do it, now that she's older."

He took a bite of biscuit and smiled at her. "And nobody can make biscuits like this. Not even my mother."

"Thank you, sir. I've been told that anytime a man tells you that you can do something *almost* as good as his mother, it's a genuine compliment. But you've taken that compliment even further. I promise never to tell your mother though."

They looked at each other, and she shook her head. "What am I saying? Unfortunately, I'll never get to meet your mother."

His eyes ran over her features, and he winked at her. "Don't be too sure about that. You never know what the future will bring."

She arched an eyebrow. "I don't think the future will bring me to Louisville."

"But you can't be sure," he said, grinning. Then he got up to check on the horses. As her eyes followed him, Grace wondered why he had said that to her. How she longed to know what he really thought of her. How tempted she was to simply ask him.

She had always prided herself on being independent, but she could feel that independence slipping. She liked to be with Jonathan so much that even now she felt a bit lonesome when he wandered off with the horses to explore the road ahead. She turned and reached for another biscuit. As she took a bite, she smiled to herself.

Maybe if they found a valuable buried treasure, she could buy her way into his heart and persuade him to stay at Riverwood. If he wanted to raise horses, he could do that very easily at their farm. And she might as well go on and tell him that she couldn't think of anything in the world she would rather do than work with horses.

She smiled to herself, feeling very good about the idea.

$\mathscr{G}$

When they were back on the trail again, Grace asked, "How much longer do you think it will take us?"

"The best I can calculate is late afternoon. I found the community of Pine Grove on my map. From the directions your mother gave me, the church should only be a mile or so east of there on the main road."

She smiled, wondering exactly what awaited them at the church.

They rode along in silence that was broken occasionally when

Jonathan talked about his childhood or told funny stories that he had heard over the years. Grace laughed with him. She thought about how compatible they were and said as much to him.

"I know," he nodded, looking at her. "I've thought how nice it would have been if only we had met in another time, another place."

She looked at the pine thicket across the road. She didn't want to think about what those words meant because they had a tragic sound to them. It was the kind of thing one would admit before you said good-bye. She blinked and looked back at the road.

Once they found the treasure, everything would change. She would be able to convince him that he belonged with her in Alabama. Yes, once they had money, everything would be all right.

They reached Pine Grove sooner than they had hoped. It was only two o'clock in the afternoon when they turned their horses down the narrow street that led through the small community.

"Do you want to stop here?" he asked.

"No, let's keep going," she said, glancing around.

As in all small communities, the few people out on the sidewalks were staring at them as they rode past. It was a relief once they were on the outskirts of Pine Grove headed in the direction of the church.

In less than an hour, they spotted the white clapboard church with its little steeple at the crest of a hill. They glanced at each other and kneed their horses to move faster toward the little building nestled in a grove of pine and oak trees. At the corner of the churchyard, Grace could see an apple tree.

Her heart beat faster as their horses climbed the hill to the church.

"It looks lonely and forlorn, don't you think?" Grace asked in a hushed voice.

"Yes. But why are you whispering?"

She glanced at him and saw the humor in his face. She laughed. "Well, I was always taught to be respectful around God's house."

She gazed up at the little steeple, a beacon to those who needed a place to worship.

"I haven't been to church in over two years," Grace said, feeling a bit guilty as they approached the small churchyard. She wasn't sure why she felt compelled to say that, but she did. She only hoped God would believe how truly sorry she was for the mean things she had said about Him.

"Well, let's start praying that we find what your father intended us to find beneath that tree," Jonathan said, taking a deep breath.

Glancing at him, she realized that he, too, was nervous. She was so excited that she could hardly stay in the saddle. She wanted to bolt down from the horse and run the rest of the way.

"Mother talked about when they came to dinners on the ground here," she said, realizing she had to talk to vent her nervousness, or else she would start screaming.

"Dinners on the ground?"

"This was before they had tables in the churchyards. Everyone brought food, and the women spread quilts over the ground like a giant tablecloth for the food."

"What about ants?"

"They just added flavor."

They reached the edge of the churchyard, and Jonathan got down from his horse and looked around. Grace scrambled off Molly before he could help her down. She couldn't wait another minute to get to that apple tree.

"The last words your father spoke before I left were about the church," Jonathan said, as he tied General to a low limb while Grace tied Molly.

"Tell me what he said one more time," Grace instructed, wishing she could have seen her father before he died.

"He said, 'Go to the church.'" Jonathan reached for Grace's hand as they began to walk toward the apple tree. "It begins to make sense now."

"I hope so." Grace replied, walking stiff-legged toward the tree. She no longer felt the ache of so many hours in the saddle, or the dull headache.

They had reached the apple tree where heavy weeds and thick grass covered the ground. Grace dropped to her knees, crawling around in the grass. Her fingers combed through the thick tufts of grass, searching for an area that might indicate a hiding place. Jonathan dropped down beside her, and together they covered every inch of ground around the apple tree. Neither spoke a word.

Slowly Grace sat back on her heels, looking all around them. Had she been mistaken? Had she just wished so hard for a miracle that she had tried to create one?

She looked across at Jonathan, who heaved a weary sigh and sat down in the grass.

"I–I'm sorry," she said, trying desperately not to cry. She couldn't bear the disappointment she felt creeping through her, ready to settle into her heart and send her hopes plummeting once again.

He reached over and squeezed her hand. "So am I." He looked back at the sturdy little tree. "I checked the area right at the base of the tree. I don't think its possible that anything has been buried here."

Grace's throat ached as fiercely as her head, and she pulled up her knees to rest her head. She couldn't bear to think of the time they had wasted or the trouble she had caused Jonathan.

"Maybe there's another apple tree around somewhere."

Her head shot up, and she winced in pain at the sudden movement. She looked all around the front of the church, but there was no other apple tree.

"Come on, let's search the entire area." He stood and extended his hand, helping her up. "We're not giving up yet."

They circled around the church to the back where the grass was knee-high. Thirty feet further, a small iron fence enclosed eight graves.

"A cemetery," Grace said, frowning at Jonathan as they walked in that direction.

The rusty old gate creaked when Jonathan pushed it open, and they entered the cemetery. Grace glanced at the tombstones. All the names were the same.

"One entire family is buried here," she said softly.

"Probably died of typhoid because all the deaths are in the same year except for one."

Grace looked at the small grave and imagined a baby had been stillborn.

"Grace, look!" Jonathan pointed toward the back of the cemetery, which was overgrown with brambles and bushes. In the very back corner, Grace spotted a small tree.

Her eyes met Jonathan's, and he grabbed her hand as they walked carefully around the grave sites until they reached the remote little tree.

An apple tree.

Grace caught her breath and squeezed Jonathan's hand. Again, her hopes were soaring. *God, please,* she silently prayed.

At the base of the tree, there appeared to be a small grave, even though weeds had sprouted over some of the bare spots. A large flat rock served as a tombstone, and on the rock was written the word Cunningham.

"Wait a minute," Jonathan frowned. "It's Cunningham. Grace, did your parents lose a baby?"

"I don't think so. Freddy was the first child. I know that because I've heard Mother talk about how much trouble she'd had giving birth to Freddy since he was the first one. He was only four years older than I. I'm certain no child was born between Freddy and me. At least I think I'm certain."

"Maybe you were too young to remember; maybe they just

never told you about another baby; the baby could have been stillborn."

Grace stared at the rock, and her heart began to beat faster.

"No, Jonathan. Father would have had a proper tombstone for one of his children. He would never use a rock on the grave. And look—even the name is crudely written."

Jonathan nodded, dropping down beside the flat rock. It was about twelve inches wide, and about twenty inches high, roughly inscribed with the words F. Cunningham, 1863.

Jonathan examined the ground underneath the rock, where no grass had grown. In the soft moist earth lay a tiny piece of something that glimmered beneath its coat of dirt. Jonathan dusted it off and held it up.

The late afternoon sunlight drifted down through the little branches of the apple tree and touched the object, which shone pure gold. "A gold coin," Jonathan said, smiling at Grace.

"Oh Jonathan. Maybe. . ." But she could say no more, for she was suddenly too nervous to speak.

"I'll get the shovel," he said, hurrying off.

Grace cast a furtive glance around the woods, then the cemetery, as she sat clutching the coin against her heart. *God, please.*

Those two words had become a litany for her that she couldn't seem to finish because she didn't know how to ask for gold. All she could whisper were those two words: *God, please.*

Chapter 9

I think I've found something," Jonathan said after shoveling out about twelve inches. "It's leather, may be a saddlebag. Yes, that's what it is!"

He carefully dug out more dirt, exposing a dark brown, almost black, leather saddlebag, badly molded and showing sign of rot and deterioration.

The leather strap he pulled on broke, so he dug out some more dirt, uncovering the full side of the upper bag. As he lifted the bag, he said, "It sure is heavy."

Grace looked right and left, her heart racing. She couldn't see a soul anywhere, nor could she hear anyone. "Is there anything else?" she whispered.

Jonathan reached down into the hole, testing the ground around it with the shovel. "I don't think so. I think this is what your father intended for us to find." He stopped digging and dropped the shovel.

"What are you going to do?" she asked, staring at him.

"Let's walk a little deeper into the woods where we're completely out of sight."

Holding the saddlebag against him, he reached for Grace's hand. They stepped through an underbrush of weeds and briars as they hurried to the edge of the woods. Grace glanced back over her shoulder when they stopped underneath an old oak.

Behind them lay the lonely little cemetery with its eight graves that contained a family. She could barely make out the dark outline of the fence and the little church, which seemed a soft white against the graying light.

Jonathan knelt down with the saddlebag. "Say your prayers," he said to her.

"I already have. A hundred times."

He untied the leather straps of the saddlebag, lifted the flap, and reached inside. He pulled out a leather bag with drawstrings pulled tight. Grace pressed against him, straining to see what was inside.

In the gray light, gold coins gleamed. Grace gasped, then covered her mouth with trembling fingers.

"There are a lot of coins," Jonathan whispered. He began to check the offside bag. "Grace, this one is full, too."

She still had her fingers clamped over her mouth, afraid to open her lips, not trusting herself to refrain from shouting with joy.

"Clear off a spot on the ground somewhere so we can count them," he said, glancing toward the base of the oak.

Grace scrambled back against the tree and began furiously yanking up weeds and shoving pebbles aside until she had cleared a small area where none of the coins could get lost in weeds or grass.

Jonathan moved back beside her and carefully emptied the bags. Together they began to count the coins. Grace stacked her coins in little piles of twenty. Jonathan methodically counted his. When they totaled up the amount, there was six hundred dollars.

They merely stared at one another for one unbelievable moment. "Quick, put them back," Jonathan said, opening the leather pouch. "Let's count the other one."

An even better surprise awaited them with the next pile of coins.

"There are 720 in this one," Jonathan said, shaking his head in disbelief.

Grace was beyond speaking. Never in her wildest imagination would she have believed that her father had managed to bury this much money and get a message to her. Then, with the help of God, she and Jonathan had found the gold that would change their lives. Yet, she was almost numb with shock. She couldn't even speak. All she could do was close her eyes and say, *Thank You, God.*

When she opened her eyes, she saw that Jonathan was praying, too. As they stood, Jonathan unbuttoned his shirt and stuffed the saddlebag against his chest. The bag was so heavy that his shirt gaped open a bit, but it was almost dark, and Grace realized it was smarter to look like two people walking the cemetery hand in hand, than two people with one carrying a saddlebag.

They moved quietly, reverently, past the graves. Although Jonathan was careful to open the gate slowly, the creak seemed to echo through the night, louder than before. Somewhere in the distance something scampered through the woods. Grace began to tremble.

"Just walk fast to the horses, mount up, and we're going to ride off in a normal fashion," Jonathan whispered.

She nodded, her teeth chattering as they marched back to the horses. A light wind whipped through the trees and cooled her skin, but she knew it was not the cool night air that made her weak-kneed. The initial shock had worn off, and she felt as though every nerve in her body was doing a crazy dance beneath her skin.

Once they reached the horses, Jonathan carefully tied the saddlebags in front of the saddle horn, then draped a blanket from his bedroll over the bags.

"I think the smartest thing to do is ride back to Pine Grove. I saw a boardinghouse on the edge of town. We'll have to stay there tonight and leave first thing in the morning."

Grace nodded. She was so grateful to have Jonathan with her to make the decisions. In spite of all her bragging about how she didn't need a man to take care of her, she knew that having the right man beside her made all the difference in the world to her.

All the way back to Pine Grove, Grace kept glancing at Jonathan, thinking he had become as important to her as the gold could ever be. Her wish had come true. Now that she had the gold, she felt certain it would solve her financial problems. Now that she had the gold, she could keep Jonathan. Everything was going to work out just fine.

When they reached the boardinghouse, most of the town had already bedded down for the night. Only a few lanterns still glowed in the windows. Grace could not imagine closing her eyes and sleeping even an hour; she was far too excited.

They pulled up to the hitching rail before the frame house with the small sign ROOMS FOR RENT in the window.

"Jonathan, I think I should do the talking," she whispered.

He nodded, and Grace imagined he, too, was recalling the unpleasant encounter back in Whites Creek.

Jonathan was careful to keep the saddlebag under the folded blanket as they walked up and knocked on the door.

An older man opened the door.

"Good evening," Grace said, smiling at him. "My brother and I are traveling and need rooms for the night. Do you have any?"

The man thrust a lantern in their faces, looking at Grace, then at Jonathan. "Come in."

He stepped aside and opened the door wide. "I'm Wallace Toney. Wife's got some soup on the stove if you're hungry."

"That would be nice," Grace said, glancing at Jonathan as he nodded politely to the man.

"First, I'll show you your rooms." He led them up some rickety steps to the second floor where half a dozen doors were closed. "You can have the first two. Me and the Mrs. Toney have the last one. Those in the middle are occupied by a schoolteacher and a cowboy."

Grace noticed that Jonathan's eyes lingered on the one Mr. Toney had indicated belonging to a cowboy.

"We'll be just fine. Thank you, Mr. Toney."

Jonathan nodded again and headed for the second door as Grace turned in the first one. She stepped inside and closed the door. Once Mr. Toney's footsteps sounded on the stairs, she opened the door again and crept down the hall to knock on Jonathan's door.

He cracked it, then opened it wider as soon as he saw it was Grace.

"I'm not leaving the room," he whispered.

"Good idea. I'll say you aren't feeling well, and I'll bring some soup up to you." She hesitated. "Could you advance me some money to pay for our rooms?"

He reached into his pocket and withdrew two crumpled bills. Grace had the distinct feeling that these might be his last ones.

"I'll be back in a minute," she whispered, slipping the bills into her pocket as she hurried down the stairs.

She followed the aroma of food down the hall to the back of the house and turned into the kitchen. She came up short in the doorway. Seated at the table was a very proper-looking, middle-aged woman, probably the schoolmarm. Opposite her sat a tall, burly-looking man with narrow dark eyes who stared lewdly at Grace. The cowboy, she decided, turning toward the stove, where a portly little woman dipped up soup into the serving bowls Mr. Toney was holding.

Grace hurried over to the stove. "My brother is not feeling well, and I'm tired, too. If you don't mind, I think I'll take our food upstairs."

Mrs. Toney turned a pleasant round face to her and smiled. "Sure, honey. That will be just fine. Wallace, get the spoons, why don't you?"

Even with her back turned, Grace felt the man at the table watching her carefully. She dared not look around. Neither he nor the woman at the table spoke a word to one another.

It seemed to take forever for Mrs. Toney to fill the soup bowls and put them on a tray, along with a napkin and spoons. "Oh, what do you want to drink, honey?"

"Just water will be fine," Grace said, smiling at her.

Another eternity seemed to pass before her tray held the necessary items. "Thank you very much," she said.

She turned and hurried from the room, back up the stairs,

and knocked again on Jonathan's door. "It's me," she whispered.

The door opened three inches as Jonathan peered out to make sure. Then as soon as he opened it wide enough, Grace darted inside, and he closed the door again and turned the key in the lock. She hurried across the room and placed the tray on a bedside table, then sank into the chair beside it.

"The schoolteacher looks unfriendly, and the so-called cowboy looks more like a thief. I don't like his looks one bit, Jonathan."

Jonathan was looking toward the door. "Well, we'll be safe enough here. I've already put Fred's bag away," he finished, grinning at Grace.

"That's good. Fred is very particular about that bag."

Then suddenly they began to laugh, and soon they were laughing so hard they had to cover their mouths to keep from being heard downstairs. They kept on laughing until Grace was holding her stomach and Jonathan was bent double on the floor. When finally their laughter had subsided and Grace was wiping tears from her eyes, Jonathan spoke up.

"I guess we needed a good laugh."

"I guess we did," Grace said with a long sigh.

She heard footsteps up the stairs, then the steps ended at her door. Her eyes shot to Jonathan when she heard a faint knock.

Jonathan crept to the door, slowly turned the key in the lock, and cracked it. "It's Mr. Toney," he whispered to Grace.

She nodded and hurried past him and out the door. Mr. Toney's eyebrow lifted in shock when she stepped out of Jonathan's room.

"I was getting some money from my brother," she said. "How much do we owe you for our rooms?"

He looked a bit relieved, although Grace wasn't sure he believed the part about Jonathan being her brother.

"A dollar per room," he answered.

Grace thought that was too much, but she was in no position to argue. She withdrew the bills, paid him, and turned toward her door. "Thank you. We'll be leaving first thing."

Once inside the door, she turned the key in the lock. Then she hesitated. She recalled the dark narrow eyes of the man Mr. Toney had described as a cowboy but who looked more like an outlaw. Reaching for a chair, she pushed it against the door and stepped back to be sure it was secure. If the so-called cowboy tried to break through her locked door, he would make enough noise to alert the entire household.

She removed her riding habit and crawled under the covers in her underclothes. Although she managed to get a few hours of sleep, most of the night she lay in the darkness and stared at the ceiling, wondering how best to use the gold.

Just after daylight, she heard a soft knock on her door. She bolted up in bed and stumbled across the room, listening.

The knocking continued, soft and gentle, then she heard Jonathan call her name softly.

"Yes?" she called to him, reminding herself she was still in her underclothes.

"I'm going to get the horses," he said. "Meet me out front."

"I'll be right there," she called back.

In spite of her fears about the man at the table who lurked in her nightmares during the night, they left Pine Grove without incident. The little community was still asleep, as it had been the night before. They walked their horses out of town, heading south again.

As the day broke, the sun shone brightly, pouring liquid gold over the treetops and lush grass in the meadows. The sweetness of honeysuckle filled the country. Grace rode along, breathing the clean country air, and ventured a glance at Jonathan.

He seemed to be deep in thought as he silently rode on General. She longed to know what he was thinking, but she reminded herself he had a right to his own thoughts without her prying. As though he knew she wondered, he turned to her, looking very serious.

"If you're up to it, I think we should press on as far as we can.

We can pay for hotel rooms with gold, and we would be wise to do that. A nice hotel is a good investment in our safety."

"I agree," she said, nodding.

They picked up the pace and didn't bother with conversation as they headed toward their destination for the night.

To Grace's immense relief, the trip passed uneventfully. She had begun the journey back a bundle of nerves. All she could think about, of course, was the gold in the saddlebags. Jonathan was very careful with it at all times, however, so she began to relax by the time they finally pulled into a small town for the night. The strain of nerves and the long trip had worn on both of them, and they kept conversation to a minimum.

They ate their meals, went to their rooms, got up, and left at daybreak each day. On the third day, they rode into Tuscaloosa. More than anything in the world, Grace longed to soak in a tub of hot water with scented soap.

She got her wish when Jonathan obtained rooms for them at the Bradford. It was by far the nicest place they had stayed at during their trip, and Grace asked to have tea and a sandwich sent to her room along with a tub of water. When finally she crawled beneath the clean linen sheets, she closed her eyes and sighed deeply. Then she said what she vowed never to forget again. "Thank You, God."

Chapter 10

Over breakfast at the hotel, Jonathan and Grace made their plans. The desk clerk had supplied her with a pen and paper to make the list, and her mind was working furiously.

"Grace, I was thinking we should talk to Mr. Douglas about helping you find some field hands," Jonathan said. "I know we can count on Reams to get us a couple of hands, but you'll need more."

Grace nodded. "Yes, I'll talk to Mr. Douglas."

At the adjoining table in the dining room, an older man and his wife were having breakfast. His accent was not that of a southerner, and Grace had glanced his way as he and his wife discussed plans for their new farm.

Finally, Jonathan turned in his chair and looked at the gentleman. "Excuse me, sir. I couldn't help overhearing your conversation. We're in town to buy supplies for her farm," he explained, as Grace turned to smile at the couple.

Jonathan stood and extended his hand. "I'm Jonathan Parker, and this is Grace Cunningham."

"How do you do," the man shook his hand. "I'm Bob Templeton, and this is my wife, Barbara."

Grace spoke to her, and they sat back down.

"We just bought a thousand-acre place right outside of Gordo," Mr. Templeton said, looking at Jonathan.

"Yes sir. And do you plan to grow cotton?"

"I certainly do. The world is demanding cotton," he said, quite emphatically. "The war reduced cotton production, and now farmers can't supply it fast enough to meet the demand."

"Where did you find your workers?" Jonathan asked with interest.

"Well, for this year, I hired hands just for the season. There are plenty of freed blacks looking for work, but they expect to be paid fairly."

"Of course," Jonathan agreed. "Miss Cunningham expects to do that." He looked back at Grace.

"Oh yes," she agreed.

"Yesterday, I found three Irishmen down at the docks who were looking for work. They're packing up to come to Gordo next week." He paused to drain his coffee cup. "Finding men to work the land isn't a problem if you're willing to pay the price."

"Yes sir, I understand," Jonathan said.

The couple stood up, preparing to leave. "It was nice meeting you," the woman said to Grace.

"Thank you. And you, too." She looked at the man. "I wish you good luck with your place at Gordo."

Grace watched the couple leave the dining room and wondered what their life would be like. She turned back to Jonathan. "No one is being rude to this man because he speaks. . ." She hesitated, wondering if he would take offense.

"Because he doesn't speak southern," Jonathan supplied, grinning.

"Yes. Oh Jonathan, maybe in some areas people are beginning to breach the gap between North and South. We mustn't believe that everyone is as terrible as Sonny."

Jonathan shrugged. "I realize that, but remember this man is obviously a man with money, and money talks. It doesn't seem fair to think of it that way, but it's true."

Grace touched his sleeve. "Well, we're prepared to do a bit of talking ourselves, Jonathan. Remember half of what we found belongs to you."

He looked at her and shook his head. "Grace, I don't feel right to take it. You need it more than I do."

"But you will take it. Otherwise, I have been dishonest in my dealings with you, and that isn't right. We made a bargain, and

I expect to keep it. Now, what do I need to buy with my half of the money?"

"I will check at the livery and buy two horses and two full sets of harness. Also, I'll find out where I can buy a two-horse wagon. You can go to the store and buy some house supplies and whatever you need. You'll need another hammer, an ax, at least four hoes, and pounds each of ten-penny and twenty-penny nails. I expect you'll want to have some work done on the buildings."

"And the house needs repairs," she added, thinking of what had to be done. For the first time, she could let her mind wander and not feel a whiplash of worry about how she would pay for it. The gold still seemed too good to be true, and she felt like pinching herself several times a day to be sure she was awake, not just dreaming.

"I'll buy some coffee and sugar; we've been out of sugar for more than two years. The first bunch of soldiers took our last sack of sugar. I'll get some salt and pepper and some spices, too. I hope to find some pretty cloth for Mother so she can make herself a new dress."

"You should buy yourself some pretty clothes. And some shoes for both of you."

She reached over to squeeze his hand. "You've been so kind and helpful. I could never thank you enough."

"You already have," he answered.

They sat staring into each other's eyes. Again, Grace was certain that Jonathan would stay at Riverwood. She had even allowed herself to dream that they might marry.

"Grace," Jonathan said seriously. "I have to say something to you now. Your father risked his life so that you and your mother could get a start with your land again. None of this belonged to me. I'm more than happy to help you and your mother. What I suggest is that you keep all the money except for two hundred dollars. That will get me back to Kentucky. I don't know what kind of situation I will find when I get there, but I will be two hundred dollars richer than I expected to be."

Grace stared at him, unwilling to believe that he would really leave. How could she persuade him to stay? What could she say? She dropped her gaze to her coffee cup, hoping he wouldn't see the disappointment in her eyes and think it was over the money.

"We'll discuss this later," she said softly.

"We can, but there's no way I will accept more than what I've offered. So, shall we be on our way?"

She looked up and nodded, forcing a smile. As her gaze met his, she wondered if the thought of saying good-bye was as painful to him as to her. There was something in the depths of his blue eyes that had not been there before. As she looked at him, she chose to believe it was sadness at the thought of leaving her.

Squaring her shoulders as they left the dining room, she decided not to accept what he had said as the last word. Somehow she would convince him to stay at Riverwood and help her.

They had decided to stay another day in Tuscaloosa to obtain most of the supplies she would need. For smaller items, she could always go into Whites Creek, but the thought of returning there did not appeal to her.

When Grace and Jonathan finally finished their shopping, she soared with joy and pride. Not only was she riding in a comfortable new wagon, but Jonathan had found her a sorrel mare, four years old. She was fourteen and a half hands high with a white blaze on her forehead and one white stocking on her right front leg. Grace named the mare Lucky for many reasons. Her father had lucked into the gold, buried it, and sent Jonathan into their lives with the good news. Even though she named her horse Lucky, Grace knew the real source of her blessings was God.

The other horse already had the name Banjo, in honor of its former owner. It was fifteen hands high, but together Banjo and

Lucky made a matched pair. When Grace bought the horses and knew they were her own, she almost burst into tears. All her life she had wanted a good horse, and now she had two.

Grace and Jonathan stopped in at the livery before leaving town to speak with the owner, Marcus Sawyers. Earlier he had told Jonathan news he had heard about high water from a week's heavy rain in northwest Alabama and Mississippi. The Sipsey and the Tombigbee Rivers had both flooded. Jonathan wanted to get the latest report before they left Tuscaloosa.

Mr. Sawyers shook his head when Jonathan inquired if he had heard any more news of the Sipsey from travelers stopping by.

"For sure. Some folks here last night said the Sipsey River was all out of its banks and in places looked to be a mile wide. How high the Tombigbee is will determine how fast the Sipsey recedes. Sipsey flows into the Tombigbee, you know; so if the Tombigbee gets high, it backs up the Sipsey. Could take a long time for the big river to get back within its banks—as much as a month."

"Oh no!" Grace gasped, looking at Jonathan.

"May not take that long," Mr. Sawyers said, noticing her concern. "What you'd better do is get back on the other side of the Warrior here so you can hit that wagon road going west. It's a well-traveled road that should be safe, and you can follow it for about six or eight miles, then you'll fork off to the left. That'll keep you on high ground. That road will take you to the ferry where you can cross the Sipsey River. But it may be a day or two wait even there; maybe not."

Jonathan looked at Grace. "That sounds like a good idea. What do you think?"

She nodded in agreement. "If you and Mr. Sawyers think that's best."

"Once you get off the ferry and travel that main road, you'll connect to the main road that you left going through Fayette County on your trip north."

Grace was disappointed to face yet another delay in getting home, but she knew she had to be sensible.

Jonathan thought for a minute. "We'd better go back to the general store and buy some more food, in case we have to wait for the ferry for a few days."

"I suppose so," Grace said as Jonathan turned the wagon around.

"Thanks for the information, Mr. Sawyers," Jonathan called as they rode off.

The news from Mr. Sawyers was the beginning of a bad turn of events for Grace. She found herself sinking into a darker mood for the first time since she and Jonathan had found the gold.

As they turned into the general store, Grace spotted a familiar face, and her heart gave a leap of joy.

"Mrs. Barton," Grace called, waving to the woman who lived near Whites Creek with her husband and family.

Mrs. Barton, dressed in a nice calico with matching sunbonnet turned and looked over her shoulder. Upon seeing Grace, she began to smile and hurry toward the wagon.

"Grace, how nice to see you!"

Grace was already getting down from the wagon to hug Mrs. Barton. She was one of the kindest people Grace had ever known, and she felt certain her kindness would extend to Jonathan.

"Oh Mrs. Barton. I can't tell you how happy I am to see you. Is Mr. Barton with you?"

Grace liked Mr. Barton as well, and since both were friends of her parents and had often visited in previous years, she began to feel a deep sense of relief sweeping over her.

"Yes, Walter Ray is down at the feed store now. We're here to buy supplies and try and restock some items for the farm."

"So are we!" Grace noticed that Mrs. Barton was looking past Grace to Jonathan, who had reached her side.

Grace made the introductions, explaining who Jonathan was and exactly why he had come to visit them. She hesitated when she got to the part about her father's message, quickly deciding not to mention it or the business with the gold.

"So he graciously agreed to bring me here for shopping."

"How nice," Mrs. Barton replied, shaking his hand. Unlike some others, Mrs. Barton was appreciative of what Jonathan had done, and she said as much to him. "We'll find Walter Ray. Of course, he'll want to see both of you. In fact, why don't you join us for dinner at the hotel?"

Jonathan hesitated, looking at Grace.

"Actually, we just stopped to buy more food here. We were on our way back to Riverwood when we heard about the river. The man at the livery suggested we take a different route."

Mrs. Barton nodded in agreement. "That's right. I heard about the river. You see, we've been here for over a week, and I'm in no hurry to leave," she said, smiling at Grace, then turned back to Jonathan. "If you wish to consider staying on, we would be pleased to have you as part of our group. In fact, we're planning to visit some relatives just out of Tuscaloosa tomorrow. They have a large home and would welcome both of you."

She had been looking from Jonathan to Grace as she spoke. Now she reached forward to squeeze Grace's hand. "Why don't you stay on a few more days? If your mother is all right, then we could travel back to Whites Creek together." She looked at Jonathan. "My husband believes there is safety in numbers."

Jonathan was nodding. "I agree. Grace, this might be the perfect solution. If the Bartons could see you safely back to Riverwood, then I could cut a day off my trip back to Louisville."

The words were like a blow to Grace, and for a moment she thought she was going to reel back into the dirt of the street. For once in her life she was absolutely speechless.

"Oh, you're planning to go back soon?" Mrs. Barton asked, sparing Grace the embarrassment of trying to make conversation.

"Yes. I have a farm in Louisville, and I'm very worried about its condition."

"Are your parents there now?" Mrs. Barton asked with interest.

Grace was conscious of the creak of wagons, the smell of leather, and the *clomp-clomp* of horses around them, but everything else seemed to be escaping her. The conversation was continuing between Mrs. Barton and Jonathan, who was carefully explaining about his father's death before the war and the plight of his mother and his sisters.

Grace's mind seemed to be locked in time. She was too stunned to move forward or backward. All along she had been certain that she could convince Jonathan to stay on at Riverwood; she hadn't been quite certain how she would do that, but believing that he loved her and knowing she loved him, she had expected their love to find a way.

As she walked beside Mrs. Barton on legs that felt as though they had turned to wood, she wondered if she had been mistaken all along about him. Maybe he didn't really love her after all; or if he did, maybe his feelings didn't go as deep as hers. If so, how could he just say good-bye to her here in Tuscaloosa and ride out of her life?

"Don't you think, Grace?"

Grace turned blank eyes to Jonathan, wondering what he had asked her. "Why don't we do some shopping and meet Mr. and Mrs. Barton in an hour for lunch at the tea room across the street?"

Grace followed his gaze across the street, and she heard herself agree. "Yes. Of course."

"Dear, I believe you stood out there in the sun too long. You look a little pale," Mrs. Barton said.

Grace felt Mrs. Barton's gloved hand upon hers, squeezing gently. She turned and looked into the kind woman's face and nodded. "Yes, I think so. We'll see you in an hour."

She had avoided looking at Jonathan for fear she would burst into tears. He had said good-bye to Mrs. Barton and placed his hand on her elbow to gently lead her into the coffee shop of the hotel.

She didn't say a word. She couldn't. It wasn't until they had taken a seat at a back table for privacy and Jonathan had ordered coffee that she felt the pressure of his hand on hers and forced herself to look at him.

His face was serious, and the blue eyes were bleak as he spoke. "I can see that you're upset. Is it because I have to leave?"

"Why?" The word sounded more like something she would have said as a child. Her voice was small and weak, and the word seemed lost in the abyss of her pain.

"Grace, you know I have to go back to Kentucky. I told you that from the very beginning, and I've done everything I can to help you." He hesitated.

The dining room was not crowded, and the waiter had quickly filled their coffee cups and was appearing at the table again.

Grace looked down at the white porcelain cup. The clear dark coffee sent a tiny breath of heat toward her. She needed the heat and the coffee to jolt her back to the person she had once been. All life seemed to have been drained from her there in the hot street with the awful announcement that Jonathan had made to Mrs. Barton.

She didn't respond until she had taken a sip of the coffee and felt the sting on her tongue. She didn't care that she had burned her tongue because she was too impatient to wait for it to cool down. Desperation pounded through her, and she knew she had to think clearly. With her strong will and sharp mind, she had found the best means of survival for her mother and herself. She had put to work the spirit her father had so often spoken about, and at times it had been the memory of her father's faith in that spirit, more than her own, that had kept her going.

Leaning back in the chair, she forced herself to look at Jonathan. She knew she had to be calm and not say anything she would regret. A deep, inner wisdom seemed to take over, refilling the void that had settled in her heart when she thought of Jonathan leaving. The panic that had overtaken her in the hot street had frightened her; she did not want to expose herself to that again, so she tried another approach.

"I understand your concern about your farm, Jonathan. And you know how appreciative my mother and I are to you for all that you've done. I guess I was just. . ." She dropped her gaze, watching her thumb nervously trace the rim of the cup handle. "Just surprised," she began again, "that since you were able to get a telegraph to your mother about being detained. . .well, I just thought you would get me safely back to Riverwood and say good-bye to Mother."

She paused, studying his face for the effect of her words. She had spoken the truth, but she knew as she did, she was also buying more time with him. She had to find a way to convince him to stay, and she felt sure that if he returned to Riverwood with her, he would not want to leave. And she hoped to talk her mother into helping her convince him to stay.

"But Grace, I don't see the necessity of my returning with you. I mean, since the Bartons are friends of your family, I feel confident that you will be safe with them. And they're going all the way back to Whites Creek. It seems like a perfectly sensible plan to me. Furthermore," he said, searching her eyes, "I think if you agree, your mother would understand. After all, she seemed very sympathetic to my situation."

Grace felt a slight twinge of temper but fought it down. "Just as I am sympathetic to your situation. But there's another reason." She paused, taking a sip of coffee, trying to think. She hated to stoop to using money as a means to an end, but she was still willing to share the money with him. After all, if he left with more money than planned, he might think the extra few days were worth his time.

"I don't feel right about only giving you two hundred dollars. You deserve more, and I can pay it. I intend to delay paying off my loan at Whites Creek until I get the farm in working order. Then Mr. Britton is more likely to advance money for next year if I need it, and I probably will. Jonathan, everything depends on getting a good cotton harvest. You've told me that. And I have no one to oversee any labor I hire. I don't have anyone to work the fields yet—"

"But Mr. Douglas and Reams will help you. And I'm certain Mr. Barton—"

She reached over and touched his arm. "If you will just help me hire some men and get them started, I won't ask you to stay any longer. And the money I would have used to pay the loan will go toward helping you meet your expenses when you return. Jonathan, for the sake of your family, you have to think of this more in a business manner."

He stared into her eyes, and as he did, something seemed to change in his face. He slipped his hand from hers and reached for his coffee cup, lifting it to take a sip. He watched her over the rim of the cup, and for a moment, Grace held her breath. She knew he was too smart to be fooled by feminine tricks, so she forced herself to think more about what she had just said to him, which did make sense. Why did he have to be so noble? If he needed money for his farm, and he obviously did, why wasn't he willing to take the money she had offered him?

"I didn't realize you were thinking of this in such a business-like manner," he said.

Grace could hear a difference in his tone of voice, and she thought she knew what that meant. But she sensed that she had hit on the right approach, one that would work, although she wasn't sure she was going to like the ultimate result of her decision to turn this into a business deal.

"How else can I think of it?" she asked, looking him squarely in the eye. "And why are you willing to be so noble? You promised my mother and me that you would take me all the way to. . ." She looked around to make sure other customers could not hear their conversation. "All the way to our destination to accomplish our mission. I understood, and she did, too, that you would get me safely back to Riverwood."

She glanced around and lowered her voice. "As for the Bartons, they are friends of ours." She looked back at Jonathan. "But they're even closer friends with the Brittons."

He leaned forward. "So are you saying that because of that friendship, you don't want them knowing your business?"

Grace nodded and made a point of glancing around the hotel coffee shop again. "Mr. Barton is much more shrewd than his wife. He's going to have a lot of questions about how I could obtain the horses and wagon and all the supplies we've bought."

"I can always say that I'm helping your family. For all they know, I could have advanced you money, could have brought money from your father. In a sense, that is exactly what has taken place."

As Grace listened, she studied his face and watched his eyes. Had he seen through her plan, or was he just testing her? Or was he merely pointing out a reasonable way to explain her money?

She nodded, studying her hands. "Yes, we could say that."

He waited for her to say more. When she did not, he touched her hand again. "The truth is, you feel that I am abandoning you, don't you, Grace?"

Her eyes shot back to him. "Yes, I do."

He sighed and shook his head wearily. "Grace, I wish there were an easy answer to this, but there isn't. I've been through four years of looking at the hard side of life, and I guess maybe I've become a bit cynical." He looked at her again. "I care for you. You know I do," he said softly. "But what chance do we have? Do you honestly think I can turn my back on my family and never go back?"

She shook her head quickly and found that she couldn't fight the tears in her eyes. "No, Jonathan, I would never want you to turn your back on your family, and of course I want you to go back. I only wish I could go with you," she said, speaking the words before she even thought about them.

She was listening to her heart again, and this time her heart had spoken instead of her mind.

"You can," he said.

She blinked back the tears, touching her eyes with the corner of her lace handkerchief as he spoke the words. Then as the impact of what he had just said registered in her mind, she looked at him in surprise.

"You can go back with me," he repeated. "We haven't thought of that as a solution, but maybe it is."

She stared at him, her eyes still bleary from the tears. "What do you mean?"

He shook his head and looked nervously around the room. "I'm not sure what I mean," he said.

As they sat in silence, trying to sort out their feelings, the thick drawl of southern voices flowed all around them, and for the first time, even Grace noticed the difference in the speech patterns. She had spent so much time listening to Jonathan the past week that to her the southern voices stood out.

Automatically, she glanced around her at the flow of people coming and going in the coffee shop. If they were sitting in a coffee shop in Louisville, the people would be listening to her voice and thinking she sounded different. And it would go further than that, she thought, as her eyes followed the figures of the various people, noticing how the contrast in their lives was paralleled in their clothing.

The better-dressed people she had seen were not Southerners but people like the couple they had met who had bought the plantation at Gordo. They were outsiders who had come in to buy up southern land. They were not *her* people. How could she, even for a minute, consider leaving Riverwood?

She would be a traitor to the South and to her own family to leave behind all that she was and who she was just to follow Jonathan back to Louisville.

"Jonathan, more people from. . .other areas. . .are coming to the South, whereas I don't believe you will find many of us in your area, buying land, or making friends with bankers and expanding their territory. Don't you see? It would be easier for you to stay here than for me to go there."

As she asked the question, she heard the conviction in her voice start to fade. Watching his face, she knew she had said the wrong thing, and she regretted it.

"Grace, I'm not staying here," he said. While he spoke in a quiet, even gentle tone of voice, Grace could not mistake the firmness in his voice. She knew he meant what he said.

"Then I guess we have nothing else to talk about."

What else could they say or do? They were both right. He couldn't live in Alabama; she couldn't live in Kentucky. Just as the war had dictated the course of events for their lives, the outcome of that conflict was changing the course of her life in ways she had not even begun to comprehend.

She started to get up from the chair, and Jonathan stood as well. She knew he was watching her closely, and she avoided his eyes for a moment as she waged a battle with her conscience. She sighed. She had lost the battle to hang onto him, if only for another week or two. She had almost resigned herself to the fact that she would become an old maid and grow old and die at Riverwood alone. She had been living in a dream world to think that would change.

"Grace, I don't want to hurt you," Jonathan said, as he came around the table to stand beside her. "That's the last thing in the world I want to do."

She nodded as she looked up into his eyes. "I know, and I believe you," she said, relieved not to be trying to be so business-like or playing any silly games with him.

"It's time to go meet the Bartons. What do you want to tell them?"

She took a deep breath. Again, she reached deep in her soul

for the strength that always seemed to reside there when she really needed it. She prayed she could be strong now, for saying good-bye to Jonathan Parker would be the most difficult thing she had ever done.

"I'll go with them," she said, as she began to walk toward the door. "And you're free to go on to Kentucky."

Chapter 11

Grace and Jonathan soon reached the yellow frame house with gingerbread trim. It was a cozy two-story home, and the first floor had been converted to a tea room to support the small family who now resided on the upper floor.

The front parlors held four linen-covered tables surrounded by cushioned, straight-backed chairs in each room, accommodating a total of thirty-two guests. A love seat and coffee table provided a space for two people, but a couple with a little girl had nestled into the love seat and ordered sandwiches and tea.

All the tables were taken, but Grace quickly spotted Mrs. Barton waving from a table where she and her husband were seated with two extra chairs reserved for Grace and Jonathan.

They walked over to the table, and Mr. Barton stood up to greet them. Mrs. Barton was smiling in her reassuring way that always put Grace at ease.

Mr. Barton was a small man with a sturdy build and a friendly round face and dark hair. His dark eyes were fixed on Jonathan with a look of interest as he extended his hand. After the introductions were made and Grace and Jonathan had taken their seats, Mr. Barton opened the conversation.

"My wife has been telling me how kind you've been to Grace and Elizabeth," he said. "And Fred. . ." He faltered on the word and looked down for a moment. "Fred was one of the finest men in the county," he continued, looking at Grace. "His family meant the world to him. He and I were together right here in Tuscaloosa when we read the list of casualties at the town hall and saw Freddy's name."

He shook his head and looked at his wife, as though needing her strength. She smiled sadly at him and reached out to pat his hand. "Mildred and I lost two babies and were grateful for our two daughters later in life. I couldn't begin to imagine the tragedy Fred felt that day when he saw his only son had lost his life."

Grace looked at Jonathan and saw that he appeared to be mesmerized by Mr. Barton and the sad story he was relating.

Mr. Barton looked at his wife and said nothing for a moment.

Mrs. Barton turned to Grace. "Dear, I can only say that as horrible as it has been for your parents to lose Freddy, it must be almost unbearable for Elizabeth to know that Fred isn't coming back to her."

She turned and looked at Jonathan. "How good of you to be so loyal to Fred and now to his family. You must be a very special man," she said, giving him the full radiance of her smile.

Jonathan seemed to have lost his voice for a moment. He merely gave her a sad smile in return, then looked across at Grace.

"It has been my honor and privilege to know Mr. Cunningham and then his wife. And Grace. I only wish I could do more for them."

As she and Jonathan looked at one another, Mr. Barton resumed the conversation. "And now Mildred tells me you are going on to Kentucky."

Jonathan slowly turned his attention to the Bartons. "I will be going back to Kentucky soon," he said. "But after talking with Grace, I have decided to see her safely back to Riverwood and say good-bye to her mother."

Grace gasped so loudly that she was certain the Bartons had heard. For a moment, no one said anything, but Mrs. Barton tactfully responded. "Well, I'm relieved to hear you say that. I must confess, I was worried that Grace would tire of our visiting relatives, but we had already promised."

"I took the liberty of checking on the condition of the river myself," Mr. Barton said. "I spoke with some people who had just come into town last night, and they confirmed what Mr. Sawyers told you. I think he is correct in the route he suggested. Furthermore, I don't believe you'll have a long wait, or rather I hope you won't. Since this is a Tuesday, it's not likely to be as crowded on the ferry as it would be if it were the weekend."

Jonathan nodded in agreement, and Grace sneaked another glance in his direction.

"That's good to hear, sir. We're purchasing some groceries, then we should get on our way. Do you mind if we don't stay for lunch?" Jonathan asked, directing the question more to Mrs. Barton.

"Of course not. In fact, I think you're wise to be on your way."

Mr. Barton stood again as Jonathan came around to assist Grace from her chair.

"Let me again express my appreciation to you, young man. And when I get back next week, if you're still in our parts, we insist on you two coming for dinner." He looked at Grace. "If Elizabeth is up to a visit, we would love to see her as well."

"Thank you, Mr. Barton."

She leaned over to hug him, then she bent down to hug Mrs. Barton. She didn't know how to thank them for being so kind and gracious to her and of course to Jonathan. They had innocently worked the miracle that she had been unable to attain. Jonathan would stay awhile longer.

As they said good-bye again and walked out of the tea room, Grace looked up at Jonathan. "You don't have to take me back. I don't want anyone to make you feel that you do. And I won't do that to you again," she said, her voice trembling.

She still felt bad about trying to talk him into staying by using money as an argument, and yet she meant to give him the money she had originally promised. She fully intended to carry out her plan of delaying her payment to Mr. Britton at the bank in the interest of getting the farm up and going again.

"Oh Grace, I can't just leave you like this," he said, sighing. "You were right. Another week isn't going to make that much difference, after all. And I realize now that I would always feel that I hadn't finished what I had promised your father I would do if I didn't see for myself that you and your mother were going to be okay when I leave."

"When I leave." The words drummed in her mind on the way back to the store to get more food. Still, she had decided to be more reasonable about everything. At least she would have Jonathan with her for another week, and he was right. They were still in desperate need of his help. For the moment, she was afraid to trust anyone but Jonathan.

She slipped her hand in his. "Thank you, Jonathan."

After buying more supplies, they climbed up on the wagon and headed west. True to Mr. Sawyer's prediction, the road was well traveled, although not overly crowded with people. At least there had been enough traffic to keep the road maintained, and occasionally people waved to them or even offered water when they stopped to rest.

It was almost dark when at last Jonathan and Grace reached the tent settlement that had sprung up around the ferry. Their hopes for a short wait before crossing on the ferry were quickly dashed. Wagons were lined up, backed up, and spread around a grove of oaks where people had set up rough campsites while they waited.

"Oh no," Jonathan moaned as he pushed back his hat and looked around the group.

Grace felt a knot of apprehension upon seeing the crowd, and she wondered if they had made a mistake.

They pulled the wagon into the grove of oaks and got out to see to the horses tied on to the rear of the wagon. Jonathan hesitated, and when Grace glanced from his face to the crowd, she saw the reason.

Unlike the agreeable Bartons, who had given them such optimism, the people who waited to catch the ferry were a different breed. They had worn-out faces, wore old work clothes, looked tired, and spoke in coarse voices using rough language. Two men were on the brink of a fight not far from the wagon, and Grace quickly walked away upon hearing the names and insults flying back and forth.

The entire scene brought to mind their encounter with Sonny, and a chill ran over her even though the heat was miserable, and her perspiration-soaked clothes were sticking to her in places.

She turned to Jonathan. "Let's go."

He scanned the crowd, saying nothing, his hands in his pockets. Even though he was dressed in riding clothes, he stood out in the crowd as a gentleman, and Grace was terrified of what might happen if someone drew them into conversation. Some of these characters would welcome a chance to vent their frustration on a Yankee, and she and Jonathan were practically defenseless against such a crowd.

Jonathan looked down at her and shook his head. "We'll stay," he said in a low voice. He took her arm, and they walked quietly away from the disgruntled people to a secluded stretch of meadow.

"I counted the people waiting, and it looks like we could board the ferry by noon tomorrow, once we get in line. I think our best bet is to stay to ourselves, bed down early, then hope the line moves fast in the morning."

Grace frowned, glancing back at the array of slab-ribbed mules, wagons with tattered canvas, and a few tired-looking horses. "Jonathan, I don't feel good about this. I think we should leave."

"Grace, look at the sky. It'll be dark before we travel two miles. And I'd rather take our chances camped here with people than on our own back there on the road. At least we can see who's around us here, and who knows? Maybe you can make friends with some of the women."

Grace thought about his words and studied the crowd once more, wondering who would want to be friends with her. "Jonathan, I'm not too tired to ride back to Tuscaloosa if you're willing."

He sighed. "That isn't safe or sensible. I think the smartest thing to do is stay put and keep to ourselves."

"Then promise me something," she said, placing her hands on his chest and looking up into his eyes.

"What's that?" The look of worry slipped away from his face as he gathered her hands in his and searched her face.

"Promise me that we *will* stay to ourselves. I don't want another fight like the one with Sonny."

He chuckled, glancing back at the group. "Neither do I. There isn't a sheriff here to come to our rescue. Somehow I don't think I'd win this fight."

Grace nodded. "I'm going to say that you're sick. That way you can stay apart from the group."

"If they think I'm sick, I imagine they'll want to stay away from me. But don't put yourself in a position that requires me to come to your defense."

"I won't. I promise."

Grace was so relieved that she smiled. And when she remembered what he had said about coming to her defense, she knew he meant it.

She tiptoed up to plant a kiss on his cheek. "I love you, Jonathan Parker," she said, then hurried off before he could respond.

It was the first time she had told him how she felt, but she no longer wished to keep her feelings to herself. She wanted him to know the truth.

As she sauntered back to the group, Grace began to look them over carefully. To her relief, the two rude men had been separated, and one was riding off on his horse.

"And don't come back," another man yelled after him.

She frowned, watching the man disappear in a cloud of dust over the road they had just traveled. Soon the men had dispersed in different directions. Two walked back to the wagons parked nearest to her own.

She stopped at her wagon and sorted through her purchases. She found the peppermint sticks she had purchased to take home and decided it was time to do some trading: candy for friendship. Pushing a smile onto her weary face, she set out for the nearest wagon.

An older woman knelt beside the ashes of a campfire. She was peeling potatoes into a big pot. Grace walked up and introduced herself with the intent of learning something about her neighbors. She soon discovered that the Adam Smith family was from Perry County. They were on their way to buy land near Tupelo, Mississippi.

"Our place was worn out before the war," Mrs. Smith told Grace. "I got an older brother settled in Tupelo. He sent word there was land near him."

Grace smiled. "I've heard Tupelo is nice."

As they continued their conversation, Grace realized this family had been on the road for days, and the rumpled clothing and tired faces were more a result of their long trip than any other reason. She learned that two of the wagons belonged to the Smiths, along with several horses, a milk cow, and two yearling calves.

In a field away from the wagons, Grace could see children playing. Mrs. Smith pointed out their two sons and a daughter who were with the group in the field. Their seventeen-year-old son, Tom, was just leaving with his father to gather firewood. A little boy was asleep in the wagon. Grace left the candy and proceeded to the next wagon.

Mrs. Smith had told her the Joe Wheeler family was traveling with them as far as Memphis. When Grace stopped to chat with Jane Wheeler, she could see the Wheelers were quite poor, but the woman was gracious to her, and Grace regretted judging them so quickly.

"Everyone seems nice," Grace remarked, handing the Wheeler's young son, Roby, a peppermint.

"Just watch out for those folk." Jane pointed toward a wagon parked by itself on the edge of the pasture. "That man's brother was the one that just got run off for trying to steal something outa the first wagon down there."

"Thank you for telling me," Grace said.

As she studied the isolated wagon, she could make out a heavyset woman with red hair tied up in braids on top of her head. The woman was stomping around the back of the wagon, dragging cooking pots out of a trunk while yelling at a small redheaded girl playing in the dirt.

"They got three more girls, all look just like their mother. And the husband—don't know where he is now—he's a drinker. Joe says he reckon he has to stay drunk to put up with the wife and girls. They only got one voice, and it's loud, from daylight to dark."

Grace laughed at the colorful description, but she didn't forget the warning to stay away from the man. She wanted to be certain Jonathan was warned.

"Well, I'll be getting back to my wagon. Jonathan is sick, and I've told him he shouldn't be around other people while he's not well."

"No, we don't want our kids getting sick."

"I know, but it was nice meeting you," Grace said with a smile, then hurried back to her wagon. She felt a lot better about the people who were camping around them. Now all they had to do was stay to themselves, as Jonathan had suggested.

Staying to themselves was easy enough for the first part of the night. But when the lanterns were being extinguished and people were settling down to sleep, the first threat of trouble appeared.

After dark, Grace had made her bed inside the wagon, and Jonathan had pitched his bedroll outside. They had been talking in low voices to each other for about a half hour when they heard a child scream.

Grace crawled to the back of the wagon and looked out.

Jonathan was already on his feet, staring toward the wagon on the edge of the pasture.

Grace followed his gaze and saw a lantern swinging precariously from its perch as a man backed against the canvas, his fists doubled. He stared down at the woman on the ground.

He was muttering something they couldn't hear as the woman kicked at him, and he kicked back.

Grace gasped, appalled by what was taking place. She had never seen a man and woman fight, but it was obvious the man was being a bully.

"Why isn't someone going over to stop him?" Jonathan asked, taking a few steps forward.

Grace's arm shot out, grabbing his sleeve. "Jonathan, we aren't going to get into this," she said, yanking even harder when it appeared he was about to take another step. She could see his tall profile silhouetted in the moonlight, and as she kept her grip on his arm and climbed out of the wagon, his face became more distinct. The muscle in his jaw started to clench.

He yanked his arm loose. "I'm not going to cower over here while a man beats a woman."

Just then a child cried out, and Grace and Jonathan watched in horror as one of the girls came out of the wagon, screaming and yelling at her father. She pulled at his sleeve as the woman crawled around in the dirt, then the man swung around and backhanded the girl, sending her flying into the grass.

Grace wrapped her arms around Jonathan, pleading with him as he started to move beneath her weight. "No, please, Jonathan. I'm begging you. Don't go over there," she sobbed, desperate to make him listen.

"Grace, what kind of person do you think I am? I'm not going to stand here and watch that bully beat a woman and child and do nothing about it."

"But you'll end up—"

"In a fight? I don't care."

He charged across the meadow. Grace stood rooted to the spot, watching in horror. Then she started running to catch up with him, hoping she could somehow intervene. But she wasn't fast enough, for Jonathan reached the man just as his fist swung out again. He hadn't seen Jonathan's approach, so Jonathan was able to grab the man's fist and haul him backward. Without saying a word, Jonathan flattened the man with two blows, while the girls screamed behind them and the lantern went flying from the wagon across the grass.

By the time Grace got to them, Adam Smith and his oldest son were running across the meadow, yelling something to Jonathan.

Just then the redheaded woman came up behind Jonathan, her arm swinging.

In the eerie light of the lantern, Grace saw a silver flash as the woman struck Jonathan's arm. His elbow swung back, knocking her away, before he even knew who was fighting him.

"Hold it," Adam warned, pointing a rifle at the man on the ground. "Tom, grab the woman," he ordered his son, who towered above all the other men.

Tom stepped forward and grasped the woman by her arms. She screamed at Jonathan while the man on the ground cursed and threatened to kill him. The girls jumped up and down, screaming at the top of their lungs.

It was the worst scene Grace had ever witnessed, but as the other men in the camp took over, Jane Wheeler extended a piece of cloth to Jonathan. "Here, put this on your arm."

Jonathan pressed the cloth against his arm and turned and walked back toward their wagon.

Grace stared after him, still sobbing and trembling. Two of the other women reached out to comfort her.

"Go on back with him," Jane said, standing beside Grace. "We'll manage here. It's not a deep cut," she added, patting Grace's shoulder. "I could see that when I handed him the cloth.

Grace nodded and plodded back toward the wagon. She felt sick after what she had just witnessed. The ugly scene and the terror that had seized her when she saw the cut on Jonathan's arm had left her weak. By the time she reached the wagon, waves of nausea rolled over her.

As she bent over double and began to retch, she felt an arm around her waist. Then Jonathan handed her a cup of cold water.

Drinking the water slowly, Grace felt her stomach settle. Jonathan led her back to the wagon, where he had lit the lantern. As she crawled up to the wagon bed, she realized he had released her and was stepping back. She looked over her shoulder, seeing in the glow of the lantern the dark look in his eyes.

"Get some sleep," he said and turned away.

"Jonathan, your arm—"

"I'm okay."

Her fear drifted away, and suddenly her numb temper came to life. He still stood in the shadows, pressing the cloth to his arm.

"Why did you have to go over there? The other men were on their way. They didn't need you."

He stepped out of the shadows and stood with his face only inches from hers. His eyes filled with anger, and his voice was tightly controlled. "I have never tucked my tail and run, and I'm not going to now. If you think that I'm going to cower down because I'm a Yank and everybody hates me, then you don't know me at all. I'll get you home, then I'm leaving this country. You see—this is the way it would be if I had allowed you to talk me into staying on. I'd rather have died in the war than be only half a man, and that's what you seem to expect of me. Well, I'm not going to do that, Grace."

He turned and stomped off around the side of the wagon, and Grace sat back on her heel, reeling with shock. She had never seen him so angry; the only time he had lost his temper was the day Sonny had challenged him. But now he was acting like a hotheaded soldier who couldn't stop fighting a war or a southerner.

"Jonathan Parker," she yelled through the canvas. "Get on your horse and go to Kentucky. I can get home by myself."

Her cry of rage seemed to resonate into the distant shadows, but there was no response. She flung herself down on the quilts and began to sob. A sick feeling began to gather in the pit of her stomach, but she knew she would rather choke before going outside to throw up again. She buried her face into the feather pillow and sobbed harder. Once she had muffled her own cries, she could hear low voices in the night, and she put her hand over her mouth and strained to hear.

Two men were talking as they approached the wagon. She sat up, terror rolling over her again.

"They're pulling out now," Adam Smith was saying. "We told them if they didn't leave now, we were sending Jeb for the sheriff in Tuscaloosa. Reckon they must have something to hide, 'cause they got real quiet then. They're breaking camp. The woman thinks you're hurt worse than you are, and we didn't tell 'em different. So you just lie low till they're gone."

Grace scrambled toward the back of the wagon. "Thank you," she called out. "We appreciate it."

The Smith boy held a lantern, and she could see more men in the background.

"Thank you, sir," Jonathan said in a loud, clear voice. "I never could tolerate a man mistreating a woman."

She held her breath. She suspected that he had deliberately spoken up to let them know he was a Yankee. Now what would happen?

"Nope, I never could tolerate that either," Mr. Smith replied. "Come on, men. Let's get back to the wagon."

Grace watched Jonathan turn and stride toward her. He looked angrier than before. "I'm glad not everyone is as worried about my voice as you are. I heard you tell me to leave, but I'll see you safely home. Then I'll be glad to go."

He disappeared around the side of the wagon, and she fell

back on the quilt, exhausted. She was beyond tears, beyond anger. She lay in the darkness, listening to the low voices melt away in the distance. She closed her eyes, but she knew she wouldn't sleep.

Much later, she heard the creak of a wagon and the plod of horses, and she sat up and peered through the back of the wagon. Two men stood by the road with lanterns. One had a rifle pointed at the wagon as it rocked off down the road. For the first time, the entire family was silent, and Grace wondered if their silence was even more threatening than their menacing shouts.

Chapter 12

Neither Jonathan nor Grace spoke the next morning as Jonathan tied the horses onto the back of the wagon, and Grace folded her quilts and tidied up. She hadn't slept more than two hours, and even then, her sleep had been riddled with nightmares of the redheaded woman bearing down on her with a knife, then the redheaded girls chasing her across the meadow, all screaming and lunging at her as they caught up.

Grace knew she had made too much fuss about their wild neighbors. Still, as they lined up with the others to get on the ferry, it was obvious that Jonathan had chosen to ignore her. He was still angry at her, but she didn't care. She was just as angry at him.

They boarded the ferry with the other families, and Grace was immensely relieved to be able to talk with the other women. It gave her an excuse to avoid Jonathan until they reached the other side of the river.

Once they did, she climbed up on the wagon and turned her head away from Jonathan. She was almost as angry at herself as she was with him. What had happened to her spirit? In the past, she would have called his bluff first thing in the morning. She would have told him again that she could manage on her own. Yet here she was saying nothing, and that gave the impression she was pouting, which was not her style. But she couldn't prod her temper enough to fuss with him, nor evoke her independent spirit to the point of dismissing him, so she sulked most of the day, and he pretended that he was alone.

Finally, after hours on the trail, Jonathan pulled the wagon into a shady grove and drew back on the horses. Pulling on the brake, he tied the reins and hopped down.

Grace sneaked a glance toward him and saw he had the water

bucket and was headed toward a line of trees that probably lined a stream. Slowly, she climbed down from the wagon. Dragging herself to the rear she petted the horses and untied Lucky. She walked the mare over to some thick grass and tethered her to a hickory sapling. Then she went back for Banjo.

"I'm glad you two get along so well," she murmured to the horse. It amazed her that she and Jonathan had so completely ruined the good relationship that once existed. Sinking down into a cool, shady area under the trees, she drew her knees up to her chin and put her head down. She had no idea how to remedy the situation, and she reminded herself it was probably useless to try. He was determined to see her safely home, then leave. She should be glad; it would be easier for everyone when he was gone.

The smell of smoke caused her to jump to her feet, wincing at her sore muscles. She ran back out into the clearing so she could check the wagon. Jonathan had built a low fire and was cooking something. Fine, let him eat; she wasn't hungry. She strolled back over to see about the horses, and as she did, her gaze met Jonathan's, and he called out to her.

"I'm warming some food."

"I'm not hungry."

He stood up and began to walk in her direction. She turned back to the horses, thinking he was probably coming over in the interest of the horses, rather than her.

"Look, Grace," he said as he stopped walking and stood regarding her from a dozen yards away. "We'll be back at your place by dark. I think we'd better settle this and not upset your mother."

She looked at him, wondering what there was to settle. "Well, you will have kept your word when we get there, so feel free to leave whenever you want."

He turned and looked to the west, in the direction they would be traveling. "All right, I'll do that."

With narrowed eyes, Grace watched him stalk back to the fire. What had she expected? Deep in her heart, she thought if she remained cool and aloof, he would give in and say something. But she had underestimated his degree of stubbornness. He was his own man, one not easily maneuvered, or maybe one who would not be maneuvered at all.

She went back to stroke Lucky's forehead. "I guess I wanted a man who could stand on his own feet," she whispered. "But maybe I didn't know that. Now it's too late." And she pressed her face against Lucky's forehead.

Jonathan had been right in his estimation of when they'd arrive at Riverwood. It had been a sunny day, but soon twilight would filter over the land. When Grace saw familiar landmarks, she felt a surge of joy. Suddenly she wanted to make peace with Jonathan.

"Thank you for getting me there and back. And for everything else," she said, turning her head slightly so that she barely looked at him.

"You're welcome."

She swallowed. He wasn't going to say anything more. "How does your arm feel? The cut, I mean."

"It's okay. I got into our medicine kit and bandaged it up before I went to bed."

Guilt tore at her conscience, and her reserve crumpled. "Jonathan, I'm so sorry. I've acted like a spoiled child. I should have bandaged your arm, cooked for you, or just. . .behaved differently. I'm so sorry," she said, and for a moment, she feared she would burst into tears.

He looked at her and smiled. "I forgive you, Grace. And I'm sorry, too."

They had made their peace just in time, for Jonathan was turning the wagon up the drive to home. Grace couldn't wait to see her mother and tell her all that had happened. As soon as they rounded the curve, she saw her mother sitting on the porch, waiting as she always did. Upon seeing them, Elizabeth stood up and walked to the edge of the porch, gripping the post with one hand.

"Hi, Mother," Grace called. "How do you like the new wagon?"

Grace watched as her mother put a hand to her mouth and began to giggle like a young girl. Suddenly, Grace was laughing, too, and so was Jonathan.

Grace jumped down from the wagon almost before Jonathan had pulled the horses to a halt, then she ran up the steps to hug her mother.

"Come into the kitchen. I have a meal waiting for you," Elizabeth said after the three had exchanged greetings.

Grace watched her curiously. From the way her mother looked, Grace thought she somehow understood everything that had taken place.

"I'll take care of the horses and put the wagon away," Jonathan said, smiling as Grace and her mother walked arm in arm back inside the house.

Once they were in the kitchen, Grace sat down with her mother at the table and told her the full story. Elizabeth did not seem as surprised as Grace expected, although she smiled and hugged Grace from time to time. When Grace finished the long story, carefully omitting her fight with Jonathan and the reason for it, she studied her mother curiously.

"Mother, you don't seem astounded by all this. To me, this is like the most wonderful dream I could ever imagine, but it's really happened. Can you believe it?"

Her mother smiled, and tears began to form in her hazel eyes. "Of course. I am surprised and overjoyed. But I always knew God would work things out. I just didn't know how He would do it."

Grace stared at her, saying nothing for a moment. Then she, too, felt the rush of tears, and she let them flow freely down her cheeks. "Mother, I love you," she said. "You have been so strong in your faith. I'll never forget the lesson you have taught me."

They sat in the kitchen, hugging one another and crying, marveling at all the blessings that had come to them. Then Jonathan's steps sounded in the hall, and Grace got up to help her mother take the meal to the dining room table.

They talked as they ate, and once or twice Grace smiled warmly at Jonathan. She had forgotten her anger and the words that had been spoken in haste, and she only hoped that Jonathan had as well.

It had been a long day, and by the time they finished their meal, darkness had settled over the house. Grace was so tired she almost hadn't noticed that her mother went about lighting the candles.

"You look absolutely exhausted," Jonathan said, his elbow on the table.

She smiled at him. Dark circles lined his eyes, and the shadow of a beard covered his jaw. "So do you. I think we've earned a good night's sleep."

He nodded and got up slowly. "I didn't realize until now that I'm practically asleep on my feet." He stretched his arms over his head, then winced.

"Jonathan, your shoulder," Grace said, worried again.

"It's healing fine. I washed off down at the watering trough when I was seeing to the horses. I checked the cut place then, and I'm strong as ever." He winked at her. "Get a good night's rest. First thing in the morning, I want to ride over and see Mr. Douglas and ask about getting you some field hands."

She nodded. "Thank you, Jonathan." As she looked across at him, she wanted to say more, so much more, but she knew she was far too tired to make sense. "I'll see you in the morning. Rest well."

He had started to walk around the table to her side when her mother entered the dining room again. Grace suspected that

Jonathan wanted to kiss her, but he was still mindful of his promise to her mother.

Elizabeth looked at Jonathan. "I've prepared the guest room for you. I pray you sleep well."

"I will," he said and patted her arm. "Good night."

Soon after Jonathan had gone upstairs, Grace left her mother in the parlor and trudged up to her own room. When she settled into her soft bed, she moaned with relief. She was glad to be home; she hoped she never had to leave again.

✍

Grace was seated on the front porch, enjoying her second cup of coffee, when Jonathan rode back up the drive, returning from a visit to the Douglas place. Her mother had just come to the door to say she had most of the supplies put away.

Grace only half heard what her mother said as she watched Jonathan walk up to the front porch. She thought about what a handsome man he was, but she knew so many more important things about him now, his kindness, his loyalty, and his honesty. He was every bit as bound to duty and honor as her father had been.

"Mr. Douglas told me to go down to the dock at Jina and ask for a man named Isaac Banks. He's working at the docks, but he wants to get back to farming," Jonathan said as he settled lazily into a chair beside her.

Watching him, Grace noticed how at ease he seemed to be. Hope sprang in her heart. Maybe now that they were back at Riverwood, he would change his mind. She wasn't going to try to persuade him not to go to Kentucky; she had learned her lesson about that. But she dared hope that somehow they could work out a plan.

"Someone told Mr. Douglas that Isaac didn't like having to live on the docks, that he wants to move back to the country. He is said to be the best worker in the county."

Grace tried to follow the conversation, reminding herself

that she should be paying closer attention. "Jina is only an hour's ride," she answered. "Would you want to go and talk with this man?" she asked, feeling a bit shy about requesting anything more of him.

Jonathan nodded. "I can, but since you're the one who's hiring him, I think you should go along so he understands who the boss is."

Grace averted her eyes. She had promised herself that she was not going to argue with Jonathan. She was so happy over all their blessings that she couldn't stir up any independent feelings.

"Yes, Grace, why don't you go with him?" her mother suggested.

Glancing over her shoulder, Grace realized that her mother had again assumed the responsibility of meals, freeing Grace to think of business. "Okay, I'll be ready in a minute."

She hurried upstairs to change clothes, and when she returned, Jonathan had saddled Banjo and Lucky. She stood for a moment, stroking first one horse, then the other. "Jonathan, I'm so grateful to have a good horse."

"I know. I thought I'd try Banjo and give General a rest."

As they rode down the drive, Grace continued stroking Lucky and looked over at Banjo. "They make a great pair, don't they?"

At his hesitation, Grace looked across and saw that Jonathan was watching her differently. The twinkle had returned to his eyes, and he was smiling at her. "Yep, a good pair."

She returned his smile, and as they rode on, Grace thought she had never in her life felt such happiness.

They reached Jina in less than an hour. The little settlement was nestled on a high bank overlooking the Tombigbee River. It bustled with activity as workers loaded freight from the dock to be shipped downriver to Mobile.

Securing their horses at the hitching post, they headed toward the small huts where the workers lived. Mr. Douglas had said Isaac lived in the first cabin on the right. As they approached the cabin, a deep bass voice belted out one of Grace's favorite songs: "Weep no more, my lady. . .oh, weep no more, I pray. . ."

The door of the cabin opened, and a huge black man stepped out. He was dressed in work clothes, a brown felt hat riding low on his broad forehead.

"Hello," Jonathan called to him. "We're looking for Isaac Banks."

"Afternoon. I'm Isaac." He removed his hat, revealing thick gray hair. In a mere half dozen steps, he caught up with them and stood towering over the couple. Grace thought he was the biggest man she had ever seen. She judged him to be at least six feet, five inches, all muscles and brawn, weighing at least 250 pounds. He had large, blunt features and a grim expression in his dark eyes.

Grace felt Jonathan's eyes on her, and she cleared her throat. "I'm Grace Cunningham. I understand you're looking for work."

"Yes'm."

"Mr. Paul Douglas sent me to see if you'd be willing to come to work for us at Riverwood," she continued.

He began to twist the worn brim of his felt hat in his large hands as he looked from Grace to Jonathan, then back again. "Are you goin' to try and grow cotton again?" he asked. "I ain't never gonna pick cotton again."

Grace heard the bitterness in his voice, and she remembered Mr. Douglas had said that this man had spent his life working cotton. He was a fierce man, she could see that, and she wanted to be sure she made her plan clear to him.

"I'm not asking you to pick cotton," she replied gently. "If we grow cotton, I would put you in charge of the other men as my overseer."

"She's interested in clearing off the fields first," Jonathan explained. "The fields haven't been farmed in a few years, so they'll need to be cleaned up and burned over."

"I don't mind doing that," Isaac answered, "but I won't pick cotton."

"Fair enough," Grace agreed.

"I make a dollar a day working at the docks," he said, still looking doubtful.

"I'll pay you that," Grace offered firmly.

"But I'd need to stay at the docks a few more days," he said. "I can't just up and quit and leave them shorthanded."

"I understand. Do you think you could come in about a week?"

"Yes'm." He clamped his hat on his head. "I reckon I can do that. You're the farm next the Mr. Douglas's place?"

"That's right. My father was Fred Cunningham."

He nodded. "He was a good fair man."

"Thank you, Isaac. If you want advance pay—"

"I don't take nothing till I've earned it."

"All right. Then I'll see you in a few days."

"Yes'm." He clapped his felt hat low on his forehead and struck a path toward the docks.

Grace looked at Jonathan. "I think he's exactly the kind of man I need to oversee the cotton."

Jonathan nodded. "I agree. Well, this was easy enough. Shall we go back now?"

They talked and laughed all the way back to Riverwood, and Grace was in high spirits as they rode back up the drive. Then she saw the fancy carriage parked in the driveway with its familiar family crest on the side of the carriage door. The driver sat under an oak tree, staring out at the pasture.

"That's the Britton carriage," Grace said, looking at Jonathan. She wondered what its presence could mean. If Mr. Britton had come calling, concerned about the money she owed, then she had some wonderful news for him.

She smiled to herself and looked over at Jonathan. "Come on inside. I want you to meet Mr. Britton. He's a very nice man."

As soon as they stepped into the hall, Grace realized it was not Mr. Britton who had come to call, but rather his wife, who was considered the town snob.

"I must say, Elizabeth, I'm shocked that you would allow such a thing." Her high-pitched voice reached Grace, and she felt as though she had just drawn her fingernails over rusty iron.

Grace turned to Jonathan. "Maybe you'd better excuse us. If you want to go on to the barn with the horses, I'll be down in a minute," she whispered, leaving Jonathan in the hall.

As Grace hurried into the parlor, Mrs. Britton whirled from the love seat, fluttering the feather in her hat. The little hat slid lower on the woman's broad silver head, and she turned to Grace with a sharp look that sliced her up and down.

"Grace, Eva Nell Douglas told me you left your mother all alone and went off with. . .that man."

"No, it wasn't like that," Elizabeth said.

"Mr. Britton and I have been hearing all sorts of things," the woman continued, gathering momentum with each word. "I understand your *houseguest* brawled in the streets with some character, and it took Sheriff Whitworth to break it up. Mrs. Primrose says you are quite friendly with this. . .this *Yankee*. Really, Grace, what are you thinking of after your father and your brother—"

Elizabeth rose to her feet, looking with contempt at Mrs. Britton. "Samantha, you have completely misconstrued the facts. Jonathan Parker is here at my invitation because he saved Fred's life—"

"Don't be gullible, Elizabeth. Naturally, he would say that. How else would he weasel his way into Riverwood? They're after southern land, you know, all of them."

Grace was so angry she forced herself to mentally count to ten before she opened her mouth. But she saw that Mrs. Britton was reaching for her purse, ready to run after her insulting little speech.

"Mrs. Britton, Jonathan Parker has a farm of his own and has no need of ours. He—"

"You can comfort yourself with that idea, Grace, but no one believes it. Furthermore, you may not have a farm much longer if you don't repay your debt to the bank. My husband has been concerned about this all along; but in view of your behavior of late, it now appears that you could get swindled out of what Fred worked so hard to give you. We intend to see that such an event doesn't happen," she said, pausing at the door to sneer at Grace again.

Her mother stood beside Grace, her hand on her arm. She could feel her mother's message: *Don't say anything more.*

So Grace kept her silence. She swallowed back her fury and waited until she heard the sound of the driver calling to the horses and the wheels of the carriage rolling down the lane.

"Mother, forget what she said," Grace cried. "I'll see Mr. Britton first thing in the morning and straighten this out."

She turned and headed toward the stairs, venting her anger with quick steps up the stairway. She would rush down to the barn and join Jonathan with the horses. She would forget. . .

At the top of the stairs, her eyes widened as she saw Jonathan close the door to the guest room and walk down the hall, his small traveling satchel in his hand.

She stared at him. "What are you doing?"

"I'm leaving, Grace."

He hurried past her and down the stairs before she could summon a response. She turned and looked after him as he strode down the hall toward the back door.

She flew down the stairs after him, her mind working. He obviously had not gone to the barn; instead, he had lingered in the hall out of concern, and he had heard every ugly word Mrs. Britton had spoken.

Well, she would explain. She would persuade him to stay overnight and talk things out.

He was already out the door, his long legs moving swiftly toward the pasture where General grazed.

"Jonathan, wait." She ran after him, catching up at the end of the yard. "Everyone knows Mrs. Britton is an ugly gossip who treats everyone unfairly. You can't let her words—"

"Some of the things she said made sense, Grace, even though you may not want to admit it. Those people have no way of knowing who I am or what my motives are. They only have my word—"

"Which is more than enough. Why, when Mr. Barton gets back—"

"At this moment, the bank owns Riverwood," Jonathan continued sternly. "You can't afford to ruffle Britton's feathers, Grace. Once you've paid him back, you can say what you want to his wife. Which brings up another point. I am still determined not to take any more of your money. You can't afford not to pay back that loan now, Grace. You have to."

Grace stood speechless, knowing deep in her heart that he was right. If she gave him as much money as she had offered, she would have to wait until the cotton harvest to repay the loan. Assuming there was a cotton harvest.

She swallowed, reaching out to restrain him as he turned to go. She knew she was losing him; it would take more than money or desperate pleas to stop him now. All she had left was the bare truth, and as he turned briefly to face her, she knew she had to give him that.

"I won't beg you to stay, but you must know this: I love you, Jonathan. Nothing can change that; nothing ever will." She looked him straight in the eye and saw his eyes brighten. She even thought he was beginning to smile.

But the smile faded as he reached for her, pulling her close to his chest. "And I love you, Grace. God only knows how hard I've tried to talk myself out of it, but it's no use. You've been honest with me when I know it must have been difficult. What's even more difficult is that I can't stay here, Grace. I have to return to Kentucky."

He hesitated, glancing over her shoulder as though considering something. Then he pulled her closer to him, hugging her against his chest as though he never wanted to let her go. "Come with me. Please. We can be happy together, I know we can. We both love horses, and we can make our dreams come true in Kentucky. Come with me, and we'll build a new life together in a different place."

"But Mother. . ." Grace began to protest, amazed that she was even thinking of leaving Riverwood. What did it matter if she spent her life alone? What did anything matter if she hadn't Jonathan to love?

"We could take your mother with us, Grace."

Grace heard the words, weighed them in her mind, even turned slowly in his arms to look back at the house. Surely her mother would understand, would want her to be happy. Perhaps she could convince her mother to come along. . . .

But then she realized that Jonathan was turning her loose, and when she looked around she saw that he had put his hand over his forehead and was backing away from her.

"What am I saying?" he asked, then looked back at her as though dazed. "Now I have really betrayed your father. Everything we've been doing is to carry out his mission for his farm and his family." He shook his head and began to walk quickly along the path to the barn.

Grace stared after him. She couldn't keep running after him; she couldn't keep begging. And he was right. If she turned Riverwood over to the bank, she would never forgive herself. Even if her mother would agree to go with them to Kentucky, Grace wouldn't feel right about it.

She turned slowly, feeling as though she had aged ten years in an hour. Her feet were leaden as she plodded back to the house, up the porch steps, and through the door. Like one in a trance, she put one foot in front of the other, climbing the stairs to her room. She closed the door, undressed, and went to bed.

She didn't think she had the energy to ever get out of bed again. She rolled over on her stomach and covered her head with the pillow so she wouldn't hear General's hoofbeats as Jonathan left her. Forever.

Chapter 13

For two days Grace remained in bed. Her mother had wisely said little, bringing her trays of food that she later removed, the food cold and untouched. On the third day, Grace noticed that her mother wore a different look on her face.

"Grace, Isaac Banks is here. He wants me to tell you that he was laid off at the docks, once his foreman heard he was planning to leave. He's here to work. You have to get up now and tell him what you want done."

For a few minutes Grace lay unmoving, staring at the ceiling. Then slowly, she sat up and swung her legs over the side of the bed. The memory of Isaac's straightforward manner reminded her that she must treat him fairly; she had promised that. She got dressed and went downstairs.

❦

Within a month, Isaac had rounded up enough men to clear the fields and burn off the old growth. He had done a splendid job of overseeing the men, and they worked from daylight to dark. Grace respected his position as overseer and only went to the fields to take food and water.

Grace had begun to join her mother on the porch each afternoon, for she felt lonely and sad, and it helped to have her mother to talk to. She was certain she would never feel really happy again, but she was at least beginning to have some satisfaction as she rode Lucky over the farm each day, inspecting the good job the men were doing.

One afternoon as she sat with her mother, she said, "Isaac has accomplished so much. He tells me he'll have the land ready to plant in seeds by the first of the week. And after Mr. Britton came out to see for himself what is being done, he told me we can get another loan next year, if necessary."

Elizabeth patted Grace's hand. "You handled the situation well by paying off the loan but not stooping to say anything about his wife."

"I don't have the strength for another battle, Mother. I don't think anyone really wins a war. Not when you weigh the cost." She turned and looked at her mother. "You've taught me a lesson I'll never forget. You never wavered in your faith. You have remained a sweet loving person in spite of all the tragedy. When I compare you to others who are so bitter, I know the value of a close relationship with God."

Elizabeth nodded. "Even if everyone in the world thinks I'm foolish to keep sitting here waiting, hoping. . . ."

Grace shook her head and looked longingly down the lane. "I would do the same if I thought I could see Jonathan riding up that drive again."

"Grace," her mother said, "can't you ask God for that and believe He will honor your faith?"

Grace looked at her mother and smiled. "I suppose I can."

The two women laughed together and sat back in their chairs, listening to the whippoorwill begin its evening song.

Grace was not sleepy that night and remained on the porch long after her mother had gone to bed. As she looked up at the vast sky overhead, amazed by all the stars and their special beauty, her mind moved on to the God who had created this beauty. She felt humbled and awed by such a God, and she stood up and walked over to the edge of the porch. Looking up in the night sky, a prayer began to form.

"Oh God, please hear my prayer. I want to thank You for sending Jonathan to us. I thank You for what my father did to try to protect and care for us. I thank You for the Bible he sent with his secret code. And I thank You for giving me the wisdom to understand that code.

"And then the gold, God. Thank You for the gold and for the difference it has made in our lives. But I have one more thing now that I must ask of You. Father, I love Jonathan, and I want to marry him and spend my life with him. I want us to have a family and to raise them in faith as my parents raised Freddy and me. I can better understand Your plan now, because of the way some things have happened. The way Father saved Jonathan, then Jonathan saved Father. Oh God, I know that was in Your plan. And I do believe You want Jonathan and me to be together. Why else did You send him to us? Why *him*?

"I know that only You can touch our lives and work another miracle. Only You can heal the awful hate and anger between North and South; only You can patch up lives and hurts to where we can be together, either here or in Kentucky. I don't know how You could do this, God, but I know that You can. You are a mighty God."

She paused, taking a breath. She remembered the other prayers she had asked for—begged for, in fact—which God had not answered. He had not spared Freddy's life nor her father's life. And she had been angry and bitter.

"Father, I know I have offended You at times with all my fussing about life and the war and everything that has happened," she continued slowly. "But please, forgive me for the things I said and did. You promise in Your Word that if we confess our sins, You are faithful to forgive us. So please forgive me. And please bless Jonathan and me and let us have a future together. Please give us a chance for happiness." She took a deep breath. Hearing her words, she realized she didn't make much sense, but sometimes dreams didn't seem sensible. "Thank You for hearing this prayer and for helping us. And I'll try to be a better person. . ."

She kept her eyes closed for a few more minutes as the night silence settled over the porch, and a lonely little whippoorwill began to sing.

⁊

That evening prayer brought Grace a sense of peace in the days to come. It was good to know she had asked God for forgiveness.

Honoring the rest of that prayer was up to God, but she had ceased to fret over the outcome.

Sitting on the porch with her mother had become part of her daily routine. Grace even began to share her mother's pot of tea. She was still trying to build her faith, although it seemed that her mother had enough faith for both of them.

On Friday afternoon, after Isaac had paid the men and everyone had left for the weekend, Grace made sandwiches from fresh tomatoes out of the garden. They were eating vegetables for lunch every day now, and she was planning to go into Whites Creek to buy some chickens.

The two women had settled comfortably into their chairs on the front porch after finishing their evening meal and were listening for the whippoorwill. Grace could hear Lucky neighing from the pasture, and she smiled to herself, thinking how grateful she was to Jonathan for all he had helped her acquire. And to her father for providing the gold.

The whinny of a horse caught her ear, then she heard gravel crunching on the drive below.

"Who's coming on a Friday evening?" Grace wondered aloud.

Her mother looked at her with a twinkle in her eyes, but Grace merely laughed and shook her head.

"Mother, it would be asking a lot for God to see Jonathan safely to Kentucky, get his business in order, then travel all the way back here in a month's time."

In spite of her words, Grace couldn't resist looking down the drive and feeling the tiny surge of hope that came to her each time a horse and rider drew near.

Two riders came around the curve and Grace sighed. "See, I told you. . ." Her voice trailed off into silence.

The first man rode a gray mare she had never seen before, and he bent forward with a hat low on his forehead so that she couldn't make out who he was. But behind the first rider, she could see the side of a black horse. It was silly. She couldn't hope. She mustn't.

Her heart defied reason, however, for Grace leaned forward in her chair in an attempt to see around the lead horse and get a better look at the black horse.

Just then, the horses spread apart on the drive, and for a moment it seemed as though her heart had stopped beating.

Grace stood, her gaze fixed on the black horse. Then she saw the blazes on his legs and on his forehead. She ran down the steps, all the hope of her life centered in her heart as she watched the black horse come into clear view. At last she could see the rider.

A cry escaped her, and she stopped running, for tears blurred her vision, and her knees felt weak.

"Hello, Grace," Jonathan called to her. He swung down from the saddle and quickly covered the distance between them. They met in a wild embrace. He lifted her off her feet and swung her in the air.

She laughed and cried at the same time as she reached out to touch his face, feeling the stubble of beard beneath her fingertips. "I can't believe it," she said, wrapping her arms around him and hugging him tightly.

From behind her she heard her mother's voice. She knew her mother would be pleased to see Jonathan, but she couldn't share him, not yet.

"I've brought a visitor," Jonathan said.

But Grace wasn't paying attention. She tilted back her tear-stained face to look into Jonathan's eyes. Why didn't he kiss her? She couldn't wait much longer.

Then she heard her mother's voice again, this time an odd, strangled cry. Grace whirled around with concern. Her mother was running down the lane toward the other horse. The man had swung down and was looking from her mother to Grace.

Grace reeled back against Jonathan. The world dipped and swayed. She couldn't believe her eyes. . .it couldn't be. But her mother's voice answered Grace's doubts. "Fred! I knew you would come back!"

Grace stood gaping in disbelief. The man was thin and stooped, but he was smiling and reaching out to her mother. As he turned and looked over his shoulder, Grace saw that he wasn't a dream. He was real. Her father had come home.

Chapter 14

It had taken an hour to settle everyone down, and in the end it had been Grace's mother who wisely suggested they go into the parlor where they would be more comfortable.

Grace hadn't left Jonathan's side; she never wanted to be separated from him again. She nestled against him on the love seat while her parents sat together, their chairs drawn close, their faces radiant with love.

"How?" Grace had asked the question a dozen times, unable to get beyond that single word.

Jonathan attempted to explain as they drank tea and left the food untouched. "After I left here that day, I couldn't forget the way your mother had waited so patiently for Mr. Cunningham; she had been so firm in her faith. And something she said to me on the porch that day continued to haunt me although I never said anything about it."

"What was it?" Elizabeth asked. Her face was radiant, her eyes glowing, and the love that softened her face gave her the appearance of a very young woman; she looked as though she were only a few years older than Grace.

"You asked me if your husband was alive when I left him. I had to admit that he was. I thought about that a lot, especially after I left here. I got to thinking, what if there is a chance he's still alive, just a chance? The more I pondered it, the more I knew I had to go back to the hospital to be sure. It was the only way I could get any peace for myself and for you."

He looked at Grace, and she saw that his eyes were filled with love for her. She wanted to cry with joy.

"When I got to the hospital, he was the first patient I saw. He was sitting out in the sun on a side porch, and I couldn't believe my eyes."

"I was going to be dismissed in a few days," Grace's father interjected, "but I hadn't wired you, Elizabeth, because the doctor had warned that we must be sure I was over the fever."

Grace listened intently as her father spoke. Her eyes drank in every feature of his face: the high arch of his brows, the wide-set gray eyes that seemed haggard and circled. Yet a light twinkled in the depths of those eyes and assured everyone that he was well.

"Jonathan told me everything that had happened." He looked from his wife to Grace, then he smiled at her. "He told me how strong and brave you have been, Grace. I am so proud of you."

"Father, I want to know how you ended up with that gold," she said. She had imagined a dozen different ways he could have acquired gold coins, and some of them were less than honorable. Yet she knew her father to be a honorable man.

"Another one of God's miracles," he said, leaning back in the chair.

Grace thought he was very thin, and he still looked terribly pale to her. Still, she knew if he had survived all that had happened to him, he would soon have all of his strength back, now that he was back at his beloved farm.

"It was the last week in September, and I was on a scouting patrol with another soldier. We were near Steven's Gap when we got ambushed by some Yanks. My buddy was killed, and my horse was killed, but I managed to hide in rocks and thick brush until morning. I climbed to the top of a mountain and looked down over the valley. I couldn't see any soldiers, so I figured they had moved on toward Chattanooga.

"In the valley, I spotted a bay horse grazing. Not seeing or hearing anyone, I crept toward the horse to investigate. As I got closer, I saw a Yankee soldier lying face down. I slipped up to him, after I was sure no one else was around. Being without a horse, my number one priority was to catch the bay. The horse kept feeding but would glance at me occasionally. Speaking gently, I walked toward the horse and noticed the nice saddle and brown leather saddlebags. The reins were still looped around the horse's neck, indicating the rider might have fallen from the saddle, possibly from illness or having been shot. Reaching the rein and tightly grasping it, I continued talking to the horse. I petted its neck with my left hand.

"My eyes were glued on the saddlebags, hoping they contained some ammunition and something to eat. I untied the leather straps of the saddlebag, lifted the flap, and looked in to see a leather bag with drawstrings pulled tight. When I picked the bag up and loosened its strings, I noticed how heavy it was. I looked inside and saw gold coins, a lot of them. Quickly I checked the offside bag. It, too, was full of coins. I hurriedly replaced the bags and retied them tightly. Then I searched the pockets of the dead soldier and found nothing but a small knife. He had no identification, nor any pistols or rifles.

"So I left him by the creek, mounted my new horse, rode to a thick, wooded area, and dismounted. Finding a clean spot on the ground, I emptied one bag and counted the money—six hundred dollars. The other bag had 720 dollars. That made a total of 1,320 dollars in gold coins."

Elizabeth reached out and touched her husband's hand. "Where do you think the money came from?"

"He wasn't an officer, and soldiers didn't carry that kind of money in their saddlebags. Because he was by himself and carrying money, I suspected it was stolen. I was alone, knowing that Yankee soldiers were in the area and more than likely between me and my outfit back on Lookout Mountain. So what should I do? If I hid the gold there and something happened to me, nobody would find it. I knew I had to find a safe place to hide the gold, a place where I could get a message to my family to go look for it. I sat praying for half an hour.

"Finally, I knew what I should do. A day's ride southwest would take me to the farm area where we lived before we moved to Pickens County. I figured if I could get on top of Sand

Mountain, I wouldn't run into any Yanks. I asked God to see me safely there, and He did. I was led to the church and the apple tree. Even found the perfect smooth rock to carve my name on to use as a grave marker."

"And then you hid the money and rode back to your army?" Grace asked, completely amazed by what her father had told them.

"I did. And we don't need to talk about what happened after that. The best thing was that I met Jonathan there, and I realized he was a man I could trust. And I was right. Jonathan, I'll be indebted to you for the rest of my life."

"I'm just as indebted to you," he said, looking from Fred to Grace. "It was the only way I could have met your daughter, and I'll have to admit, sir, that I haven't had a moment's peace since I left her."

"Nor have I," Grace said, smiling into his eyes.

"Fred, why don't we take your things upstairs? I'm sure you need to rest after the long ride," Elizabeth suggested.

"How have you been?" Jonathan asked Grace after her parents had left the room.

Grace was vaguely aware that her parents had left them alone. She suspected they knew there were important things to be discussed, and this time Grace wasn't going to let Jonathan ride out of her life.

"I've been lonely. And sad. For all of my bragging about how much I loved this place, it didn't keep me from being lonely or from missing you with all my heart."

She reached forward and pressed her lips to his cheek. He took her in his arms. "Guess your mother will forgive me for breaking my promise, just this once," he said.

He drew her closer, and they kissed again and again. Finally he pulled away from her and stood. "Want to go with me to take care of the horses?"

She laughed. "Of course I do." As they walked out to the

yard to lead the horses to the barn, she was already thinking how awful it would be when he started talking about leaving. She wanted to know how long he planned to stay, but she was too nervous to ask.

"Your father and I saw the fields and pastures. Everything looks nice, Grace."

"Isaac has been a miracle worker."

He reached out to pull her into his arms as they led the horses to the trough. "And I expect you've been quite the boss."

She laughed. "Actually, no. Isaac is his own man, you know. I didn't want to run the risk of losing him."

As they rubbed the horses down, Jonathan asked more questions about the farm, the cotton crop, even Reams and his wife.

She related everything to him, talking until she was almost hoarse. Then, as they walked back up to the house, she turned and looked at him.

"How long can you stay?" she asked, for she had to know.

"I sent another wire from Chattanooga," he said, looking serious. "This time I promised to be leaving here within the week."

"Oh." She nodded and looked down at the freshly cut grass beneath her feet. How could she say good-bye to him again? It would tear her heart out to spend time with him again, then watch him leave. She drew a deep breath. "I'll try hard not to beg you to stay," she said, but as she spoke, her throat tightened. She cast a glance toward her healthy garden, admiring row upon row of healthy vegetables that were her pride and delight.

Jonathan took her arm and turned her slowly to face him. "I believe we were standing about right here the last time I asked you to go home with me. You said you couldn't leave your mother alone. She's no longer alone," he said, trying to smile.

Grace searched his eyes, then turned and cast a glance toward the house. Her mind stumbled over his words, weighed them out, and as she did she wondered if she could really leave the only home she had ever known.

"I. . .don't know," she said, feeling his arms wrap around her. As she turned and looked into the deep blue eyes, she felt her heart start to beat in the way it always did whenever she was close to him. "I. . .Father just came home."

"Yes. That's why I planned to stay on a few days so you would have time to spend with him. Then, if you're willing, I thought maybe there could be a little service over in that church across the road."

"They're already having services—" She broke off as she saw the twinkle in his eyes. "You mean like—?"

"Like a wedding," he said, tilting her chin back and smiling into her eyes. "Grace, if you'll marry me, I promise to do my best to be a good husband, a good father. I promise to be the kind of Christian man you deserve."

"You're already that kind of man, Jonathan," she said. "Do you really want to marry me?" she asked, suddenly feeling shy.

"As soon as I can. I don't know how much longer I can keep that promise to your mother."

They both laughed as they walked hand in hand back to the house. When they reached the kitchen, Grace's mother was busy preparing fresh vegetables.

"I can't wait to prepare a good meal for your father. And for you, Jonathan," Elizabeth said, smiling at him. "But first, Grace," she turned to look at her daughter, "your father wants to visit with you for a few minutes. He's resting in his bed."

"Of course." She looked at Jonathan.

"I'll stay here in the kitchen and see if your mother needs me to sample anything."

Grace laughed and left him settled at the table. She flew up the stairs to her parents' bedroom. Her father was not in bed, as she had expected. Instead he was seated in a rocking chair by the window. While her first impression of him had been that he was very thin and very tired, she knew when he turned his face to her and smiled that he was also very happy.

"Father, I'm so glad you're home." She ran to his side, throwing her arms around him and hugging him gently. She could feel his shoulder blades jutting out beneath his cotton shirt, but she knew between her mother and all the vegetables they had, he would soon be in good health again.

"Daughter, you can't possibly know how glad I am to be home." He turned and looked out the window.

Grace followed his gaze and saw that he was looking out on the cotton fields.

"You've done an amazing job, Grace. Jonathan has told me everything,"

"We have a wonderful overseer, Father. Isaac has accomplished miracles. Oh, I'm so glad you're here."

He looked at her, smiling affectionately. "There were times I wondered if I would ever see you and your mother again."

"She never stopped believing you would come home, Father. She never stopped looking and waiting for you. She always knew you would return. She has remarkable faith, and she has taught me a lot about waiting and trusting."

Grace paused, wondering how much Jonathan had told him about what they felt for each other.

"Pull up a chair," her father said, tilting his head back to study her thoughtfully. "You've turned into a beautiful woman, but then I always knew you would. And now I have something to ask you. How do you feel about Jonathan?"

Grace hesitated. She longed to tell him all that was in her heart, but she didn't want him to worry about her leaving. Now that she was sitting with him talking about Riverwood, she had begun to wonder if she could leave, even though she knew she was desperately in love.

"Speak up," he encouraged. "Are you half as smitten as he is? It's easy to see he is very much in love with you, Grace."

"And I'm that much in love with him, Father." She sighed, looking at her hands. "I just don't know what we can do about it."

"What do you mean?" He watched her closely, and she was certain she couldn't bear to hurt him. He had just come home to them; how could she tell him she wanted to leave?

"Well...he won't stay here, Father. I already asked him before."

"Of course not," her father readily agreed. "He has a farm in Kentucky, and he's long overdue to go see about it."

"But Father, he asked me to marry him," she blurted out. "He asked me to go back to Kentucky with him, and I can't do that." She was fighting not to cry, and she kept her head lowered so he wouldn't see the tears once they started rolling down her cheeks.

"Why can't you?" her father asked quietly.

For a moment Grace wasn't sure she had heard him correctly. Then slowly she lifted her head and looked into his eyes. When she did she saw the sheen of tears veiling his eyes.

She caught her breath. "Oh Father, I won't leave you. Please don't be sad. I would never make you sad after what you've been through."

He shook his head and reached for her hand. "These are tears of joy. Grace, when I think of how blessed I have been to have a woman like Elizabeth, it chokes me up. I hate to think how empty my life would have been without her. As much as I love this farm, it would have meant nothing if I hadn't had Elizabeth as my wife, as the mother of our children. The joy and happiness of a good marriage is one of God's greatest gifts. Don't throw away that opportunity."

She stared at him, wondering if he understood that if she married Jonathan she would be leaving him and her mother.

"I would never want you to miss out on the happiness that your mother and I have known. Jonathan Parker is one of the finest men I have ever known. I would be proud to welcome him into our family."

"Father, I love him with all of my heart," she said, "but to marry him and move to Kentucky would be—"

"Would be what? Seems to me the man is planning a good

life. He has talked to me a great deal about his ideas, and I can see that he's as crazy over horses as you've always been."

"Yes, he is." Grace laughed. "There's nothing I would rather do. But— Oh Father, do you really think it would be all right for me to leave?"

He reached for her hand and held it against his chest. "Grace, no one could have been more brave or more conscientious than you have been in carrying on my work here. I'm not so selfish that I want to hang onto you for the rest of your life though. And neither is your mother. We feel you deserve to be happy, and if you choose to find happiness with Jonathan, then you have our blessing."

"Oh Father!" Grace leaned over to hug him as tears began to roll down her cheeks in spite of her efforts.

She knew she could wait no longer to tell Jonathan. All the sadness in her life had been magically wiped away, and she had been given an opportunity to live with Jonathan as his wife.

"Just be sure this is what you want," her father said, squeezing her hand.

She spoke slowly, confidently, for her words came straight from the heart. "I've never been more sure of anything in my life."

"Then I guess you and your mother had better get busy planning a wedding."

"I guess so." She laughed, then ran out of the room and down the stairs to the kitchen, wondering how to break the news to her mother. And what would Jonathan say when she told him she was going to accept his proposal?

Grace found them both in the kitchen, and her mother smiled at her, but there were tears in her eyes as well.

"You know?" Grace asked, looking at her mother carefully.

She nodded. "I've known all along."

Grace laughed and turned to Jonathan, who wrapped his arms around her. She thought she saw a light mist in his eyes as well.

He smiled and said, "The question is, do you know what *you* want to do?"

A lazy smile settled over her face. She took a deep breath and thought about their life together. "I know exactly what I want to do," she said, staring dreamily into his face. "I want to go to Kentucky as a bride, and I want to spend my life with you—and your horses," she added. They all broke into joyous laughter.

"Let's walk down to the garden," Jonathan suggested, glancing back at her mother. "I'm afraid if you start talking like that, it will be hard for me to keep my promise to your mother."

Grace laughed and nestled against his chest. "Soon you won't have to."

She could hear her mother's laughter following them down the hall as they went out on the front porch to gaze across the lawn. Twilight was settling over the land, and Grace could hear the whippoorwill starting its night song from the oak tree.

"I've waited here with Mother for what seems like an eternity," Grace said. "I've waited for you, Jonathan. I prayed for you to come back to me. And now you have." She shook her head in amazement. She still couldn't believe all that had happened.

"Yes, now I have," he said, wrapping her in his arms again. "And I never want to leave you again."

She smiled as he lowered his lips to hers. "I won't let you leave me."

She knew she sounded a bit sassy, but she could feel her teasing spirit surging forth again. She felt something else, though, something much stronger. She felt the deep abiding love that she knew her parents shared. With that knowledge, like her mother, she would always be waiting for Jonathan to ride home each evening, to take her in his arms, and to share the rest of their lives together.

Peggy Darty authored more than thirty novels before she passed away in 2011. She worked in film, researched for CBS, and taught in writing workshops around the country. She was a wife, mother, and grandmother who most recently made her home in Alabama.